Shades and Shadows

BOOK ONE: SARA'S STORY BEGINS

A NOVEL BY MIMI MITCHELL

This book is a work of fiction employing historical facts and persons. No other persons living now or in the past are represented in the book. Any similarity to others, living or the dead, is purely coincidental, and should not be construed as real. I proffer my apologies to history and to the real U.S. Congressmen from Louisiana who served during the time the fictional Joseph Thierry does in the book.

I wish to thank my husband, daughter, son-in-law, and niece, A.S., for their labors and suggestions. I am deeply grateful to my friend, M.K., and to my friend and sister, C.L. for their wonderful reviews of this work. Many others were generous with encouragement and suggestions. I wish to thank my father who provided part of the genesis of this novel. My father has given me hope for the world, showing that we can change and grow over time.

- Mimi Mitchell

FOREWORD

What do we know about ourselves, our history? We grow accustomed to myths, believing and repeating old stories for generations. Our memories are often confabulated. I am recounting here, as well as I am able, my story, being fully certain that it contains distortions that I cannot untangle. Still, my story is as true as anyone's can be, and I tell it here because I am compelled to, hoping someone will remember that I and my loved ones walked the earth, breathed the air, and shared the same loves and disappointments as you.

- Sara

White Genealogy

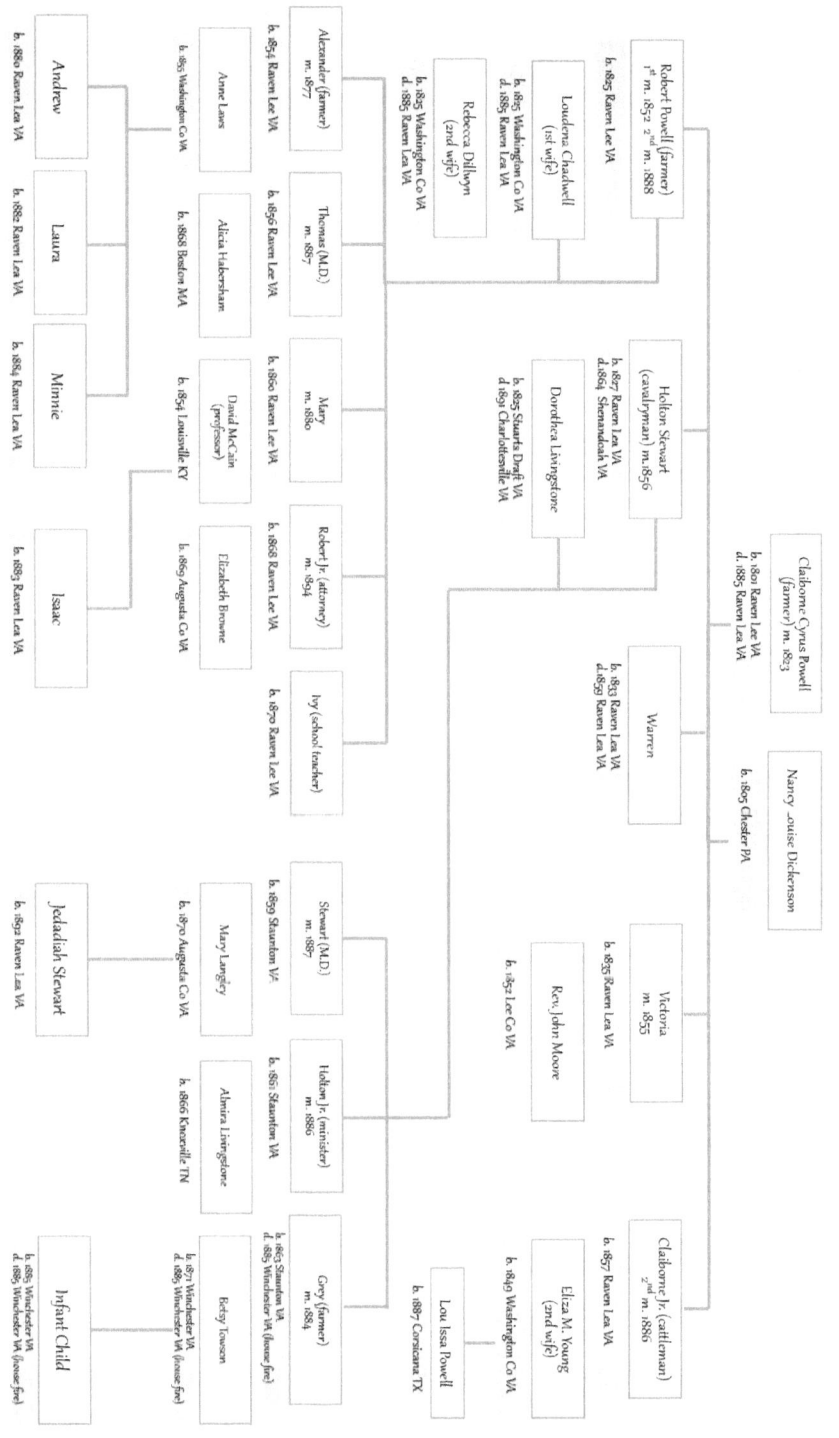

Black / White Genealogy

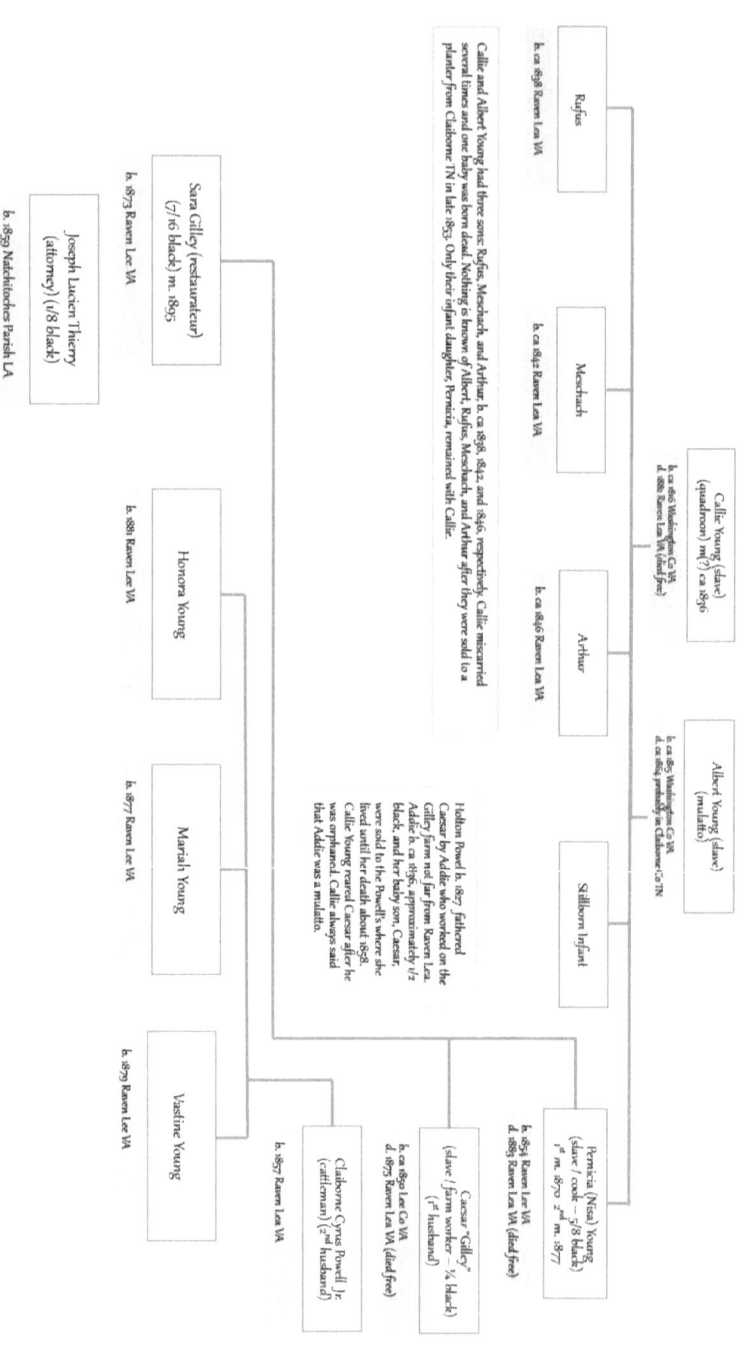

Rufus — b. ca 1838 Raven Lea VA

Meschach — b. ca 1842 Raven Lea VA

Arthur — b. ca 1846 Raven Lea VA

Stillborn Infant

Callie Young (slave) (quadroon) m(?) ca 1856; b. ca 1825 Washington Co VA, d. 1881 Raven Lea VA (died free)

Albert Young (slave) (mulatto); b. ca 1825 Washington Co VA, d. ca 1863 probably in Claiborne Co TN

Callie and Albert Young had three sons: Rufus, Meschach, and Arthur, b. ca 1838, 1842, and 1846, respectively. Callie miscarried several times and one baby was born dead. Nothing is known of Albert. Rufus, Meschach, and Arthur after they were sold to a planter from Claiborne TN in late 1853. Only their infant daughter, Permicia, remained with Callie.

Permicia (Nisa) Young (slave / cook — 5/8 black); 1st m. 1870 2nd m. 1877; b. 1853 Raven Lea VA, d. 1883 Raven Lea VA (died free)

Caesar "Gilley" (slave / farm worker — ¾ black) (1st husband); b. ca 1851 Lee Co VA, d. 1875 Raven Lea VA (died free)

Claiborne Cyrus Powell Jr. (cattleman) (2nd husband)

Hollon Powell b. 1807 fathered Caesar by Addie who worked on the Gilley farm not far from Raven Lea. Addie b. ca 1836, approximately 1/2 black, and her baby son, Caesar, were sold to the Powell's where she lived until her death about 1858. Callie Young reared Caesar after he was orphaned. Callie always said that Addie was a mulatto.

Sara Gilley (restaurateur) (7/16 black) m. 1895; b. 1873 Raven Lea VA

Honora Young; b. 1881 Raven Lea VA

Mariah Young; b. 1877 Raven Lea VA

Vastine Young; b. 1879 Raven Lea VA

Joseph Lucien Thierry (attorney) (1/8 black); b. 1859 Natchitoches Parish LA

TABLE OF CONTENTS

CHAPTER 1: MOTHERS

A Shade upon the mind there passes
As when on Noon
A Cloud the mighty Sun encloses
Remembering
That some there be too numb to notice
Oh God
Why give if Thou must take away
The Loved?

Emily Dickenson

We live our lives in the progression of one day to the next, but we certainly don't remember that way. I will try to tell my story in the order it occurred, but there may be digressions to better explain what happened.

I was born in southwest Virginia to ex-slaves. Even though I was born after slavery was abolished, not much had changed for black folks in the eight intervening years. Most negroes, in particular the rural ones in the south, were abysmally poor, but so were most white folks there after the Civil War. As a child, like all children I expect, I lived my life, accepting everything. If I were hungry, cold, feverish, the condition was temporary. Momma, Papa or Ole Mammie would see to me soon.

The first two or three years of my life, I lived with my papa, momma and my grandmother, Ole Mammie, in what was still referred to as a "slave cabin." The slave cabins were on a hill about an eighth of a mile above the Big House. I had no concept of big or small so long as my body fit the space. Mine fit the cabin. Evidently I was a small girl from birth, but that never mattered to me. All grown-ups looked like giants to me and there were very few small children on the hill in the cabins to compare myself to. Anyway I was in the Big House much of the time with the white children. The Powell family owned the property and three and four generations of them lived there together when I did. I always called the two eldest, Ole Missus and Ole Massah. When I was young, I never concerned myself with whether my life was peculiar or commonplace. It just was.

Ole Mammie was the person I spent the most time with while I was small. Ole Mammie passed when I was nine or ten years old. I can't remember the day exactly. I do remember being a handful as she watched me while Momma worked in the kitchen at the Big House. When Ole Mammie put our clothes on lines or bushes to dry or to go searching for wild food, she trailed me behind her on a rope she tied 'round my waist and to her apron. Seems as if I always got loose and got a whipping for her troubles. After the whipping she'd usually get me a piece of dried apple or, if we had just made sorghum in the fall, I might get a cookie. I always got a hug and her reminding me for the hundredth time to stay near her as I might get hurt if I went off by myself. As with most children, I suspect, I had no idea what kind of danger she meant. I doubted it could have been much worse than the switching she gave me when she found me.

Ole Mammie said more times than I can count, "Sarie, there is angels and devils on this Earth and we can't always tell which be which. You can't tell by the color of a person's skin and you sure can't tell by how good looking they is or how ugly. Stay near me 'til you is old enough to figger people better." I must have worried that old woman something awful. But, oh my goodness, I loved her.

Ole Mammie was what folks in those times called a quadroon. In her case that meant that one of her grandparents was white. She always thought it was most likely her mother's daddy because her mother came from a farm where there were a good many mulattoes. She herself could barely remember her parents. She calculated that she only lived in the same cabin with both parents until she was about six or so. Her father was sold to another farm, and she and her two older sisters lived with her mother until the older girls were also sold. Her mother passed when Ole Mammie was barely eight.

Because Ole Mammie was little, as were Momma and I, she was a house slave. I don't believe she could have done field work as well as owners wanted. Her original master sold her to the Powell's when her mother passed. Ole Missus Powell had seen my grandmother on that other farm and Little Callie had impressed her with her quick intellect and her delicate features. Missus Powell, whom we colored folks all called Ole Missus, asked her new husband if she could take the girl and train her as a personal maid. In those early days of marriage, I was told, Ole Massah would do anything for Ole Missus. In fact, I don't remember him ever arguing with her over anything she ever wanted. Ole Missus ruled the Big House. Ole Massah and Massah Robert ruled the fields, barns and finances.

Many slaves didn't formally marry and in some states, during certain periods before emancipation, they were forbidden by law to marry. On the other hand, sometimes and in some states during the era of slavery, marriage among slaves was strongly encouraged. Seems as if white folks couldn't decide whether slaves marrying was a good thing or a bad thing. It didn't matter much anyhow as couples were split up anytime the masters decided to sell one or both, but many slaves did marry according to their own customs. I was told that sometimes this involved the bride and groom jumping across a broomstick. I never saw such a thing, but it sounded as if it were fun.

I never learned whether my grandmother Callie and grandpap Albert were officially married or not. She did wear a thin gold band on her left ring finger as long as I could remember. It seems Ole Mammie and Grandpap Albert formed a household together when Callie was about 20 and Albert was roughly the same age. Over time, Albert became the supervisor of the field hands, especially in the tobacco. I was told he treated the other slaves with respect, but expected a day of real labor when they worked.

My grandparents had four live children by the time Grandpap Albert and the three boys were sold off the farm. They had lost several children over the years to miscarriage and still birth. Ole Missus, or Mrs. Claiborne Powell, had miscarried more than once herself and one son had been born deaf. Because he couldn't hear, he never learned to speak, only to make noises that the family interpreted with varying degrees of success. He had died years before I was born. But the two women, one white and one black, suffered similar heartaches over their children and for years they were as close as mistress and slave could have been.

A great deal of the mothering of Mrs. Powell's children fell onto my grandmother who seemed to love children indiscriminately whether they were hers or someone else's. She always said, though, that Massah Robert was her favorite as he had been born shortly after she came to Raven Lea.

Missus Powell taught Ole Mammie to read and write a little even though it was strictly against the law at the time. Ole Mammie's grammar was never as good as Mrs. Powell wanted, but it was a sight better than the field hands. Ole Mammie was neat and tidy in her appearance and with her work as Mrs. Powell's maid; she was, in most ways, highly acceptable.

Ole Missus had grown up in a northern household, believing that slavery was an abomination before God. I never heard her speak to a black servant in any way that she would not have used with a white one and, evidently, she behaved the same way before slavery ended. She was as strict and miserly with white help and trades' people as with blacks. She was just as acerbic and quick to point out imperfections even to white guests when she saw fit as she was to correct black folk.

She was a paradox to me in many ways, but in particular her beliefs about slavery. Ole Missus had lived a life of relative luxury greatly due to the fact that her husband owned a large farm that was prosperous because of slave labor. She liked fine furnishings and dressed elegantly even so far out in the country. She had given extravagant parties in the days before the War. Those parties were only possible because of the fruits of slave labor, but she disliked the fact that she and Ole Massah Powell owned slaves. I was told she refused to be told when her husband sold some slaves or bought others.

Ole Missus Powell said slaves should be able to read a Bible for the benefit of their souls and for the good of society. She couldn't understand or agree with those who legislated against education for the negro. The Bible was the "Good Book." To believe reading the Good Book could corrupt slaves was complete heresy to her and she had no intention of abiding by an immoral law! People might have argued with her logic and may have pointed out to her that it wasn't Bible-reading they feared from slaves' literacy, but they would have been wasting their breaths trying to make such a distinction to Ole Missus. The very fact that many whites feared what slaves might do if they could read and write spoke volumes against the oft-stated white opinion that negroes were inferior to whites. If black folks were so inferior, how could they learn to read, write, count, and sow insurrection?

Ole Missus' daughter-in-law Miz Loudena, Massah Robert's wife, taught my momma to read and write from the time my momma was small. Miz 'Dena was born into a household that had only a few slaves, nothing as grand as the Powell farm, but something in her rebelled at treating slaves like animals. She said that anyone who had lived closely with black folks could see intelligence and spirituality in them. She said she couldn't see any difference in the characters of white folks and black folks. Miz 'Dena stated emphatically, defending the little education that she gave to my momma and a few others, that it was a general nuisance to have help that couldn't read or write. Thanks largely to Miz 'Dena, Momma soaked up knowledge from everything. Momma's speech was nearly as good as the white household's and a heap sight better than most other white folks we met.

Ole Mammie had hair the color of the tinplate roof on the barn when the sun hit it. She braided it into one thick plait and wrapped it 'round her head. She never wore a scarf not in the winter cold or the summer heat - not Ole Mammie.

"I earn ever last silver hair on this old head," she'd say. "And I'm proud to show the whole world that God reward me with it!"

She always called her hair "silver" as if it were a precious metal and from the things she told me (and what I learned years later) I guess she had earned her precious hair. As a child, I loved Ole Mammie, but I didn't know, and I couldn't appreciate then, how her life affected all of us on the Powell farm for generations, long after she was gone.

As I've said, by the time I was born, the old slave days were gone. We were free, but I couldn't imagine that being free made much of a difference in the way we negroes lived. Most negroes still lived in the old one-room cabins on the big farms. The floor was hard-packed dirt. Meals were cooked over a fire in the hearth, making the cabin swelter in the summer unless you attempted to cook over an open fire outdoors and risk damage from weather or animals to your dinner. Only the elderly and infirm were at home during daylight hours from early March until late November to watch a fire and prepare food. There were often no bed frames, just pallets on the floor. Whatever possessions a black family owned could be loaded into the back of a wagon with room to spare for half a dozen children!

Most negroes wore whatever old clothes the white folks gave them. And wore them and wore them until they were rags sewn on top of rags. I think that was why after I could buy my own cloth or clothing, I kept my clothing clean and in good repair. If it couldn't be mended to look almost like new, I put it in the rag bag. I was intensely aware as I grew older when I was wearing those hand-me-downs that Miss Ivy Powell or Miz 'Dena Powell had worn before. I knew that they were wearing much nicer things if I was given their old things. Later my sisters and brother wore better, too.

Most of us ate what was grown on the farm and wasn't consumed at the Big House or sold for cash. Once in a blue moon one of the negroes would snare a rabbit or catch a mess of fish. Even wild game was scarce after the War because so much of the livestock was gone that folks had to depend on game, over killing much of it. What the Yankees didn't "appropriate" often did poorly because of too little fodder or because Massah Robert sold the feed for cash to buy other things we needed. When the folk up at the cabins caught game they'd send some to other folks if their own family couldn't use it before it went bad. Sometimes they'd even send some down to the Big House if they caught something as big as a deer or a wild hog, but that wasn't often.

It was good to have our black friends up on the hill. They didn't send their extras to the hog pens and the chicken lots as we did at the Big House. Of course we all knew that the livestock had to eat if we were to eat it. But times were lean when I was little and it seemed to me that things were never going to change for negroes.

That "mule and forty acres" slaves had been promised before I was born must have missed us some way or another. Seems that it missed all the other negroes I ever knew too. I allowed all this to Ole Mammie one day the summer before she passed. I was about nine at the time. I got one of the worst whipping's in my life for it.

"Sarie, you got no idea what you talking about! I never want to hear such words outta your mouth again!" She gave me several sharp smacks on my naked legs with whatever she could break off that despised old apple tree.

I can't eat an apple to this day, not even in a pie, because of that tree. I didn't dare squirm too much or yelp as that would just make Ole Mammie mad enough to hit me harder.

"Ole Massah ain't never going be able to sell you away from your momma and me like he done with all my children excepting your momma. Solt one of the best men God ever made from me after we was together for 20 years. Solt my three little boys away from me too. I beg Ole Massah not do it. I cry, Lord, I cry! I get down on my knees and I beg, but Ole Massah had Albert lift me off the ground. It look like Albert gonna cry too, so I try to calm down, but I can't." At this point Ole Mammie looked like she might cry now, but she didn't. She sat down stiffly on her old, short three-legged stool, scratching at the dry, dusty ground with the switch as if she could draw a picture of her lost little boys.

"Hush, Callie," Albert whisper. "Ole Massah got de law behind him. We be lucky he ain't done this afore now."

"Ole Massah say to us, I don't like doing this, but we've got to have some cash. The last two years have been hard. My railroad investments - oh, neither one of you will understand any of that! Albert and your boys are the best I have, Callie. I'd give my right arm to be able to keep them, but they'll bring the best price."

Ole Mammie looked down at her bare feet, "I'd give my right arm too if he just let them stay with me. Mayhap his telling me that supposed to make me feel better. Well, it not work that way. I cry even harder 'cause I know just how good they are. Ole Massah threaten to beat me if I don't stop wailing, but I can't stop. Ole Massah a hard man, but he ain't as bad as some I could tell you about. I never saw him beat but one negro and that one violated one of the women field hands. Ole Massah don't tolerate women folk being mistreated, white or black. That slave never violate another woman again. Couldn't." She said flatly. My young brain didn't know what to make of that and I never learned exactly what Ole Massah did to prevent the man from harming another woman.

"Ole Massah finally agreed, though, to sell them all to one buyer, if he could. That way, at least, Albert and the boys be on the same farm. Sweet Jesus answer my prayers the day Ole Massah find a man who take them all four, but he took them all the way down in Tennessee almost to Georgia. I never seed them agin, though Miz Victoria, who live way down Tennessee visit that farm when she and the Rev'rand move to

Monteagle. She see Albert and my boys. She write to her mama to tell me they was well and well-treated and were glad to hear that me and the baby was, too. But that was a long, long time ago when Nisa still young enough to go naked in the summer time."

Ole Mammie shifted her skinny legs in front of her. "Sometime I think only reason Ole Massah didn't sell ya momma was she still a baby and looked like she gonna pass any day." Ole Mammie put the switch away and readjusted her whole body on the stool, trying to find a spot that didn't ache from the rheumatism. Her hands and feet were too crippled from arthritis to allow her to work much at anything anymore, but the Ole Massah and Massah Robert saw that she was provided for.

She was in a talking mood now and she had more to say. She patted the ground between her legs, letting me know I should sit there because I had more to hear. She idly began to run her fingers through my hair, trying to straighten it. What a useless effort that always was, as I would run under the big old yew looking for whatever might be hiding there and get sap and twigs in my hair or do something else just as messy. But I so loved the feel of her knobby hands in my hair and on my head!

"I was afraid my milk would turn sour I cry so hard and so long when my boys and they papa leave. It get no chance to sour because all that bawling dry the milk up. I so worried about that baby that I take a chance and steal milk from the ewes. Good thing Nisa need milk in the springtime. Mayhap I take too much from one of them sheep as its lamb die. I worry a long time that Ole Massah or Massah Robert figure the lamb die because I stole its milk. I fed that child anything I could find that wouldn't poison her. On mill day, I scrape the chaff off the floor afore the rats could get it. I gets Big Cook to let me have some seeds from punkens and squash so's I could grind them up. Those seeds and that chaff make a few hoecakes for my baby. Jesus hear those prayers too. The ones where I beg Him to let my baby live."

"No, missy, never deny what a miracle God give us the day Mister Abra'am Lincoln set us free. We be poor, that's certain, but we ain't slaves no more to be whipped and chained and sold!"

Her words haunted me for years. Ole Mammie believed things had changed radically with the end of slavery. I'm glad she didn't live twenty years more to see how slowly things change and how hatred can erase much of what we negroes saw as progress.

So my momma, Nisa, was born into slavery, too. Timing may be all the difference in our lives. Had Ole Massah needed cash eight or nine years later he wouldn't have been able to sell my grandpap and my uncles. Some families did split up after the War to find work somewhere else, but that was their choice and they could either send for their families later or return to visit them. And that happened on our farm too. Ole Mammie said that as many as ten families left together at the end of the War. They might have left before but the Union army had discouraged slaves from leaving their masters during the war as there was really no place for them to go and survive. Several more families left in a few years after the South was defeated. The grown men folk of another three families had since gone north to find work. Ole Mammie said the farm was nothing like it had been before the War. White folks had to help one another with the field work now. There weren't enough black laborers around to work, not even for hire.

Ole Mammie said, "There was work winter and summer, girl. Plowing, planting, weeding, reaping. All the time something going on outside if the weather was good. When the weather was bad, we spin, mill, repair, and sew. The Ole Missus and Massah had parties and all sorts of gaiety all through the year." She looked down at her feet again as if she was remembering times past - the good and the bad.

"Course in the old times before the War, they had all that gaiety and big to-dos 'cause they only paid they help in bad food, little stifling houses and cast off rags. And they could make us work from before sunup 'til dark. If we complain or get sickly too often, they could sell us to some place worse." She sighed heavily and heaved herself off the stool, returning to whatever she'd been doing before I mouthed off.

Course, I remember many things about my Momma. Momma was a light skinned woman about the color of a cup of coffee with more milk than coffee, as was I. Neither Momma's eyes nor any of her children's were black like Ole Mammie's, although my eyes were the darkest. Ole Mammie said Momma had light skin and soft brown eyes because her papa, my Grandpap Albert, was a mulatto. He wasn't born on our farm, so Ole Mammie said, "Don't be calling Ole Massah a 'dulterer! He not be the one!"

Momma was short and small boned with just enough meat on her to look soft instead of scrawny. She might have been five feet tall, but no more than that. I thought her size was the only way I resembled her. I don't know how she managed all the heavy lifting she did, but she compared herself to a donkey, small, but sturdy and strong. She had a smile like the sun coming through just after a storm. You had to smile back when you saw it. And she was always humming or singing as she worked. She had a beautiful voice that I learned as an adult is called "soprano." Years after Momma passed, I heard Rosa Ponselle sing for a select group of people in her home in Baltimore. She made me think of my momma so much when she sang "The Last Rose of Summer" that I had to stifle sobs. I think God took Momma to heaven to teach the angels how to sing!

I don't remember my papa much at all. Oh, how I wish I could! Both Ole Mammie and Momma allowed as how he was probably the best man they ever knew. Momma said he was a real Christian, not just one as says so. I can remember his laugh because it was so loud and it made me laugh too. I also remember him swinging me up in the air or setting me on his shoulders. I think that's one of the best things I can remember in my whole life - feeling like a bird up so high and hearing and feeling my papa's deep laugh. As young as I was, I do remember my momma and Ole Mammie wailing and wailing when Papa passed.

Papa was hauling rocks up the hill to the slave cemetery when the doubletree on the wagon broke. Not the harnesses. The metal rings didn't separate. The doubletree broke! The horses bolted and the wagon turned over, the rocks and wagon crushing my papa.

Momma and Ole Mammie both allowed as how there must have been evil doing's the day Papa passed, what with him dying on the way to the cemetery because a doubletree broke. We never heard anything more about it, so we never knew how it happened that the doubletree broke. In my entire life I never heard of another instance of such a thing, but I have been told that it sometimes happens.

Momma said that Ole Massah and Ole Missus both came to the cemetery when Papa passed. Momma said it was because they esteemed Papa so much. Papa had saved Ole Massah's best American Saddlebred mare when it came down with the colic. That horse came within an ace of dying. Seems Ole Ab'ram who lived above the stables let that horse eat too much dry food in the spring when the horse was also eating new sweet grass all day. If the mare had died, Ole Massah would've lost a valuable foal as well. I was told that my Papa managed to get to the horse without getting hurt and got that horse up off the ground by rubbing her muzzle softly and speaking to her in his quiet gentle voice.

Ole Massah allowed as he had never in his life seen anyone as good with a horse as Papa. The only person who even came near to papa with horses, Massah Robert allowed, was his brother Holton and he had been killed in the War by that time. No one else had been able to get near the mare because she was in such pain, rolling and thrashing around too much to get close to her. Papa had helped train that mare from the time she was a foal, so maybe her knowledge of him kept her a little quieter until he got a rein on her. My papa walked that horse around and around in the paddock for close to an hour as she settled down, the colic easing. Ole Massah cursed and yelled at Ole Ab'ram to clean the mare's stall right then as it was the least he could do after almost letting her die. Papa put the mare into the stall and stayed with her all night to be sure the colic didn't return.

When Ole Mammie was recounting this story, it seemed strange to me. I couldn't see as how a horse could eat too much, after all, they eat grass all day. They seemed to need a constant supply. A pig might eat too much maybe. But a horse?

When I said this out loud, Ole Mammie rebuked me, "Sarie, when you knows something 'bout horses, then you can tell us what you opine! You've had a belly ache from eating green plums, ain't you? Well a horse can eat the wrong stuff too. Girl, I'm not certain you even knows the front end of a horse from the rear." The words might have sounded stern except for the fact that Ole Mammie was laughing her funny grin with about half her teeth missing. "Til you do, girl, keep your mouth shut and learn from your betters!" That was probably the best advice Ole Mammie ever gave me - about a great many things.

Anyway, I was told that Papa saving that mare got Ole Mammie, Momma and me into the room behind the kitchen. As it happened, Big Cook passed just a week or so after Papa did. That was a case of good timing for a change because Ole Massah and Ole Missus decided my Momma had worked as Second Cook so long, she should have the Big Cook's job. Even though Big Cook passed soon after Papa, Momma allowed as how that wasn't strange. Big Cook was really old, older even that Ole Massah, and she had been feeling poorly for a long time, leaving Momma to do most of her work anyway.

Times were hard for all of us on the farm for years after the War, so the only help Momma had in the kitchen was Ole Mammie and, later, me. Ole Mammie and I were Momma's Second Cook!

Even in the winter, Momma could whip up a dinner of collard greens with ham hocks, mashed potatoes, crackling bread with butter, green beans, pickled beets and cucumber pickles that wouldn't put a Lord to shame. What she could do with fresh vegetables and pullets in the summer was pure magic! It makes my mouth water just remembering. She taught me how to cook all kinds of things including tomato pudding, rhubarb pie, pound cake, fruit cake, chess pie. Those were some of Ole Massah's favorite dishes. He and Massah Robert were right partial to sweet things.

Momma said that room behind the kitchen was actually smaller than the cabin we lived in before, but now there were just three of us, so smaller was alright. I can't remember the cabin on the hill, but Ole Mammie and Momma allowed as how we were much better off in the little room behind the kitchen. We actually had a bed up off the floor and the room had a glass window with shutters. Momma said the room was warmer in the winter because the big kitchen stove was on the other side of the wall and it was cooler in the summer because we cooked in the summer kitchen then. Ole Mammie said the slave cabin was hotter in the summer than the place bad folks go, but her favorite things about the new room was, "Girl, we don't have to carry water so far now and we got our very own outhouse much more close than what we have before!" Ole Mammie allowed as how the nearness of an outhouse was really important, especially when you are old.

Momma always said she never stopped missing Papa. When I got older, I wondered about that. Growing up on a farm, I learned young how babies come into the world. I was too little to know about men and women when Momma was still with us, but I saw the animals in the fields and in their pens.

I don't recollect my sister Rhi being born. Somehow it seems that she was always there, even though I know she wasn't. Rhi was four years younger than I. My papa and Rhi's papa were different men. Had to be as Papa was dead a couple of years before Rhi was born. Rhi was almost as white as Massah Robert and Miz 'Dena's children. I do remember the new shoes I got when Rhi was born. Momma said they weren't very practical, but they were beautiful! They were shiny, patent leather. I used a biscuit to shine them on Sundays before church. I was so proud of those shoes. I cried and cried when Momma said months later that they were too little for me. To stop my caterwauling, Momma cut the toes out so I could wear them a little longer.

I do remember when Vaz was born two years after Rhi. He looked half grown when he came along. Ole Mammie said he was the biggest new baby she ever saw, and he was always taller than average at every age. Vaz was very light skinned with yellow, curly hair as a child. Vaz's eyes turned green when he was about six or seven months old. Green! Can you imagine a negro with yellow hair and green eyes? And I believe that Ole Missus got that boy confused with the Baby Jesus. The way she carried on over him! New shoes came again in celebration of Vaz's birth too. And not just new shoes. We got new clothes, too. Not hand-me-downs from the Big House, but brand new clothes including a jacket for each of us, and one for Momma.

The day Ole Missus brought the new clothes when Vaz was born, she told Ole Mammie and me to use some of the precious sugar and make "a nice, delicate cake" just for us. Not for the white folks. Just for us, although Ole Missus insisted that she have a piece with us. I didn't know what to think. Ole Missus sat in the kitchen, holding Vaz on her lap and ate cake - with us! That was probably the first time I thought Ole Missus had lost her mind. It sure wouldn't be the last.

A little while after Vaz was born I realized that young Mr. Claybone came tapping on our door many nights after we were all in bed. I knew it was him because I could smell his soap. Nobody else in the House used that soap. It smelled nice, like some kind of spices. Mr. Claybone often came to the kitchen during the day too, carrying one of the children around, talking "baby talk" to the children and silly talk to Momma, often in low whispers. Once I even saw him kiss Momma's forehead. I'd never seen anyone kiss another human except for Ole Mammie and Momma kissing one of us children. Momma laughed and told him he needed to hurry out to the hayfield - or the tobacco - and help with the harvest. He bowed to her, put whatever child he was holding down and left laughing.

Mr. Claybone was always considerate of Ole Mammie and me. When he brought candy for the little ones, he always brought some for Ole Mammie and me too, but I was jealous of the way he and Momma laughed together as if they knew funny things we didn't. Momma was happiest when Mr. Claybone was with us, it seemed. When he tapped on the door at night, Momma would get up quietly and leave the room. Most of the time I don't remember her coming back, but she was there in the morning, smelling like Mr. Claybone's soap.

Vaz was about two when Nora was born. She looked like one of the dolls Miz 'Dena's children had stored carefully in the attic for the next generation of girls to play with. I thought Nora was the most beautiful baby I ever saw. To this day, I believe she was. And she smiled almost as soon as she was born. That, and her size, were the features she got from Momma. Mr. Claybone gave Momma a pair of gold hoops for her ears when Nora was born, taking the time to put them on for her. And once again, Ole Missus brought gifts for the whole family, but the things she gave "Mariah" and "Vastine" were better quality than what Ole Mammie and I received. I noticed the difference, but it was several years before I realized why Ole Missus took on so over those children.

Ole Missus named every one of Momma's younger children. She allowed as how they would grow to suit dignified names. What kind of negro names were "Mariah," " Vastine," and "Honora"? Ole Mammie, Momma, and I always called them "Rhi," "Vaz," and "Nora." So did all the other negroes.

Ole Mammie took bad sick on Christmas Day one year. I reckon it was the year of our Lord 1882. Momma and I mixed flour, water and ground up mustard seeds, put that mess on warm flannel rags and laid it on her chest, turned her over after awhile and put fresh flannels with the mustard plaster on her back. I even got a pint of applejack from Ole Ab'ram and put cane syrup in it for Ole Mammie's cough. She refused the spirits at first and she complained about everything for the first few days. I reckoned Ole Mammie was going to pass just to spite us for putting that plaster on her! But she got so sick that she couldn't complain and she even drank the spirits, thanking me, between fits of coughing and sips of applejack for making the "cough medicine" which I had watched her make for others many times. Maybe the applejack helped cut the phlegm, but mostly it just put her into a stupor.

Just before she passed, Ole Mammie said it was time for her to join Albert. She had long said Grandpap Albert must have passed awhile back or he would have found her after the War. Ole Mammie took Momma's hand and told her that she didn't think "bad" about the babies being born like they were.

"Children is gifts from God, Nisa, and you're young still with life left in you," she told Momma between fits of hard, dry coughing, struggling to breathe. She whispered her last words "You be sure this family treat you and the children right. Massah Robert promised me that! And Clay vowed that much too!"

She looked over at me and smiled sweetly. "I'm not going far, Sarie. I'll watch after you." She closed her eyes in sleep and died later that night, never waking. Ole Mammie's last words seemed strange to me then, but Momma seemed to understand exactly. And for years I thought I saw Ole Mammie watching me. Sometimes smiling. Sometimes not.

Ole Massah had sent for the doctor, but the doctor came too late. She had the pneumonia, he said. "Miz Callie's been with you a long time." the doctor told Massah Robert and Miz 'Dena within my hearing, "Please help her daughter and grandchildren."

I had always called her "Ole Mammie," but she was only 62 years old when she passed, and no one ever loved me the same way again in my whole life.

Momma passed just a couple of months later trying to birth another baby, a little girl. It passed too. Momma sent me to fetch Miz 'Dena and Mr. Claybone when the bleeding began, but they couldn't save her. Was I too slow? She had urged me to hurry! Should I have stayed with her? She sent me away to find help and Miz 'Dena asked me to take the babies to the rear parlor and keep them there until she came for me. Momma told Miz 'Dena to tell us to be good children and obey her and Mr. Claybone. Miz 'Dena said that she expressed her love of us children in the last few words she spoke. My sweet momma.

I truly believe I would have laid down and died myself if I didn't have three little children crying mostly because I was crying. They refused to let go of me. I carried Nora in a sack with Vaz in my arms, his own little arms wrapped tightly around my neck. Rhi held tightly to my skirt tail. I was barely ten years old. I was scared - mortally scared. How was I to take care of the four of us and keep us together? I had to stand on a stool to help Momma in the kitchen. What job was I fit for?

I had awful nightmares off and on for a couple of years after Momma's death about the Second Coming. Jesus came to earth, taking the just and the saved, leaving me on Earth to manage as best I could during the Tribulation. Jesus took the children, but not me. I wasn't even fit to go to Heaven.

I recollect most of what happened at Momma's funeral as if it was yesterday, but I don't recollect a word of the service. Seems to me like a preacher didn't need to be there. Funerals are for the living anyway and I could have done without words. I felt dead myself.

The sleet and snow came down that morning as if God Himself was angry over Momma's passing. The wagon carrying her body slipped backwards several times as we went up the hollow to the cemetery. One old horse could barely pull even such a light load as Momma and the little dead, unnamed baby up that muddy, slick track. I was carrying Nora in the sack I always slung around my neck for her. I had carried her like that since she was a newborn. She was used to me. Several people from the hill asked if they could carry her or take care of Rhi and Vaz for me. The children would cling tighter to my skirts and wail if anyone looked like taking them away from me. Rhi clutched one side of my sodden skirts and Vaz clutched the other. All of us were wet head to foot except Nora. I was wearing Momma's jacket because it was big enough to cover Nora in the sack. It kept her dry. The only part of me that was dry was my front where Nora lay. My teeth chattered so hard from the cold that I thought they might break!

We couldn't get our regular minister for the service. He was away for another funeral and the weather was so bad he couldn't get back in time. I would've liked kind Miz Victoria's husband to say the words, but they were way down in Tennessee and couldn't get there in time either. So Deacon Young said something just before four older negro men nailed the lid shut on the single wooden casket and laid Momma and the baby down into that watery hole. Their shrouds had been pure white down at the Big House, but they had somehow gotten slightly muddy.

Momma was buried right next to Papa's grave. I was in such a state that I thought I saw a man I believed to be Papa smiling from beside the tree nearest their graves. I never spoke of this to anyone else. Ever. I was either crazy, which is most likely the explanation, or I saw my father's ghost celebrating Momma joining him.

We all sang Were You There because it was Momma's favorite and, as bad as the weather was, it was only two weeks until Easter. In my mind I could hear Momma singing with us.

Were you there when they laid Him in the tomb?
Were you there when they laid Him in the tomb?
Oh, oh, oh, oh, sometimes it causes me to tremble, tremble, tremble.
Were your there when they laid Him in the tomb?

I wanted to *jump into that grave* taking all three children, letting them pour dirt over the four of us! Maybe then Papa could be completely happy! The image I thought was Papa shook his head as if to say, "No,"

19

but he smiled lovingly at me. I couldn't jump anyway. My feet were so heavy I couldn't move. My heart was heavier still - so heavy I couldn't breathe.

   I think Ole Massah must have spoken to me a couple of times before I realized it. Finally, Miz 'Dena put her gloved hand on my arm, got me to look up at her and nodded toward Ole Massah. I looked at Ole Massah and I believe he might have been crying too, though maybe it was just melting sleet. Ole Massah cleared his throat and spoke to me.

   "Sara? Your name is Sara?" he asked. I think I nodded at him. Sadly he murmured. "You look like your father a little, but more like your mother, I think." I wondered if he'd ever noticed me at all. I'd lived in his house for eight years or so.

   "Well, Sara," he continued softly, "this is a hard day for you and these babies. I know because I lost my own mother when I was only eleven. I am more sorry than I can express at your losses today and last December. Your grandmother was a good woman her *whole* life. No one can ever say different, and your mother was a fine, fine woman, too. She was like a member of the family. If you need anything, help or money, go to my son Robbie." He dofffed his hat to me and turned toward Mr. 'Zander who was helping to steady his grandfather on the uneven ground.

   Massah Robert helped Ole Missus up beside us. Ole Missus was moaning and carrying on as if it were her mother who had been laid in that cold, silent unrepentant ground. She seemed more grieved than I would ever have suspected. She tried several times to speak, but seemed unable. Miz 'Dena put an arm around her mother-in-law and said to me, "Sara, your mother was the best cook we ever had. We trusted her with everything. The cooking, the food budget. Everything! My mother-in-law and I have talked and we agree that you probably learned your mother's recipes." I saw Miz 'Dena look at Ole Missus quickly as if she were about to say something Ole Missus might not like. She quickly continued.

"If we get someone bigger and stronger to come down every day to help you, would you like to be the new cook? We know you are very young, but we've seen how quick you are to learn things." Ole Missus looked like Miz 'Dena had said too much, but Massah Robert spoke up.

"Sara, you and the children can continue to stay in the room behind the kitchen. My father and I are going to look at our accounts later this week to see if we can't pay you more for your work. Times have changed and we don't want to lose you to people who might pay you better, but who won't appreciate you as much. Can you give us your decision about taking the job of cook after Mr. Powell and I talk about what we can pay? We'll send a girl down tomorrow to help you. If she doesn't work to suit you, let Mrs. Powell know. Mrs. *Loudena* Powell. *We*'ll look until we find someone who suits you." He doffed his hat and helped his sputtering mother back to their carriage.

I turned to look as I heard Ole Missus tell her son in an angry voice, "Robbie, I want those babies upstairs with a proper nanny! How long are we going to pay that old woman back? We don't owe that oldest child anything special, but of course, I won't just put the girl out! Let her assist the new cook when we hire one. The girl can live with one of the families on the hill."

"Mother, if I have anything to say about it those children will *all* remain together, and I'm certain that eventually Clay will get his mind back and want it that way, too. If the little ones go upstairs, Sara goes as well. How's that going to set with everyone? That old woman saved us more than once, and I shall *never* forget it. Even you cannot be so selfish as to remove those children from that girl. Look at them! Why, I think all four of them might die if you did!" He replied firmly. Ole Missus looked startled at that. "Nisa worked so much that little Sara has been the biggest caretaker of those babies. She's the real mother to them!"

"That girl knows next to nothing about anyone on the hill. She's lived most of her life in our house!" Massah Robert muttered as if through clenched teeth, "And it may just be that we *do owe that oldest child* more than you, in all your infinite knowledge, are aware of!"

"Oldest child?" My head was spinning. What were they talking about? Did they mean me?

That's when I finally started sobbing and dropped to the ground. Relief at still having a home for the four of us broke the tight knot that had almost cut off my air. I gulped air between sobs. My crying woke Nora who took her thumb out of her mouth and started howling. Rhi and Vaz began to clutch me harder and all four of us were sitting there in the mud wailing and moaning.

Ole Ab'ram, who nearly let Ole Massah's American Saddlebred mare die, came over with Aunt Priss and Sookie. They helped us up and into the back of the wagon that had hauled Momma and the poor, little unnamed baby up the hollow. Young Mr. 'Zander and his Missus put a horse blanket over us. It was muddy, which explained how the shrouds had gotten dirty, and it probably stank, but it kept the sharp wind from hitting us in our wet clothes on the way back down the hollow to the Big House. The white folks rode ahead in their covered carriages and the negroes walked behind us, singing mournful dirges all the way home.

I barely remember the rest of the day, but someone had been thoughtful enough to heat water and fill the tub we used for bathing and to lay out dry clothing for us so we could change from our muddy, sodden clothes on our return from the cemetery. Aunt Priss and Sookie helped us into the house. They helped us clean up and change before they led us into the dining room where food was laid out for the white family *and the negroes*. I never knew who made the food or cleaned up when we were finished. I seem to remember Miz 'Dena helping the children and me into our room, pulling off our shoes, and putting a quilt over us after the four of us climbed into the fresh clean bed with its new mattress. I may have dreamed it, but I thought I felt Ole Missus stoop over us and kiss Rhi, Vaz and Nora. It seemed she even stroked my cheek gently. If she did, it was the only physical affection she ever showed me. So I probably dreamed it.

It never struck me 'til the next day that everybody on the farm was at the funeral unless they were too young or too ill to be there. Mr. and Miz 'Zander's little boy, Andy, had a cold and the weather was too bad for him to be out. Miz Mary had come home to be with her mother for the birth of her first baby, due any day, so she stayed at home with young Andy, but her husband Professor McCain, was at the funeral. Rob and Miss Ivy were there too, but Mr. Claybone was not.

Massah Robert and Miz 'Dena's youngest children, Rob and his sister Miss Ivy, came to the kitchen the next morning personally to offer their condolences. They amazed me by insisting on helping until we could get someone to help permanently. If they had never done another thing for me, I would have loved them forever for their kindness that morning.

"We can carry dishes in and out of the dining room for you." Miss Ivy said softly, "And, later, I can read recipes to you. Of course, you already know how to cook most of what we eat, but from time-to-time, the family will want something special."

I did know how to make the usual stuff, not just because I had been Second Cook, but because I acted as Big Cook when Momma was sickly which had been a good deal of the time with the last poor dead baby. Momma had been nearby then where I could easily ask questions about what I was doing, but I was alone now.

Rob said, as he looked at the big kitchen stove with the heavy kitchen pots and pans, "I can carry those things to the sink for you and help put them on the stove when you need them back there. Since it's winter, the black boys on the hill don't have so much to do, so we can get a boy to carry wood and water for you. We know that Mother is looking to find a girl who will be a real help for you, but until she sends someone down, Ivy and I will help."

I started crying again. Lord, I was like a bucket full of holes in those days. Everything made my eyes - and nose - leak. "Thank you kindly. I expect I'm going to need help for a long while." I finally managed to speak.

They talked for several minutes about what they would do and when. Rob and Miss Ivy actually made *all* the decisions. I just *tried to pay attention* and agreed with whatever they decided. Deciding anything was more than I could do at ten years of age with my head spinning from grief. Finally, Miss Ivy said, "Mother will come see you shortly and set up a schedule with you for your kitchen tasks." She looked at her brother as if to send him a private message.

Thinking back I expect Miz 'Dena hadn't thought I'd need so much help, but Miss Ivy, who was only fifteen herself, was wise enough to know that her mother was the best person to help me. She was a kind, smart girl. A true friend as long as she lived.

"If you can handle just the cooking and washing up today, Rob and I will take care of everything else, including serving and carrying the soiled dishes back to the kitchen. Is that satisfactory, Sara?"

"And, remember, I'll get one of the boys to carry water and fire wood in for you. You are not to try to move the big heavy cast iron pots by yourself, Little Sara!" Rob admonished me firmly. He almost always addressed me as "Little Sara," and although I called his sister "Miss Ivy" I never called him "Mister." There was a sweetness about him that made him especially dear to me even then. Later he always behaved as if he were my older brother just as he was Ivy's.

Almost as an afterthought I asked, "Miss Ivy, Rob, is your Uncle Claybone ill? He didn't come to the service with the rest of the family yesterday."

They both sniffed scornfully, but Rob said, "Yes! I reckon you could call it that!"

"Well, I hope he feels better soon," I said. They looked at each other in that same confidential way again, as if they felt sorrier for me than ever before.

"Don't worry about Mr. Claiborne," Rob said firmly, "He will be completely well sooner than anyone would expect!"

Lately, Miss Ivy and Rob scowled if Mr. Claybone's name was so much as mentioned, as if he were the devil or something. Since he was their uncle, you might think they would hold him in high regard as my sisters and brother did, but, indeed they did not think well of him at all. Miss Ivy and Rob left with promises to return before dinner needed to be served.

I was so confused in the kitchen that day that I'm not sure what I prepared, but the worry over what to make and how to go about it on my own served as a distraction from giving way completely to grief. I would be fine for an hour at a time, then collapse into Ole Mammie's rocker and bawl until I realized I was upsetting the little ones. Then I'd rise and try to get some work done. I did a lot of silent crying for a long time trying not to upset the babies.

The house maid, "Silly S'rena," as Ole Mammie and I always called her as a private jest, stopped in the kitchen on her way to burn rubbish and dump things in the trash pit. She said as how she was sorry Momma passed as Momma had helped every family on the hill. Seems like Momma sent leftovers to those who needed them.

The folks in the Big House weren't hurt by it and the hogs got big and fat by fall anyway. The chickens laid all the eggs we needed. So it seemed like no one was hurt and the seven families, or parts of families, who still lived on the hill were better for Momma's ways of stretching victuals. S'rena often told things she ought not have, but I always had a little soft spot in my heart for her for telling me how good my Momma had been and how much the black folk all loved her. But the rest of what S'rena told that day was most revealing to me, not so much then, as later when my thinking grew clearer.

The day of my Momma and my baby sister's funeral, S'rena had to get her work finished fast. She wanted to be at the service. She said she went into the front parlor without knocking as it was almost never used, but since the Deacon and his missus were there the evening before, she needed to clean the grate and dust the furniture. She said Mr. Claybone was crying so hard he never heard her come in. She backed out of the room as quietly as she could, deciding to clean the room after the funeral was over. When she came back later, after the service, she saw Mr. Claybone was still in the room. This time he was lying face down, his feet hanging off the settee, with a nearly empty bottle of Ole Massah's best Kentucky bourbon in his hand and another empty one on the floor. By this time, S'rena reckoned as how she better clean as quietly as possible and risk Mr. Claybone's ire over Ole Missus' come the next morning. She said he stirred once, long enough to mumble, "Nisa! Nisa! Don't go, Nisa!"

S'rena asked me if he was talking about my Momma. I was only ten, but I was smart enough not to answer that. It wasn't as if Nisa was a common name or anyone else we ever knew had been called that! Anyhow, I figured S'rena made the whole thing up until I saw the empty bourbon bottle in the trash pit several days later.

CHAPTER 2: MIZ 'DENA

One shade the more, one ray the less,
Had half impair'd the nameless grace
Which waves in every raven tress,
Or softly lighten o'er her face;
Where thoughts serenely sweet express
How pure, how dear their dwelling place.

from She Walks in Beauty Like the Night,
George Gordon, Lord Byron

Either white folks believe that black folks can't hear or, more likely, can't understand what they hear because much of what I know about my own life, I learned from hearing things not intended for my ears. Not because I was eavesdropping, but because white folks didn't seem to notice I was there.

Miz 'Dena came down real sick early the year of our Lord 1885. This was a heavy blow to the entire household, including me. Miz 'Dena had been mother to me for the two years since Momma passed. She had encouraged and praised my efforts in the kitchen, helping me to become useful and resourceful in the kitchen and as good a parent as I could be at such a young age. She was the heart and soul of the family, so we all grieved while trying to put on pleasant faces around her.

Miz 'Dena had discovered too late just how ill she was. The doctor said there wasn't much he could do for her except to try to keep her comfortable. She was stoic, initially refusing the opium that Dr. Young left for her pain.

"I'd rather be in pain than out of my head!" she argued, but the pain became worse. Then she said, "Just a drop of my medicine, Ivy. Then I'll take some of the delicious broth you made, Sara." I insisted on spoon feeding Miz 'Dena because she would sometimes eat just to please me when she wouldn't touch food for anyone else, not even Miss Ivy or Massah Robert.

Every morning Miz Anne peeked into Miz 'Dena's room to be sure Miz 'Dena was awake for her bath. Miz Anne bathed her as gently as if she had been one of the babies. Miz Anne had always seemed aloof to me, but she was the epitome of Christian love and filial duty with her mother-in-law.

I don't think it ever entered Ole Missus's head to try to feed or bathe Miz 'Dena, but Ole Missus read part of the newspaper to her every day, inserting her opinions on everything and everyone mentioned. Although the paper and mail were delivered daily by the private carrier the Powell's paid to bring it from the local post office, the paper was still several days stale by the time we received it. Ole Missus insisted on a Richmond paper declaring that she wanted to know the comings and goings in bigger places than our little community. She didn't care that "a good time was had by all" at the local box luncheons to raise money for Confederate veterans and widows. Of course we also received the weekly local paper which she read when no one was watching.

Massah Robert and Rob would carry Miz 'Dena to and from the chaise lounge by the window so she could see something besides the walls of her room. On nice days they would throw open the door to the second floor porch and let in the warm breeze perfumed by the blossoming fruit in the nearby orchard. Toward the end, even the breeze hurt her so much she'd refuse to have the door open. She no longer wanted to be moved to the window. Fortunately for her dignity, she was so thin by then that it required only one of the household women or the nurse to help her to the chamber pot.

Her son Dr. Thomas Powell travelled down from Boston where he was in his final year as a resident. He thought he might be able to help with his mother's illness as he was specializing in genito-urinary problems and her cancer seemed to have started in her lower abdomen, probably in her ovaries Dr. Young had said. But Dr. Thomas was too late to help her medically, so he sat and read poetry to her for several half hour periods each day until he returned to Boston a short week after his arrival and just a month before Miz 'Dena passed. She especially loved Longfellow's poems and I always associate her with the ever faithful *Evangeline*.

Mr. 'Zander was descended from neither of his parents as best I could tell. Although he looked like Massah Robert, where Massah Robert was always kind and courteous, Mr. 'Zander was practical, to the point of coolness, stiffly courteous. He went through charitable motions similar to those of his mother, but whereas Miz 'Dena never made anyone feel beholding or subservient, somehow Mr. 'Zander always left the impression that he was acting from a sense of noblesse oblige.

Out of duty I'm convinced, because he never did so before his brother led the way, Mr. 'Zander read to his mother for an hour every morning before beginning his workday on the estate. Whereas Dr. Thomas had read lovely, sometimes thrilling poetry, Mr. 'Zander read from the *King James I Version of the Bible*. It seemed to me that Miz 'Dena much preferred poetry, but she loved all her children and I never heard her complain, not even in her worst pain, to any of them about anything. I wanted so badly to tell Mr. 'Zander that all the reading about the "wages of sin" was completely unnecessary. Miz 'Dena lived her Christian love for others with a smile on her face, and a bit of kick to her gait.

Miz Mary came home the last month of her mother's life with the intention of allowing her mother to spend precious time with young Master Isaac while she helped with her mother's care. That was well meant, but a three-year old is not much delight to a dying person, even such a loving grandmother as Miz 'Dena. When Miz Mary and the little boy came into Miz 'Dena's room, Miz Mary would have to hold squirming Master Isaac on her lap. Miz 'Dena could never have held him nor tolerated him sitting beside her, jostling her on her bed, although clearly from the loving expression on her face she would have liked to. Master Isaac, of course, wanted down to explore the new room. Miz 'Dena did laugh at that a couple of times, and she laughed at the boy's incorrect pronunciations, but after about fifteen minutes of the child's rambunctious ways, she would tell her daughter to take the boy outside in the spring air for awhile.

"Mary, dear, let him run some of that young energy off," she'd say, "Then come back when the boy is having his nap. I like looking at your pretty face."

Only Miz 'Dena could have seen "pretty" in poor lantern-jawed Miz Mary, but the smile her mother's compliment put on that face justified any exaggeration.

Later when the pain became really bad, Miz 'Dena would whisper to Miss Ivy, Rob or even Massah Robert, "Some of my drops, plea-a-se!"

I'd wait until the pain eased some and pick up her spoon to give her some broth. Too often then she would shake her head slightly, "No, thank you, Sara. You're a good girl to make the broth just for me. Go back to your brother and sisters. I'll try to take some later. I promise."

But she almost never could stomach even my carefully prepared and highly diluted broth in the last couple of weeks. Those last two weeks she neither ate nor drank anything except her medicine. Dr. Young said it was just as well. She wasn't going to get better. Let her go on to God and the two infants she buried long ago.

Massah Robert walked around looking older and grayer every day while Miz 'Dena was dying. Two days before she died I heard her weak voice saying to him, "Robbie, you've been a perfect husband and the best father. Thank you, my love. I've had a blessed life with you and our wonderful children." She lapsed into a coma later that day, never saying anything more.

When I found Massah Robert alone crying in the back yard the day after she was buried, he was holding a pink Memorial Day piney up to his nose. He saw me, took his handkerchief out, blew his nose, and, holding the piney out where I could see it better, said, "Loudena liked pineys better than roses." He laughed a little, "She said pineys didn't have thorns!" He started to cry softly again, walking away toward the front yard.

He turned back to me, maybe because I had started to cry too, saying kindly, "Don't cry, Sara. It will be alright. God doesn't give us more trouble than we and He can handle together. My sweet Loudena is not in pain now. If any of us gets to Heaven, we'll find Loudena there!" He turned back to the front yard and walked out of sight. He must have heard the same litany from his mother that Rhi repeated to me from time to time.

If I hadn't seen or heard spirits in that house before, I certainly began to see them from the corners of my eyes then. They were everywhere.

CHAPTER 3: MR. CLAY MOVES TO TEXAS

The souls of those I love are on high stars.
How good that there's no-one left to lose
And one can weep. All created in order
To sing songs, this air of Tsarskoye Selo's.

The river bank's silver willow
Touches the bright September stream.
Rising from the past, my shadow
Is running in silence to meet me.

Anna Akhmatova

Later that summer I got a real education about my family. I was sitting
in a chair on the kitchen porch, stringing and snapping beans to put out
to dry the next day. It was almost nine o'clock at night. I was usually
asleep by then, but there was still some light and the beans wouldn't
string themselves. Someone would bring me another bushel or two
tomorrow or the next day and I'd have this to do all over again. The girl
we hired to help in the kitchen didn't seem to see well enough to get all
the bug spots and strings off properly. While Violet was a great help in
many ways, she was very little help with beans.

The children were all in bed asleep. At first I only heard the insects
humming and the whippoorwill calling. I loved to hear the insects at
twilight. The sound made me feel satisfied deep inside. Satisfied to have
earned a few minutes to appreciate nature. Satisfied to have earned my
nightly rest. But there's something about a whippoorwill's call that
made me sad, sometimes to the point of crying. Made me lonely to hear
one bird calling to its mate at the end of day. I had to wipe my eyes with
my apron that evening. When I put the tail of my apron down I saw
Massah Robert and Mr. Claybone coming between the hedges from the
stables. At first I couldn't hear them, then I could. It wasn't that they

came closer. They had stopped. They both were speaking much louder - angrier.

"You are a complete ne'er-do-well, Clay! You're 28 years old, for God' sake! You've got children sown all over this damned county!" Massah Robert shouted at his brother.

Mr. Claybone laughed, but it didn't sound like a happy laugh. "Whoa, Robbie," he interrupted, "I don't travel the whole damned county - maybe one or two over in Russell County!"

I knew I ought to go inside because this argument was not meant for my ears, but I'd already heard too much. Besides, if I had gone inside, that squeaky kitchen door would have given me away and that might be embarrassing for them.

Massah Robert sounded like he might grab Mr. Claybone by the throat, "It's nothing to laugh about, you jackass! There are little bastard Powell's all over the place, black and white and every color in-between! Those children ought to be taken care of - by you! Instead, Daddy is trying to do it, and at his age! Our Daddy who never in his life would have treated a woman the way you've treated these girls. Why, I think you've become a booming business for some of them. Just last week Daddy arranged for John Speers to marry Ann Kendall. John Speers!" Massah Robert was clearly disgusted.

"That's what that poor girl's come down to! He's at least 75 years old! He was too sorry to serve in the War, so she won't even get a war widow's pension from him! I think Daddy gave him a couple of hundred dollars to marry her, and I know he slipped *her* at least twenty dollars when old Speers wasn't looking. She looked like she'd rather die than marry that old moonshiner, but what other choice did she have? No honest farmer will marry her now that she's brooding."

It was very strange for me to hear Massah Robert talk loudly or to use coarse language. I was still young, naïve, but I knew what they were talking about.

"When you start messing with poor, unmarried, *decent* girls, you've gone too far!"

"I'm not sure any of those girls are decent, Robbie. I never *ravished* any of them, and certainly not Ann Kendall! In fact, I never promised any of those women anything! They thought if they lifted their skirts for me, they'd get more than a roll in the hay! I'm no fool. I like the company of pretty girls, but I am not going to marry because some gal got herself in the family way trying to catch a rich husband! Not if I couldn't live openly with the only woman I ever wanted to marry - a Virginia marriage was illegal, and the whole damn county would've run her off if we'd tried to live together openly!"

Massah Robert was choking, he was so mad, "Good God, Clay! Don't you dare tell me you would have married Nisa! She was a lovely girl, but…"

"Nisa was beautiful, but that wasn't what attracted me to her in the beginning." Mr. Claybone said wistfully."Right after I came back from Williamsburg, I came home late one night, well actually one morning. I heard this enchanting singing coming from the other side of the house. I went round to the herb garden and saw Nisa there picking herbs and singing. It must have been about six o'clock. The rising sun hit her hair making it look like a halo around her head!"

Massah Robert snorted, "You were still drunk I'd guess!"

"May have been, but the red in her hair looked like a flaming halo and she was signing something, something about rosemary being for remembering. I tell you, Robbie, I was gone, hook, line and sinker from the minute she lifted her face and smiled at me! I never had a thing to do with another woman when Nisa was alive! I wish to God that we had run off. I tried to persuade her to go to France, but I didn't have much money and she wouldn't leave her old mama and her oldest child anyway. So don't you say a word, not one word, against Pernicia. She was the finest woman you or I will ever know!"

There was a scuffle. From what I could see in the ever darkening twilight, Massah Robert knocked Mr. Claybone down. "My Loudena was the finest woman you or I will ever know!" he said between gritted teeth.

Mr. Claybone sat quietly for a minute or two on the dew-wet grass with his hands behind him, supporting himself. He finally sighed heavily, "I guess she was, Robbie, 'cause she never said an unkind word against Pernicia or me, and she cared for our children after Nisa died. I don't think Mother could have managed without 'Dena when Sara was still so young, even though Mother loves my babies."

Almost no one ever called my momma Pernicia, her given name. Clearly Mr. Claybone knew her well. And he would've married my momma! A white man and a negro woman. Well, she was what some folks call "high yeller," and I had heard more than one person, white and black, refer to her as "real perty," but still… I was past moving inside now. I was completely stuck in that chair. I'm surprised I didn't let that big pan of beans fall off my lap onto the porch floor I was shaking so hard.

Mr. Claybone put his hand up to his head, "Why'd you hit me so damned hard, Robbie? You're an old man! I didn't know you could still hit that hard or I wouldn't have started this row with you!"

He was chuckling a little, but I believe Massah Robert had hit him hard. Dismissing Miz 'Dena's saintliness was a way to get permanently on Massah Robert's bad side.

Massah Robert laughed a little and sat down on a bench beside the path. "You're still a shiftless good-for-nothing, Clay, so don't try to make me laugh! I wish Nisa was still alive. If for no other reason than the girl had a way of getting you to toe the line. You were a stranger to work before you hooked up with Nisa and you've been a stranger to it ever since she passed! The girl was a miracle worker. I don't know how in the world she got you to work. "

"She did it the oldest way in the world." Mr. Claybone laughed. "She said she worked hard for her family and if I didn't work too, there'd be no playing - at least not with her!"

Massah Robert laughed immediately at that. He had his hands clasped between his knees and his back bent over so that he and Mr. Claybone were nearly eye-to-eye.

"Things have got to change, Clay! Old Daddy Claiborne is dying. He'll be dead before winter, and I will not feed and house someone who does nothing to earn his keep and everything to ruin his life and as many others as possible! Do you hear me?" he said firmly. As if to himself, he mumbled, then they both were quiet for a moment before Massah Robert resumed, "There will be no more payments to girls carrying your babies," he said resolutely. "Mother has coddled you to the point of ruination, and Daddy never tried to stop her. Maybe it was because Warren was like he was. I don't know, but I won't allow it. The only hope for you is to throw you out on your own where you either sink or swim!"

They were both silent for what seemed like a long time, then Mr. Claybone spoke, "Robbie, funny this should all come out tonight. For a while now I've been thinking 'bout going to Texas. There's land to be had reasonably in a promising area near East Dallas if I move quickly."

"Promising of what?" Massah Robert asked warily as if he didn't trust what he was hearing.

"Raising cattle."

Knowing his brother as he did, Mr. Claybone quickly added, "Now, don't get your back up against it before I even explain it to you. Eliza Young will get about $2,000 when she marries. She's wanted to marry me forever. I've seen her ankles and cleavage more times than I care to talk about and neither one is all that worth seeing! And I refuse to pick her handkerchief up off the floor one more time. She's misplaced her shawl ten times if she's lost it once. And, she wears far too much scent for a decent woman!" he added for emphasis as he got up, dusting his breeches off and sat on the bench across the path from Massah Robert.

Massah Robert laughed. "How much older than you is Eliza? Ten years?"

Mr. Claybone laughed too for a second. "Seven years, but that's just it, Robbie, she is getting past marriage material. Her loins are not likely to produce children much longer. She is desperate to get married to most anyone under most any conditions. Her brother and his wife will inherit her father's place soon. The old man can't live forever. He's all of ninety now! Eliza doesn't see herself as an old-maid auntie to Alfred and Imaline Young's passel of brats, and I know for a fact that Al is going to put a stop to Eliza's extravagant dresses and trips to Richmond every fall!"

Massah Robert replied, "Well, seeing as how she's our first cousin, it might be a good thing if she doesn't have any children! You remember Warren, even if you were a baby when he died. Warren was deaf and dumb from birth and Mother and Daddy are *second* cousins several times removed. Odd that I have Warren so much on my mind tonight." He stopped in thought for a minute, then went on, "But I wouldn't dismiss Eliza just yet as a brood mare! Mother was over fifty when you were born!"

"Great Jehoshaphat! Robbie, you can't compare anybody in the country to Mother! Damnation, God broke the mold when he made her!" Mr. Claybone cursed. "That woman will live longer than you or I, and *don't be surprised* when she marries again after Daddy dies! Go ahead and laugh, but I'm telling you…"

Massah Robert laughed heartily at that. After a long silence he said, "Nevertheless, what makes you think Eliza will give you money to fund your ranch?"

I could hear Mr. Claybone smile even in the dark, "'Cause she will, Robbie! 'Cause she will! But - I need more than $2,000 to buy the land, the stock and set up housekeeping. Eliza won't give me a penny unless we marry here with a big to-do. I know that woman's pride. She will insist on going with me, damn it all!"

"Oh, Clay, you've not even married yet and already you're looking to get rid of the poor thing!" Massah Robert teased.

"Poor thing, my horse's ass!" Clay said emphatically. "The reason she's not married yet is not because of her looks or her family. She used to be well-enough to look at, getting a little grey now and her teeth are not white anymore." Massah Robert protested, but Mr. Claybone went on. "The damned woman drinks *tea* all day long. But, dammit all, Robbie, *she's not married because she's the orneriest female this side of hell!*" He sounded determined now. "She's about as far from my sweet, funny Nisa as a woman can be. But, I'll shake her off within a month of moving to Texas! She won't like the shack we'll live in down on the property I buy. She won't like the dust either. She'll miss wearing her finery to parties - and she won't find me very attractive either, if you know what I mean. I'll buy her a decent house in East Dallas and she can deal with cowmen and railroad men's wives. She'll love flinging all her Virginia connections and gentility in their faces." He guffawed at this vision.

"How much more, Clay?" Massah Robert asked after he stopped laughing.

"How much more what?" Mr. Clay had drifted away. "Oh, how much more money? I don't know exactly. It's not easy to figure, but to become operational I need about $4,000 all together, plus whatever else that damned woman will require."

Massah Robert stood, "Bring me more accurate figures tomorrow and we'll see what can be done. I'm willing to finance this if you show me you're willing to work and that it's a project *worth* financing, but…" he stopped to be sure he had his brother's attention completely, "I will expect *half* the profits until you've repaid me. I'll place half of what I receive in an account for each of Nisa's three children by you and I'll keep the rest." I heard all this, but it was years before I understood it.

"But, Robbie, it could be very slim pickings for some time!" Mr. Claybone complained.

"Then, I suggest, Sir, that you work very hard and that you buy good breeding stock. After all, these are the children by the one woman you say you would have married if you could have! See me tomorrow with details. I'll draw up the paperwork."

With that Massah Robert stood and began to walk down the path to the front yard. He turned back to Mr. Claybone, "And, Clay, whatever Eliza Young is, she's no fool, either. She may want more than a marriage license in writing. Don't sign anything too quickly. And don't be afraid to modify any agreement she wants you to sign. If she's as desperate as you say…" He left the rest unsaid.

As he passed me, sitting in the dark on the porch, he nodded, "Evening, Sara." I could barely get the words out, but I wished him a good evening as well.

Mr. Claybone sat on the bench for a long time. It was too dark now for me to see the beans, so I got up and went inside. I didn't care if the door did squeak. Mr. Claybone may have known I was there all along. Massah Robert certainly did.

I dreamed of Momma that night. She was walking with Mr. Claybone down a church aisle toward Miz Eliza. She put his hand in Miz Eliza's hand and the dream ended.

Mr. Claybone, who I began to call Mr. Clay after overhearing his conversation with his brother that sultry summer evening, signed papers with Massah Robert and probably with Miz Eliza, too. Mr. Clay and Miz Eliza married early in September with the pomp and ceremony predicted months before. Ole Missus even found a way for Rhi, Vaz,

Nora and me to be there, though she made us swear to stay out of sight as much as possible.

"If Miss Eliza Young sees the children, Sara," Ole Missus warned, "she may well call off the wedding. That woman is so proud she'd cut her nose off to spite her face!"

Ole Missus had been crying off and on since the engagement was announced. She blew her nose softly and added, "God knows I don't want Clay to go away, but he's made up his mind and Robbie assures me that this is a good opportunity for Clay to make his way in the world. I can't talk this over with Mr. Powell as he doesn't remember *anything* these days. He doesn't even know who I am some days." She stated this as fact, not wistfully as many women would have. "I suppose I must let Claiborne try." She sighed heavily.

Once again, Ole Missus had caused my mouth to drop open. I was wondering when she had *ever* talked anything over with Ole Massah, or he with her for that matter. They met at the table, but seemed to live entirely separate lives otherwise.

Ole Missus and I never said in words that Rhi, Vaz and Nora were Mr. Clay's children, but *I* understood that she knew they were and *she* understood that I knew. She had come to accept me as a necessary partner in their rearing, although I think she wished she could do without me and manage on her own. The children knew that Mr. Clay was their father. I think he must have told them soon after he and Massah Robert talked.

Although Mr. Clay had been in and out of the kitchen almost as long as I could remember, talking to my mother when she was alive or spending time with the children, after the conversation I overheard in the yard that night, he began coming almost every day. He talked with the children, played board games with them, told funny stories. He went fishing with Vaz 'most every afternoon if the weather was nice. He bought them a pony and cart and taught Rhi and Vaz how to drive it.

He put an old child's saddle on the pony and gave all three children riding lessons before breakfast every day. Since Nora couldn't drive the cart yet, he'd put her up with him on his black Tennessee Walker and ride her around the farm for about an hour just before supper most days.

He never interfered with Miss Ivy's lessons. Ole Missus had placed Ivy in charge of educating the children shortly after Momma passed. Since it was summer, lessons were scheduled mid-morning and mid-afternoon. The children were back in the kitchen sharply at ten every morning with their hands and faces washed, ready to learn.

The day before the wedding Mr. Clay sat at the kitchen table, praising the children for being "handsome, smart, *good* children. Just as your sweet mother would have wanted you to be."

His voice was gruff as if filled with emotion he was trying not to show, "I loved your mother more than I loved my life, but I cannot bring her back for you or for myself. I must find some peace in this world or I may go mad." He looked straight at me for understanding, then he laughed. I think the laugh was for the little ones' sakes.

"Besides the three of you will need a great many things in the coming years. It's time I went to work again to provide for you, but for now…" he gave each child a five dollar gold piece.

"Sara and Ole Missus, as you call her, know what's best for you. *Mind them* now, you hear? *Promise me*! And promise to work hard at your lessons. Learn everything Ivy can teach you. Do as I ask, children." They nodded.

"I will write to you from time to time and I want you to write to me. Will you do that? Miss Ivy will help you. It will mean all the world to me to hear what's happening in your lives."

Last he made a promise I wasn't sure he could or would keep, "If I do well in Texas, I will see that you children have a *very* comfortable life." But he certainly kept his promise to write to them.

Well, I thought we were comfortable enough, but I reckoned white folk's, particularly these white folks, ideas of "comfortable" and my ideas were different. Mr. Clay stood, bent down and kissed the girls on the tops of their heads. He shook Vaz's hand and laughed, "Try, son, not to get into as much mischief as I did when I was a boy!" He quickly pressed something into my hand and hurried out of the room. I opened my hand to find a small bag with five $20 dollar gold pieces! I knew he meant it for hard times. I used that money and, having lived frugally, I used most of what the family paid me as Big Cook when the time came to be sure my own life was "comfortable."

The children and I went to the wedding, which was on Eliza's father's farm. We were supposed to help clean glasses and dishes, but during the ceremony, which was on the front lawn under the big oaks, we stood in the parlor and looked out the open front windows just like the negro house servants were doing. There was quite a crowd. It looked as if half the county was there, but the only ones we looked at were the bride and groom. Ole Massah was too frail to go to the wedding, but all the rest of the family went.

Miss Eliza looked happy, and, I must say, pretty which I'd never thought before. Mr. Clay looked pale as buttermilk and we never actually heard his vows because he spoke them so quietly. When they turned to face their family and friends, Mr. Clay looked immediately towards the front parlor windows and slowly and significantly nodded at us. He even raised his hand as he smiled in our direction. That's the only time I saw him smile all day. I loved him for that open acknowledgment of his children.

It took courage because half that crowd almost certainly knew those "high-yeller" children were his. The men probably were amused by it, but I'm sure the women hated Mr. Clay. He didn't care what they knew now that the vows were said! That apple sure didn't fall far from Ole Missus's tree for, low and behold, Ole Missus turned and looked at us too. She smiled like it was the Second Coming and she didn't care who knew either!

It was about three weeks before the first letter came from Mr. Clay, and it was some letter.

October 11, 1885

Claiborne Powell, C/O John Crockett, Esq. Law Offices

Dallas, Texas

To my dear ones - Mother, Daddy, Brother, Niece-in-Law, Niece, Nephews, Great Nieces, Grand Nephew, Mariah, Vastine, Nora, and Sara, (maybe I should have just mailed this to the local paper),

Mrs. Powell and I traveled by bateau from Hawkins Ferry down the Powell River to the Clinch and eventually to the Tennessee River up to Paducah, Kentucky. She and I were in the second boat being pulled by the one in front. Our personal goods were in a third boat behind us. The scenery was lovely and I dragged a fishing line much of the daylight hours as Mrs. Powell suffered with 'mal de mer' and reclined on the bedding we put under the canvas on one end of our boat. As Vastine knows, fishing is no great hardship for me. I actually caught several varieties of fish that our cook cleaned and fried for my dinner, his, and the dinners of the other two crewmen. Mrs. Powell drank tea and ate only a few tea biscuits all the way to Paducah where we arrived on Tuesday. We spent the night in a hotel there, as the steamboat to New Orleans was not due to leave until the next morning. Eliza ate a good dinner but went early to bed as her head still ached from the glare of the sun on the river.

I enjoyed traveling on the Natchez very much. This was either the sixth or seventh such boat that Captain Leathers built. It was a lovely boat with the paddle wheels at the stern which is a change from his usual side-wheel design. The Natchez has stained glass windows and several paintings of Natchez Indians, including one of an Indian woman jumping off a cliff to her death. Our stateroom was ornamented in the latest fashion. Mrs. Powell seemed to enjoy it well enough as she spent the entire trip there. The humidity, the sun, and the noise of the engines seemed to cause her much discomfort. I am glad to say that she did not suffer from 'mal de mer' on this luxurious vessel. She did eat regularly on this three-day trip, but not fish. The room steward brought her anything she wanted from the dining room menu. I enjoyed the gaming room both evenings and actually won 230 dollars. I lost no money, although I do think several sharps thought they would fleece me!

When we arrived at the port in New Orleans, I purchased tickets on a faster steamer to take us to Galveston Bay. We spent the evening in New Orleans and Eliza wore her finest new gown when we dined at Antoine's. She pronounced the cuisine to be the finest she has ever tasted. She actually ate fish in Antoine's, although how she knew that it was fish, I can't conceive. I thought there was too much gravy (they call it 'sauce') as every dish seemed to come with some kind or other. Please tell Sara that I hope she will never offer sauces with ALL her dishes. They actually cook and EAT crawdads in New Orleans. That's a waste of good fish bait, but then, they also eat SNAILS with a great deal of garlic SAUCE! Eliza thought the snails were "exotic" and delicious. Some people rave over the coffee in New Orleans. They can keep all their chicory. I thought it gave the coffee a decidedly off flavor. I must say, however, that their pastry called bey-yehs, or something like that, is delicious. If Sara could learn to make these she could open a shop in some fair-sized town and make a fortune. But the best thing about New Orleans is their beautiful dark-haired, dark-eyed Creole women.

It took us another day to get to Galveston which is largely wharfs, warehouses, and cotton presses down by the water, but there are several handsome buildings downtown, especially a particular chapel and the railroad building. Nevertheless, I was ready to be on my way so, with little delay, we boarded a train headed northwestward to Houston as soon as we could get our goods transferred. We took one train to Houston and another to Dallas. Our first night in Dallas we stayed in a fine hotel. The next day we called on an old friend of Eliza's father, John Crockett, Esq. Mr. Crockett was Mayor of Dallas three times! He insisted that we stay with him until we could find a place of our own. His grand-niece gave us much help in locating rental properties and in finding a couple to help Eliza manage while I am away looking at property near Corsicana. Eliza felt unwell the next morning when we were to look at properties, so I went alone and found a good, comfortable house in East Dallas. The house is not large, but not too small as there is a room for the help. The house rents with a small stable. (Anne, you might agree with Eliza that I should have allowed her to see the place before I sealed the deal, but then, if it were you I was dealing with, I would have. You are a reasonable, accommodating woman, and not apt to feel faint at the least exertion.)

I had the trunks and crates moved into the rented house that very same day.

(Mother, I dutifully oversaw the disposition of our luggage and household belongings from one vehicle to the next all the way to our house in East Dallas. I had the stevedores be extra careful with the crate containing the new china you purchased as Eliza requested. The Havilland was in excellent condition when we uncrated it. They took great care with the crate containing your mother's silver, as well. Nothing was damaged. I did notice, however, that one of the teaspoons looked as if it had been bitten repeatedly. I like to think that YOU did this as a little girl).

I liked the couple Mrs. Bowdoin (Mr. Crockett's niece) had suggested and I hired Lupe and her husband, Jorge, the same day. They will move in the same day we do as they have been living in a relative's small house. I thought it was a very fruitful day, but Eliza threw a hairbrush which I almost dodged. I have a pump knot on my head that makes it so tender I can't wear my hat. I WILL break her from her antics if it kills her! (Daddy, I never raised a hand to the woman. You would be proud of me.) Pump knot or no pump knot, we thanked Mr. Crockett for his generosity and moved over to the new place immediately after supper. Lupe had made up a bed, filled the lamps with oil, and put towels near the wash basin with a full water pitcher. We had what we needed for the evening. If Eliza discharges Lupe and Jorge while I'm down country looking at land, SHE will have to find new help by herself or do without!

(Robbie, as you counseled, I established accounts with reasonable, but not extravagant limits, for Eliza at the grocer's, a department store, and an apothecary. I have also given her an allowance of 50 dollars which seems a vast amount for the three or four weeks I expect to be away. As we used nearly a third of her money to get us here, I have placed the balance into an account payable to her if I should die. Mr. Crockett's law partner will pay Lupe and Jorge weekly from an account he is managing for me. The majority of my funds is in the bank. The money I won at poker, I "gambled" by buying several shares in a business Mr. Munger is developing to make parts for his new ginning system).

I stayed in the rented house long enough to see Lupe and Jorge put everything to rights as Eliza instructed. Then I went to find a small horse and carriage for Eliza. I also purchased a fine sturdy pony for myself. I call him by the ridiculous name of Gaylord. I miss my Walker, but I know that young Vastine will take good care of him for me. Gaylord and I are leaving tomorrow to look at land down around Corsicana. I've told Eliza she should not come down until I at least have land and some sort of shelter. I believe she is looking forward to my absence, although she did apologize quite prettily for throwing the brush. She said she intended to miss me, but when I swerved - I will try to write to you from Corsicana.

With dutiful regards,

Clay

P.S. Please give ALL the little ones hugs from me and remind them to do their lessons carefully.

The next letter arrived about two weeks later. It wasn't as thick. Mr. Clay had been busy in those two weeks.

October 27, 1885

Claiborne Powell, C/O John Crockett, Esq. Law Office

Dallas, Texas

To my dear ones - Mother, Daddy, Brother, Niece-in-Law, Niece, Nephews, Great Nieces, Grand Nephew, Mariah, Vastine, Honora, and Sara,

I look forward to hearing the news from home when I return to Dallas in about three weeks time. I reckon that it will take that long to transact my business here. I have been down here in the Corsicana area now for almost two weeks. I have talked to prospectors, farmers, and businessmen, to anyone who would talk to me.

I have changed some of my plans. Cotton is dirt cheap right now and there are many cotton farms for sale at pitifully low prices. Pitiful for the sellers, good for buyers, which are few and far between because people are afraid this recession will last forever. (Robbie, I may never have done a deal of work, but I've observed a great deal of it. Especially farming!) There is one small property I like about ten miles outside of town, roughly 75 acres, with a spring-fed creek running through. It is for sale for $1,000! I hate to steal the property, but I think I can get the seller to take $750 and throw in the farm equipment. The seller is a widow who wants to move back to Lubbock with her two school-aged children as soon as she can. Sadly, I don't think they have enough money for food for the winter.

The house (a shack really) needs a new roof and a good deal of general maintenance. I am not handy, but if I can persuade a good carpenter to work with me, I can learn. After I get the house in livable condition I intend to find a sharecropper to work the land for me. Because cotton is selling so low right now, there are many negroes, many with large families to feed, looking for work.

Daddy, I know that cotton wears the land out as badly as tobacco and I have learned from you to rotate crops, planting rye and clover to renew the soil. I will till the fields and plant them in rye as soon as I purchase the place. The soil is so poor

46

that nothing but the most noxious weeds thrive. I'm thinking of planting about half the land come spring in corn and sugar cane, see how they do, and alternate crops as scientifically as I can manage. Let me know your suggestions. I will put a small herd of 25 to 35 cattle in the fallow field as soon as I can get some fencing up. There is an iron works company in town that I want to invest in. This place is about to BOOM and prices are still good for buyers. I feel it deeply in my Powell bones!

I have received a letter from Eliza. She is satisfied, for now, with the house and with Lupe and Jorge. She has found the lending library in town and has used the mule drawn street cars almost daily to go somewhere or other. I don't like her going out alone in a town she doesn't know, but I dare not tell her this as she would obstinately do it even more! Now that the weather is cooler, she seems to feel much better.

This letter is all business and cannot be very interesting to most of you. I want you to know, however, that I think of each one of you every day. I hope to have more interesting news for the next letter. Please give all the little ones big hugs from me and remind them to study their lessons!

With dutiful regards,

Clay

I do not know what Massah Robert replied to his brother about crops and cows, but I don't believe Ole Massah had the ability to even consider what Mr. Clay should do. He was a little more feeble and forgetful every day. The poor old man had to wear diapers, like a baby. When he ate, he got food all over himself, on the floor, everywhere. Ole Missus hired a white nurse, Miz Bowen, to come live in the Big House. Miz Bowen slept on a cot in his room as he needed care all day and all night. He no longer came downstairs as he couldn't do it by himself and he was so big, even withered as he was, that Massah Robert and Mr. 'Zander were afraid they'd let him fall if they tried to help him down. Ole Missus left the door open between her bedroom and his so she would know how he was doing.

I had never cared one way or t'other 'bout Ole Massah, but it hurt my heart to see *anyone* in such condition. I don't think you can live your whole life in the same house and not feel for someone when they evaporate like water from a pond before your very eyes. There was so much sickness and death in the house that year that it seemed the gloom might last forever. And Mr. Clay, although he was an acknowledged scoundrel, was not around to make us all laugh at his ridiculous jokes and stories. Scoundrel or not, he was at least entertaining.

Thankfully, Ole Massah passed soon, before we even received Mr. Clay's next letter. Ole Massah was 84 years old when he passed. He had three living children, 21 grandchildren, and about six great-grandchildren at the time of his passing. His descendants would include farmers, doctors, teachers, professors, attorneys, a sculptor, a minister, restaurateurs, and many other things, *including* a movie mogul - there were even a few disreputable individuals who are best left unmentioned.

Mr. Clay sent regular letters updating us on his progress. He told us more about crops and finance than his children *or I* wanted to know. He bought the property for a little less than even he thought he could. It turned out the equipment was simple and not very useful, but the widow sold him a pair of oxen complete with yokes for next to nothing so he could start plowing the *fallow* fields right away. He found an excellent negro carpenter, Willis Allen, who evidently was skilled as well at many things other than woodworking. Mr. Allen and his family repaired the house and the barn.

The widow had not been able to harvest what cotton there was in the fields when she sold it. Mr. Clay had Willis and his family of ten children pick the cotton. Mr. Clay sent the widow a check for half of what the cotton brought. He sent the rest, after deducting the expenses for buying winter wheat and rye seed, harvesting and transporting the cotton to market to Massah Robert. Massah Robert divided this small check four ways: half was divided into three separate accounts for each of Mr. Clay's children, and the last half he kept toward repaying the loan he had extended to Mr. Clay. I knew this because Massah Robert showed me the children's bank books, explaining what he had done. It was not much, but it was the beginning of their father's financial support. Little did I imagine at the time how much Mr. Clay would give them.

Mr. Clay planted his wheat and rye in December with the help of the Allen family. He, Willis and Willis' oldest two sons spent the next couple of months fencing. Mr. Clay would not let the younger children help. He insisted that they go to school during the school year. He reported that the winter was miserable and cold with high, drying winds most days. He hoped never to have to work that hard again!

As soon as the fencing was up, Mr. Clay bought cattle. The breed was new to the United States so the cows were expensive and he bought far fewer than he had hoped, but they were immune to Texas cattle fever. He bought mostly Herefords which he claimed were excellent beef cattle. He also bought a few Texas Longhorns because they had a history of surviving the Texas weather extremes. He told us that the one three-year old Hereford bull he bought cost almost as much as *all the cows* he purchased! He planned to sell no cows the first year and to keep the best bull-calf produced from that first breeding. He had become a thoughtful, responsible rancher, seemingly overnight.

Mr. Clay planted sorghum in mid-April on roughly 10 acres and planted 20 acres of corn. He planted the rest in cover crops or put cattle on it. He had hired Willis and the oldest two girls full time. The girls, who had finished six years of school, cooked, cleaned and did the washing for Mr. Clay. The girls and Willis worked six days a week. "Sunday," he told them, "is for rest and *church*. If you leave me a loaf of your delicious bread, Thea and Queenie, I can feed *myself* on Sundays!" I wondered if Mr. Clay went to church on Sundays. If I were a betting person, I'd have bet *not*. He had never gone to church when he lived in the Big House.

But his letter in October after they'd been in Texas a full year amazed us all.

October 20, 1886

Claiborne Powell,

C/O General Delivery, Corsicana, Texas

To my dear ones - Mother, Brother, Niece-in-Law, Niece, Nephews, Great Nieces, Grand Nephew, Mariah, Vastine, Honora, and Sara,

Until now, Eliza and I have seen each other only a few days each month since we moved here, so it is astounding, but true. Eliza is in the family way! The baby is due sometime in mid-April next year. We are not renewing the lease on the house in East Dallas. As a matter of fact, Eliza is here in Corsicana to stay. She made quite a face when she first saw the place, even though we had white-washed the outside of the house and the outbuildings, and painted the inside rooms. She found it clean enough and even praised the Allen girls for their work. She likes the kind of cooking the Allen girls do, finding it more like HOME than Lupe's Mexican cooking.

Jorge has brought our household goods up here. That leaves us in a bit of a dilemma, as Eliza is very fond of Lupe and Jorge, and I like the work Willis and his family do. One of Willis' girls is getting married soon and will be moving to Oklahoma. That is one less person to pay, but I don't know how I can afford Lupe AND Thea. Eliza says that Lupe will be a perfect nanny and can help Thea clean and cook. She has even agreed to pay Lupe's wages until the farm begins to make some real money.

The money I inherited from Daddy's death is paying for a stone and brick house at the top of the hill. Willis is a good builder and I am paying him half of what I normally would, promising, IN WRITING, that he and his family can live rent-free for five years in our current house when the new one is finished. Eliza insists that a room be built for Lupe and Jorge in the new house. She also insists that the new place have indoor plumbing, including two water closets, one for us and one for the help! The house plans get bigger every day. Right now we are building four bedrooms just for our family. I wish sincerely that I could have us all together, but that is not a good idea for a number of reasons.

Things began rather badly between Eliza and me, but living alone has improved her disposition - and maybe mine as well. She is so happy about the baby that she even likes to please me instead of arguing about everything under the sun. We go along very well most days. Remarkably she has not thrown a shoe, a hairbrush, a glass of water, or anything else for almost three months now. I've learned not to dodge, and, as she is an excellent marksman, she always misses me. Later she apologizes so sweetly that I have to forgive her temper.

Unbelievably, the local chapter of what once would've been called the Ku Klux Klan (before the federal government started riding them hard) approached me about joining. ME! I think they now call themselves the White League here, but in some places they are known as the Red Shirts. As Will Shakespeare reminded us 'A rose by any other name would still smell…' These men are acting partially out of fear because, it is true, there is lawlessness in the country right now. Lawlessness from negroes and whites. I believe it's due to the fact that many people are without work. I tried to be respectful in declining their offer, but I'm fairly certain I made some enemies. They told me it was 'a white man's duty to preserve law and order.' I believe I said something to the effect that the best way to preserve law and order is to abide by the law yourself and to elect capable, honest people to office, especially the sheriff's office.

Well, I won't allow Eliza to wander alone around Corsicana after that. I'm not sure that Lupe or Jorge are enough to protect her, but I don't have the time to go every time she wants to buy some gewgaw or other in town. She had a derringer pistol even before we left Virginia. I insist that she carry it loaded in her handbag. Jorge carries a rifle under the buckboard. I have seen to it that Willis' family has three rifles with plenty of ammunition. Willis is cool-headed and is respected by white folks and negroes alike, but you never can tell what someone will get in their craw. I work with a pistol strapped into a holster, a loaded rifle on Gaylord's saddle, and another in the wagon if I've brought a wagon. I look like a stereotype of a Westerner!

I don't want to scare any of you. We don't carry weapons just to protect us from malicious people. There are several species of snakes here that are poisonous, similar to what you have in Virginia, but there are many more of them, and occasionally you can come upon a single wolf, or, at night, a pack. I can take care of my own here, but I want you to understand that it is not Eliza who keeps me from asking my children to move here. I want them to grow up without having to worry about such things as the KKK, the Red Shirts, the White League, or whatever they call themselves these days! Please let them know that I think of them every day and I hope that they are minding Sara and learning what Ivy tries to teach them.

Enclosed is one-half, minus the harvesting, labor, and transportation expenses, of the cotton sale this year. It isn't much as we planted so little and the prices are still low, but I am happy to be able to send it. I thank you, Robbie, for financing this venture. Please give hugs to my dear ones!

With dutiful regards,
Clay

Well, never in my life did I expect Mr. Clay, even as devil-may-care as he was, to openly tell his whole family what they already knew anyway, that Rhi, Vaz and Nora were his! You could have knocked me over with a feather. I think the family was more shocked by the fact that Miz Eliza was in the family way and that she and Mr. Clay were *getting along well* together.

Miz Eliza birthed a little girl in late March the year of our Lord 1887. They named her Lou Issa because Ole Missus' middle name was Louise and after poor dead Miz 'Dena whose name was really Loudena. They sent a family picture when the baby was about three. The little girl was beautiful. In fact, except that Lou Issa's skin was a little lighter than Nora's and her hair was not as curly, Lou Issa and Nora looked like the sisters they were. It was not until several years later that they realized little Lou Issa was not normal. She had been slow to sit, walk and talk. Then they learned her thinking was slow. After Lou Issa's birth, Miz Eliza had no more babies. The doctor said that the trauma of delivering a first baby at Miz Eliza's age sometimes did that. But that child was always treated like a princess by her mother, father, Lupe and Jorge.

CHAPTER 4: VAZ GETS A LICKING

Silence invades the breathing wood
Where drowsy limbs a treasure keep,
Now greenly falls the learned shade
Across the sleeping brows
And stirs their secret to a smile.

Restored! Returned! The lost are borne
On seas of shipwreck home at last:
See! In a fire of praising burns
The dry dumb past, and we
Our life-day long shall part no more.

W.H. Auden

Things were not easy for a long time after Momma passed. I had spent a great deal of time taking care of my little sisters and brother before her passing, so it wasn't that they missed Momma so much. But, Lord up above, I did. 'Deed I still do after all this time. Seems as if I cried everyday for at least the first year. And it was all because I missed Momma, although burning the beans or putting too little salt in the cornbread or such things always started the bawling. Then sweet Miz 'Dena passed too, humorous Mr. Clay left, and Ole Massah passed. There for awhile, life looked like a succession of grayer day after gray day.

Rhi was my very best friend in those days. She'd put her long, scrawny arms around my shoulders when I was in the "Valley of Despair" as we laughingly called it. At eight she was almost as tall as I was at twelve, she'd lead me to the rickety rocker that had belonged to Ole Mammie and set me down in it. Then she'd climb up in my lap, and, while she was tearing up herself, she'd say, "Sara, don't cry. It's going to be alright. You'll see. Ole Missus says Jesus don't put nothing on us that *He and we* can't handle together."

"Doesn't put *anything*, sweet girl," I'd correct her grammar.

Well, I never put a whole lot of store in what Ole Missus said, but I sure hoped she was right about this, though I often wondered just how much a person could bear and still carry on with living.

If Jesus was so good why'd we have to suffer so much in the first place? Except for having very little faith, I couldn't see as how I'd done enough bad things in my young life to earn the kind of punishment I was receiving - and Sunday sermons on Job never helped much because I couldn't understand why God let the devil inflict all that misery on Job *either*! The story of Adam and Eve and original sin made even less sense to me. Why didn't God just punish *them? Use them as an example! Maybe the rest of us would've obeyed better!* I never voiced these opinions to the children because I hoped they'd believe in God's goodness when I couldn't.

I could just imagine the whipping I would have had from Ole Mammie if I'd ever said anything to her about such thoughts. Why I was downright *afraid* she knew my thoughts from all the way up in heaven - if there was such a place. More likely in my mind in those days, she was over in the dark corners watching me as she said she would. It was enough to make me think before I spoke!

Rhi and I would rock in that chair for a few minutes with her humming some song we usually sang on Sundays or she'd sing something else, almost as good as I remember Momma doing. I loved "Oh, Lucinda." I never learned how Rhi came to know it, but she'd point to me when she got to the part about Lucinda having "such lovely jet black eyes and long black curly hair." Neither my hair nor my eyes were black, but I suppose Rhi thought they were dark enough to call black. I'd kiss the top of her head and we'd get up and go on about our business - because I had to and Vaz and little Nora were jealously demanding our attention to them.

I was the Big Cook now and I had to tell Violet what to do. Violet was a good girl and would do anything I asked. As long as I lived I always referred to her as a girl. She was probably ten, maybe twelve years older than I and plump even then. She had been kicked in the head by a mule when she was little and had trouble remembering things. She was always somewhat childlike.

Actually, calling her memory *trouble* doesn't really tell how bad off she was. Some days were worse than others and I wanted to scream at her. But I tried not to get mad when she asked me to tell her for the third and fourth or even fifth time how she should do something or to repeat what I had just said. Here she was old enough to marry if anyone had wanted to marry her, looking as good as the rest of us except for the indentation on her left forehead. She was almost as tall as Massah Robert who stood well over six feet, but she was *childlike*. Actually, I think little Nora had more sense by the time she was five than Violet ever did. I finally got enough sense just to tell her one thing at a time and have her do the same things in the same order every day. Change always disrupted Violet's ability to cope.

Because I needed her so much and she truly was a pitiful thing, I always said something like "Thank you kindly, Violet, I sure couldn't have done it without you!" or, "Violet, you're a wonder with those pots. I could never get them as clean as you do!" She'd smile as if I gave her a bag of gold except I don't believe the poor thing ever knew what gold was. She did like it when I'd give her a few cookies or a big piece of cake to take home to share with her mother, who we all called "Aunt Prissy," and her brother, Carl Thomas.

Violet was, however, *amazingly good* with the children. On nice days, I often asked her to take them outside and play tag, toss, or catch after most of our work was done. It's strange how *she never forgot things about the children.* She watched them very carefully. She was firm in her language with them if they were doing something that might cause them harm, but she never spanked or tattled. I often saw her pick them up and take them away from danger, scolding mildly. And she really *was* good at cleaning the big pots and scrubbing the kitchen floor. I didn't exaggerate that. Violet kept the kitchen immaculately clean and she carried the heavy stuff that I couldn't carry 'til I was grown.

But Ole Missus *refused* to let her come into the dining room. It was as if Ole Missus thought you could catch feeble mindedness. That left me to carry food to the table, refill bowls when the family wanted more of something, and take the dishes away after they were through eating, besides all the cooking that still needed tending in the kitchen. Thank God Rhi was a smart little girl and strong for her age. She was able to help more and more in the dining room. Ole Missus actually liked Rhi in there with them. I believe if Miz Anne and Mr. 'Zander had been comfortable with the idea, Ole Missus would've let Rhi, Vaz and Nora all eat at the big table with the white folks. It was her house so I'm surprised she didn't insist on it, but it was years before my brother and sisters ate there.

Ole Missus loved Momma's last three children as if they were her own. By the time Momma passed, many of Ole Missus' children and grandchildren were grown and out of the house. It wasn't that Mr. 'Zander's children didn't love her, but they saw her as antiquated and odd, so maybe she was lonesome for the company of little ones.

Ole Missus was not childlike in any other way except for her complete adoration of those three children, especially Vaz. She used to come sit by me when I was shelling peas or snapping beans or anything where I was stationary for a while. Ole Missus corrected my speech and would often hit my cheek lightly with her fan if I "misused the English language!" I resented it mightily then, but the training came in quite useful later.

"The children spend most of their time with you, Sara. It is very important that you set a good example," she'd say. "Children learn what they see and hear! You are not to say 'de' for 'the' or 'dem' for 'them.' You are never to say 'ain't' and, *of course*, no crude or coarse language, but I never heard your mother or grandmother speak an ugly word, so I expect you don't either."

I was listening, probably with my mouth wide open, as, at that age, I couldn't imagine how in the world a *word* could be "ugly." A 'possum's "ugly." A chicken hawk's "ugly." And sure as certain old Miz Gilbert Laws, Miz Anne's mother, was "ugly" with that great long nose of hers and the hog-like bristles on her chin. But a *word*! How was that possible? Ole Missus had some fanciful notions!

Ole Missus had a good deal to say about the "proper rearing of children." And, although I often wished she'd hurry up and finish what she was lecturing me about so I could go about my work instead of sitting listening to her babble, I sure needed to learn about the "proper rearing of children." I knew so little and there was no one else to teach me. So I obediently listened and tried to learn from what conversation I heard in the dining room how to speak "correctly." I know I sometimes "misused the English language," and it's certain I had an accent, but I spoke better than the negroes I was raised with - mind you though, I know full well that *speaking* better doesn't make a person *better*! I learned that the hard way over the years.

It was not enough for Ole Missus that those children should wash in a basin as most of us negroes had to. In fact, I expect most white people cleaned themselves the same way in those days - at least the ones who tried to keep clean. Her little "angels" had to have a tub bath every Saturday with a shampoo just like the white folks in the house and they had to be washed from head to toe daily. They also wore shoes summer and winter. Now that's not *natural* for black children. It's probably unnatural for white children too. Feet need to breathe, but Ole Missus wouldn't have those children "running around like heathens." Ole Missus saw to it that come Sundays they wore clothes as fine as anything Massah Robert's children or grandchildren wore.

Ole Missus wouldn't stand for me physically punishing my sisters or brother either. Rhi and Nora were good children, but Vaz was a *scoundrel* from the time he could crawl! The only time Ole Missus was ever really mean to me was because of Vaz, and, I'm sorry to admit it, I never forgave her for it.

It was a hot, humid day in early July and the children, Violet and I were working in the summer kitchen making blackberry jelly. We had wet kitchen towels tied around our heads and necks to try to keep us cool, but the towels dried out so quickly and our hands were too busy to re-wet them often. The girls had washed the jars and picked the beetles and stems out of the berries. They'd eaten enough while they were doing this that their teeth, tongue, and lips were stained a deep purple. I laughed at the sight, and they grinned really big so I would laugh even more. Of course all of us had purple hands. Vaz had washed his hands and was sitting in the corner shooting marbles. After the juice was extracted from the berries, Vaz was supposed to dump the solids onto the compost pile near the garden, carry jars up for us to use, then, later, help Violet carry the cooled jelly jars to the cellar.

While I was cooking jelly, I was also trying to make dinner. The white folks expected their dinner on the table by half past twelve. It had been a very busy morning and Vaz chose to disappear just as the jelly couldn't be left. I was fuming, but I figured he'd be back in time for his own dinner. He was not.

Rhi and I carried food to the dining room which was further from the summer kitchen than the regular kitchen. Then we ate our own dinner quickly, and picked up the dinner remains at about two. I asked Rhi and Nora to wash up the summer kitchen and finish clearing the dining room table. Violet had cleaned the big jelly pots and was to scrub both kitchen floors. I made a couple of blackberry cobblers for supper that evening. I had to wait near the summer kitchen for them to finish baking as I couldn't rely on Violet to remember them before they burned. I pulled them out to cool before I left to look for Vaz. By that time it must have been 3:30 with no sign of him still.

He was almost eight years old and as tall as I. He was certainly big enough to know better, but he was still too young for me not to worry about. I hollered and hollered for that boy! I walked all around the Big House, up on the hill to look down at the workers in the two large tobacco fields, the cow pasture on the other side of the hill and in the garden across the road. It was so hot what cows weren't lying under a grove of poplars in the center of the pasture were standing udder deep in the pond. I checked the barns and stables. Vaz always wore a big straw hat with a hawk feather stuck in the band. If he'd been anywhere in the open fields I would have known it was Vaz and not one of the workers.

I went across the road and all the way down to the river because I knew the boy loved to fish. On such a hot day, I thought he might even be swimming there. I forbade him to go down there alone and he usually went with Miz Anne's boy, Andy, but Andy had been at the dinner table. When I asked Andy, he said he'd not seen Vaz since right after breakfast when Vaz was carrying jars from the cellar.

There were two ancient negro women sitting under a big sycamore tree fishing. They knew Vaz. "No, Sarie, we hain't seen him."

I called as loudly as I could to a couple of elderly white men on the other side of the river and asked about Vaz. Seemed as if only the old folks had time to fish that day. Everyone else was in the fields because the weeds were at the peak of their season and had to be chopped out. The old men shook their heads to indicate that they hadn't seen him either. Vaz knew everyone and everyone knew and liked him.

I could hear distant thunder and see tall bilious clouds rolling out of the west toward us, so I started back along the path, up the hill toward the road and the Big House. I wasn't too worried about a storm yet as the clouds were still white, but a storm was coming. I could sense it. The leaves on the trees were turned up and the air felt heavy.

I caught up with the old women as they were nearly to the road going home, carrying their poles and empty lines over their shoulders.

"Too hot even fer fish!" one of them laughed.

"Let me carry your poles." I offered.

"Shaw, Sarie," one of them said, "Tain't nothin' to carry! Don't weigh nothin' without fish! But you are your momma's child, girl! Allus thinkin' 'bout someun else."

Even though they had farther to travel up the hill than I, the other one said, "Gal, you bettah get home soon! Dem clouds lookin' mighty fearsome!" she commented as the clouds began to darken in the western sky. The storm was approaching faster than I had expected.

"Fergit 'bout that boy! He's smart as a whip an' he's alright som'eres."

"Yes'um," the other one said somewhat out of breath from the climb up to the road, "but I'd give him a hidin' he wouldn't fergit iffen I wuz you, Sarie!" She laughed a toothless laugh. "Only thang wrong wit dat boy is he needs a good whoopin' frum time to time!"

"Yep," the other one nodded, "Ole Missus spoil him as bad as she spoil his daddy if you let her!" It was simply a fact. Everyone knew my brother and sisters were Mr. Clay's. But the negroes didn't seem to resent the children because of it as white folk did.

I'd been looking for Vaz for well over an hour. I had to get home and finish supper or there'd be the devil to pay. "You better stop at the stables and rest. You'll never make it all the way home before the storm breaks!" I called out to the old women. Then I ran across the road, kicking up dust, and around to the back of the house. I barely got into the summer kitchen before hailstones began to pelt down. Out the open door, I could see my poor old neighbors. No luck fishing and now hail! They dropped their fishing poles, tried to cover their heads from the icy pellets and hobbled as quickly as age and infirmities allowed toward the stables.

"Did you find him?" Nora asked nervously.

I shook my head "No," as I looked at the clock we kept in the kitchen. "Oh, no! It's half past five!" I groaned. I'd been looking for Vaz longer than I thought. Without another word, Violet, Rhi, Nora and I began peeling potatoes and flouring whatever we fried for supper that night. Supper had to be on the table by six-thirty. One of us made cabbage and onions, I remember because always afterwards I associated the smell of them with storms.

Violet and I covered Rhi and Nora with a large oilcloth as they carried supper from the summer kitchen, onto the kitchen porch and down to the dining room door that opened directly onto the side lawn. The food was not hurt by the rain, but those covering the food were soaked. Of course, one of the soaked was Violet who wasn't supposed to go into the dining room once the family was seated. That would leave her in the pouring rain until she could get back up to the regular kitchen door off the porch.

We were actually a little early and only the younger family members were at the table. I quietly told Violet to hurry into the dining room where she could slip into the regular kitchen through the inside door. Violet was just slipping out of the room into the kitchen when Ole Missus came in. Ole Missus saw her and started to say something sharp to me about it, but Massah Robert spoke up, "Poor creature! I hope she doesn't get ill from such a soaking. Sara, see that she sits by a fire with some hot tea or coffee. Wrap her in a blanket, too!"

Well, even though it was raining, it still must have been at least 75 degrees. We had been so hot earlier that we welcomed the cooling rain. I was every bit as wet as Violet! I never argued with their ludicrous notions, but, Lordie, white folks could be so strange.

Rhi, Nora and I went into the regular kitchen from the dining room. Our supper was in the summer kitchen, but we weren't going back out with it raining so hard. It wouldn't rain like that forever. I figured the storm must pass soon as it had already been going on for about an hour, but, unexpectedly, the storm actually intensified. Lightning zigzagged all over the sky lighting up the now dark kitchen, and shaking the house it was so close. About five minutes after the family sat down to eat, lightning hit the big oak on the front lawn with a terrible cracking, booming sound. It shook the whole house and we actually smelled sulfur! It turned out that lightening split the top out of the tree. The tree even caught fire for a few minutes until the rain extinguished it.

I started to shake but not just because of the tree. Where was Vaz? I was thinking maybe I should let Ole Missus know that he was missing, but she'd probably have a fit and die - after she killed me.

I had to sit down in Ole Mammie's rocker because my legs wouldn't support me. I could hear the commotion in the dining room as the family ran to the front porch to see what had happened. When eight or so people run out of a room, clambering, it's hard to hear yourself think, but I could hear Ole Missus praying loudly from her seat at the end of the dining room table. "Lord Jesus!" she was saying over and over, "Lord Jesus, preserve us and forgive us for our iniquities!"

About the same time I heard feet pounding up the steps of the cellar just beneath where I was sitting in the rocker. The cellar door banged open onto the porch and feet pounded to the kitchen door. Vaz flung the door open, demanding, "What was that, Sara? Sounded like a cannon!" He started running towards the dining room door to see what had happened.

I can't remember grabbing the stick of kindling or catching Vaz by one of his long skinny arms, but I remember flailing furiously at his backside with that thin stick of wood. I don't know if I ever hit him as he was squirming so hard and crying out that I was killing him! Ole Missus heard this ruckus even above the storm and the excited babble from the front porch. She rushed into the kitchen. Quick as if she were a twenty-year old, she grabbed that piece of wood from my hand and flung it across the kitchen, breaking a window, letting the rain pour in. Vaz was telling her he didn't know why I was hitting him. He'd done nothing. Missed his supper, but he wasn't hungry.

I tried to tell Ole Missus why I was upset with Vaz when, "Whap!" That old woman slapped me so hard across my face that I skidded backwards on the wet floor, and hit the side of my head on the big oak work table! Blood poured down into my shoulder, into my left eye, down my cheek and onto the floor. Ole Missus looked at me and yelled, "Get a rag and mop that floor before it stains!"

Mop the floor? I'm near to passing out and she's worried about the floor. That's how important Sara Gilley was to this family!

Violet and Rhi got rags, one for the floor and one for my head. Little Nora stood silently near the stove with her knuckles in her mouth, gaping ashen-faced at the lot of us. Ole Missus began to calm down, but she looked vengefully at me, "Girl, if you ever lay another hand on this boy - I repeat, do not lay so much as a finger on Vastine or you'll find yourself up on the hill married to some big black negro who won't tolerate your shenanigans! If he needs disciplining you tell me what he's done and I will take care of it. Do you understand?" I might have nodded - probably not. I was hurt, confused and really angry all at once.

Ole Missus walked to the other end of the table, picked up a long knife, frightening me out of any more growth I might ever have. I was sure she was going to come at me again, this time with a knife, but she simply proceeded to cut a huge slice of bread, slathered butter and blackberry jelly on it.

"Vastine, sit down and eat some supper. Mariah, get your brother a glass of milk." She seemed to scrutinize Vaz carefully, "Where did your sister hit you?"

The young scapegrace did have enough honesty to blush, replying, "Grandmother, I don't think she ever actually struck…"

"Listen, Missus Powell…" I began angrily, my voice dripping with indignation.

"Ma'am," Mariah addressed her grandmother firmly, interrupting me without moving an inch toward the milk. "Vaz has been missing since before dinner. He scared all of us out of our wits and Sara especially. She looked for him half the afternoon. If a boy ever deserved a whipping, Vaz did! Sara has never hit any of us, but I can't blame her for taking a stick to Vaz today! You should not have slapped Sara, Ma'am. She was trying to teach Vaz right from wrong." I might have been trying to teach him right from wrong, if I'd thought about it, but picking up the kindling was an angry, impulsive reaction to the frustration I'd felt all afternoon. I was a little ashamed of my own behavior, but not much!

Rhi was my sister and my defender and she had just celebrated her tenth birthday. What a lioness, even then! She was enough like her grandmother, that she wouldn't allow what she saw as an injustice to pass - not even if it meant standing up to the devil himself. After having her say, she made her way to the milk jug. "By the way, Grandmother, none of us has eaten, including you."

Nora had come over to me and was clutching my skirts, crying with her face against my hip. I patted her on the head and whispered, "Hush, little angel. I'm alright. Everything is alright." I slumped into Ole Mammie's rocker and pulled Nora up into my lap, rocking her and kissing the top of her curly blonde head as Violet tied a bandage around my head, covering the wound.

Ole Missus gave one of her, "Harrumps!" Then she said to all of us, "Maybe I should have been slower to act, but I will not have any of you abused by *anyone*." That was as close to an apology as she was ever going to make.

Her tone softened when she spoke again, "Honora, Grandmother didn't really hurt Sara. Head wounds bleed a great deal. It doesn't signify a serious wound. I didn't hit her very hard, but the floor was wet, and she fell into the table."

"No," I thought. "You didn't hit me very hard? I just imagined I saw stars and that was before I hit my head on the table and nearly passed out!" But I kept quiet for the baby's sake. Nora had her face hidden in the bodice of my bloody dress. She'd have to have a bath and a shampoo tonight before she could go to bed. She began to hiccough from crying so hard.

When Rhi handed Vaz the glass of milk, he stuck his tongue out at her for her troubles. Of course his grandmother didn't see that.

Ole Missus sat down next to Vaz and watched him eat as if he were the King of Egypt. It was that day I decided that somehow, some way I was going to make myself independent enough so that no one could ever treat me like that again and get away with it.

Later that evening when we were all in bed, Vaz got up off his pallet on the floor and tried to climb into bed with his sisters and me. He put one leg up on the bed and his long skinny arms around my neck. I pushed him away because there was very little room and also because I was still quite angry with him. He was a persistent little cuss though. He kissed my cheek and said, "Sara, I was bad today. It was just so hot and the cellar was cool. I didn't mean to be gone so long, but I fell asleep. I'm sorry that Grandmother hit you. I never meant to get you in trouble. Does your head still hurt?" I nodded, but I couldn't stay mad at the little scoundrel.

"Vastine," I mimicked Ole Missus's voice, "don't do that to me again. You scared me out of a year's growth! I thought lightning had killed you!" I was trying to make an impression on him and I think the tears that began to run down my face were far more effective than words.

He kissed me sweetly on my forehead, "I'm sorry, Sara, that you were scared?" I nodded and Vaz patted my cheek. I pulled him up next to me. The storm had cooled the air considerably so one more body was welcome warmth. We all went to sleep together in that small bed. It's a memory I treasure of my family lying safely together with the rain, gently drumming on the tin roof of our little annexed room.

CHAPTER 5: MASSAH ROBERT REMARRIES

He was a haughty person in the world;
nor is there any goodness which adorns
his memory; hence his shade is furious here.

The Divine Comedy, Inferno VIII,
The Wrathful and the Sullen,
Dante Alighieri

About a year after Momma passed, Ole Missus had assigned Miss Ivy, Massah Robert and Miz 'Dena's youngest, to teach Rhi and Vaz their letters and numbers. Nora was still too little and I had work to do. I'm fairly sure that Ole Missus would not have worried if I learned very much even if I didn't have work. Vaz had just turned five when the lessons began, but that boy was a whiz and soaked up everything Miss Ivy challenged him to do.

During the school year Ivy was still in school herself, so the lessons proceeded when she came home in the afternoons, but she assigned homework for them to do in the mornings. In less than a year, Vaz could read well, count, and subtract. It just so happened that I learned some reading and arithmetic almost natural-like just by being in the room with them. Then Rhi began telling me things, teaching me, as they did their homework. She taught me multiplication tables and simple division by having me repeat them over and over. I could already read and print letters, but I began to learn apace as well.

When Miss Ivy discovered this, she gave me lessons to do when I had the time. For Christmas the first year after Miss Ivy started teaching me, she gave me a wonderful Christmas gift - a cooking book. It had recipes for all kinds of things, many that I had never heard of, but I started trying a few new things. The white folk always said as how they liked the new things and asked if I would make them again. I learned that I was a good cook. I had learned techniques from Momma and the rest became fairly simple.

Although Rhi did quite well and I was a good student too when I had time to work on lessons, Vaz was Miss Ivy's star pupil. Miss Ivy said quietly for my ears only that Vaz was the brightest child she'd ever seen, and, she added, Rhi was almost as smart as her precocious brother.

After Mr. Clay moved to Texas, Vaz wrote a long letter to his father every week. Rhi would add a paragraph or two and help Nora to print a sentence or two even before Nora's formal lessons began.

Miss Ivy taught us at the kitchen table for four years. She even taught me how to spell, write and sign my name in cursive letters. I was really proud to be able to write "Sara Gilley." By that time Ole Massah had passed, and the only two in the Big House who remembered my papa at all were Ole Missus and Massah Robert, and soon Ole Missus would probably be gone too. Everyone else was either dead or had moved. It was important to me that my papa's name still live even if he didn't. Sounds foolish, I suppose, but that's how I felt. Gilley remained part of my legal name for the rest of my life.

Massah Robert was terribly lonely after Miz 'Dena passed. About two years after her death, Massah became well acquainted with an attractive widow who had seven children, four of them still young. Massah Robert married her, I believe, in the hope of filling the house again with laughter. The former widow brought her four youngest children to the Big House to live. Her older children stayed in their former home. To say that major changes took place at the Big House is a gross understatement.

About this time Ole Missus decided it was time for Rhi to become a "house servant." I thought she was already a "house servant" as she worked in the kitchen and dining room. Ole Missus had never been best pleased with S'rena as a maid, so as soon as she heard S'rena was courting heavily, she encouraged S'rena to marry that good-for-nothing, Benjamin, from down the county.

"You don't want to be giving away what he ought to marry you for, Serena. Do you understand me?" Ole Missus asked S'rena sternly in the kitchen in front of me.

Ole Missus never employed subtlety. Not with her family, and certainly not with the help. Sometimes her frankness bordered on what she herself would call in others "ugly" behavior. It seemed out-and-out rudeness to me even though I wasn't expected to have any delicacy, seeing as how I was a "negro." I didn't want to hear her talk to the girl about such intimate things. The girl had a mother after all.

"The Bible says it's a sin to fornicate. I repeat, fornication is a sin! You know what fornication is don't you, S'rena? You do still go to church, don't you? You don't want *to go to perdition* do you, gal?" S'rena almost turned white. I doubt that S'rena knew what "perdition" was, but she knew it couldn't be good from Ole Missus' tone!

I already knew S'rena had been "giving it away" for months and was expecting a baby in six months or so, but I was not going to open my mouth about that, not even in privacy. I don't know how her mother would've managed without her income, small as it was. Ole Missus would've fired S'rena right out and run her off the property. She might even have sent S'rena's mother away too for failing to "raise the girl better."

S'rena had told me more about intimacy and procreation than I ever wanted to hear. Lord, I blushed my live-long days when I remembered how she described what she and Benjamin did together. Ole Missus treated me as if I were still a little ten-year old instead of nearing fifteen. I learned about "nature" from Miss Ivy who swore me to secrecy lest Ole Missus know that Miss Ivy knew about intimacy in marriage. Miss Ivy said I ought to know because I was safer from the wiles of bad men if I did. It was *good* that Miss Ivy told me because several of the boys from up on the hill and down in the village had already tried to get me to walk out with them at night. Miss Ivy said if their intentions were any good, they would've asked me to walk with them to church and back or to sit in the shade of the big maple tree in the back yard where everyone could see that we were behaving properly. Evidently, Ole Missus thought "nature" was something you learned by experience. Miss Ivy said she was glad her own mother had not been so "antiquated."

"We can't use Ben… Bennie… Benjamin on the farm right now," Ole Missus lied to S'rena, "but I'll give you a good recommendation wherever you two want to go." I know she lied because Massah Robert had been looking for a good man for over a month to help in the tobacco fields. He'd asked me if I'd heard of anyone looking for work. I don't know how he thought I'd hear about it if they were. I had just about zero time to gabble with the neighbors - ever!

S'rena was so puffed up over that low-down, sorry Benjamin that she didn't realize Ole Missus was getting rid of her. I expect Ole Missus knew exactly what I knew - that S'rena was prematurely in the family way. Ole Missus was getting on in years, but she was no wise ignorant.

"Lord A'mighty! Missus Powell, I shore would take it mos' kindly iffen you writes a letter to Missus Graham telling her how good I is. 'Jamine, he got a good job with dem and dat's whar we gonna live." Ole Missus was so glad to send her on her way that she didn't even raise dust over S'rena blaspheming!

"Gal, what are you going to do about your poor elderly mother? She's not able to live entirely alone anymore. She's welcome to live here for the rest of her natural life, but I can't be *seeing to her*." Ole Missus acted a little feeble as this came out. I think Vaz must have inherited his acting talent from her.

"Un, hun!" I thought, "Ole Missus certainly knows the girl's increasing. She wants to get rid of daughter *and mother*."

"Why… why… I hadn't thought 'bout dat." S'rena stuttered.

"Well, I could tell Miz Graham what a good seamstress your mother is. Least she used to be before her eyes went bad. But I guess she can still do simple needlework."

Ole Missus was willing to shape the truth in all kinds of fashions when it came to getting her way. I knew she'd find a solution for S'rena to suit her wishes. She didn't care in the least that S'rena and Benjamin might have preferred living without others in their household just then. To be fair to Ole Missus, according to her lights, the girl should be taking care of her elderly, nearly blind mother. That was a daughter's duty, especially as there were no other relatives nearby.

Later that same week Ole Missus gave the girl an old sheet so threadbare it didn't look as if it could stand one more washing, a pillow that had lost most of its feathers, a moth-eaten blanket and a half-dollar! I hated to spend my money because I had plans for the future perking in my head, but I felt so sorry for the girl that I bought her several pieces of crockery when I went to town to trade that week. She was so grateful and pleased with the pretty flowered pattern that I was completely ashamed over my reluctance to spend the two dollars on her.

We'd seen what Ole Missus had bestowed on S'rena so when she came into the kitchen carrying a parcel later in the week, we all figured she must have been cleaning more closets and had more trash to hand out to someone instead of burning it. She sat down at the table and asked Rhi to come over and sit next to her.

"Mariah, you will probably have to earn your living unless Clay makes a lot of money down there in Texas or you marry a well-to-do man, so I want you to take S'rena's place as the house servant. That way, you'll learn how to do things properly and can find *inside work* if you need to work later in your life. You have a home with me as long as you need one, but I won't live forever. One must, after all, be prepared for future possibilities." Ole Missus said all of this in a rather sad voice as if the thought of Rhi having to work for someone truly bothered her.

"Here, girl, open this up." She handed Rhi the package. Rhi opened the package carefully so as not to tear the paper. Paper was scarce. Inside were two sky-blue dresses with white collars edged with lace. "Mariah" was embroidered on the left shoulders. There were two white aprons and two white lace-edged caps. There were also two pretty nightgowns with little pink roses on them and a pair of shoes with buttons. There was something else - a few skeins of fine white wool, a couple of yards of good-quality white cotton, and a couple of yards of a different lace than was on the caps and dresses.

"Mariah, you and your sister can knit some hosiery and make you some new undergarments. I know the two of you knit well." She explained the wool, cotton, and lace in the package. She looked over at Vaz and said, "Vastine, I apologize for talking about women's delicate clothing in front of you, but she is, after all, your sister, so I expect you already know what she wears under her dress."

Unbelievably, Vaz actually turned the color of a cooked beet. Of course he knew what she wore under her dress. He knew what each of his sisters wore under our dresses. We all three slept in them - our petticoats.

"Mariah, tomorrow I want you to move Honora's things and your things up to the yellow attic bedroom. The room hasn't been used since my grandchild, Miz Mary's son, visited at Christmas, so you will want to open the windows and clean the curtains and bed linens. It's dusty, very dusty in there. You'll want to take the rug out, beat it well, I repeat, beat it really hard, and scrub the floor. From now on that's where you two will sleep. Honora is still too young to be a house servant, so she can come down here every morning and help Sara when she is not doing her lessons. Have you understood me?"

Mariah nodded and Ole Missus continued, "My grand-daughter-in-law, Miz Alexander Powell, Miz Anne that is, will walk you through the house after breakfast tomorrow, telling you what you are to do as a house servant. I'm going to let my daughter-in-law, Miz Rebecca Powell, know that I've asked Anne to do this to take the burden off her. Anne has been here longer. She knows how we like things done. Maybe Miz Rebecca will leave you alone that way. I hope so. She can be so," she stopped for a second, "so, hmm, *thorny*, sometimes." She looked at Vaz who by now was back to his normal color, "Vastine, next year, I will give you the blue attic bedroom." Having said what she came to say, Ole Missus lifted herself slowly out of the chair and left in a rustle of taffeta and a tap-tap of her cane.

We knew the implications of her asking Miz Anne to show Rhi around. The new Mrs. Robert Powell was not well liked by Ole Missus. In fact, the two women barely disguised their utter disdain of one another.

We all looked silently at each other for what must have been two full minutes after Ole Missus left then we burst out laughing. Vaz stood up, imitating his grandmother to perfection as he gave an impromptu lecture on good housekeeping.

"Mariah, one does not, I repeat, simply does *not* forget to dust behind the picture frames!" Vaz sashayed around the room for our amusement. "And you must, I repeat, *must* either use fresh flowers every day or replace the water every day, giving older flower stems a new cut! Have you understood that?" For emphasis he had picked up the broom and was tapping the handle on the floor imitating his grandmother's use of her cane.

I still don't know why we laughed and laughed 'til tears rolled down our faces. It was a good day. Later when I was low, I tried to remember that day.

We all knew, and knew well, that Miz Rebecca Powell did not get along with poor, sweet, dead Miz 'Dena's children any better than she got along with Ole Missus. Rob had been in Charlottesville studying for almost two years now, having left in a hurry a short two months after his father remarried, and several months sooner than planned. Mr.

'Zander was cooI, but civil to his mother-in-law - barely. Ole Missus, Miss Ivy, and Miz Anne tried to occupy most of their table-talk with one another and Massah Robert, including Miz 'Becca in their conversations only enough to manage the minimum of politeness. The honeymoon phase of Massah's second marriage was ancient history having lasted maybe as long as three months into the marriage. He also said very little to his wife at table. Mr. 'Zander and Miz Anne's three children usually sat quietly and obediently at the table as Miz 'Becca's four imps squirmed, picked at their food and made ugly faces or kicked at one another under the table when no one was watching. It was the quietest table you can imagine and usually with thirteen people present!

It was no wonder most of the family tried to avoid interacting with Miz 'Becca. She was one of the most obnoxious human beings I have ever encountered, but in such a way that her behavior made you feel awful, but you couldn't really respond in an "ugly" way or you'd just succeed in making yourself look like the fool.

Even when Miz 'Becca gave a rare compliment, always delivered with a false smile, she managed to ruin any pleasure you might have had in it.

She might say, "The turkey is so flavorful, Sara. It's too bad it finished cooking so early that it dried out," or, "Mariah, the flowers in the parlor are beautiful, but the hortensias are so lovely by themselves, why not make separate arrangements just with them?" How can you respond to such comments?

She usually was overly sweet around Massah Robert. Massah was always a courteous man, even when firing someone, but he had justifiably earned the reputation for being a man you did not run afoul of. More than once I heard people remark that "Robert Powell does not abide fools well." And so it was the rest of us who really suffered from the new Missus Robert Powell's sour disposition and Queen of the May haughtiness.

In fact, the only family member who could tolerate Miz 'Becca was Captain Holton Powell's widow, Massah Robert's sister-in-law. She resided in Fairfax County and Charlottesville, alternating living with her two sons and never actually met Miz 'Becca. They wrote letters to one another. I never met Miz Holton Powell, but the family always said she was a good woman who tragically lost her husband during the War and recently lost her youngest son and grandbaby in a house fire. They say she was never the same again, so she lived six months of the year first with one son, a minister, and then with the other son, a doctor.

The time Miz Victoria and her husband, another Reverend, and six of their ten children still living at home visited her mother and brother, I overheard Miz Victoria in the front parlor praying, asking God to forgive her bad thoughts about Miz 'Becca, asking for more patience. "Help me to forgive, as You forgive us," she prayed. This was the very day after they arrived. The Reverend and his family, *all good people*, left a week earlier than they had planned. That woman was so provoking that good Christian people had to flee the house to keep from committing sins left and right! How were the rest of us supposed to manage?

Even Miz 'Becca's children from her first marriage didn't really like her. The three oldest stayed at their home place, coming once a month, out of filial duty, for Sunday dinner. The four younger ones had no choice but to move with their mother to the Big House. And a more miserable bunch of children you never saw! They quarreled all the time, pinched one another, kicked, and even *spit* on each other. At least once a week, one of them punched another one so hard, he or she couldn't go to school that day. They had behaved so badly on the school wagon that they all had to walk to school because the driver refused to let them ride any more. So in bad weather Old Abraham drove them to school. I think he grumbled the day long every time it rained or snowed.

Those children were rude to everyone *except Massah Robert* who would never have abided it. So they were also *sneaky*. Mr. 'Zander's daughters were too young to be of any interest to Miz 'Becca's children, but Andy sometimes tried to play with Miz 'Becca's two youngest, Miss Elvira and Master Mark. More often than not, either Mr. 'Zander or Miz Anne had to separate them because they began hitting or kicking one another. I don't know how Miz 'Becca's children survived to adulthood without someone braining them!

Andy and Vaz were best of friends and Vaz was so tall, even then, that he would never have stood for anyone of them mistreating Andy when he was around, but Miz 'Becca refused to let her children play with one of Clay's "by-blows." Vaz bided his time over that insult and added it to the growing list of reasons he hated her.

No indeed, things were not well in the house after Massah remarried. I overheard too many unhappy conversations either with Miz 'Becca and a family member or about Miz 'Becca.

From the kitchen one morning when Ole Missus and Miz 'Becca were both in the front parlor for some reason, I overheard them. "Dear Mama," Miz 'Becca said in her overly sweet way to Ole Missus (none of her own children had ever dared call Ole Missus "Mama"), "don't you think it's time to repaper this room. The paper is so old-fashioned and dismal. Don't you think a shade of red would be divinely elegant in here? See this illustration. It says this pattern is red and gold." She must have tried to show Ole Missus something in a periodical.

From the kitchen even I could hear Ole Missus suck in her breath, "Yes, Rebecca, it would certainly be elegant if this house were *a bordello, I repeat,* a bordello!" Then I heard Miz 'Becca gasp as Ole Missus kept on talking. "I bought that paper with my own money when Mr. Powell and I first built this house in 1847. That paper came all the way from France! It cost a small fortune, and it is still in excellent condition. That chimney was built so well that the fireplace has never smoked and the servants pull the curtains against the afternoon sun to prevent fading. I repeat, Madam, the paper is in excellent condition. It would be folly to spend money to replace it. Do you understand me? Folly!"

Miz 'Becca was not to be dismissed yet, "Well, Mama," she said a little less sweetly, "I reckon I need not be in such a hurry to redo the room. It's still your house. By the by, Mama, I was wondering the other day just how old you'll be on your birthday next month. Eighty-four?"

Ole Missus never liked references to her age, so I was surprised to hear her laugh at this. "Rebecca," she said firmly in her old, gravelly voice, "When I pass, you can do whatever Robbie will allow, but I wouldn't count on red paper in the front parlor if I were you!" I heard a swishing of skirts and the cane tapping as Ole Missus turned to the hall door and mumbled loudly enough for Miz 'Becca (and me) to hear, "I'll live long enough to dance on your grave anyway." The door closed firmly behind her.

Miz 'Becca talked to herself for what seemed to be 30 minutes after Ole Missus left, but I could only understand a little of what she said.

"Old besom!"

"Dance on my grave, will she?"

"Maybe I'll get lucky and the old witch will tumble down the stairs and break her scrawny turkey neck!"

She said some *ugly*, mean things that morning. Maybe that's why God let Ole Missus live long enough to attend Miz 'Becca's funeral a few years later - if she had chosen to go.

Ole Missus may have laughed at Miz 'Becca as she departed the parlor, but she was in her bed for the next three days with one of her rare "spells." She had, unfortunately, developed a habit of confiding in Vaz who at ten looked nearly grown and could carry on a conversation with any adult. Ole Missus failed to realize that Vaz was still a child in some ways. He often acted too quickly without considering the repercussions. The next day when Vaz went up to learn how Ole Missus was, she confided the conversation she'd had with Miz 'Becca to him. He told me furiously about it later the same day. I had to talk him out of the tree tops. He had flown into such a fury. He was already plotting to put a piece of wire across Miz 'Becca's doorway that night so that she'd fall on her face when she came out in the morning!

From the kitchen one morning soon afterwards, I overheard Miz' Becca, Miz Anne and Miss Ivy talking after the children and the men left the dining table. Miss Ivy was talking about a new dress she was having made for the senior dance at school in April.

"Oh, Anne, it is the loveliest shade of green! Not a dark green, but a pale blue green, almost as blue as it is green. It even has *a bustle* with ruffles descending to the hem. It has scalloping at the hem that reveals a white silk underskirt. There are white silk roses embroidered just above the scalloping, white lace from the bosom up to a high fitted neck, large white lace standing out from the shoulders over long sleeves. I objected to the long sleeves and the high neck, but Daddy and Grandmother have insisted that this is southwestern Virginia, not New York or Paris!" She was so excited and *so* happy describing her first evening gown.

"Well, dear," Miz 'Becca began in that quiet, silky voice she used to plunge her tongue into people, "It ought to be beautiful, considering no one else will be getting a stitch of anything for some time. Mr. Powell says your dress is costing a right pretty penny. Now we must all economize until the tobacco is sold in the fall. My own dear children need new clothing now because they've all grown so much."

I knew this to be a twisted version of the truth, and I expect that Miss Ivy knew so as well, because, for one thing, however expensive the dress was, Ole Missus was paying for it. I also had overheard Massah Robert telling Miz 'Becca to buy her children new clothes with the money he'd put into her expense account. *He* told *her* that her children had outgrown their old things. Yet, I couldn't say anything.

Miz Anne tried to pass over her Mama-in Law's comments. "Oh, Ivy, the next time you go to the dressmaker's, may I come too? I can't wait until April to see this dress! I may have to have one made, in a different color of course, along the same lines. It sounds so beautiful. Who are you going to the dance with?"

This was too much for Miz 'Becca, "Good gracious me! Now you, Anne, want to spend a fortune on a dress for which you have no occasion to wear!"

Miz Anne tried to utter a response, but couldn't get it out before Miz 'Becca went on sourly, "I hope, you're not going with that pimple-faced nephew of Miz Eliza's. He's a head shorter than you and is always tongue-tied around me."

I wondered who in God's creation could blame the boy for having enough *good sense* to keep his mouth shut around Miz 'Becca.

Of course, her second cousin was going to the dance with her. They were in the same class together and Miss Ivy felt sorry for him, knowing he would not be brave enough to ask any other girl. Nor would anyone accept him, despite his family connections, with his skin in such a condition. Years later when the pimples were ancient history and he was a highly successful financier in New York City married to a leading socialite fifteen years his junior, he wrote Miss Ivy a lovely note on her 40th birthday, remembering her kindness that long ago spring - and gifting her with a magnificent Packard touring automobile! How that would have stuck in Miz 'Becca's craw if she had been alive to know of it.

I could almost feel Miss Ivy turn red, but Miss Ivy was Ole Missus's granddaughter! "Step-Mama, *a little* kindness on your part would be appreciated by everyone in this house, especially me. I am sure that Cyrus Young has never given you any reason to be so hateful! Cyrus has something you will never have for all of Daddy's money. Manners and good taste!" I heard a chair scrape on the floor and Miss Ivy's fast long steps as she headed out the hall door.

"Well," Miz ' Becca sighed, heavily aggrieved, "Where does she get the audacity to speak to one of her elders in such a fashion? Why, my mother would've locked me…"

"Oh, dear Mama-in-Law," Miz Anne interrupted, "You fired the first volley and you know it! Ivy will not be quiet when a dear friend is maligned. I can't blame her for her response to you."

"Well, I never meant any unkindness. I was just stating facts. The boy is homely and abnormally shy. Well," she sighed again and said, as if to herself, "what can you expect, Ivy is no great beauty herself."

Miz Anne evidently stood up because her voice came from near the hallway door, "I'm sure you don't want my opinion, Rebecca, but you're about to hear it anyway." Miz Anne didn't wait for a comment. "Ivy is so smart, so humorous and so kind that if she lacks *your great conventional beauty* it never keeps the young men away. They all like her very much and her father has already turned down two good proposals of marriage saying that she is still too young and he doesn't want to lose his baby girl just yet."

As Miz Anne opened the door, she shot back to Miz 'Becca, "And, furthermore, Rebecca, I think you very much intended to be unkind because you can't stand to see anyone happy, particularly Ivy who reminds us constantly of her dear, sweet mother!" The door didn't quite slam, but it was louder than necessary when it closed. It seemed that Miz Anne didn't suffer fools gladly either.

"Well!" was all I heard from Miz 'Becca that time.

It was only a few days later that Rhi, with Miz Anne just behind her, came into the kitchen crying as hard as ever I saw her cry. She ran past me and into the room we had shared until very recently. She flung herself face down on the bed with her feet hanging over the side.

"Rhi, what's wrong?" I figured somebody had passed away the way she was carrying on. "Honey, tell me what's happened." I sat down beside her on the bed. She sat up slowly and I dried her cheeks with the hem of my apron. "Why are you crying like this?" I noticed finally that she had her apron pressed to the back of her head.

"Oh, Sara, that woman is horrible!"

"What woman are you talking about? Miz Anne? Ole Missus?"

"Of course not Miz Anne! She'd never treat me like that and if Grandmother finds out about this she may kill her!" Rhi started to cry again. "I don't want Ole Missus upset, Sara. Promise you won't tell her! Promise!" She demanded.

"I can't tell her *anything* right now, Rhi, because I don't know *anything*. Tell me what's upset you so much!"

Rhi had to grab the wash basin on the stand and vomit before she could dry her tears, and the anger poured out. "Who's the most hateful human being you ever met, Sara? Miz' Becca!" she declared. "God will have to build a special place in hell for her. She's so lowdown!"

"What has she done this time?" It wasn't the first time Miz 'Becca had upset Rhi, but this time it must have been especially bad.

"Do you see that I don't have my cap on?" Rhi reached up and gingerly touched her scalp. I noticed then that her braids were loose and there were many loose strands of her pretty chestnut hair clinging to her head and loose on her shoulders. She also had a long deep scratch on her forehead near her hairline.

"What did that woman do to you, Rhi?" I asked between my teeth as I stood to get a better look at her head. "Tell me now because I don't think Ole Missus is going to get a chance to kill her!" There was a pump knot the size of a goose egg on the back of her head and it was already turning a deep blue. The scratch had happened, from the looks of it, when her hair had been yanked loose from her braid. "

Rhi ran to my wash basin and threw up again. I poured water onto a face cloth, had her lie down again and gave her the cloth, "For your head, sweetheart." I explained.

"Oh, Sara, you can't start something with her. Massah Robert would fire you. Promise me you won't go after her! Why they'd put you under the jail for attacking a white woman! Promise or I won't tell you!" Rhi was clearly scared of what I might do if I knew.

"Alright, Rhi, I won't go after Miz 'Becca." But I never promised not to speak to Massah Robert!

That's just what I did after dinner that afternoon. I heard Massah Robert's heavy footsteps going down the hall towards his office. I told Violet and Nora to clean the kitchen and the dining room and to be quiet about it as Rhi was lying on my bed feeling very poorly. She had a bad headache, and I didn't care if the whole house was filthy. Rhi was suffering, and I knew Ole Missus would want her to lie down if she was sick. I left an old pail near her in case she needed to puke again. I had important business to take care of. I waited about five minutes before I headed down the hall to talk to Massah Robert.

I knocked firmly on Massah Robert's office door. I was plenty angry still. In fact I was probably even angrier for having held it in for two hours. If I had seen Miz 'Becca, who had *not* come down to dinner, I believe I would've broken my promise to Rhi and actually struck the woman. Massah Robert called for me to "Come on in!"

He looked up, surprised that it was me. "Why, Sara, what brings you to see me?" He smiled and actually motioned for me to take a seat which I did not do. I was too angry to be still and I was afraid I might lose my nerve if I allowed his good manners to calm me.

"Massah Robert, I am no tale carrier. You know that."

"What's upset you so, Sara? No you handle your own business without tattle-telling." He looked grave knowing that I didn't complain about trivial things. Not even big things, usually. "You're a good girl. Your mother and grandmother must be very proud…"

I could wait no longer so I think I stopped him mid-sentence. "Sir, my sister, Rhi -Mariah, that is - has been severely mistreated by a member of this family! Badly mistreated, Sir! She has been physically injured, and I want you to take steps so that it never happens again!" Whew! I'd gotten that much out without falling down in a limp heap.

"Who? What?" he demanded. "Those brats of Missus Powell!" he roared, jumping to a logical, but wrong, conclusion.

"No Sir!" I said hastily. "But you are *correct* to call the little SNEAKS 'brats.' They are, but they learned it first-hand from their mother!"

He looked shocked at my vehemence and started to rebuke me, "Sara, I'm very fond of you, but I can't allow you say such things about my wife!"

"I have worse to say, Massah! Please hear what leads me to say anything to you at all about Miz 'Becca."

I don't know if he would have allowed me to go on if Miz Anne had not tapped lightly on his office door, entering without waiting for a reply.

As soon as she closed his door behind herself, she held up one hand and said, "Daddy Robbie, please hear me if you won't hear Sara."

He sighed as if he was resigned finally to hear it all. "Please, sit down - both of you. He got up and locked the door. "That way there'll be no interruptions. Sara, please go on."

I told him about Rhi coming to me sobbing inconsolably. I told him what Rhi had finally told me.

"Miz 'Becca accused Rhi of stealing a piece of jewelry from her. It isn't the first time this has happened, but Rhi usually doesn't answer her back except to say she doesn't have whatever it is. Almost every time it has happened, before the day is out, the piece turns up on Miz 'Becca's person. If not that day, then the next. She has never once apologized, and Miz 'Becca acts as if it's her right to make ridiculous accusations, threatening to get Rhi thrown out of the house even when the charges are false. Later she acts as if it was all a simple mistake, a misunderstanding."

Massah looked at Anne, 'Did you know this?"

"Yes, Daddy Robbie. All of us have heard Rebecca accuse Mariah, saying, 'that little by-blow of Clay's has sticky fingers. She took...' whatever was missing at the time. We'd see the pin or bracelet on Rebecca later that day or the next and tell her how glad we are that she had found it. She laughs when that happens as if she may say anything she pleases and owes no one an explanation or apology! I believe the woman thinks she's royalty! Her haughtiness is beyond bearing! Casually she remarks that it was in a pocket of another dress, or even in the jewelry box and she had simply overlooked it." Anne coughed, cleared her throat as if she was on uncertain ground, but proceeded.

"Daddy Robbie, she has called Mariah a by-blow to her face. Told her she is Clay's bastard child. Called her high yellow. Told her that if her daddy cared anything about her, she'd be with him in Texas. Called her over-grown and homely, and I don't know what all else." She cleared her throat again.

Miz Anne continued, "I don't like race mixing. You all know how I feel about it. I've never made a secret of it. I didn't approve of what Clay did, but I dislike cruelty much, much more, particularly to a child! Mariah is not thirteen years old yet, and she is a really good girl. Daddy Robbie, you, Sara, and I know that if Grandmother Nancy learns of this, she will throw Rebecca out of the house, and *you too* if you defend her. We've all kept quiet for Grandmother Nancy's sake and for yours, but we've seen how she treats that child. And," she might as well unburden herself further, "she doesn't treat the rest of us, especially Ivy, much better. But this time, she's gone too far."

"What happened this time, Sara?" Massah asked sadly, gently, clasping his hands on the desk in front of him.

"Rhi had enough, Sir. She's not a dog that can be kicked and kicked and will still lick your hand if you feed it! As a matter of fact, I'm rather surprised she stood it this long. Rhi is a polite girl, but she has a bit of Ole Missus' temper if she sees something unfair. This time, instead of just denying having it, Rhi told Miz 'Becca to look in her pockets, her purse, her dresser anywhere the pearls might be - because she had not taken them." I bent over, my arms folded in front of me, beginning to cry, not sure I wasn't going to throw up myself. My twelve-year old sister had to defend herself against this monster because the adults allowed Miz 'Becca to get away with her cruelty.

Stifling sobs I explained, "That, evidently, was all it took for Miz 'Becca to fly into a rage and snatch the cap off Rhi's head so roughly that she scratched Rhi's face. It was still bleeding when she came into the kitchen. She pulled out several large chunks of hair! Rhi said Miz 'Becca threw her cap on the floor and stomped on it. Then she ordered Rhi to pick it up and get out of her sight. Rhi opened the door to leave without retrieving her cap. Then, Miz 'Becca threw a pewter paperweight hitting Rhi in the back of the head. HARD! Rhi is lying on my bed now with a cold rag on her head and the shutters closed. Miz Anne, I let young Andy go with Vaz to fetch the doctor. I didn't want to waste time explaining to him why he should stay here. Please pardon my not asking for your permission." Miz Anne nodded her acceptance.

"Rhi has a sick headache so bad she cannot even get a cup of tea down right now. She's puked several times since she came to me."

Miss Anne added, "I saw Rebecca throw the paperweight that hit Mariah. I'm surprised it didn't kill her. She threw it with considerable force. We're not talking of something soft like a pillow, Daddy Robbie.

I had to help the child down the stairs and to the kitchen because she was *reeling* from the blow. Rebecca is now laid up with a headache, afraid someone might actually tell you this time what she's done. I don't think she knows I saw her because as soon as she hit Mariah she slammed the door. We haven't told you how uncivil and downright *mean* the woman is. We didn't want to carry tales, and we didn't want to upset you. We were *wrong*! We should have told you when it first started. Mariah may have a serious head injury and if Grandmother Nancy hears of it - *Heaven help us all*!"

"Massah Robert," I added quietly, but firmly, "If you don't take care of this, I will leave. I will take my sisters and brother out of this house as soon as Rhi can travel. Then Ole Missus will know and, as Miz Anne says, H*eaven help you all*!"

Miz Anne smiled slightly. "Daddy Robbie, Grandmother Nancy may murder her, and, I'm sorry to tell you, that I'm thinking about now it might be *justice*! Mariah has *every legal right* to file criminal charges. The northern Republicans have gone now, but things are not like they were during the old days when a white person could strike a black person with impunity, especially if a white witness, such as myself, gives evidence!" She stood up and left, walking me out the door in front of her. Considering the increase in lynching's of blacks, I wasn't sure Miz Anne was correct, but what she said should have been so.

The doctor came and, over the course of four days, Rhi returned to normal, except for her vision which was always slightly poor after that blow. Ole Missus took Rhi to have spectacles made as soon as we realized her sight was a problem. Until about a year later, none of us told Ole Missus what we believed caused her eyesight to become so poor so suddenly. I kept all three children in my room for the rest of the week. Eight-year old Nora, Ivy and I managed what house cleaning got done while Rhi was still dizzy and nauseous. We told Ole Missus that she had a bad sore throat, asked her to stay away from Rhi, telling her that we didn't want her to catch it.

Whatever Massah Robert said to his wife, she never laid a finger on any of us again. In fact, she only spoke to the white folks after that. Somehow Ole Missus never found out what was up then, and that was no small blessing because I do believe she would've shot Miz 'Becca. Rhi, Vaz, Nora and I were all delighted when Miz 'Becca never spoke to us, but sometimes it made it awkward having to hear her requests from a second person.

She didn't speak to the four of us, but she exacted vengeance in small hateful ways just the same. Rhi said Miz 'Becca's clothing would be thrown in heaps on the bedroom floor, not just to be hung up, but needing to be pressed and hung up. Her bedding was always so disheveled that the whole thing had to be remade every day. She must have intentionally spilt food, wine, coffee, and tea on the floor and table cloth so that after every meal the cloth had to be changed and the floor mopped! She had a fire started in her room almost every night and in the front parlor every morning, no matter how warm it was, requiring the grates to be cleaned daily. She would purposely walk straight up to us and stop, forcing us to go around her, often with heavy loads in our arms. The woman emitted anger like a fire exuding heat. You could feel it. I expected they'd find Rhi and Nora dead in their attic bedroom one morning and Vaz and me dead in our room. We started to lock our doors at night.

The day Miss Ivy told us that she was going away to college to learn how to teach, Vaz cut one big shine. She told us she'd be away except for holidays. We wouldn't see her again before Christmas and only for a week or so then. Vaz was almost eleven, could read anything, could write in fancy letters, and could multiply and divide big numbers *in his head.* Little Nora had just begun to read, add, and subtract. She was the one who still needed Miss Ivy the most. Rhi and I were alright. We could teach ourselves many things just by reading. Neither Ole Missus nor Massah Robert minded us reading anything in the bookcases. The old days when whites and the law forbade the education of negroes were long gone. Thankfully.

"Ivy, why do you have to go away to learn to teach?" Vaz demanded, shouting at her. Vaz never called her *Miss* Ivy. "You've been teaching us for five years, and you've done fine." By now he was stomping around the kitchen, shoving a chair out of his way, kicking at the cat that ran away just in time. Acting as if he were the Massah, Vaz strode to the dining room door going to find his personal savior, Ole Missus.

"Ivy, I will not *let* you go! I shall talk to Ole Missus about this! *She* won't let you go either!"

Ivy was wringing her hands as if she didn't know what to do. I'd never seen her act like this before. She shouted back at Vaz when she had never raised her voice to any of us.

As if to dare him to tell his grandmother, she said him, "It's not for you, Master Vastine, nor my Grandmother to stop me. If you must know who put the final seal of approval on my going it was my dear Step-Mama!"

Yes, Miss Ivy liked to teach, but I think going away to school was her way to leave such an insane asylum as her home had become.

Probably the worst offenses Miz 'Becca committed in Vaz's eyes were that she was short tempered with Ole Missus who was getting frailer by the day, and she had been rude to Miss Ivy and his sisters. For what she had done to Rhi, I think he wanted to put Miz 'Becca in a dungeon somewhere and throw away the key. Thankfully, Miz 'Becca ignored Nora.

Vaz started sputtering over what Miss Ivy said, but he felt sorry for her because of her terrible step-mama. Vaz always possessed great loyalty to the people he cared about. Added to his keen intelligence was his dark desire to exact vengeance when he thought those he loved had been injured. He gave the water bucket waiting by the door to be filled a hefty kick and mumbled something under his breath that sounded like what Ole Missus would label an *ugly* word.

"Ivy, I hate that woman!" he declared loudly. "She's mean! She's hateful! She's a liar! And she gets people mad at each other just for her own delight! Why did your papa marry that old harridan?"

Harridan must have been one of the words he had just learned, but I knew what it meant by the way he said it. "I think the devil came into this house riding *under* her skirts!"

I looked quickly at my sisters to see if they caught Vaz's implications. Seemingly, they did not.

"Hush, Vastine," Miss Ivy said sternly, but she smiled at him, showing him that she wasn't terribly angry. She said softly, "Harridan is sufficient, Vastine, as it already means an old woman who behaves like my sweet Mama-in-Law. In my presence and in the presence of your sisters, do not make another inference such as you just did. If that old harridan hears you, grandmother will have to save your hide from a licking by Daddy."

Ivy strode around the kitchen, up righting the overturned water pail before continuing, "My Step-Mama didn't behave this way before Daddy married her. She was cunning and determined to marry the richest widower in the county. I see the way Daddy stoops over these days. He regrets marrying her. He's *miserable*. But he married her, for better or for worse. And his honor requires him to defend her from all of us."

Ivy sat down in a chair as if she was weary before musing aloud, " 'Course Grandmother doesn't give a fig at this point in her life who she makes mad, but she is getting a bit on in age to argue with Rebecca all the time." She rose slowly and walked over to Vaz, giving him a soft slap on his cheek, more in fun than serious. "You young scoundrel, that old woman loves you so much, you ought to be trying to make her life easier instead of raising one ruckus after another!"

She sat down at the table again, beckoning for us all to sit with her. "In the meantime, we still have several days of lessons before I leave. I have asked Grandmother to see about getting a tutor to work with all of you. Grandmother thinks the new Methodist minister in Gates Gap might like a little extra money, seeing as how he has so many children. Fourteen, I believe, God bless them. She's going to inquire about him tutoring you several days a week. Anyway, we shall see. Shall we begin lessons?"

"Ivy, one more thing," Vastine said as if resigned to the changes. Ivy sighed heavily as if she was afraid of what Vaz might say or do now. "When and where are you going to school?" He asked sadly, accepting that he was going to lose his Ivy. Although she was technically a cousin, she was his first love. I believe he looked for the rest of his life for someone like Ivy.

"Children, I'm leaving next Monday. I will be very tired from all the jostling but I am so looking forward to seeing something outside this county! I'm going to stay with Aunt Dorothea Powell, her son Stewart and his new wife for several days and spend some time with my brother Rob. They're all in Charlottesville. Then on Saturday or early Sunday, Rob will drive me over to Staunton where I will start school on Monday. I'm so looking forward - Oh, I just said that, didn't I?" She laughed at herself and patted the table. "Let's begin. Daylight's burning!"

Life went on after Miss Ivy left though it felt as if she took the final crumb of happiness from the house when she did. The new tutor, Reverend Pickle, started coming on Tuesdays and Thursdays, about two weeks after Miss Ivy went away. He was not much interested in teaching girls, but Ole Missus said as how he *was* to teach Nora since she didn't know much yet. Vaz's lessons were too hard for Rhi and me and Nora's lessons were too easy, so we couldn't just learn by listening to their lessons. Rhi and I read together at night after the work was done. Reverend Pickle (and his name perfectly suited his pinch-faced appearance and sour disposition) produced long lists of homework for Vaz to do on the days he wasn't there, but he must've believed Miss Ivy hadn't given the boy much of a challenge, because what he gave Vaz was far too easy. Vaz went through those assignments like water through a sieve.

Thankfully, Miss Ivy wrote to us every week and she would send Vaz more advanced lessons, especially in mathematics and history. Once Vaz told Miss Ivy that the Reverend wasn't teaching Rhi and me, she always sent assignments for us as well. We had fun reading Miss Ivy's letters and doing the work she asked us to do. We would write back telling her how we got on with her lessons and what was happening on the farm. Of course, Vaz was also writing to his father about our educational progress and the Reverend Pickle's errors in Latin and mathematics.

CHAPTER 6: INTRODUCING JOSEPH THIERRY

I love you as certain dark things are to be loved,
in secret, between the shadow and the soul.

from 100 Love Sonnets,
Pablo Neruda

The year of our Lord 1890 is stuck in my head more firmly than yesterday. So much happened to alter the course of my life forever. It's so woven together that it's hard for me to tell what happened first, but I believe it happened in this order.

Mr. Clay wrote regularly as he said he would, but one mid-afternoon in April when I had rare free time, a very special messenger arrived with news of Mr. Clay. I was sitting in the spring sunshine on the kitchen porch reading *The Princess Casamassima* by Henry James.

My eyes were full of tears because I had just read that Hyacinth's "mother," Miss Pynsent, was passing. The sound of scrunching steps approaching the house caused me to lift my eyes from the book to see who was coming from the stables at that time of day. It was a man, about five-feet nine or ten inches tall, no wise as tall as Massah Robert. At first he seemed to be an unknown black man, but when I wiped the tears away, I saw him more clearly. I didn't know him, but he was not as white as the Powell's nor dark like the negroes. He was swarthy with dark brown skin, dark hair, dark eyes and a curled-up moustache. I thought he was quite handsome, swaggering down the walk as if he owned the place wearing a very good, if dusty, suit, carrying his hat in his hand.

He smiled broadly showing teeth that were remarkably white in contrast to his skin and moustache. "Are you Miss Gilley?" he asked in an accent I'd never heard before, removing his hat and bowing slightly towards me.

I stood, put my bookmark carefully in place and laid the book on the chair where I had been sitting. I was uncomfortable and I was rarely uncomfortable around people; it wasn't that I was afraid of him. I just felt awkward, unkempt, and ill-prepared to meet the likes of this man. Standing on the porch with him on the ground below, we were about eye level, but I couldn't look into his eyes.

"Yes. Who wants to know?" I asked with what I thought was suitable formality.

He laughed as if I'd said something funny. "My name is Joseph Thierry and I have brought parcels and a letter from Mr. Claiborne Powell." He took two paces and was at the steps now. I could see that he was older than I had first thought. He might have been younger than the early 30's, but he'd spent a good deal of time outdoors so it was difficult to tell what caused the crinkling around his eyes - age, sun or laughter.

"I'll take you around to the front door. Follow me." I said without lifting my eyes to his face, starting down the steps. I was so conscious of being barefooted, in my oldest, most faded dress, and wearing a terrible old country bonnet to keep the sun out of my eyes while I read. I feared the tears I had just shed might have left trails down my possibly dusty face.

"Wait." He stopped me in mid-step as I started off the porch. "I've come with specific instructions to see *you* and Mr. Clay Powell's children first!"

"Instructions from whom?" I blurted.

"From Mr. Clay Powell, of course!" I looked up at him then. I must have seemed not only unsophisticated, but stupid as well. He'd just told me who the messages were from. He was still smiling, but more natural instead of posturing.

"Well, I shall have to find the children. I don't know where they are right now." I tried to think where they might be. I happened to look down at his boots to try to concentrate better. I saw that his boots were very dusty but, like his suit, of excellent quality. Hastily I looked up. I'd acted as if I had no manners when I had actually been brought up with *a few*.

"Why, you must be thirsty! Can I get you some water? Tea? Coffee? Buttermilk?"

He bowed slightly again. "Yes, Ma'am. I'd appreciate a glass of buttermilk very much. It's so good to find a civilized person who still offers a guest buttermilk! I've been traveling since daylight. But if you don't mind, first, I'll go clear the dust from my throat with water from the pump over there."

I don't remember ever being called "Ma'am" before, so I was taken aback, but I picked up my book, and motioned for him to help himself at the pump. I waited for him to swish his face and hands lightly. He gathered water in his hands several times, drinking thirstily.

"Please have a seat." I motioned to Ole Mammie's rocker that I'd dragged out of the kitchen to sit in while I read. I turned to the kitchen door, then turned back towards him. "Is someone attending to your horse?"

"I took care of D'Artagnan and the ponies before I came to the house, Ma'am. Thank you for asking." He seemed genuinely pleased that I had thought about his livestock, but he gave me a look as if he couldn't imagine what I was thinking.

"Are you wondering about the horse's name, Miss Gilley?" He asked smiling broadly.

"It *is* unusual, but then Rhi, that is Mariah, and Vastine have named one of the house cats Lothario. I suppose a person of literary leanings

94

might name their animal after a character in a book." I was amused and smiling.

He was headed up the steps to the porch. "Please use those if you need to." I pointed to the pitcher, basin and soap at the end of the porch as I started inside again. "Oh, there's no towel there!" Without a thought I untied my apron and tossed it to him as if he were one of the children. Deftly he caught it and laughed heartily. I know I blushed because my face was on fire as I went inside. I had very little opportunity to learn how to behave around guests as I was usually busy somewhere else when they were about. Lord! I must have seemed like a total rube - well, after all, that's what I was.

I found Nora and Violet playing checkers at the big kitchen table. Nora always won. I don't think it could have been much fun for her, but Violet loved to play.

"Do either of you know where Vaz is?" I asked.

"He and Andy were hoop rolling on the front drive, last thing I knew." Nora replied. "That was right after dinner. They could be anywhere by now." And probably were, I thought with dismay.

"Violet, please pour a big glass of buttermilk, and leave the pitcher on the table. Nora, make a ham sandwich using some of the fresh lettuce. Make two, in fact. Set the table here. Then ask the gentleman on the back porch to come in and have a bite." I started for the hall door to find Rhi.

"Tell Mr. Terry," or something like that I muttered to myself, "that I've gone to find 'Mariah' and 'Vastine.' Introduce yourselves. Violet, please *do not leave the room until I return* or until one of the other children comes in."

"No, Sarie." Violet nodded.

I found Rhi scrubbing the front stairs, sent her off to her room as soon as she could put her cleaning supplies and big old scrubbing apron away. "Wash your hands and face, and straighten your hair and clothes. Then go down to the kitchen and introduce yourself to Mr. Terry. He's here with a message from your father."

It seemed forever before I found Vaz and Andy looking for dry land fish in the midst of a stand of pines. They had actually found several dry land fish even though it was still early in the season.

"You boys didn't eat any before I could sort them, did you?" While it's difficult to confuse dry land fish, also known as morels in other parts of the country, with poisonous mushrooms, it can happen. I wanted them to use caution as they were still new to mushrooming and I didn't want them sick.

"No, Sara," Andy answered. "We've seen what mushroom poisoning can do. Remember Aunt Victoria's boys getting sick last spring from eating bad mushrooms?"

"Yes, I do. Those boys were sick for about 12 hours." I reached out and took their small collection from them. "Let's go home. Vaz has company."

"Who? Who is it, Sara? What do they want?" Vaz demanded, jumping round me like a cat agitating for its dinner. I understood his excitement. We very rarely had company.

"You'll see. Except for the fact that he's got news from Mr. Clay, I don't know why he's here either. Before you see him, you need to wash your face and hands." I happened to look down, "And your feet, too, from the looks of them!"

I looked at my own feet. Vaz's feet weren't the only feet in need of washing. "Your grandmother may have a word or two for you, Andy, about *how heathens behave*!" I looked pointedly at his bare feet. "Better clean yours and find your shoes and stockings!"

We three went by the water pump where I always left soap and a scrub brush for just such emergencies as this. Vaz, Andy and I washed our faces, hands and feet in that cold, cold water. I had thrown my bonnet off in the kitchen earlier, but my hair was a real mess now from stepping under tree branches and getting caught in briers! I took my fingers, trying to straighten my braids like Ole Mammie used to do. I hoped it helped. We went inside where Mr. Terry was entertaining the girls. I introduced Vaz to the stranger, excused myself for a few minutes to go into my room and change from the old, *now torn*, dress into a newer one. I found a clean apron and put on my shoes and stockings. It would have taken me half an hour to unbraid and re-braid my hair, so I just straightened it a bit more.

When I returned to the kitchen I found Andy still there. I asked him to go find Miz 'Becca's children and play as Mr. Clay had sent private greetings to the children.

"You can join the children and their guest later, Andy." I added to soften his dismissal as I sent Violet off to the summer kitchen with rags, polish and a load of silver to clean. "If you finish the silver before I send for you, please set about cleaning that mess of creasy greens in the bushel basket on the back porch. Be sure to rinse them three times, Violet. Three times now." I always had to remind and remind Violet. By the time she finished the silver she would have forgotten what she was supposed to do next, so she'd be back in the kitchen in about an hour.

Violet smiled her shy, crooked smile, dipped an awkward curtsy toward Mr. Terry and left.

"Good bye, Violet. Maybe I will see you again later." He said graciously to the girl.

"Mr. Terry…" I started.

Gently, "Thierry," he corrected, pronouncing his name "T'ierry", "but please just call me Joseph. Clay has spoken of y'all so much that I feel like I'm your uncle, children."

He told the children about Clay's ranch, about the baby, about Eliza, about the cows, the cotton - all sorts of things. Then he told us how he and Clay met.

"I have a ranch in Sabine Parish, Louisiana. I'm not much of a dab at ranching, but it's been in my family for generations, ever since the Thierry's left Nova Scotia and settled in Louisiana about 140 years ago," he began.

"The Sabine River is actually the border between Louisiana and Texas, so some of my cattle came down with this Texas cow fever. A rancher I know from up near Natchitoches (not to be confused with Nacogdoches, Texas, now!) suggested I might want to talk to this newcomer ranching around Corsicana. I wrote to Clay Powell. He wrote back, and I went up to look at his herd. He finally agreed to sell me his next Hereford bull-calf. And from then on we've been fast friends." Joseph pronounced.

"Well, Mr. Thierry," Vaz stated firmly, "That can't be so very long since Daddy's only been in Texas five years now."

Joseph Thierry roared with laughter. "Your father knows you pretty well, son, to have been away from you for five years! He said you are savvy and..." he was looking for the right word. I supplied one.

"Impudent!" I looked my brother in the eye and scolded, "You don't know this man, Vaz. He's come a long way to bring news of Mr. Clay. Mind your manners!"

Vaz grinned first at me, then at the stranger. "Ah, Sister Sara, come off your high horse! Men talk to men differently, don't they Mr. Thierry?"

Again, Joseph Thierry laughed. "Yes, son, they do, but usually a young man has some respect for an old man's age!" He raised a hand as if to say, "No offense taken."

"Young ladies," he said to Rhi and Nora, "I've brought y'all gifts from your father - from Mr. Clay." This time he caught what he feared might be an error. I flipped my hand sideways as if to say, "It's alright. They know."

"The presents are in a pack I left in the stables. If Vastine will go with me to help carry them, I'll be back shortly." Joseph Thierry and Vaz got up from the table and started for the kitchen door. Mr. Thierry turned to me, "Thank you ever so much for the food, Ma'am. I was completely ravenous!" He turned his attention to Rhi. "And, Miss Mariah, the ginger bread was the perfect finish to my repast." The man talked as if he were a book!

Mr. Clay had sent maps and a set of encyclopedias. He must have ordered them from New York or even London for it was the latest edition of the Encyclopaedia Britannica.

"What a heavy load you've toted up here for these children!" I exclaimed. "Did you bring a wagon, too?" I was probably more excited about the encyclopedias than the children were. Now I could learn about anything!

"No, Miss Gilley, but I did have two Western ponies in train on the way up. They carried the packages. The ponies are gifts for Mariah and Vastine, as well." He looked over at Nora and added, "Your father says he will send you a pony too when you are older, but he expects the one he gave the three of you before he left still works for you, Miss Honora." The smile on her little nine-year old face lit the room up. He'd called her "*Miss* Honora."

"Yes, Sir. I don't think I could manage a bigger animal right now than our old pony, Marshall."

Mr. Clay and Miz Eliza had sent an embroidered, fringed buckskin jacket for Vaz. It was a bit large, but the boy was growing so fast, it would most likely be a perfect fit by cool weather in the fall. They'd also included a pair of handsome Western boots that were also a little too big just yet.

"Look, Sara," gone was Vaz's usual nonchalance. He was so proud of the gifts that he was turning round and round so I could get a look at the jacket from all sides. "A real Western jacket! Just like cowboys wear! And look at these boots. I'll be almost as tall as Uncle Robbie in these!"

Mr. Thierry cleared his throat, "Actually, son, most cowboys don't own such a fine jacket as this. But Buffalo Bill Cody wears one very like it. Least he did when I last saw him in Colorado. No. Wait a minute. Let me think. Not Colorado." He took his pointer finger and smoothed one side of his moustache as if it were habitual when he was trying to recall something.

"I've got it now! It was in Connecticut - of all places - I met Buffalo Bill! It was a few years back, about 1885. I can't remember now *why* I was in Connecticut! Shipping business, I suppose."

"Did you meet Buffalo Bill?" Vaz asked enthusiastically in awe.

"Not only did I *meet* William Cody, for that's his real name, but I met *Chief Sitting Bull* too. His real name is Tatanka Yotanka. That Indian is even more independent than you, young gentleman. He left Cody's show after only one season and went back into federal custody rather than appear before crowds of booing white people - but he made a *great deal of money* in one season."

"He went back to jail?" Rhi asked in surprise.

"Well, not a jail as you think of it, but he is supposed to stay on the reservation. He can leave it only with permission from federal authorities. It's a large territory that was not good for much to white men until gold was discovered about 10 to 12 years back. I'm not sure the Indian wars are over yet, but *God help the Sioux* if they rise up again for they cannot win against the U.S. government. There are too many of us and too few of them." He seemed to think on what he'd said for a few minutes before saying more.

"Sitting Bull thought the shows were sensational. The Indians in the shows wear garbs usually reserved for ceremonies. Lakotas rarely wear those big war bonnets when they go into battle, but Cody and his audiences like the theatricality of it. Then there was some discussion about Sitting Bull's excessive drinking…"

I gave him a look to indicate he need say no more on the subject of alcohol.

Mr. Thierry picked up one of the boots and pointed to the heel, "There's a practical reason for the heels on these boots, son. They're there not just to make you taller, although as I'm not a tall man myself I find it helps with the ladies if I seem taller." He pointed down to his own Western boots, "The high heel keeps your foot from slipping through the stirrup. That's really helpful if you're galloping."

Vaz plopped into a seat at the table and looked at Mr. Thierry as if he were a god. "Oh, how I wish I could meet Bill Cody and Sitting Bull!" Vaz exclaimed.

Looking back on the conversation about Sitting Bull, it seemed prescient. When the Sioux began to practice the Ghost Dance ceremony, the U.S. government discouraged and feared the practice. They sent agents to Sitting Bull's home on the reservation to take him into custody, not because he had violated a law, but because they feared he was encouraging other Indians to practice the feared pagan ceremony. Sitting Bull refused to mount a horse and be taken into custody. His neighbors grew angry and shot at the Indian agents who were attempting to arrest their chief. Two of the agents, themselves of Indian heritage, shot and killed Sitting Bull in December of the same year Joseph told us about the great chief. Sitting Bull himself had no weapon.

Rhi made a little grimace at Vaz, but Nora was too busy examining the yellow light-weight wool gown with embroidered white daisies just beneath a dainty row of white lace around the neck. Mr. Clay, and, more likely, Miz Eliza, had included a white velvet bonnet, lined in yellow satin with a big white bow on one side. The dress was fairly unornamented which was good for someone as small as Nora. She was unaware that the rest of us were even in the room.

Rhi had received a beautiful dark blue velvet coat trimmed in seal skin around the neck and down the front. It was designed to be full length, but Rhi was so tall that it struck her mid-calf. I thought that was actually better. They'd included a new bonnet for her too. The velvet matched the coat and it was trimmed with a white bow and white silk flowers.

"Rhi, let us see you in the coat!" I coaxed. "I've never seen anything so beautiful!"

Rhi stood, pulling the coat on gingerly. She looked like a princess! The smile on her face was worth every penny Mr. Clay had expended on such an extravagant garment.

Mr. Thierry held out a small package to me. I didn't reach to take it. Having had so few gifts in my life, I thought he was confused or wanted me to open something for the children. "What's this?" I nodded towards the package.

"Why don't you open it and find out?" He said softly. "Mr. and Missus Powell thought of you as well."

I hesitantly took the package and began gently to unwrap it so as not to tear the paper. Inside was a small beautiful box made of different kinds of wood that created a design of dogwood blossoms. Later I learned that wood put together this way is called marquetry. All I knew then was that the box was lovely and delicate. I "oohed" softly in appreciation.

"It opens, Miss Gilley!" Mr. Thierry said. "Lift the top off the box."

I lifted the lid and peered in at the blue satin lining. Inside was a brooch watch. It looked like real gold!

"Oh," I gasped. The bar above the watch had three baby birds sitting in a nest made of what appeared to be real, but small, pearls. The baby birds had blue stones for eyes. I couldn't take my eyes off it. There *was* something more beautiful than Rhi's coat after all - that watch!

Mr. Thierry turned the watch over and there was my name engraved on the back - Sara Gilley. "The eyes are sapphires, Miss Gilley. The nest is real pearls. This is a very nice piece of jewelry. Mr. and Missus Powell wanted to give you something to always remind you of the children you're raising." He nodded at each of the children.

"Oh," he picked up the box from the table and turned it over. He began to turn a metal stem on the bottom and set the box on the table while it played a melody I did not know. I looked up, puzzled at the music. It was soft, dreamy, and vaguely sad.

"Miss Gilley, it is a piece written by a German composer named Robert Schumann. He died much, much too young. This piece is exquisite, yet so simple. It is called *Reverie*. That means…"

"Yes! Of course, it sounds like a *reverie*!" I looked up, realizing I had interrupted and that he was a little taken aback that I knew what *reverie* meant. I smiled at him. "I read a *great deal*. I don't have much free time, but what I have is usually spent reading, winter and summer. Please tell me more."

"Well, I don't think there's much more I can tell you as I am not an expert on Schumann, but I hope you enjoy the music. The German name is *Träumerei*. No one, but a German, would call it that."

"Gracious, Mr. Thierry," Rhi asked, "do you speak German?"

"Ja, ich spreche ein bisschen Deutsch, abu ein bisschen, mind you - only a little. I studied Latin, French and German at the University of

Louisiana, now Tulane University. The French was easy as most of my family speaks French mixed with English, although we often mangle a beautiful language! I needed the Latin for law, so I am fair with Latin, but I must admit I could never get my tongue in the right places to speak German well!" He laughed a charmingly deprecating laugh.

Quietly Mr. Thierry continued, "Clay said the song made him think of your mother. I thought that was fanciful until I saw you on the porch reading and crying. There must be quite a bit of your mother in you, Miss Gilley."

I didn't respond at first. We listened to the music one more time. Then I said, "I hope there's a *great deal* of my mother in me, Sir. Seems to me that she was always busy at one thing or another, but she *took* the time to look at a hummingbird and call it to our attention, to bring a hyacinth into the kitchen so we could enjoy its fragrance. And she sang as she worked. Oh my! *Momma could sing*! And she made up delightful stories for us which she told us almost every evening at bedtime. Stories about magic and little people who could fly and forests where the animals talked to one another…" I felt everyone staring at me.

Nora couldn't remember Momma at all. I was the only mother she ever knew. Rhi had a few memories of Momma making up those bedtime stories accompanied by the little songs she also made up. Vaz's memories were sensory. He remembered that she smelled like the lavender soap she bathed with before bedtime and how soft her lips were when she kissed his cheeks "hello" in the morning and "goodnight" in the evening. Here I was carrying on about someone no one else knew! I blushed again.

"Don't feel embarrassed, Sara," Vaz said softly. "I wish you'd talk to us more often about our mother. We were so little when she passed… "

To take attention away from my discomfort, I tried to pin the watch on, but my hands were shaking too much. "Ma'am, may I?" Mr. Thierry asked. I nodded bashfully and let him put that pin on my next-to-oldest dress. "You do honor to your mother and to yourself in telling us how special she was."

I've worn that watch brooch almost every day of my life. I had the watch sent to a shop for repairs only twice in all the years I had it. Over the years my dresses became "gowns." I wore silk stockings instead of cotton, satin slippers and long kid gloves, but I ever owned only one other piece of jewelry that I cared about more.

"Thank you." I almost whispered. The girls came over and oohed and aahed. Vaz took a quick look and went back to peacocking around the kitchen in his Western jacket, making the fringe swing back and forth.

I had to move quickly to get supper prepared, so I asked Rhi, Vaz and Nora to escort Mr. Thierry around to the front of the house and find either Ole Missus, Miz Anne, Massah Robert or anyone *except* Miz 'Becca.

Rhi came bursting into the kitchen in about half an hour saying, "Mr. Thierry is staying a few days. So we need to lay an extra place at table for awhile. And, Sara, you'll never guess *who he is*!"

"You mean he's not Joseph Thierry, Mr. Clay's friend…"

"Oh, he's that alright!" Vaz had run in to the kitchen right behind his sister. "He's also a big shot lawyer from Baton Rouge on his way to open an office in Washington, D.C. He studied law under one of the current Supreme Court Justices. I can't remember which one, but Mr. Thierry studied with him in Washington a few years back ." He was almost jumping up and down, "Just you wait, Sara! We're going to hear some big things about Mr. Joseph Thierry!"

"Well, right about now we may hear his stomach grumbling. Vaz, help Rhi get the table set. Then, Rhi, I want you to put fresh linen in whatever bedroom he will be sleeping. When the table's set, Vaz, get a silver tray from the pantry and the small wine glasses. Put a clean napkin across your arm like Ole Missus showed you. Carry the tray into the front parlor and take the blackberry wine out of the cherry shrunk. Pour about three glasses first. Then offer wine to anyone except the children. Only fill as many glasses as you need to. Be careful not to spill it! It's almost the last we have before I can make more in the summer."

"Nora, how about you break off a few redbud twigs and get a few daffodils for the table." I turned back to the stove where I was getting ready to fry the dry land fish the boys had collected, but there weren't many. I'd have to cut them into smaller pieces and serve them surrounding something - not the fresh creasy greens and ham hocks I had just cooked. The mushrooms would become soggy. They'd just have to stand on their own and I could hope that the children wouldn't take them all before they made their way around the table!

"Violet, please start shelling the peas. I wish I'd known Mr. Thierry was staying before now. We could've killed a couple of chickens."

I ran down to the cellar and picked out a couple of jars, one of pickled beets and a second one with pickled okra. I took the last of the fall pecans to toast and put on top of goat cheese with a bit raspberry jam. I knew there was fresh asparagus waiting in the kitchen for supper. Before I went back to the kitchen I ran to the dairy, grabbed the last of the goat cheese I made the month before. My hands and apron were full as I started back towards the kitchen, wondering what else I could do. I'd make corn muffins! Just as I rushed up out of the dairy, I met Mr. Thierry walking back from the stables with a travel bag. I know I had cobwebs in my hair from going into the back of the cellar and my apron was dirty where I'd wiped the dust from the jars. I gasped in surprise. *Of course,* he laughed!

"Miss Gilley, where are you going in such a rush?"

"To try to make a supper *fit* for you to eat!" I blurted out. He laughed harder.

"I'm not particular. Which is not to say I don't enjoy fine food, but I've eaten enough boarding house fare to learn to accept what comes to the table." He took several items from my apron and we walked back towards the kitchen.

I was thinking of Ole Missus often saying that "Beggars can't be choosers!" But this time I had enough sense not to express it aloud.

I started up the steps to the back door and reached for the cheese so he could go on around to the front. He smiled up at me and seemed to speak to himself, "Good God! You are the *prettiest girl* I've seen in a long, long time!"

I couldn't speak. No one had ever called me pretty except Ole Mammie. I turned quickly away from him, embarrassed and ashamed. He said, "Miss Gilley, I am so sorry! I meant no insult! In fact, I didn't know that was going to come out of my mouth. I am a man who usually thinks carefully before… Please, excuse my brazenness! It's just… well, *you are*!"

I felt strangled with shock and anger, standing there in my faded dress with dirt on my apron and cobwebs in my hair. I thought he was making fun of me, but I managed to say, without turning to look at him, "Just because I'm poor, I'm plain, and I'm black, you may think I'm vulnerable to compliments." I did turn and stare at his astonished face. "It's better that we forget this because you have been so kind to the children and to me. But don't ever speak so to me again!" I practically ran into the house, but I heard him laugh uproariously.

I lived in dread of his telling one of my elders how I had rebuked him when in fact he may have made a totally innocent comment. Had I not felt so awkward and inferior, no doubt, I would have handled the situation differently. Maybe even making a joke of it instead of such a highly played tragedy!

Mr. Thierry stayed with the Powell's for a total of four days. I made every dish I'd ever gotten a compliment on while he was there from chicken liver pate to my version of apple pie, to risen rolls, to roasted squabs in wine sauce, made with the last of the wine. Although he spent

107

a great deal of time with Vaz, and talking with Rhi and Nora, I never saw Mr. Thierry close enough to speak to him again until the evening before he left.

It was after supper, but still light outside. Mr. Thierry stuck his head into the kitchen from the porch door. Violet and Nora were cleaning up and I was making yeast dough for the beignets I intended to impress him with the next morning.

"Miss Gilley, please *stop*! *Please*!" he said forcefully, but with a broad smile of his face.

I was stunned. "Stop what, Sir?"

He laughed a little, "Stop fattening me up so much. My horse will not be able to carry me to D.C. if I go on eating like this! My clothes will be too small and I'll have the devil of a time finding a good tailor in a hurry!"

I started to laugh too. He almost certainly knew I was vainly trying to show him how accomplished I was at seventeen. I wiped the flour from my hands and covered the dough with a damp cloth.

"Come on in. You remind me of Mr. Clay and Vaz - Vastine." I wagged a finger in his direction. "They can always get around me no matter how hard I try to stay stern with them!"

He came in looking very handsome in a clean pressed suit and tie. I think I had to catch my breath. It seemed like we just stood there looking at each other for so long it became uncomfortable.

"And why, Miss Gilley, would you want to be stern with me?" He teased. I felt sure he knew I still smarted from his comments the day of his arrival.

I shook my head from side to side, refusing to respond to that. I don't believe he expected an answer anyway.

"It's still light out. Will you walk with me out to the two benches on either side of the path so we can talk privately?" he asked.

I shook my head, "No." I said breathlessly.

"What if Mariah and Honora sit on the porch in plain sight of us? I just want to talk to you for about ten minutes before I must leave immediately after breakfast tomorrow. Please."

He sounded so earnest that I gave in and asked the girls to sit on the porch while Mr. Thierry and I talked. "Girls, you know what people are. Please sit on the edge of the porch so there can be no gossip."

Mr. Thierry and I walked out to the gap in the hedges and sat one on each side of the path. We could see the girls. They could see, but not hear us.

He looked straight into my eyes as he talked, "Miss Gilley, I am a complete jackanapes to have so boldly told you that I think you are lovely. It certainly must have seemed like a very inept attempt at seduction." At this point I wondered how this could be any kind of real apology. I think I made some kind of a grimace as he smiled and held up both hands.

"Sir!"

"Come now, you are a well-read young woman even if you have spent your whole life in the country. I am not trying to seduce you now nor was I then. I am trying to apologize. If I'm awkward at it, it's probably because I'm not used to apologizing. Forgive me, Sara." Not until later did I realize he'd called me by my given name.

"I… I accept your… your apology." I stammered. "We're not likely to meet again, so just let's forget the whole…"

"That's the saddest thing about this for me." He looked down at his hands and folded and unfolded them. "I don't have children of my own and the time I've spent with Clay's has meant so much to me, and I

109

want to get to know *you*. You make me *laugh* like no one has in a long while. Just *looking at you* makes me happy!"

"You're a young man, Mr. Thierry, you can marry and have a dozen children of your own!" I exclaimed.

"Well, I suppose *I could*, Sara, but I currently have a wife who *refuses* to have children. She won't hear of adoption either. In fact, she won't hear of a divorce without raising a big hullabaloo. I can legally get a bill of divorcement without any problem from the courts, but there is a great deal more at stake here than either her or my reputation." He looked embarrassed to say these things to me. There seemed to be much that he was omitting, but I had no right to hear even the little he had said. He owed me no explanation of his personal life.

I was truly at a loss for words as I now realized, to my shame, why I had been so uncomfortable around Mr. Thierry from first meeting him. I was completely taken with him. I dropped my head so he couldn't see my face, but he had to know *why and what* distressed me.

"Sara," he said softly, "I have no right to say another word to you about your loveliness, your joie de vivre, your naturalness. I am a married man, and to say more, would make me an out-and-out scoundrel! Let me just say that I *never* meant to insult you. As for you being poor - well, I work for a living myself. Why should that matter to me?" Much later I would learn that by my standards he was far, far from poor.

"As for you being *black*, I'm certain my grandmother was, what I expect you are, half white, half black or nearly so, but I can't remember her color at all! All I remember is her incomparable food and how, as a little boy, I loved to sit on her lap as she told me stories about the olden days! And, how in the name of God, can you imagine yourself as *plain*?" He hit his fist into his palm, angry now. "This is why I *had* to speak to you before I leave! You are lovely compared to white women, black women, or any color in between! You've lived your whole life here where these white people define beauty according to their own appearance! If you aren't blonde, blue-eyed, and in-bred, you're not attractive!"

I looked up at him at this. I accepted his apology, and I accepted his compliment! I smiled at him as I teased softly, "Why, Sir! Do you mean to tell me that people in Louisiana don't marry their relatives the same as they do here?"

He shook his head as if to clear it, then he laughed heartily. "Well, Sara, you've got me there! My wife is actually my second cousin!" He playfully shook his finger at me this time, "I'm not through with you just yet, little wag! I want you to promise me that you will not marry anyone unless he treats you like the sweet, lovely girl you are! You deserve respect and kindness. Be sure the man you marry gives you *both*!"

No one had ever talked to me about so much as a possibility of marriage except Old Missus when she threatened to marry me off to a black man who would beat me. She and I both knew that was an idle threat because she could not force me to marry or find a black man we knew who would ever lay a mean hand on me. Tears filled my eyes and I tried desperately to keep them there instead of allowing them to fall as I managed to say, "I have no intentions of ever marrying."

He stood up, came over, and took his handkerchief out. He dried my cheeks and gruffly told me to blow my nose. I obeyed. Then he said, "Nonsense! How old are you? Eighteen?"

"Almost." I sniffed.

"Gar ici! You a vielle fille! Alohrs pas! You, an old maid? Never!" he translated. "You will find someone… "He touched my cheek softly with his bare fingers and I shivered. I think he did as well.

"You'd better go inside. It's getting dark and it's getting cold." He turned on his heels, to go to the stables, but I put my hand on his arm.

When he'd taken his fingers from my face, I felt so utterly alone. He wheeled back around, "Oh, Sara, if I write to you will you write back?" Then he took my hand off his arm, brought it up to his lips, kissing it passionately. I thought I was going to sink to the ground, but when he let go of my hand and strode off to the stables, I stumbled to the bench.

Rhi and Nora came running to me. They'd seen him kiss my hand. God only knows what they made of that! They never asked and I never told them what it meant to me for, truth be told, I wasn't sure then what it meant!

I had made no promise to write and, indeed, I refused to write for the first six months that he wrote to me. There was something very wrong about writing to a married man. But Vaz found a devious way to get me to correspond with Mr. Thierry.

"Sara, the man meets *all kinds of people*. He travels all over, including to Europe on family business. He knows so much that you could learn about! All you'd have to do is ask him about the things you want to know."

I suppose all I needed was a good rationalization to convince me that my writing to him was innocent, that it could further my education. Vaz supplied it and I fell into the habit of sending one long letter a week to which he never failed to respond. I didn't see him again for three long years, but we came to know each other very well through long, soul-revealing letters.

CHAPTER 7: MIZ 'BECCA
GETS HER COMEUPPANCE

...and listen to their marvelous tales of ghosts and goblins,
and haunted fields and haunted brooks,
and haunted bridges and haunted houses...
But if there was a pleasure in all this...
it was dearly purchased by the terrors
of his subsequent walk homewards.
What fearful shapes and shadows beset his path...

from The Legend of Sleepy Hollow,
Washington Irving

Even with the new tutor and Miss Ivy's mailed lessons, Vaz did not have enough to keep him out of mischief. He was not normally sneaky, not he, being cocksure that he had a right to behave as he wanted, but something Miss Ivy said about making life easier for Ole Missus must have stuck in his head. Vaz knew that Miz 'Becca hated dogs in the house and was deathly *afraid* of cats. Vaz hated the woman with a vengeance for her mistreatment of Rhi and Ivy. He hated that she referred always to me as that "nigger cook." He hated her affectations and artificial sweetness around his Uncle Robert whom he truly esteemed.

Somehow or other the dogs would get in the house, all the way up to the second floor, always into Miz 'Becca's bedroom. Massah Robert slept in the room beside hers, and the dogs never bothered him. There were consequences of the dogs being upstairs. It's not good to leave a dog too long inside.

Miz 'Becca appropriated the front, formal parlor for a private hour every morning after breakfast for her daily Bible reading. I always wondered if she ever read a word or simply wanted to impress us with her piety. If she did read, it seemed to bear no fruition in her behavior, but maybe that was because it became almost a daily thing for the cats to leave their little "gifts" of dead animals on the Aubusson carpet there. Odd thing about the dead prey in the front parlor, the cats had always left their killings on the porch near the kitchen door until the last few weeks.

   The woman *never failed* to scream when she saw the cats' dead prey on the rug. She must have screamed ten times over a dead mole or a mouse or a bird. And the time there was a dead rat, a really ugly, scruffy Norwegian rat - well, she didn't stop shaking until dinner, then ate nothing, but complained the whole time she was at the table, describing the carnage over and over in great detail to those who were *trying* to eat! You would have thought she'd become accustomed to it, but not so.

   When she discovered an ugly hog-nosed snake crawling on her bedroom floor one night, she woke the whole house. Odd about the snake, too. I don't recall in my fourteen years or so in the Big House that a snake was ever found inside. I suppose there's always a first time. She screamed 'til we all came running to see *who had died*. Even I came up from the ground floor and Rhi and Nora came down from the attic. Massah Robert removed the snake, all the time assuring her it was harmless. I must say that Miz 'Becca looked a sight better with her false teeth in than she did that night.

   It almost seemed there for awhile as if the plagues visited on Egypt's pharaoh were being sent to torment Miz 'Becca. She found frogs in her shoes accompanied by maggots and flies on their dead bodies. The water in her boudoir pitcher was blood red several times. Then there were a number of days in a row when the privy was occupied almost all morning. Miz 'Becca would go to the "necessary," as Ole Missus called it, see that the door was locked, walk back into the house or sit on the front porch only to go through the same routine several more times during the morning. The men had no problems when they came in from the barns and fields. The privy was available then.

Miz 'Becca would finally run upstairs to her room and chamber pot - if it were there. Like many well-kept homes of the day, a pot was not used during daylight hours as it was only cleaned once a day, after the room's occupants left in the morning, and was often left to air outside until near bedtime.

I knew of Miz 'Becca's difficulties only because she had asked Violet to please bring her pot upstairs. Violet never had much of a sense of humor, but she grinned when she told me about it. However much I disliked the woman, even I found this trick lowdown and mean. I had every intention of taking Vaz to task over it as I never doubted for a second that he was the privy culprit. And the dog, cat, snake, frog and red water culprit. But, as it turned out, Vaz stopped locking the privy for other reasons.

Vaz went fishing one morning and caught a great mess of fish. Because of his good fortune, he came back to the house later than usual. Mr. 'Zander was banging on the privy door with one of his daughters, Lucy, I think, Andy and Massah Robert standing behind him, all waiting to get inside. I had stepped to the end of the back porch to see what all the fuss was behind the summer kitchen. Vaz quickly handed me his heavy creel and bluffed before the truth was discovered.

"Ah, the latch has been dropping on its own after you shut the door! Especially if you shut it hard." Vaz embellished his mendacity. "Too much play in it, I guess. I meant to either fix it or ask someone else to fix it, but this is how I get it open."

He proceeded to show them how he used a flat hard piece of wood he kept on top of the privy roof. The stick was long enough, and thin enough to stick through the crack between the boards on the latch side of the door and reach the bar. He pushed up on the wooden bar, freeing the door.

"I'm surprised," Vaz said ever so innocent-sounding, "that you've never had this problem before given the design of the locking bar. It ought to be pushed horizontally rather than dropped to prevent just such a problem!" I wished I had what was not then available, a recording. He gave a classic performance.

A wire angled just the right way with a loop large enough to fit the wooden bar could have pulled the bar down from the outside if the door was shut. No one ever left the door agape for olfactory reasons, and no one thought to question Vaz's explanation because Miz 'Becca had been too embarrassed to complain about her privy problems! Rhi found the looped wire right on top of the privy where I asked her to look since I was too short to find it without climbing.

Maybe these things were why Miz 'Becca became meaner and meaner. She was afraid to go to sleep because of things that might be slithering around in her room. Her daily Bible reading was interrupted about four days of every week and Rhi could never totally eliminate the smell of dog excrement from Miz 'Becca's bedroom rugs.

For the life of me I don't know why that *old harridan* failed to lock her bedroom door or why she never suspected Vaz, but then he was always *so polite and considerate* to her face. "It's chilly in here, Miz 'Becca, may I get the lovely shawl you left in the rear parlor for you?" or "Miz 'Becca, here, let me put this stool under your feet so you can sit more comfortably." or "Miz 'Becca I picked raspberries this morning for Sara to make jam, but I know how you like them. Here is a bowl full just for you." Had she tasted the red water in her pitcher, it probably would have been raspberry or beet-flavored. What a young hypocrite Vaz was!

Too bad that Vaz was never the suspect because it seemed that Miz 'Becca always thought it was young Master Andy, Mr. 'Zander and Miz Anne's boy. She knew better than to accuse him without evidence, and Vaz was most careful that there *was no evidence* of the perpetrator's identity. It was just as likely that one of her own children left the doors agape for the animals to come and go or took impish pleasure in bedeviling their mother. So Miz 'Becca stewed like a piece of tough meat that had to be cooked a long time. She'd remind everybody eight, nine, ten times a day to "close the doors firmly!" Which was a clear signal for all of us to slam the doors as hard as we dared. I'm ashamed to admit it, but even I sometimes slammed them.

She walked around fussing just loud enough to be heard, "Why must we have all these animals? One dog. One cat. That would be enough! I could stop one dog from messing my carpet. I could keep one cat out of the parlor." It must have been at this point she concocted a plan to reduce our animal population.

The next time we needed provisions from town, Miz 'Becca said she was going along as she required some medicaments from the apothecary. Ole Ab'ram drove the carriage with Miz 'Becca inside and me sitting up next to him in the blowing rain. She was not going to allow the "nigger kitchen help," as she called me, to sit inside next to her.

Miz 'Becca went into the apothecary, came out in a few minutes, and sat in the carriage eating the bonbons she bought inside. I had crossed the street to buy the things we needed from the dry goods store. I wasn't there long. Ole Ab'ram was standing under an awning almost out of the blowing rain. He helped me put our supplies in the carriage on the floor next to Miz 'Becca. I had hoped the rain would stop before we had to return home, but it seemed to be heavier than before. When we got back to the carriage Miz 'Becca opened her window and said to Ole Ab'ram, "Have Sara go across to the apothecary and pick up the package the pharmacist is putting together for me. I don't want to get wet. I've just about dried out from the first drenching! Here's some money. She should be sure to bring me all my change and the *receipt*."

I lifted my skirts and ran or sloshed, more like, across to the shop to pick up the package. I asked for the package and the receipt. The nearly blind clerk, if the thickness of his spectacles were any indication, handed me back the change and I started for the door. I looked at the receipt. I counted the change. The clerk had given me ten cents too much change. I went back to him, handed him the receipt and explained what had happened. Since he had given me a fifty-cent piece in change, I couldn't just hand him ten cents to straighten it out. He read the receipt out loud, but the only word I heard was "laudanum."

The clerk smiled at me and said, "Thanks, Missy. Tell your employer that William Donnelly said you are an honest girl!" I barely heard what he was saying as the word "laudanum" was echoing in my head!

He handed me a clean rag and said, "Dry what you can with this, Missy. Do you have something catching that Miz Powell won't let you sit inside the carriage? No need for you and Ab'ram both to get a'soaking. She's a right quare one!" He criticized Miz 'Becca.

"Thank you for the cloth. My umbrella broke in the wind coming into town." I didn't respond to his comments about Miz 'Becca. White folks could and did say unkind things about other white folks, but if I had followed suit... No, that wouldn't do. Even then, nearing the 20th century, negroes could get into serious trouble for being too uppity!

Why did Miz 'Becca want laudanum? I knew what it was from reading *The Sign of Four* by Arthur Conan Doyle the previous winter. I expected then that was what the family had given Miz 'Dena in *very* carefully measured drops. I was also fairly certain that Miz 'Becca would never think that I might know what laudanum was. I was just the poor, ignorant negro cook. Maybe Miz 'Becca had decided to try to calm her nerves with laudanum. The good Lord knew she needed something! But I had deep feelings of misgiving about it. Laudanum was a powerful drug, the use of which could get easily out of hand.

I felt so uneasy that I examined Miz 'Becca very carefully, and I hoped surreptitiously, for the next several days to see if she showed any of the effects that the drops produced in Miz 'Dena. I must have looked too closely or too long one morning as she peevishly asked, "Didn't anyone ever tell that girl that staring is *rude?*" She told the breakfast table occupants, nodding at me. She still never spoke directly to me or to Mr. Clay's children, except Vaz.

At the question Ole Missus tutted and responded to her daughter-in-law, "Rebecca, I expect she's concerned that you are sickening with something. You look *awful* I repeat, you look like the living dead. Purple marks under your eyes, lank hair, skin is as yellow as summer squash." Ole Missus actually had the gall to laugh as she turned and addressed her next remark directly to me.

"Sara, I think you'd better brew some of your special tea for jaundice. What is it Miss Callie taught you to make? Some kind of rosemary tea?"

I knew no good would come from this taunting by Ole Missus, but I responded politely to her. "Not for jaundice, Ma'am. She made a concoction of applejack, slippery elm, wild cherry bark, honey, and a little rosemary to disguise the slippery elm as a cough syrup. For liver and jaundice, she made a tea of burdock root." I said matter-of-factly as I placed a platter of eggs on the table next to the sausages and biscuits.

"Spirits?" Miz 'Becca almost yelled. After the word "applejack" she evidently heard nothing else.

"AL-CO-HOL?" She squeezed the word out through stiff lips and a tightly clenched jaw.

"Sounds to me as if it's something I might need." Massah Robert pretended to cough, trying to ease the tension with humor.

Mr. 'Zander made one of his rare attempts to be humorous, "Sara, see that I have a flagon of this cough syrup as soon as may be, but go easy on the slippery elm. In fact, go easy on all the herbs!" He gave a hacking cough..

"I'll be glad to do that, Sir, but more than a little rosemary and alcohol is actually *bad* for you." Massah Robert and Mr. 'Zander laughed loudly at that.

I must have looked distressed because Miz Anne waved her hand back towards the kitchen. "Y'all stop. Poor Sara knows you men well enough to know you'd drink enough to *kill* your selves!"

"Surely not, Anne! I must take issue with that!" Miz 'Becca began. "Robert only drinks medicinally and moderately."

I left the dining room as quickly as possible to the sounds of Ole Missus snorting in derision, Massah Robert trying to diffuse the tension with humor, Mr. 'Zander telling his children to finish breakfast or they'd be late for the school wagon, and Miz 'Becca muttering, defending her statement.

Miz 'Becca *was* somewhat more cheerful in the next couple of days than she had been, but I didn't see any signs of grogginess or slower movement. When the Powell children's favorite dog, Boggs the English bulldog, showed up dead on the front porch later in the week, everything came together in my head! Boggs was almost always the dog found in Miz 'Becca's room. Boggs would come to anyone who had a biscuit. He was not much more than a puppy and he had been very healthy.

I called Rhi and Vaz out onto the kitchen porch to tell them what I suspected. Vaz looked grim and Rhi started to cry because, "The children loved Boggs so much. How could *anyone* poison him? *Even* Miz 'Becca!"

"She's not just *anyone*, Rhi! She's the devil *incarnate*! Before Andy and I cull the barn kittens, that would probably die of starvation *if we didn't*, we at least pray over them and give them a swift, clean death." Vaz muttered through clenched teeth. Then he looked down at his shoes and said pitifully, "But I expect I caused Boggs' death. Poor Boggs."

I knew what Vaz meant by that, but I also knew well enough that he'd find a way to get revenge for Boggs - and for the death two days later of the calico that had been our best mouser.

Miz 'Becca had finally begun to lock her bedroom door, but that didn't protect her or her property. Vaz was agile and strong at eleven years of age. There was a large maple out from Miz 'Becca's bedroom that a healthy young boy could use to enter her room. One limb, slender, but strong enough to hold Vaz's weight, almost touched her window. In fine weather, we usually left the windows wide open. In those days, we had no window screens.

I heard Vaz and Andy making plans the day after Delilah, another cat, was found dead. One dog and two cats! The house was now acquiring the shades of animals that had untimely deaths. I sometimes fancied that I heard their plaintive meows and whining.

Andy was supposed to keep guard the next afternoon while the ladies took their afternoon nap. He was to stand just outside the back parlor window and hoot like an owl if Miz 'Becca left the parlor before Vaz got back. Vaz argued with Andy that the ladies wouldn't think twice about an owl hooting in the daylight. Vaz planned to shimmy up the maple, crawl along the limb that went almost to Miz 'Becca's bedroom window and climb inside. If it rained the next afternoon, they'd do this the first dry afternoon. There were to be no footprints outside or in.

Andy and Vaz were the same age and good friends in spite of the fact that Miz Anne didn't encourage the relationship. She was always kind to us, but she didn't really want her boy and a negro boy, even Mr. Clay's much petted and beloved son, being best friends - even if they were technically cousins. Nevertheless, the boys were inseparable much of the time and Andy wanted to be the one who climbed in. Boggs, Andy pointed out, was, after all, *his dog*! But Vaz insisted that if anyone was going to get hurt, or be *caught*, in this adventure, it was going to be him. We all knew that Mr. 'Zander and Miz Anne were strict disciplinarians with their children and believed that "sparing the rod" would indeed "spoil the child." Vaz was likely to get away much more leniently if caught. It did rain the next afternoon and their plans were delayed.

The next morning after breakfast, the three Powell children were walking to the stables with their grandfather, Massah Robert, who had promised to ride with them that day. They found the collie, Bess, lying dead just beyond the hedges. The children had been upset over Boggs' death, but they hadn't seen him dead. Bess, lying there with her legs stiff in the air, sent the girls screaming to clutch their grandfather's legs and Andy threw up his breakfast almost on his grandfather's boots.

Massah Robert didn't know what to think. Was there some sort of disease, like distemper maybe, killing the dogs and cats? Was someone poisoning them? He picked up his youngest granddaughter and took the children all back to the house to their mother.

Massah Robert came into the kitchen to ask me if I had seen anything amiss concerning the animals lately.

"No sir." I answered firmly. "They've eaten well, run with the children, and, generally been fine! I've seen *no signs of disease* like we had a few years back with the cats."

"Thank you, Sara. That confirms my suspicions that someone is poisoning them." From the look on his face, he already had someone in mind. I kept my own counsel, adding no more.

After dinner, as was their custom, the ladies retired to the back parlor to sew a little, then nap. Miz 'Becca did get up before napping, and I heard the owl hoot, but she only went to the privy. She returned to the parlor very shortly. The owl hooted the "all clear" signal and the plan went forward.

Just before supper, I heard Massah Robert loudly and sternly speaking to someone in the front parlor. Again, I wasn't eavesdropping. I was arranging the dining room table with roses and other late spring flowers for Mr. 'Zander and Miz Anne's anniversary supper. I must admit though that I did not leave so as *not* to overhear the conversation.

"Why, Mrs. Powell, is this bottle of laudanum labeled for *you*? Are you *ill*?" Massah demanded harshly, loudly. I could imagine him holding up the bottle I had retrieved from the apothecary little more than a week before for Miz 'Becca.

"Mr. Powell! How dare you speak to me in *such* tones! Were you *snooping* in my bureau?" Her voice was pitched higher than usual as she tried to sound offended.

"No, Madam, I am *no* spy! I found the bottle on the floor in my room next to the *locked* door between our rooms. Locked from your side, I might add! Now, answer me! Why do you have this?"

"Locked door? How could the laudanum…?" Miz 'Becca began and changed course, "Well, my nerves…"

"Your nerves, Madam? Judging from the date this was filled and the amount that is missing, you could have calmed the nerves of half the county!" he thundered.

She began to cry. From the muffled sounds she must have lain down on the settee. "Are there *ghosts* in this house? My doors were all locked!" She actually sounded afraid.

"There may well be ghosts. I can tell you that ghosts would probably allow adults to settle their own affairs, but they would *never* stand for what's been going on here this last week!" Massah thundered then he ordered, "Sit up this instant and tell me what you used this narcotic for!"

"Robert, it takes more laudanum than you might imagine to calm someone's nerves." She sniffed, obviously sitting up now.

"Nerves be damned!" He yelled. "I know very well how much laudanum is required *to knock a person out*! We gave laudanum to Loudena for the last two months of her life!"

"I am so sick of hearing about *the sainted Loudena*! Please stop throwing her in my face every chance you get! And, Sir, please *remember* that you are a gentleman and do not use coarse, field language with me."

"I apologize for swearing." He muttered, "But tell me truthfully what you have been doing with this!"

"I told you.."

"You are, Madame, I am sorry to say, a bald-faced liar!" he accused. I'd never heard Massah talk that way to *anyone*.

"Sir! I will not stay here to be abused." she was moving toward the hallway door. "When you are ready to *apologize*, let me know."

"Madam, I don't *want* you to stay. In fact," he said coldly, "I insist that you and your children move out of this house no later than the day after tomorrow or I will have you *carted out*." I heard no more footsteps. Evidently Miz 'Becca had stopped.

"I will not be forced from my home! When you married me…" she dared him.

At that moment I heard Ole Missus interrupt. She must have entered the room silently from the hallway. Matter-of-factly, "It's not *yours or Robert's* yet, Rebecca. It's *mine*. My son, is, of course, welcome here as long as I live. *You* poisoned the children's animals. I *cannot trust* anyone so low to live in my home. How can I be sure any of us is safe? You are to go the day after tomorrow, or *I will help* Robert file a bill of divorcement!"

"I never hurt…"

"Don't dissemble, Rebecca. Lying is an awful sin." Ole Missus said evenly.

"On what grounds could Mr. Powell divorce me?" Miz 'Becca bluffed.

"Oh," Ole Missus said quite calmly, "we'll think of something, or maybe we'll just have you committed to a *lunatic asylum* which is where you *rightly belong*!" The door closed quietly as Ole Missus came out of the parlor and into the dining room to find me standing, gaping in stunned silence. To this day, I swear the old woman *winked* at me, then looked upwards as if to thank Jesus for delivering us of Miz 'Becca. I knew it was really Vaz who had delivered us, and I was pretty sure that he had talked it over with Ole Missus *before* he did it!

Massah Robert said, "When you struck my niece Mariah, nearly killing her, I gave you one more chance to remain with this family. I should have moved you out of here then. You've broken faith with me *completely*. Leave on Thursday and I'll never divulge to the world why you left. We can just say that we deal better apart. I've heard the last word I ever want to hear from you, Madame! Any communication you have for me can be handled through James Oldwell, my attorney. I'll see that you have the same allowance as you've had here."

"I'll need more back at home… There are repairs that need…"

He interrupted her in midsentence, "Then ask your son for more because I won't give you another nickel. You could have lived here the rest of your days in complete comfort had you dealt with us amicably. You wanted to rule the roost, Rebecca! Now there is no roost *here* for you to rule. Good evening, Madame!" With that Massah Robert walked into the dining room to join his family who had just filed in silently for supper. He quietly asked Mr. 'Zander to go fetch Carl Thomas in the event that we had to deal with Mrs. Powell harshly. Her children ate in polite silence for the first time since they had come to the Big House. They'd heard enough, just as the rest had.

Andy and Vaz looked so innocent and yet so smug at the same time. I saw Massah Robert eyeing them to see if there was any evidence of complicity on their part. I'm pretty certain that Massah Robert did not believe ghosts had placed evidence in his room of Miz 'Becca's evil doings. Since Ole Missus was also looking innocent and smug, I think

Massah Robert summed up the situation accurately. To my surprise, he seemed happier than he had in months. On his way from the dining room, he clapped Andy and Vaz on their shoulders as if to thank them for their services. There can't have been another household in the country that operated as ours did!

I never laid eyes on the woman again, thank God. She and her poor brats were gone by noon the next day. Her children came to the breakfast table, looking as if they were *happy* to be going "home," but Miz 'Becca never came down to eat nor asked for food to be sent up. Personally, I didn't care if she starved. Anyone who would poison helpless animals - and, of much greater importance to me, anyone who would hurt one of my precious children...

Vaz and Andy asked me to make a special cake to celebrate her departure. I didn't think that was appropriate since this had come about at such a cost, but I did make a batch of cookies and let the children have a picnic in the back yard the day after she left.

Miz 'Becca had a good income from Massah Robert back in her old home and, from what I heard, she *did* rule the roost there. Seems her family and the help were all afraid of her awful temper. They were right to be afraid. Three years after Massah Robert cast her out, Miz 'Becca died. Poor Miz 'Dena had suffered miserably for months before her passing and that wretched creature, Miz 'Becca, passed peacefully in her sleep. Seems to me there is *no justice* here for the wicked and even less for the righteous.

Massah Robert lived ten years longer than Miz 'Becca, but he'd lost his beloved first wife Loudena far too soon and never really recovered from it. Massah Robert had his first stroke about nine months after Miz 'Becca left. That's when Mr. 'Zander took over the complete management of the farm.

CHAPTER 8: MASSAH ROBERT AND SARA TALK

Hanging from the beam,
Slowly swaying (such the law),
Gaunt the shadow on your green,
Shenandoah!
The cut is on the crown
(Lo, John Brown),
And the stabs shall heal no more.

Herman Melville

The combination of a letter and his first stroke evidently brought great uneasiness to Massah Robert's soul. The letter came from his nephew Dr. Stewart Powell advising that Mrs. Holton Powell, Dr. Stewart's mother and Massah's sister-in-law, had passed. Fortunately, Massah's first stroke only weakened his left leg. His speech was still clear and he got around fairly well with two canes. He sent word via Miz Anne after supper one evening early in March of 1891 that he wanted to see me in his office. I was to bring a pot of strong coffee with some sugar and cream, and some of that Christmas fruitcake if any was still left.

I knew from the mention of sweets that I hadn't displeased him, so I was not worried, but of course I was curious. He had never summoned me before. His office smelled of leather, good cigars, and burning hickory logs. It was a comfortable place for a man, I thought. Away from women gabbling in the family parlor, but near enough to know your loved ones are close.

I put the tray down on a table and started to pour some coffee for him.

"Whoa, Sara! Wait a minute. I need some Dutch courage - well, more like Kentucky courage, I guess." He laughed a little at his attempted humor. He pointed to a book shelf behind me, saying, "See that bottle of bourbon. Fill about half my teacup with bourbon. Then add the coffee, two sugars, and a touch of cream. I can still stir, I think." He laughed again in self-deprecation. "I hope you brought a cup for yourself."

I had, but it was getting late for me to be drinking coffee. "Help yourself, Miss, and add a jigger of bourbon to your own cup!"

"Massah, I don't... I've never... I don't drink hard spirits. Thank you!" I stammered in total surprise. The complete truth was that I'd never drunk any spirits, hard or soft. Ole Mammie pounded it into my head that spirits were okay for medicinal purposes and communion wine was acceptable, but she claimed alcohol caused most of the problems in the world, one way or the other.

"Well, you may change your mind when you hear what I've got to say. Keep the bottle close. I'm *sure* I'll need more! Sit down, Sara. Be easy!"

I was half way toward running out of the room, thinking Massah had another stroke and lost his reason this time, but habit is difficult to abandon. I obeyed.

He drank most of his "coffee," then began with an odd question. "Sara, did it ever occur to you to wonder how this farm managed to remain relatively prosperous after the War? After over half the negroes left? After the stock and the crops were almost wiped out?" I don't think he really expected an answer, but I didn't have one anyway. I didn't *know any other existence* than what we had, and from where I was, it certainly was *not* prosperous!

He looked up from his memories to ask for a glass of bourbon and water this time. The glasses and a pitcher were on the shelf behind me. "How much water, Massah?"

"*For God's sake*, child!" he barked at me, "Don't call me *that*! After you *hear* what I have to say you may want to leave the house *tomorrow*!" I stood there in stunned silence. He'd *never spoken angrily* to me before, and he'd certainly never called me *"child"* in such a familiar way either. After hearing what he had to say, I tried to remember to address him simply as Mr. Robert for the rest of his life. It made him more comfortable.

"Very little water - oh, hell, girl! Forget the water! Make yourself a cup of mostly coffee with a couple of drops of bourbon, sugar and cream, *please*." he insisted. "I think you'll handle this better that way, but even if *you don't, I will*!" Again he laughed a little, as if at himself.

And so began the story of how the Powell's survived the War, even prospering in comparison to their neighbors.

Mr. Robert was 35 years old when Virginia entered the War on the side of the Confederacy. He had three young children at home that made it difficult for him to call for war, but he was no advocate of secession anyway. However, duty was duty and if General Robert E. Lee, a loyal Virginian and the greatest general in the country, had refused to lead the Union, choosing the South, Massah felt obliged to help.

He told me that he had fought in several skirmishes down near Cumberland Gap, but he was wounded seriously in a skirmish in Jonesville early January 1864. It was his last fight. He nearly died from the infection. His cousin Alfred Young, Miz Eliza's much older brother, carried him home lying face down on the back of a dead man's horse. Mr. Robert allowed as how Ole Mammie saved his life.

He laughed and said, "I blame your grandmother Callie for the fact that here I sit 65 years old, with only my mother and God older than I am. I'm glad to be alive nevertheless." So he told the story of Ole Mammie's medical skills that cold January.

When Alfred Young brought Massah home, Ole Massah Claiborne and Miz 'Dena helped place his large inert body on the big kitchen table. Ole Mammie was already in the kitchen ironing some of Ole Missus' dresses. Ole Massah knew of Callie's healing skills, so he asked her to tend to Mr. Robert while he sent one of the other negroes after the doctor. He sent Big Cook to the summer kitchen to start a fire and prepare the day's meals there.

Miz 'Dena later compared Mr. Robert's color to that of the snow that was on the ground that morning. She thought he was dead his breathing was so shallow, but Ole Mammie assured her he was not dead. Ole Mammie helped them strip his wet, dirty clothes off and had Miz 'Dena give him a bath, while she threw more wood into the big kitchen range. She covered him with a quilt ten-tear old Master 'Zander brought down, then she asked 'Zander to keep his grandmother, little sister and brother, and Master Clay occupied and out of the room while she took care of his father. She wanted Ole Massah to leave too, but he refused to leave his first-born child.

Ole Mammie laid a slender knife on the top of the kitchen stove, and had Ole Massah and Alfred pour moonshine carefully down Mr. Robert's throat as he lay on the big kitchen table. She let the knife cool slightly as she soaked the dried blood from his body and removed the old rags on his arm that Alfred Young had used to staunch the blood. She threw the rags into the fire. She asked Miz 'Dena to light all the oil lamps in the kitchen though it was light outside. She poured moonshine around and into the wound, took a small swig for herself, and *dug* the bullet out of his arm with the hot knife from the stove.

Mr. Robert was told how Ole Mammie performed her surgery because the moonshine worked as well as she intended, knocking him out. Although unconscious, Mr. Robert had flinched when she soaked the wound. Miz 'Dena thanked God at this sight of life in her husband.

Ole Mammie allowed as how it was good the shot had not hit a bone and splintered, but she took her time digging the cloth out that had entered with the bullet. She reheated and cooled the knife a couple of times during this procedure.

"He was shot yesterday mornin'! *What took ya'll so long to get home, Massah Alfred?*" If Alfred Young answered her, Mr. Robert never learned what he said. I expect she was trying to distract everyone from the pain she was inflicting by cleaning the wound thoroughly.

Mr. Robert said he must have been groaning because he was told that his father had asked Ole Mammie to stop *several times*. "*If* you *want Young Massah to die*, I can stop!" Mr. Robert repeated what he'd been told she said, "But there's shredded cotton and wool down in that hole. Massah Powell, I reckon on saving his life, *if you'll let me do what I know how to do*!" She evidently peered carefully inside the wound having Miz 'Dena hold a lantern directly over it.

"Daddy Claiborne, please don't interfere! Callie has tended to about *everyone* of us at some point. Let her work!" Mr. Robert said he was told that Miz 'Dena was adamant - and determined enough to risk her father-in-law's ire at her temerity. "Robbie won't remember the pain when he comes to. He'd want Callie to do her best!"

"I'm certain there's no maggots in it, thank the Blessed Jesus, it's so cold everything's *froze solid*. The cold may have helped slow the bleeding, though 'lowing that arm to hang down on the way home *wasn't the best thing*. Still, I reckon Massah Alfred did as good as he could just to get him home alive." With that she allowed that she had removed all the material she could see.

They had called the doctor, but he had been working on the injured down near where the fighting occurred. Mr. Robert said he was glad the doctor *couldn't* get there because the doctor would likely have sawn his arm off up near the shoulder. He'd already lost so much blood, surgery such as that would have likely killed him.

What Ole Mammie did *was not soothing work*, but it eventually helped him heal. She reheated that knife when she finished digging, Mr. Robert said, and stuck the *hot knife* into the wound, turning it completely around. He said they told him his flesh sizzled and he nearly came off the table even though he was still knocked out. Then she poured moonshine in and around the wound. Last of all, she put varnish on top of the wound and wrapped it all tightly in clean bandages. When the doctor finally arrived the next day, he said he couldn't have done better himself, although he was of the opinion that he'd have to return later in the week and remove a gangrene arm.

Mr Robert said Ole Mammie came to his bedroom morning, noon, and night to change those bandages. She had Cook make pork jelly, beef essence, milk toast, all sorts of light but healthful dishes, and Miz 'Dena fed him *a tablespoon at a time* all throughout the day. He said he nearly died the third day after he was shot, but Ole Mammie sat in his room with Miz 'Dena and the two of them fed him snow to help cool his fever and keep him from losing too much fluid. As they worked, they prayed.

Ole Missus stayed away until the second week by which time the danger was past. She claimed she would've had one of her "spells" if she'd seen her son in such poor condition. Everyone was just as glad she didn't enter the room when he was still so ill.

"I've heard some fine, sincere prayers in my day, Sara, but I've never heard anything like what Miz Callie could do. I believe *God listened* to her just to hear *the music* and *feeling* in her prayers!"

I smiled because I knew exactly what he was talking about, but, in my opinion, it wasn't the music and fervor God responded to. It was the fact that Ole Mammie *wouldn't shut up* until she was satisfied with the outcome. She and Ole Missus had stubbornness and perseverance in common.

"Why, I think she prayed for every soldier in the Confederacy, half of them *by name*, including Lt. Colonel Pridemore." He laughed, remembering how long her prayers could be.

"Why, she even asked God to be with the captured Union troops, particularly those headed for Andersonville. I even prayed myself for God to help the unlucky bastards!" If Mr. Robert noticed his profanity, he showed no signs of it. It didn't offend me. He was simply comfortable around me, and getting a bit deep in his cups.

I certainly was *not* comfortable enough around him to tell him I didn't reckon God had a whole lot to do with the War between the States. *If He had*, things might not have been so bloody! Couldn't God have just opened up a sea somewhere like he did for Moses and the Israelites and let my people *walk to freedom* without all those massacres? I was still young when Mr. Robert told me these things, but I suppose I knew enough even then about human nature to know that a bunch of *stiff-necked* Southerners and *self-righteous* Yankees (or should that be stiff-necked *Yankees* and self-righteous *Southerners*?) wouldn't have stopped when Pharaoh did. Or maybe, come to think of it, they did, because Pharaoh's soldiers *drowned*. With such thoughts, I shook my head vigorously for a brief second. That little bit of bourbon had gone straight to my head. I hoped Ole Mammie was not in a dark corner watching me, reading my thoughts!

Mr. Robert mused, "I don't know which was *worse*, our Andersonville or their Fort Douglas! Sherman *was a devil*, so when he said *'War is hell*,' he knew whereof he spoke." He sat silently, *grimly* for awhile.

"I lived and recovered the full use of that arm, but *my brother Holton*, whom I was so close to, died later that same year fighting in the Shenandoah. It was his widow who just passed."

This time it was Mr. Robert who shook his head as if to clear it, "God in Heaven, I only saw a few skirmishes with just a few people killed and injured. That was awful enough to last me for a lifetime! I sometimes still dream, almost 30 years later, of horses and men screaming, cannons booming, men laying on that frozen ground *dead or dying*. Can you image the carnage at Gettysburg, Chicamauga, Chancellorsville, Spotsylvania, Shiloh, and so many other hellacious places? Probably not. It's too horrible for most people to conceive! *None of us* ever thought the War would cost *so much* in human life or last so long. We were all naïve, even those of us who tried to prevent it." He drank the rest of the bourbon in the glass.

"There were over 600,000 men killed, many of them not much older than Andy and Vastine. God only knows how many sustained permanent injuries or died from disease. I've read that at least another 400,000 were maimed or passed from illnesses contracted in the camps. I can't even *count* to a million, Sara!" He sat quietly for several minutes before he began to speak again.

"*So young*. A whole generation of men, North and South." He seemed deep in his thoughts again for a long time. I expect ten or fifteen minutes passed before he spoke. I must have nodded off because it seemed that his voice called me back into the room from wherever my mind had gone.

Finally, he waved his good arm toward the fire, "Please put another log on, Sara, and pour me another glass. Is that fruitcake there on the tray?" He pointed at the cake, "Can you pass me a slice? Seems I didn't eat much supper tonight. Help yourself to another drop of bourbon, Sara." He laughed because I had taken so little.

The first sip had burned like fire going down my throat, as small as it was. I declined any more. By now I had concluded that the stroke had impaired Mr. Robert's mental facilities somewhat, otherwise he would never have *offered* me spirits. Nevertheless, I felt content, sitting there by the fire, listening to tales I'm not sure Mr. Robert had shared with his own family. Even though the stories were of horrible things, horrible times, I felt a sense of camaraderie with Mr. Robert.

"Sara," Mr. Robert said gently, "spirits may loosen a tongue and encourage evil doers to do their evil, but it's not what you put in your mouth that's the problem. *It's what comes out of it*. Still, you are young and I expect you are right about how much, if any, you should drink."

"Yes, Sir," was all I replied.

After a minute or so of reflection I asked, "were you especially kind to Momma and me because Ole Mammie helped save your life?" I ventured to ask.

He looked me straight in the eyes, "Only *partially*, Sara. And your grandmother didn't *help* save my life. *She did save it. Twice!*"

He took another big swig of bourbon and said, "I wouldn't be here now nor would Rob, Jr. and Ivy be here if she hadn't. *Miz Callie saved my life twice. She saved this farm, and, at least, part of our fortune!* This family could never properly repay her! *Never!*"

Mr. Robert gave me a brief history lesson about the use of money during the War. Contrary to what some folks denied, there was gold lying around in hidey-holes during and after the War. In fact, I had part of that gold in my possession - the $20 gold pieces Mr. Clay gave me when he moved to Texas. Some folks talked of gold bars. I never saw any, nor did Mr. Robert speak of gold bars. Hoarding legal coinage and gold during the War was certainly considered unpatriotic in the North and in the South, but, nevertheless, it was hoarded to such an extent that merchants resorted to the use of unofficial privately-minted tokens to facilitate trade. In the spring of 1864, the U.S law made private minting illegal, and minted official small denomination coins.

Before the War, the Powell's had been one of the wealthiest families in the Virginia Appalachians. Ole Massah had been smart enough to invest in industry, even in the North, especially in coal, iron, and railroads. I guess Mr. Clay acquired his financial savvy from Ole Massah.

There was *talk* of war *long* before war came - *"Wars and rumors of wars,"* the Bible says. Most Virginians were not warmongers, even those who held slaves. Virginia had a great deal of industry, especially in and around Richmond and Petersburg with rail lines and ports giving them access to commerce north and south. Informed Virginians believed that War with the North would likely be *devastating* to the South, especially so to Virginia as it was close to northern industrial sites and carried on so much trade with the northeast.

"And, Sara," Mr. Robert told me bitterly, "*I am a true son of the South*, a wounded CSA veteran, but it is hogwash that the '*Cause*' was largely about states' rights. Of course it was about that, too, but mostly it was about *slavery*! The vice president of the CSA, Alexander Stephens, said in a public address that the *cornerstone* of the Confederate government was based on the '*Great Truth,*' *as* he called it, that black men are not as endowed by the Creator as white men and that slavery is a justifiable order because of that inferiority."

He went on to give me another history lesson I had not been able to read. There were histories available about the War, but they seemed to either glorify the Union's destruction of the South for the lofty, righteous purpose of freeing slaves or to glorify the South's valiant and noble defense of its states' rights, its genteel way of life.

Mr. Robert told me that there were several states with a higher percentage of slaves to free people than existed in Virginia at the beginning of the War, but *the largest population of slaves* was in Virginia. Slaves were *valuable*. The sale of slaves was often far more profitable than the sale of cash crops, particularly in Virginia. The federal government knew this, yet there was never a serious discussion among legislators to reimburse slaveholders any money if they freed the slaves in whom they were heavily invested. A meager amount of money was given to certain slaveholders who freed slaves, but it came largely from private religious groups.

"Sara, most of the time, if you want to know the truth about history, follow the resources, the money. People can, *and will*, wrap all sorts of nasty behaviors in religion, patriotism, brotherhood as if their cause is some grand gift wrapped in pretty, pious speeches! But if you remove all economic considerations you'll soon see different actions and different reactions!" He poured more bourbon, but he put the glass down. "I know I'm a cynic. You are *so young* that this must sound harsh, but the only thing I know that tops the economy as a reason for hatred and war is *family,* and sometimes, sad to say, the economy even tops that!"

Since January 1, 1808 it had been illegal to import slaves into the United States, although smuggling slaves up and down the southern coast was not uncommon. Thus, *interstate trade in slaves* became an important and *legal* industry. In Virginia slaves were used frequently as *commodities,* meaning they were bought or bred *to be sold* to southern neighbors who often held much larger tracts of land and badly needed their labor. Cotton farmers and rice plantations, although in decline, paid high prices for high quality slaves. Mr. Robert told me that a reasonably young, strong man slave, particularly a skilled one, generally sold for about $800 in 1860. In the event that I didn't think that was a significant sum, he said, "Sara, in 1890's currency, that is about $1800. Slaves represented big money to the South - to the seller and to the buyer!"

I think hearing about selling slaves to *make money* made me even sicker somehow than knowing how they had been worked! At least when they were worked, part of the output of their labor, small as it might have been, came back to them in the form of food, housing, and clothing. But Mr. Robert telling me this should have been no surprise because Ole Mammie had told me the same thing - how she lost my Grandpap and uncles when they were sold away from the farm. Somehow Mr. Robert's telling me reinforced the idea that it happened *often.*

As most Southerners did, Virginians considered themselves largely autonomous from the federal government. "The tsar was far away," and that was a good thing. It had been so all the way back to the founding of the United States. A confederation was impractical, but preferred by many southerners. Most Virginians, including Robert E. Lee, saw themselves foremost as *Virginians,* then, as Americans.

Although, the average white Southerner *never owned even one slave,* those who did had a whole way of life built around cheap, slave labor. Giving up slaves in order to join the Union was *unthinkable to slaveholders.*

Virginia might have made a deal to keep slaves and join the Union under the same conditions as had Kentucky, Missouri, Maryland, the part of Virginia that split off, and parts of Louisiana, including New Orleans, but they never did.

After most southern states seceded in the final days of 1860 and early days of 1861, Mr. Robert and his father went to Richmond in February 1861 as part of the Convention on secession. That same month the federal government announced plans to put steam-powered men-of-war in major southern ports to insure the collection of the onerous new Morrill tariff. The tariff greatly threatened King Cotton profits by taxing the gunny sacks and bags used in the cotton industry. Warships were to be placed in southern harbors to blockade the exportation of cotton unless the tariffs were paid. They were also there to coerce the seceded states back into the Union.

Initially, the Virginia delegates were overwhelmingly against secession, but they came to perceive the Union as unyielding. Warships in U.S. harbors had the effect of an embargo since they were there as a *threat,* not as defense. *Embargos are acts of war!* The Union was waging war on its own citizens, southerners, many of whom had been anti-secessionist up until the embargo. When Lincoln asked the non-seceding slave-holding states to provide troops to retake federal properties seized by seceding states, it was the last straw for Virginia. They would not attack their southern neighbors. In July, Virginia voted to secede. Mr. Robert said that he and his father were both dismayed, but they went home to do whatever was necessary to keep their family and property as intact as possible.

Maybe it was the bourbon, but I couldn't help but question why the Powell's didn't just free their slaves and start a new life not built on a need for cheap labor. The Powell family had been on this land for more than a hundred years when war broke out. The Cherokees had claimed the area as hunting grounds far longer. I never knew exactly what part of Africa my negro ancestors came from before they were captured, sold, and relocated, but they weren't born in America originally. It seemed to me that people have moved, freely or of necessity, since Adam and Eve were put out of Eden. The Powell's didn't relocate because they figured on *surviving the War* intact, as Mr. Robert had just told me. I said nothing.

Mr. Robert cleared his voice and began his narration again. "Our plans in case of war actually began earlier. When we read as early as August 1858 that Free-Staters and pro-slavery proponents both rejected the LeCompton Constitution for Kansas, Daddy Claiborne and I began to feel war was inevitable. Up until then we had hope that reasonable men could deal with their differences, well, *reasonably*. Without exaggeration, *blood* ran in the streets of Kansas towns when reason failed." He looked at his watch and began to wind it, gathering his thoughts.

I was beginning to see that however compassionate and fair-minded Mr. Robert tried to be, these attributes had not extended to the freeing of his slaves. "Reasonable men" might not have freed their slaves, but surely *upright men* would have and paid them as free laborers for their work. It was before I was ever born. I kept my silence.

"My father and I travelled to Philadelphia in the spring of 1859, sold most of our stock holdings in northern businesses, converting the profits into gold coins, small enough in denomination so as not to attract too much attention if war came. We also bought 20 Springfield rifles, 10 Colt revolvers and two crates of ammunition. Our merchandise *filled about half a train car*. It was a heavy load and I remember keeping my hand inside my jacket near my own new revolver the whole train ride home. Holton and Old Abraham met us at the train depot with two wagons and several of their old rifles. The crates were labeled as if they carried books, furniture, and other household goods. Indeed, we had packed lightweight household goods on and around the gold and guns. We never had the first problem bringing the gold home, but I worried the whole way back."

"When Lincoln was elected, but before his inauguration, South Carolina and five other states seceded. War seemed eminent. We removed the gold from the safes here in the house and buried it during a new moon. We buried it in three different places. It seemed unlikely that anyone could ever find all three. And, indeed, no one ever did. There's not much left now, a little more than $500, I think, all of it back in the house. But, if it hadn't been for Miz Callie, at least one stash would've been found and, I have not a single doubt, that my family would've been hurt, maybe some of them killed."

It is difficult for me to repeat what Mr. Robert told me that evening, but it's a story that must be told.

By late 1864, the Confederate Army was falling apart all over the South, especially in places where there was no longer ammunition, clothing, or rations. Many Rebel soldiers had simply walked away from their units and were trying to get home, looking for food and shelter on the way. Many knew there wouldn't be much to go home to. They'd seen the burned houses and barns. They'd seen the empty fields - empty of crops and empty of livestock.

By early 1865, many Southerners who'd come through the War in fair condition, meaning their houses still stood and they had a milk cow and a few chickens, were not very generous with what they still had because they weren't sure how much longer they could keep it. It looked as if the War was ending, but people up North were *aggrieved and angry* over their own war dead. Many Yankees felt the war had been caused by the greed of the Southern *"aristocracy."*

People in the South, especially Virginia, maybe because they were firmly in the middle of avenging Union soldiers and deserting Rebels, lived in constant fear of strangers. Ole Massah and Mr. Robert had given the remaining negro families on the hill weapons and bullets, and told them to shoot any stranger who wouldn't stay their distance, *white or black*. They had told the negroes that *we were all in danger* of retreating soldiers, Yankee or Rebel, and from a few displaced negroes who had nowhere to go and nothing left to lose.

Please forgive me for calling my Ole Mammie *"Callie,"* but the story Mr. Robert told me that night should never have been part of my beloved Ole Mammie's life! In my mind, I've attached this story to *Miz Callie.*

One cold, nearly cloudless night in early February 1865, the loud, persistent barking of dogs woke Mr. Robert. He said he pulled on his boots, grabbed his loaded rifle from under his bed and went downstairs without waking Miz 'Dena. He happened to look out the windows up toward the slave houses where the dogs were raising such a fuss. He saw a woman being pulled down the hill by two men carrying rifles. He knew that it was Miz Callie by the way she never wore a scarf and even then her hair was silvery in the moonlight. It appeared that her cabin was ablaze.

Miz Callie was angry with herself as her thinking had been too slow, waking up to someone banging on her door and the kennel dogs and neighbors' dogs howling outside. She was too disoriented to grab the pistol *and* shove ten-year old Nisa, who was scared half to death, into the tunnel they'd prepared. She chose to get my momma, Nisa, out, quickly kicking the bed covers over the tunnel opening. The intruders quickly succeeded at knocking the door so hard that the inside bar fell off, allowing them entrance.

Mr. Robert said that he put on a coat and quietly let himself out the front door so he could ease his way around the side of the house without being seen. He heard someone leave the front bedroom where Master Clay, Master 'Zander, and Master Thomas slept. He heard the bedroom door close slightly. One of the boys came down, quietly, but several of the stairs squeaked. Master Clay quietly opened the front door, and Mr. Robert had to turn back to stop him from coming out in the yard to him. Master Clay was not quite eight years old and that cotton head of his would be an easy target by the light of the moon.

"Clay, *get back inside!*" Mr. Robert told him, having his hand firmly on Clay's mouth. "Don't speak. Go back upstairs and wake Daddy. Tell him to help you get everyone out of the house quietly by the *office door.* Wrap the women folk and the babies in quilts and stand under the big magnolias, like we planned. Hurry! No questions!" He was asking Clay to help get seven other people safely out of the house.

"And, Clay, get your pistol, and tell 'Zander and Thomas to get theirs, too. *Keep the safety's on* like Daddy taught you!" He shoved the boy back in the house and proceeded to the side of the house again. By this time the two strangers and Miz Callie were almost down the path to where it forked either toward the Big House or toward the stables. Mr. Robert said he saw Miz Callie lift a hand to her head as if she had been hit hard before they dragged her off the hill. He could see their breaths in the cold air, so he pulled his coat collar up around his own mouth and nose. He didn't know if they were going to the stables or coming toward the house. If they didn't have Miz Callie between them, he could have shot both of them before they got any closer, but he figured deserters wouldn't hesitate to use her as a shield or to kill her.

Miz Callie started talking, and talking *loudly*. "You young men look like you from good families. You don't got to take nothing from this family. They'll *give you* food, clothing even a warm place to sleep tonight. These are Christian folks. Let me take you into the kitchen *where it's warm* and get you some food." Miz Callie knew the plan was for the white folks to leave the house quietly by whatever door was farthest from intruders. She was trying to send the family a signal. One of the men turned and slapped Miz Callie hard in the face. "Shut up, Nigger! I wouldn't eat anythin' *you* give me. Prob'ly try to pison us!"

Mr. Robert said Miz Callie spit several times, probably spitting blood out of her mouth. Then she started talking again.

"Mister, they is no one here who'd do such a low thing. I am a Christian woman."

"Maybe. Maybe not. But, you *sure bite*, don't you? Who were you protecting up on the hill? You got a passel of brats in that shack? If you do, they'll be roasted by now!" He laughed as if he'd said something funny.

"I got no children no more. They've all been sold." She lied loudly.

She had been protecting my momma. By now, Momma would've gone out the tunnel. The negroes had all been instructed to dig a tunnel in the floor and under the cabin wall to the outside. The tunnel opening was to be covered with a rug, a basket, something. Anyone who needed to escape through a tunnel was to go quickly and quietly to a neighbor as far from danger as possible.

The big black dog, Solomon, had been away from Miz Callie's cabin when the trouble began, probably treeing a 'coon, but the commotion from the other dogs brought him home. He found Momma. His job was to protect Momma first and Miz Callie next. He ran the five cabins down with Momma to Uncle Reuben and Aunt Cici's cabin.

Momma told Mr. Robert later that she shook so hard she bit the insides of her cheeks, and if Solomon had not been with her, she would probably have disobeyed her mother and run after her. Momma said that Solomon whined and looked back for Miz Callie the whole time he was going with her to the old folks down the row.

Solomon's baying didn't need to waken Uncle Reuben and Aunt Cici. There was enough noise on the hill that night to wake the dead. Every dog up there and Massah's hunters in their kennels were all yelping and baying. No sooner had Momma knocked on the door and cried out to them than the door opened. They were up already and Uncle Reuben had his rifle ready. When he opened the door, he saw Miz Callie's cabin on fire, and tried to pull Momma in. She wouldn't go in without the dog, so in Solomon went too. The dog kept whining at the door wanting out. After a long while, Momma calmed enough to let him leave.

Aunt Cici and Uncle Reuben kept my Momma safe that night. They assured Momma that Solomon would find her mother and take care of her. I'm sorry never to have met them. They died before I was born.

All the negroes had emergency plans they were to use if something like this happened. Mr. Robert said the negroes had been told to protect themselves, but not to interfere away from their own cabin, their own family. He didn't want them hanged for crimes against whites.

"Whar's this stash of gold they have?" One of Miz Callie's captors asked. Miz Callie always said they'd heard of the gold before she ever saw them. No one ever learned how they knew of it, but Mr. Robert always thought one of the neighbor boys who had served in the Confederate army may have passed information along one boring evening or another about his wealthy neighbor who paid for goods in gold. He was likely trying to impress others when, in fact, he didn't know anything. But when the deserters showed up at Miz Callie's trying to kick open the barred door, demanding she take them to the owner, she told them she knew where the gold was - no reason to bother the family. The family was big, and she knew where the gold was anyway. Mr. Robert always said she must have been very convincing. The fact that they went with her probably saved his family a great deal of trouble. There were quite a few youngsters in the house then and his mother was always easily agitated, subject to spells with her heart.

"Follow me." Miz Callie said, "And, for the love of God, don't hit my head again! I can't show you *any gold if I'm dead!*" Feisty. Ole Mammie was always feisty!

"It's up the holler on t'other side of the stables. We may need a light and we for certain gonna need a shovel." Mr. Robert said she was trying to tell him what they were going to do and *where* they were going.

Miz Callie and the two unknown white men went behind the hedges toward the stables. The quickest way to follow them was on the path, but it scrunched when you walked on it, so Mr. Robert walked carefully on the icy grass. Miz Callie had them pick up a shovel and a lantern in the stables, "It's better prob'ly if we don't light the lantern 'til we out of sight of the stables and the house." Miz Callie said.

She was leading them up the hollow to the slave cemetery where, indeed, one of the gold stashes was hidden. He learned much later how Miz Callie *knew* where that one stash was, but he was completely puzzled about it that night. He had to stay a fair distance behind them in order not to be heard. He was afraid they would kill her before he could shoot them both, and, truth was, at least one of them would likely have shot him in the process.

Mr. Robert had no light other than the full moon which was peeking in and out of clouds. He also wished he'd brought a pistol. Miz Callie, he said, was in her nightgown and appeared barefooted. He never understood how she was able to go up that rocky, frozen trail like that except she was doing it to protect her loved ones. Later she said she thought there might have been a couple of other stragglers nearby, so she wanted to get these two separated from them. Seems she was right about that because *Ole Massah shot at someone* sneaking around the stables shortly after Miz Callie had led the two up the hollow. They never found a body, but they did find a trail of blood all the way down to the river. If several deserters were together they could certainly have forced the family to give up at least part of the gold, and might have killed some or all of them - or worse.

The hollow widened into an open field. They climbed a gradual rise to the top of the long field. Mr. Robert stayed far to the right side in the shade of the pines and red cedars growing at the edge of the field. Miz Callie seemed to stop when she got up to the cemetery. Mr. Robert could see her looking around.

"Things look different at night," she said. "But I think it's over there under that big rock. It will take two of you to move that rock. It's a big un."

She had pointed, intending for *them* to go to the rock and attempt to move it. One of them pushed her hard in the back with his rifle butt. "You nigger women are strong. You an' Omar git that rock up!"

She had intended to escape through the thick cedar woods on the far side of the cemetery when the men began to try to move the rock, but it hadn't worked out that way. She and the one named Omar shoved the rock, trying to roll it. Part of the problem was that the rock was frozen to the hard, cold ground.

Omar looked up at his crony, "Goddamn it, Virgil, git your sorry ass ovah here an' hep us."

Virgil came over and they all shoved, trying to move the rock. "Omar, can you find your way back to the stable an' bring a hoss an' rope?"

"Iffen I could, I wouldn't. By now the fahr you set in the cabin has got the whole damn country roused up. No way, I'm goin' back *alone*! I think I heered a shot as we come up the holler. I bet someone's kilt. Eithah they've kilt that desertah's been follerin' us fer two days, or he's kilt one of them."

Omar turned, took a few steps toward the road they'd just climbed, and looked down the hollow from where they'd come, expecting to see someone. Mr. Robert said about that time, he tried to duck into the cover of a big pine when one of his icy boot heels slid on the naked bedrock that formed part of the road. He lost his grip on his rifle, which discharged when it hit the ground, stock first, business end up in the air. Accidently and providentially, the shot hit the one called Omar in the face. Omar got off one shot before he fell face down - dead. When Omar's rifle went off, Mr. Robert said he scrambled for his rifle but couldn't find it. Between the flares of the gun fire and a stray cloud covering the moon, he could see nothing. Virgil lifted his own rifle looking for someone to shoot. Mr. Robert rolled as quietly as he could to the side of the trail an *down* the hill a little. When the moon peaked out from behind the cloud, Virgil started cautiously down the path looking for whoever shot Omar.

"He's dead, too." Miz Callie said in a teary voice, "I saw the shot hit him in the back. If he ain't dead yet, he will be by morning. He ain't going nowhere with *that back*!"

"Well, I didn't see it!" Virgil snarled. Just then Virgil's foot struck Mr. Robert's gun. He reached down and picked it up.

"If he was alive you'd hear him running for help. Come, *help me* with this limb. I think I got this rock to budge a little!" Then cunningly, softly, sadly, "When we get the gold out will you *take me* with you out of this awful place? They going to know I'm the one show you where it is."

"How long you been without a man?" Virgil sidled up next to her, fondling her almost naked backside .

"Oh, Ole Massah sold the only man I ever had. Solt him 'bout ten years ago." Miz Callie was buying time for Mr. Robert to get away and get help. She figured he didn't have another weapon with him or he would've used it by now.

She later told Mr. Robert that she remembered thinking, "Get help, Massah, and *get it soon*, but be quiet! This man won't think twice 'bout killing you and me both!"

"So, you *a upright Nigger*, then? Not laid with ever' man in the country?"

"No, Sir, *that be sin*! I am a *Christian woman*!" She looked over at him, "Let's try to get this big ole rock up! Let me light that lantern so's we can see what we doing. Then if you take that other limb maybe with two limbs we can shift it."

And shift it they did. Miz Callie said she tried to delay actually moving the rock by pretending to be weak and tired. "Give me a minute to ketch my wind." She'd say, "Look I'm just *a little woman*. I'm not a field hand! I'm a maid."

Virgil threatened her if she didn't get back to work, but she resisted. "I can *help*. I know we can get that rock up, *but I got to ketch my wind first*." But she could only delay so long. Finally they managed to heave the rock off the treasure.

Under the rock lay a large metal box with a padlock on it. Virgil hit the lock several times with his rifle butt before the lock broke. Inside the box were several denominations of coins and *lots of them*. Miz Callie told Mr. Robert it was as if the very sight of gold made the man called Virgil drunk! She said he picked up several coins and rubbed them against his face, bit one or two to be sure they were real, laughing and doing a little jig the whole time. Then he reached out, grabbed her and kissed her hard, biting her lips, her cheeks. She pushed him backwards and he shoved her hard to the ground on top of the jumble of rocks that was all around, kicked her hard in the side, pinned her arms under her and ravished her.

He rolled off her and rolled her forcefully face down onto the stones, but her arms and hands were in a position to pick up one of the rocks lying all about. She could pick up a rock from that position, but it was impossible to use one forcefully like that. She had to endure what seemed unendurable, lying there until he rolled over and began to snore. She never once cried out during the vicious attack. She didn't want Mr. Robert to come back to try to save her and be killed for his troubles. She wanted Virgil to think she was dead or unconscious. She knew she had to think and think hard to survive because *that man wanted her dead.*

When he had snored for a couple of minutes and she felt sure he was asleep, Miz Callie got on to her knees and slammed the rock she held in rapid succession first into his nose, then his forehead and finally into his temple, hearing bones crunch every time! Until she had crushed Virgil's skull she had felt little pain, but all the pain came at once almost as soon as she realized he was dead. Somehow she dragged her frozen body, with several broken ribs, blood coming from her own nose, her mouth - so many places *she* wasn't sure if any part of her *wasn't bleeding,* along the ground over to the other dead man.

Thankfully Omar had fallen on his face, Miz Callie recounted, because that made it easier to pull off his coat. She said she could only free a few inches at a time before she had to stop and rest, her breathing excruciating, shallow and hard. She wanted to sleep just for a few minutes, but she knew if she did she would freeze to death. The boots must have been stolen, she said, because they were too big for the man called Omar and came off without much resistance. Getting them on her own feet, however, was impossibly painful.

Because she slept in winter with heavy wool socks on, her feet were covered although the socks were damp from the frost she'd walked in. Miz Callie covered as much of herself as she could with the coat. Every breath she took almost caused her to fall out. She couldn't smell the filth on Omar's coat because her nose was bleeding. Had she smelled it she might not have put on that filthy, flea-ridden rag that probably kept her from freezing to death that night. It was so long on her that it covered her toes. She rolled over into the soft pine needles and fell into oblivion .

Mr. Robert, Ole Massah, and Uncle Reuben found her just before daylight. They never expected to find her alive, but they brought a blanket in case, knowing she had been only in her nightgown. She was slightly off the path under the pine trees, with Solomon lying up tight against her. He whined until they found her, but when they tried to touch her, he snarled and growled at them all. Solomon didn't trust anyone to take care of his mistress. Finally, Miz Callie whispered, "Hush, boy! Good dog. Show some manners!"

She never opened her eyes nor sat up. She probably was incapable of doing either as her eyes were swollen shut and she was stiff from her injuries and the cold. They thought she was dead until she had spoken

149

to her faithful dog. Not until daylight, back at the Big House, did they realize just how close she had come to death.

Mr. Robert said, "I can't even take credit for killing the one deserter since that was an accident. But there lay two dead deserters and sure as the sun comes up in the east every morning, Miz Callie killed that second one! Unfortunately, I think she killed him with the first blow. He deserved to die a *slow, mean, painful death*." He motioned to the doors at the bottom of the bookcase.

"Get another bottle, Sara. I need another dram or two." He looked sober for a minute or so, "The shovel was already on the hill. The big rock had been moved already. We pulled the box out and threw the trash in, covering them both with that big rock."

He stopped for a minute. "After the War was over, Miz Callie asked a favor of me. 'Get them evildoers out of that cemetery. They don't belong there with the rest of those good people.' Of course we moved them."

When I'd poured him another glass, refusing any more for myself, he went on, "The doctor had to stitch your grandmother in all kinds of places. My sweet Loudena was with her the whole time, leaving her side only for necessities. After the second week, Miz Callie finally *ran* Loudena out of the room we'd put her in upstairs. I think she said, 'Miz 'Dena, you're getting to look like all *those other sickly white women*! Get *yourself some sunshine*!'"

"Miz Callie was ill a long time. She had about three broken ribs, probably a collapsed lung, a broken jaw and a broken ankle besides the other stuff. But, do you know what caused her the *most pain*?" I shook my head, crying at last.

"*She killed a man.* A sorry, low-down *mad dog* rapist! But it hurt her conscience to *kill* the bastard! She didn't mind so much killing him as not giving the son-of-a… him *time to make his peace with God*!" He stopped talking for a couple of minutes while I cried and blew my nose on my handkerchief. The hall clock chimed midnight. I had no idea so much time had passed!

"Your momma stayed with Uncle Reuben and Aunt Cici until Miz Callie was well enough to go back to the new cabin we built for her. She didn't want any jealousy or hard feelings on the hill. She *wouldn't allow us to do much for her* afterwards," he sighed.

"Miz Callie raised your father after he was orphaned. Caesar was about eight or nine when his own mother died. It so happened that Caesar was working in the stables with Abraham by the time of this awful trouble. The farrier couldn't come to us for some reason or other and we had several horses that needed shoeing. Caesar and Abraham had left that day for an overnight trip to have those horses shod. Your daddy would *never* have allowed Miz Callie to be taken off that hill, not even as young as he was! He would've *killed* those two men or they would've *killed him*. We never knew whether to be glad or sad about his not being there that night!"

My head was spinning either from the bourbon or the new revelation. No one had ever told me that my father and mother had grown up in the same house!

Mr. Robert went on as if in a dream, "Miz Callie did allow us to make your Momma second cook. She made us take a solemn oath to see to the care of *her children, and she considered Caesar her child, too, and grandchildren*. My father and I both promised her that neither her children nor her grandchildren would ever suffer any hardship if we could help it. Daddy gave your grandmother, Nisa and Caesar their freedom. Miz Callie had asked for the children's freedom, but she didn't want that broadcast about, and, as they were well employed here, here they stayed. The end of the War really made those freedom papers just symbols, but Miz Callie always said she appreciated the act. Daddy even tried to get Albert and her boys back, but they'd been sold at least one other time, and then *the boys disappeared into freedom*. Seems Albert died just before the War started." Mr. Robert shifted in his chair, raising his arms up over his head to stretch. He had one more thing to say.

"The gold that is still in the safe is yours, Sara. I know your sisters and brother are Miz Callie's grandchildren, too, but *Clay* is providing for them. *I'm* leaving *you* the gold in my will, but if you decide to leave us before I pass, I'll turn it over to you when you go. This family benefited from your grandmother's sacrifice! See this as *her legacy* to you."

Love or guilt? Even from my own dealings in the world, I'm not sure which is the stronger motivation. They are so often entangled anyway.

I knew for certain that evening that I never wanted to set foot in that cemetery again.

CHAPTER 9: MISS IVY RETURNS HOME

Mr. Robert invited *everyone* to the party he gave when Miss Ivy and Rob returned home in 1892. Miss Ivy decided to teach in the school she had attended nearby rather than to accept several offers elsewhere. I expect that she did it in part out of filial duty, but mostly due to sincere affection for her father. She had outgrown the cultural amenities that were locally available and would miss theatricals, concerts and the like. Her return, however, seemed to be the one consolation Mr. Robert had in years.

Rob's graduation from The University of Virginia Law School at the same time created great excitement. Mr. Robert was very proud, not only of his youngest two, Ivy and Rob, but of each child. 'Zander was managing the farm profitably. There was not great money to be made farming there at that time, but it was more than enough to keep his family in comfort and to pay his laborers decently. Dr. Thomas was practicing medicine in Chicago and Mary had a handsome son and a husband who was well-thought-of in the academic community throughout the mid-south.

The house was full to the rafters with visiting family. Dr. Thomas and his pretty red-haired wife, Alicia, and their two little ones came. Miz Mary and the professor came with young Isaac who, at ten, was almost as tall as his father. Miz Victoria and the Reverend came with the two granddaughters they had been raising since their son's death three years back. The girls were nearly grown. They had not been with their grandparents on their last visit. I was stunned at how old Miz Victoria and the Reverend both looked. Losing a child is difficult, it seemed, no matter how old the child was.

Cousins came as well. Dr. Stewart Powell and his bride came from Charlottesville. She was about to deliver their first baby very soon. The Reverend Holton Powell and his wife traveled also to be there.

To the great surprise of everyone, Mr. Clay came for a brief visit. Miz Eliza remained in Texas since five year-old Lou Issa was never easy to handle away from her familiar surroundings, and she was delicate and sickly at the time.

Vaz had long since had the second attic bedroom and his sisters shared the other one. Ole Missus would *not* have them displaced and the rooms were quite small anyway. She decided to put Mr. Clay in with his son. Miss Ivy had her old room, but she shared it with Miz Victoria (whose room it was once long ago), the granddaughters, and her sister, Miz Mary. Five in that room! Pallets were taken from the attic storage area for the younger ladies. Rob shared a room with his brother-in-law, Miz Mary's husband the professor, and his Aunt Vicky's husband, the Reverend. Rob laughingly told me twice that the two older gentlemen snored constantly and one, or both, had problems with flatulence. Dr. Thomas, his wife, and their children shared a room. Dr. Stewart and his wife had their own room, as did Reverend Holton and his wife. This was confusing for all of us. I don't know how these folks knew where to sleep and, although Mr. Robert had installed a water closet on the second floor, I believe folks must have stood in line if they wanted a bath! At any rate, the household relied on older sanitary conveniences, such as pitchers and wash bowls and, of course, the privy.

All this company meant that Mr. 'Zander and Miz Anne's two girls had to find a corner somewhere to bunk down as their room was taken by guests. Young Andy and Isaac slept with their granddaddy Robert who said, to their great merriment, that they were the most restless scoundrels he ever shared a bed with. Miz Anne and Mr. 'Zander's two girls begged to put a cot in my room. I told them I didn't think this was seemly since my own sisters weren't sleeping in there anymore, but they begged until Miz Anne finally said that if it were alright with me, she didn't mind. Miz Anne agreed on the condition that her girls help get food on the table and clean the dining room after every meal.

Something in Miz Anne had changed towards me, a softening, a respect that I had not seen when I first became Big Cook. Maybe sharing a house, managing children, and general day-to-day living brought this about. I expect we come to appreciate some characteristics in those we live with and deal as well as we can with the things we don't like. At any rate, I came to respect her as well. For one thing, she wasn't shy about working herself and she expected her children to do some honest labor as well. No queen was she! She was a fair, decent woman and certainly warmer than her husband.

"Girls," Miz Anne said, "Sara has a great responsibility on her small shoulders with all this company. Being in her room, you will disturb her sleep no matter how quiet and considerate you are. You may sleep there only if you can be a *real help* to her! You've pleaded to be with your *dear Sara*," she laughingly teased them. "Be sure you are true friends to her and do as she asks."

It turned out, even as young as they were, those two girls were a considerable help in feeding so many people three meals a day, and often tea too.

Rob, after two sleepless nights with the snorers, decided to sleep on the upstairs porch even if it were chilly at night. He asked Rhi for an extra quilt and a pillow so he could sleep in the swing on the upstairs porch. I had to laugh, just imagining his big feet and long legs hanging off that swing!

"Alright, Little Smarty Sara," he addressed me when I laughed in his face over it, "you are short enough to fit the swing perfectly. Let me have your bed!"

"No, Uncle Rob," Miz Anne's Laura cried, defending my bed space, "we can't sleep in a room with you! And Sara needs a good night's rest to feed all this company!"

He laughed at Laura and pulled one of her pigtails, "I was joking of course. I would never take Sara's bed. She earns the right *every* day to have the softest bed in the house which I am sure it certainly is not!"

I felt sorry for the laundress, Sudie, even though she earned extra money that week. There seemed to be a line full of face towels, shirts, bodices, under garments and the like every day behind the summer kitchen. The big laundry cauldrons were always full and her two boys kept carrying water from the pumps for her.

Violet was not enough help in the kitchen since Rhi and Nora were busy most of the day cleaning house, so we brought Mabel down from the hill. Mabel was twelve. She had a quick mind, but a contrary spirit - just the opposite of Violet. It would've been nice to have a girl who was *smart and cooperative*, but that wasn't to be. The girl questioned every request I made of her. I tried to be patient, but I think I probably said to her at least once, "Hush up, Mabel, and just do what I'm asking! I don't have time to explain everything and you *ought* to know why anyway!"

Rhi had outgrown two perfectly good uniforms, so She gave them to Mabel. You would've thought Mabel was a society lady the way she lah-de-dahed around. In fact, she became so highfaluting that she tried to give orders to Violet whom she saw as an inferior. That was Mabel's undoing. Trying to order Violet to do anything was like trying to herd cats. Violet would walk away pitifully, coming back without a clue as to what Mabel had said before, and doing exactly what she had done many times before, in the same way. It so frustrated Mabel that she was pulling at her own hair by the end of the second day!

I never wore a uniform. I don't believe I would've worn one had Ole Missus ordered me to. Something in me revolted at the idea. I did have a few good, plain dresses in solid colors, and I had aplenty of clean aprons, so I was always presentable. I had long ago insisted that Violet be given two good plain dresses to work in as none of Rhi's castoffs would fit her. Violet was taller even than Rhi and considerably stouter.

The children, including Vaz, Rhi and Nora, ate on an improvised table on the back kitchen porch that week because, as big as the dining room table was, it couldn't handle twenty-some people, plus the occasional neighbors who were invited. The children enjoyed the freedom from adult supervision, and the new dogs had a great deal of extra attention, most of it involving table scraps. I believe someone had the idea that it would be fun to teach the dogs tricks with the leftovers - at least they assured me they only used the scraps from their plates.

The children never seemed to mind that Violet was "different," and she loved waiting on them, especially Dr. Thomas' toddlers, who were supposed to be under the supervision of Miz Victoria's granddaughters. Violet would hum off key as she served the children's table and the children would laugh and make up silly words to go along with her tunes. The sillier the words were, the more they all, even the older ones, enjoyed it. Once in awhile, Violet would add her own silly words. I still remember one verse she created as it became an instant hit and was frequently repeated by Miz Anne's children over the years when they wanted to poke fun at someone. It was most likely the silliest song of them all.

There used to be a man who was white, black and tan,
Like his hound dog! Ho-o-o-w-l! Ho-o-o-w-l!
He sang for his mule when the mule came home from school.
The mule tried long to teach the man a different song.
Like the hound dog! Ho-o-o-w-l! H-o-o-o-w-l!

The children all had great fun especially the evening it rained while they were eating supper. Every time the wind blew they got a misting and the yelps of laughter made wonderful music to my ears. Several times I laughed just hearing them enjoying a good time together as cousins. I never had experienced that; I was a little jealous. The truth was Rhi, Vaz and Nora never had much of it either. We needed more children's laughter in the house.

Miss Ivy and Rob's celebration party was on the front lawn. We hung lanterns in the trees and put several long planks on saw horses, covered them with linen, took the chairs from the kitchen, the dining room, and borrowed some from neighbors for the lawn seating. Everyone ate and danced under the stars.

Miss Ivy was the belle of the ball that night. She wore a beautiful gown of the softest pink ornamented with white lace and a cascading bustle down the back. Some of her old beaus had married, moved away, or gotten engaged while she was at school, but there were still two who courted her that night, Mr. Adam Griswold and Judge George Huntley. The Judge was a widower, but he was not much older than Dr. Thomas, and, from what little I saw of his three children, they were quite well-behaved. Of course, his sister, their Aunt, kept a tight rein on them. But Miss Ivy preferred Mr. Griswold. Those of us who knew her well could see that, even though she tried not to show favoritism.

Miz Mary Powell fell over in a heap on the lawn about eleven in the evening while the small orchestra took a twenty minute break to get some refreshment. Her husband was standing on the opposite side of the lawn talking to the other doctor in the family and our local physician. Young Andy ran to get his uncle while Rob and the Judge started to lift Miz Mary off the ground. She had not fainted, but she had been stunned when her water broke. The doctors, including Miz Mary's husband, hurriedly walked across the lawn toward the crowd that was gathering around Miz Mary. It seemed to be all men immediately around her and the poor thing was so embarrassed. Her skirt hem and slippers were wet. The poor lady was more embarrassed than in pain. Miss Ivy and her sister Miz Mary McCain pushed the men aside, "Excuse me, Sir!" and "Your pardon, Sir!" until they could get close enough to protect her modesty.

"Sara," Miss Ivy looked over to me where I was refilling another punch bowl, "May I have your apron?" she mouthed. I immediately took off my big, long apron and made my way to the women. I tied that apron as well as I could around Miz Mary Powell. Her distended abdomen took up a lot of apron, but her husband lifted her in his arms and the women surrounded her until he could get her inside.

Before morning we had another life to celebrate, a handsome red-faced, wrinkled little boy they named Jedadiah Stewart Powell. Ole Missus was once again enthralled over a new life. She insisted on holding him as soon as he was cleaned up. Miz Mary was too weary to protest which was just as well since Ole Missus always got her way.

A few days later all the guests, except Mr. Clay, decamped for other places. Miss Ivy, Ole Missus, and Mr. Clay called us to a meeting at the dining room table. I had very rarely sat there. I wondered if we were all being sent away.

"Children, I've included your sister in this conversation as she has raised you body and soul." Mr. Clay said. Ole Missus would've argued with him, I think, if he hadn't given her that "Mother, don't interfere!" look.

"I've looked into a number of fine colleges, hoping that you, Mariah, Vastine, and Honora, would choose to attend college for at least two years and, preferably, four."

Mr. Clay was intense with them as he rarely ever was. "If I'd stayed in college, I might have made you children wealthy. Like you, I was a good student, but…"

"Where did you go to college? I never knew you went to college!" As always Vaz would interrupt even the minister in his pulpit if he wanted.

Mr. Clay smiled, seemingly ashamed which I'd never seen him. "If I said William and Mary, would you believe me?"

"Oh, my!" Rhi gasped. "Where Thomas Jefferson went to school?"

"Yes, sweetheart, the very same. I went away at the age of sixteen. I only needed a few months before I would've graduated, but I'd already been given too many chances to redeem myself. I lasted 'til my twentieth birthday before I managed to get kicked out for my - well, shall we say, my *transgressions*. And, unlike my loving, doting mother, I will know if *you* stray *long before* you get sent down! Woe on your backside, young gent," he looked pointedly at Vaz, "if I have to take action!" Then he reached over and patted Vaz on the shoulder, "But I trust you've got *enough of your mother* in you to have better sense than I did!"

"Are we *old enough, ready* for college?" Rhi asked curiously.

"No, Mariah." Ivy said. "You are certainly *not* old enough yet, but I'm going to determine where you need extra work and *you will be ready* by the time you're sixteen, just as your daddy was," she looked around the table to see if that term caused any embarrassment. It did not. We'd all grown used to the word long ago. "That's only a year from now, young lady, but I don't see any problems. You've worked hard *ever since I can remember*." She turned and teased Vaz, "Now *this scoundrel* is another matter!" She pulled his ear a little.

Vaz grinned because he knew how advanced he was. In the spring, he had often corrected the tutor, especially with Latin translations and history. The Reverend Pickle had complained to Ole Missus that Vaz was *insolent*. I don't know what she replied, but he shut the front door very hard as he left and the only time we saw him again was when he came to get his final pay.

Ole Missus gave her favorite grandchild a sad, loving smile. "Son, I can't bear," her voice cracked with emotion, "the thought of any of you going away except for *one* reason - to *ensure a good life* for yourself. A college degree won't make that happen, but it makes it much easier. I've used most of any money I ever had, but I've told your daddy and Ivy that *I will use the last cent I have*, if necessary, to see that all three of you have whatever college education you can get. Your daddy has looked into several schools that are financially possible for us and that still offer a first-rate education for males and females, whites and blacks."

"We're *not colored*!" Vaz said hot temperedly.

"No, son," Mr. Clay said, "You are not even technically mulattoes, as your mother was part white. Away from here, it is unlikely that anyone would ever even question that you are anything but white, especially with those light eyes."

"Well, *I'm not ashamed of being colored*!" Mariah fired up. She rarely got angry, but the color thing always brought out her temper. "The best person I know is darker than I am!" She looked at me. I dropped my head and my eyes started to mist. She never denied her mother's people even when it might have been an advantage for her to do so.

"Children!" Mr. Clay put up a hand and looked sympathetically at Nora for having to endure another argument between her brother and sister about color. "It makes *no* difference to me if you choose to live your life as colored, white, or mixed. I expect, though, that living your life straddling two worlds, white and colored, has to be the most difficult, and you've done that right here!"

Nora spoke and it was characteristically sweet of her, "It's never *felt difficult*, Daddy. Everyone has always been good to us, except, Miz 'Becca and Uncle Robert sent her packing when he found out everything she'd done. Grandmother wouldn't allow her to mistreat us. Miz Anne even took up for us."

"Just as she should have!" Miss Ivy said strongly.

"That awful woman!" Ole Missus interjected. "See Mariah's spectacles!" she pointed.

"She wears those because that *witch* hit her in the head, nearly killing her. And, even then, Robbie let her stay because she cried and apologized and promised not ever to hurt any of the children again. I don't know if I'll ever forgive him for that! They all kept the reason for Mariah's sight difficulties from me until Rebecca was given the boot!" Ole Missus was angry all over again.

"Daddy," Nora went on, "I don't think even Miz 'Becca was mean to us *because* we are colored, although she did remark on that often enough. *She was mean to everyone* except Uncle Robert!" Mr. Clay got out of his chair and picked Nora up, sat down in her chair, and held her in his arms, gently rocking back and forth as if she were a baby. He looked so sad, I wanted to hug *him*. Nora was eleven years old, but she was about the size of a nine year old. Mariah went over to her father and put her arms around his neck. He reached up and took one of her hands and kissed it.

Mr. Clay put his chin down on top of Nora's head, "That old hag! *Who does she think she is* to *mistreat my babies* - and *over something I did* and they couldn't help!" He looked over Nora's head at me and said very quietly, "I believe I'll see Mrs. Rebecca Powell before I return home."

"Oh, Dad," Vaz said matter-of-factly, "Don't stir things up. We got our own back! 'Course it backfired some, and that *was* really awful, but she went too far, and that's when Uncle Robert got rid of her."

"When did you start calling my brother 'Uncle Robert,' and what does he say about that?" Mr. Clay was laughing as he rubbed Vaz's head with his knuckles.

Once again, I thought that there couldn't have been another house in the South where families lived the way we did. The neighbors thought we were "quare" folk, but they didn't bother us much about our mixedness or anything else. Just a stare from Mr. Robert or Ole Missus hushed tongues. Sometimes I even fancied that Ole Missus was Medusa. She could turn you into stone with just a look.

"Oh, he told us to call him 'Uncle' a long time ago." Rhi stated matter-of-factly.

"Well, by Jove!" Mr. Clay exclaimed, "I guess I owe my brother a bunch of apologies! Now tell me how did you rid the house of that she-devil he married!"

"I'll tell you about it later. Don't think I'd let that harridan mistreat my sisters, or my grandmother, or Ivy, and she did all of those things and worse!" He raised himself up to show just how grown he was. At thirteen he was as tall as Rhi and they were each taller than I.

"Okay, back to the topic of schools." Ivy said. "Your daddy thinks either Oberlin Institute in Ohio or Berea College in Kentucky would be excellent. They both admit men and women, colored and white. Berea is actually tuition-free, but, of course, there are still some expenses such as room and board. You can work at either school and, as a matter of fact, you *must* work at Berea. Oberlin is farther away. Oberlin is affiliated with the Presbyterian Church and Berea is non-denominational, but church or chapel attendance is required at both schools."

She sounded like advertisements you might receive explaining the programs.

"No!" Vaz interjected. "I'm not into all that Bible-thumping!"

"Hush, Son," Ole Missus said. "It wouldn't *hurt you* to open your Bible a little more often and it might do you a *world of good*, you young heathen!" But she laughed.

"It doesn't much matter where you go to college, Vastine," Mr. Clay weighed in, "there's almost assuredly going to be some religious involvement and requirements. So stop nit-picking over everything. What matters is how good is the education you can get there, and I can't find a hair's difference, except - well, the State of Kentucky keeps making noises about forbidding interracial education. If that should happen after you start at Berea, that could derail your education, at least for a time - if anyone knew you were technically, at least in the states of Virginia and Kentucky, a negro." He looked over at me significantly.

"I have a very good friend in Washington who is working at the behest of a Supreme Court Justice, originally from Kentucky. My friend is from Louisiana where they have already passed a law saying that certain facilities must separate whites from coloreds. The hope is to overturn the Louisiana law when it comes before the Supreme Court. If that can be done, then it's unlikely Kentucky would try to pass such a law just to have it struck down." Mr. Clay explained.

"I told you, Sara!" Vaz was on his feet too fired up to sit still. "Didn't I tell you? He's talking about Joseph Thierry! Dad! Dad! Mr. Thierry writes to us almost every week. Of course, most of it is a sealed letter to Sara inside the letter to us! But he tells us what he's been reading, what cases he's working on. Things like that!"

I must have been about the color of Old Miz Laws' (Miz Anne's mother) red wig. I could've crawled through one of the cracks in the floor boards I was so embarrassed. The whole purpose of putting a letter for me *inside* the one to the children was so the whole world wouldn't know Joseph, as I now thought of him, had written specifically to me. Vaz had always had a big mouth.

Mr. Clay and Miss Ivy started laughing. Ole Missus just sat there as if she never heard a word, *which meant she had known for some time* about the private letters.

"Will you please excuse me?" I mumbled, "I really must start supper if we're to eat on time." I probably stumbled out of the room and out to the summer kitchen where I sat down, expecting to cry, but found myself laughing at what a fool I was to believe there was anything private in that house!

After the talk in the dining room had gone on for some time, Mr. Clay took the children out to ride. Violet and I almost had supper ready when I heard them return from the stables, stop at the pump, and sluice some of the dirt off. The children went on to the porch and up the outside stairs to clean up a little better before supper. Mr. Clay came into the summer kitchen and asked if he could have a private word with me. Violet said she'd go to the dining room and be sure everything was set up properly.

"Sara," Mr. Clay said solemnly, "Joseph Thierry is a *good man*. If he makes a promise you can expect he will either keep it or die trying. But *he is still a man*, sweetheart. And a man whose wife is incapable of loving anyone but herself. If I thought ill of Eliza before I married her, I did her a great injustice. Eliza just needed to be loved and treated with a firm hand. But all the things I thought about Eliza were *trivial* compared to Olivia Marie Thierry's character. Without exaggeration, she is the most wicked woman I have ever met."

"Why are you telling…" I started.

"Don't deny the attraction, Sara. I've seen the man around women! *He can't help himself.* He's like a flame for moths. Women can't seem to help themselves. Even Eliza remarks on his charm! I know he had a woman in Baton Rouge that he kept for *convenience*. She was much older than you and was well paid for her companionship, but he doesn't live the life of a monk. His wife has never minded so long as he was discreet and regularly returned to New Orleans to escort her to balls and dinners and other fetes. In fact, Olivia Marie likes his having a mistress because it means *she* doesn't have to share a bed with him."

Mr. Clay went on, "She *refuses* to have babies. She went to an old Voodoo priestess to end at least two pregnancies. Voodoo witches usually won't practice abortion because they see it as a sin, but Olivia Marie evidently convinced this one that she would die if she carried the baby til its birth. And *I, of all people*, fully understand a woman aborting a child if she is fairly sure birthing it will kill her. *I wish to God that your*

165

mother had…" He shook himself almost like a wet dog. "But Olivia Marie's fear has no basis that any of us knows about! She is healthy, at least physically. I think she's mentally…" He left the rest to my imagination.

"Although she is quite the coquette in public, she wants no men in her bedchamber unless they are willing to engage in behaviors that won't create a baby."

I must have looked totally at sea. At that time I had no conception that men and women could be intimate in any other way. I must have been red faced again because he put a gentle hand on my shoulder.

"I am *not* the person to explain those things to you, Sara. I know Mother won't, and it's likely Ivy doesn't know anymore about that than you do. You'll learn in time." He seemed to be searching for words before he continued.

"I know that Joseph is quite taken with you. If he'd been around you more, I might even believe him when he says he has deep affection and the highest regard for you, but he married a cold woman and has relations with women who are paid to be - shall I say, *'affectionate.'* He's as susceptible as you are, I think. I also know that he wants you to move to Washington as soon as may be even though he is *not* divorced."

Something hot inside me rose up in self-defense at his carefully worded, but obvious discouragement of any involvement with Joseph. "Does the *whole world* expect me to live like a nun? To cook and raise those three children that I had no choice but to raise when I was so little I couldn't even pick up Rhi and Vaz?" I waived my hand towards the upstairs. "Don't misunderstand me! I *love those children* enough to lie down and die for any one of them, but I never had any say…" He looked stunned. The cork was out of my mouth now and I couldn't stop what came out.

"Am I supposed to be pure and untouched *because my momma did what she did?* Because my momma was your whore? Am I supposed to atone

166

for Momma?" As soon as the words were out of my mouth I became sick to my stomach over what I'd said about my sweet momma. "Oh, Lord. No! *Momma, forgive me*!" I was gagging trying to hold back the bitter bile that had risen to my mouth.

He took his hand off my shoulder suddenly and turned his face from mine. I couldn't tell what he was feeling, but he turned around with deep anger on his face.

"How *dare you speak in such a way about your mother*? How *dare you*? I almost *struck* you! Never defile your mother's name again! Your mother and I were married before I ever - I loved her and she loved me. We would have had to leave the country to live openly together in peace! She wouldn't put you, or me, for that matter, in a position where we would be made miserable by public opinion. Mother and your grandmother were witnesses to our marriage! We had to travel to New York to marry as our union would have been impossible or questionable any place nearer. It would never be legally recognized in Virginia, so I have had to adopt *my own children* - and even that action is questionable in some states! Daddy knew all along that Nisa and I were married. Why the rest never knew, I'm uncertain. Maybe Mother feared that if too many people knew someone would blab it about the county and get us arrested for miscegenation - marriage between a black person and a white person." He strode around the kitchen several times as if to calm himself.

"The day Nisa died because no one could stop the bleeding in time, the best part of me died too! I was holding her hand when she passed telling her to hold on that we'd sent for the doctor..." His voice broke and he sat at the kitchen table, crying like a baby. I stood at the stove, bent over, sobbing and trying not to vomit because of what I'd said.

Finally when he stopped crying, I asked, "Why did no one ever tell *me* you were married? Why let me go on believing that my sweet mother..."

"Because I was *deeply ashamed* of never having lived with her publicly, openly, acknowledging her as she *deserved* to be acknowledged. Ashamed for not telling the world to be damned if they didn't like it! I couldn't do any good for Nisa after she was dead!"

He blew his nose on his handkerchief and said quietly, "You resemble her so much that *it hurts my heart* to *look at you*! You were still so young when I left for Texas seven years ago. You are a woman now." he mused, "I see why Joseph says you are the loveliest girl he's ever seen. Nisa was so beautiful and *so good*."

He stood up, "No, none of us has a right to ask you to live the life of a nun, or to ask anything at all of you. You've been a good sister and a good daughter. I say these things because I *don't want you to get hurt*. I don't think Joseph will ever divorce his wife although he has the legal grounds to do so. Color *is the reason* he won't do it. Not yours. *His*. In Louisiana he would be considered 'colored,' even though he is only one-eighth negro and doesn't look as if he has any African heritage. He would lose all political power in Louisiana if it were known. He might even lose some in D.C. And that *awful woman* would find a way for the whole world to know if he divorces her! He's involved in something now that could affect *so many people* and he doesn't want to jeopardize the outcome."

He walked over to me and folded me in his arms. "Daughter, be careful with your precious heart. I warned Joseph that hurting you would end what has been a very good friendship." He kissed my cheek, turned to go, and vehemently said, "*These ridiculous notions* that folks, *white and colored*, have about who a person should or should not love. What an *awful heap of heartache* it causes!"

CHAPTER 10: MARIAH GOES TO COLLEGE

And if, as weeks go round, in the dark of the moon
my spirit darkens and goes out, and soft strange gloom
pervades my movements and my thoughts and words
then I shall know that I am walking still
with God, we are close together now the moon's in shadow.

D.H. Lawrence

Rhi worked as a house servant in the Big House from the age of ten until she was sixteen. Ten may seem young to scrub floors, clean grates, wash windows, change linen, beat rugs, dust high and low, and a myriad of other duties, but it was not uncommon in 1887 for young *poor* girls to do these things, especially if they were as tall and strong as Rhi.

When she turned sixteen, Miss Ivy and Ole Missus decided Rhi knew enough and was sensible enough to leave home for college. Oh, how I resisted the idea! I didn't want my sister, my best friend, to go away - not 50 miles away, and certainly not more than 350. That might as well have been in China, it seemed so far to me.

Miss Ivy, Ole Missus, Clay, and Mariah came to a decision that Oberlin College would be better for her than other schools that might be nearer. Oberlin had long traditions preceding even the Civil War of teaching whites, blacks, males, and females. The area around Oberlin also seemed to be more conducive to her safety and happiness than that of the next best option. The political climate in Kentucky was fragile at the time, with a great deal of pressure to ban all school integration.

After Rhi's acceptance, Ole Missus gave Miss Ivy the duty of seeing Rhi outfitted suitably to go that far away, to look presentable, and to *survive* the cold snowy winters. Miss Ivy was the logical person for the job. Not only did she have good taste and could manage a budget skillfully, but Miss Ivy had spent four years away at college herself. The beautiful coat that Rhi's father had given her just a few years before was too small, but the fur was in good shape and came in handy to adorn a new coat and hat. The beautiful velvet made into a lovely jacket with jet beads on the collar. We had to improvise the closings with frogs as there was not enough material to make buttonholes and button closings. Miss Ivy and Rhi purchased numerous personal supplies in quantity, including soap, olive oil for hair care, talcum powder, tooth powder, etc., a small piece of luggage she could manage by herself, and a large leather trunk. Rhi would not be home again until she finished her education, except, possibly, at Christmas, so it was necessary to take clothing for warm and cold weather. It was a large production with *two* seamstresses working on dresses and the rest of us working on undergarments, socks, and anything else Ole Missus got it into her head that Rhi might need.

Good winter boots had to be *made* and that required an overnight trip to the nearest good boot maker. Rhi had never spent a night away from me and had been practically nowhere in her entire life. She was nervous and giddy with excitement. She, Miss Ivy and Miz Anne stayed in a hotel, ate dinner in a fine restaurant, and saw a play as well as having Rhi fitted for boots. I was jealous of my sister for the first time in my life.

How I would have loved to go with them - and I could have *gone*, but I would have been relegated to a hotel room unless I wanted to create a great deal of discomfort in the dining room as my skin was too dark. At that time it was *not illegal* for me to eat with them or to sit with them in the theater, but managers could make it very uncomfortable for all of us if I did. Rhi looked as white as many whites, her hair was a luxuriant chestnut color, and her eyes were grey. She, Vaz and Nora had been legally adopted by their father so even her name was the same as the rest of the entourage. However, the fact that she was accompanied by two distinguished ladies who were obviously white made her absolutely acceptable. No one questioned that she was anything other than white.

Lightweight and woolen underwear had to be procured. They bought a pair of silk stockings for special occasions, but I was enlisted to knit several pairs of heavier wool socks and two wool shawls, one in a light color (I decided on pink as Rhi was so lovely in pink) and one in a dark color - black, of course. Ole Missus complained that pink wasn't practical as it couldn't go with all of Rhi's clothes, so she had a black, white and grey paisley shawl sent from Scotland for her. I never saw another shawl quite so handsome! Rhi had six skirts and bodices, eight day dresses and four dresses suitable, with a bit of added ornamentation, for soirees, half of each was made in a lighter fabric and half in heavier material.

It seemed to me that Rhi received a fortune in gifts. As I recall, she cried over every one. Miss Ivy gave Rhi a small serviceable, but attractive gold watch pin. It may have cost her half a year's teaching salary, but she was so very proud of her protégé. Rob sent her a pair of drop pearl earrings, requiring us to pierce her ears since they had never been pierced. She certainly cried over that! Dr. Thomas sent a leather bag just the right size to carry books from class to class with her initials stamped into the leather - *M.P.* Miz Mary and her husband gave her letters of introduction to several faculty members they had met over the years *and* a good fountain pen. Her father, of course, paid all necessary expenses and established a small bank account from which she could draw for unforeseen necessities. Ole Missus paid for her new clothing. I think she nearly bankrupted herself in doing so, but she smiled as I hadn't seen her smile in a long time when "Mariah" modeled her new wardrobe.

Mr. Robert gave her a gold locket with a photograph of Vaz, Nora, herself and me inside. He had insisted we sit for the portrait some months before she left. I had a larger, framed version in my room, as did Ole Missus. Miz Anne gave her two exquisite lace collars that she had tatted. Mr. 'Zander, ever practical, gave her a good dictionary. Nora knitted her two mufflers and two pairs of mittens, saying she knew Rhi would misplace a mitten and need more! She had also knitted a "sweater" for Rhi. This new fashion was not very attractive, according to Ole Missus, but it was certainly more suitable for sitting in a classroom taking notes than constantly pulling a shawl back up as it slipped off the shoulders. Rhi was thrilled with the charcoal grey woolen garment. As I handed her my gift of a diary, paper for note taking, stationery and stamps, I told Rhi that I didn't think a princess had so much.

All we females cried as Rhi got into the carriage with Mr. 'Zander and Miz Anne to go to the train station. Vaz helped his sister into the carriage and gave her a loving kiss on her cheek as he put his own small gift into her hands. It was Christmas before I knew that he had used all the money his father had sent him up to that time to buy her a gold ring with her initials engraved on top, surrounded by eight small diamonds. Many years later, Rhi told me that she never took the ring off except when she had to have it resized to fit her arthritic fingers. By that time she could have worn a diamond ring a queen would've been proud to wear, but she only wore the one Vaz gave her. I was so very proud that day and so *miserably lonely*!

Rhi's first letter home came about five days after she left for school.

September 8, 1893

Baldwin Cottage Women's Collective

Oberlin College

Oberlin, Ohio

Dear Grandmother, Uncle Robert, Mr. 'Zander, Miz Anne, Miss Ivy, Andy, Lucy, Minnie, Sara, Vastine and Honora,

What a long, tiresome trip the train and stage rides were. For the first several hours I enjoyed the new sights and gawked at everything. After about five hours of that, I became tired of sitting, watching scenery pass. Long before supper, I had consumed my tea and I wanted nothing more than to walk from car to car on the train to stretch my legs, but I heeded your advice and limited my walking. I must say, though, that no one looked unseemly. There were several businessmen, snoring loudly in their seats, and a number of families with children in various stages of rowdiness.

"Oh dear," I exclaimed aloud, "I told her that you can't tell by looking at people whether they are proper folks or rogues and scalawags!"

"Hush, Sara," Vaz said impatiently. "Please keep reading, Grandmother."

When I finally arrived at Oberlin, an upperclass woman met me at the station, helped me load my belongings on a cart and had the driver take us to Baldwin Cottage. I have enclosed a postcard of what they refer to as a cottage. Isn't it beautiful? It looks like a castle to me.

"Grandmother," Vaz exclaimed sticking his hand out toward her, "may I see the card?"

"Yes, Vastine, but don't soil and wrinkle it. Pass it to your sisters when you've had your look."

I attended a welcoming ceremony in another dormitory. Then we were free to unpack and explore the campus until supper - only they call it "dinner" here. We will have to change for dinner every day. No ink stained cuffs or muddy shoes in the dining room. The male students will join us for dinner every day. They are required to wear cravats to dinner.

The first few days all freshmen will be tested both in writing and orally to find out what classes we should be placed in. I am anxious about this, but I know I had the best teacher I could have in you, Miss Ivy. I will remember what you told me and tell only what I know. I will also ask for clarification if I fail to understand the questions. I will let you know in my next letter what classes I will be taking.

My roommates are both very nice girls, a little older than I, but shorter. I'm sure you are not surprised by that! One is a negro girl named Cassander Hall and the other is a white girl (although she may be mixed like me) named Irma Hochsteder. Cassander is from Albany, New York. She has travelled some distance to get here.

It's difficult for me to believe, but Cassie had farther to travel than I did. I must look this up in an atlas when I can get to the library to see how this is possible. Irma is from Zanesville, Ohio, which is only a half-day's journey. I think the three of us shall deal well together, and it is certainly nice not to be completely alone in a strange place.

There is to be a bonfire after supper tonight to boost the spirits of the football team. Tomorrow they will scrimmage, in preparation for their regular season games. I'm not sure they even have a complete team yet with new students still arriving. I'm hoping the placement tests will not go on during the scrimmage. I have never seen football played, and I understand that the games are very exciting.

I want to write to Daddy and Step-Mama and get both letters in the post today so I will stop here.

With my dearest affection to you all,

Mariah Powell

The next letter arrived the following week.

September 14, 1893

Dearest Family,

I can hardly believe it, but the college has given me credit for a full two semesters of English, U.S. history, algebra, geography (despite my doubts that Albany could be as far from Oberlin as Roanoke is!), Latin, and hygiene. They have given me credit for three semesters of American literature, and one semester's credit for European history and religion. It seems that all the reading we did, Sara, was highly beneficial to my college education, but I must give the greatest credit to you, Miss Ivy. You should be teaching in a college somewhere!

This is my fall schedule:

Mondays, Wednesdays, and Fridays - 8:00 AM European history, 10:00 AM geometry, 1:00 PM biology, 3:00 PM gymnastic training (I think I will like basketball best)

Tuesdays, Thursdays, and Saturdays - 8:00 AM European literature, 10:00 AM religion.

It is a daunting schedule of six courses, which is at least one course more than a student usually takes, but the dean believes I can manage this and finish my degree in education within two years. That should save Daddy some money, I think. Next semester I will finish with geometry, biology and European literature and add chemistry, geology, and gymnastic training as well.

Next summer, I will be going to New York City, Chicago, Boston, and Washington D.C. We expect to spend about two weeks in each city studying the art and architecture there and working with immigrants and their children. This travel will give me credit for a semester of art history and a semester of social issues if I pass the examinations when we return to Oberlin. The travel is not as expensive as it might be as we six (Dean Moore and five female students) will be staying on college campuses in each city and teaching English several hours each day to immigrants and their children. The cities will pay for our rooms and board instead of giving us wages. So it will cost Daddy only for the travel. I was very reluctant to ask him for the money, but Dean Moore wrote to him personally to tell him she thinks I should add this to my curriculum. Daddy agreed saying that it sounds like an important part of a good education. I'm so excited at the prospect of being useful to those less fortunate! I will send detailed letters from each city.

Next fall I will finish with chemistry and geology, add a third semester of more advanced algebra, a semester of rhetoric, a semester discussing world events, and, of course, gymnastics. I will spend the Spring of 1895 assisting in high school classrooms for half a day, five days a week and take the last semester of advanced algebra and gymnastics three days a week. The other two days I will teach, under supervision, high school mathematics and science classes. In the summer, I will sit for examinations and travel to Dallas for the remainder of the summer before I begin to work. Daddy and Step-Mama have pleaded with me to stay at least a month.

Is this ambitious enough, or maybe overly ambitious? Please give me your thoughts. I know all the details about what classes I will have may be boring to you, Grandmother, and probably to Sara as well, but I expect Ivy wants to know and it is good for Vaz to get an idea about these things.

My dearest affection,

Mariah

P.S. I have met a very interesting young man here. He is in his third year and is in my European history class. He was born in Jamaica, but grew up in New York City. More about Rohan Clarke at another time - if there's anything more to tell.

I'm certain that my words were not carefully considered when I responded to this letter. It seems that Rhi cried bitterly when she received it and the knowledge that I had caused her tears when she was far from home trying to do well, struck me to the core. She had never had much of a social life: Sunday school, choir practice, the occasional outing with her brother, sister, and me. She had a right to find some happiness, some diversions, and it all seemed so innocent. Was I *jealous* that she found a nice boy appealing while all I had was a drawer full of letters tied in a pink ribbon from a married man? It's true that I had praised her ambitious academic plans, but I also warned her not to overtax herself. To this, Rhi responded that she had far less to do at Oberlin than she usually did at home. But I also had reminded her that she was at Oberlin to study and get a degree, and at considerable expense to everyone who loved her. It was several letters before she responded to my chiding her to stick to her studies. This letter she addressed just to me.

October 12, 1893

Dearest Sister Sara,

Please forgive me for not assuring you before now that I am completely serious about my education. I waited until now to write because I was so hurt and angry when I first received your comments encouraging me to stick to the straight and narrow concerning my studies that I dared not write until time had mellowed my emotions. I know absolutely that you said what you did out of love and concern for my good. I am not angry anymore, but I still cry when I think you might believe that I could so quickly forget what it has cost to send me here.

I know, dear Sara, that you have sacrificed any pleasure you might have had in a man's company in order to see that Vaz, Nora and I are raised well. No one can know this better than I. You have been mother, sister, and friend to me and I love you more than I can ever tell you. There is no way I can repay your sacrifice. No way.

Rohan and I study European history together. You might think he would have a better grasp of it than I because he was born in a British country, but his parents were so anti-English when they came here that they discouraged education in things European, and, in particular, things English. We are fond of each other, but, at the moment, this fondness involves walking on campus, having a picnic on the lawn, going to concerts and lectures together, and studying. We have not even held hands. And, my pretty sister, he has certainly never kissed my hand as Mr. Thierry kissed yours!

I will finish my education. That I promise you, but, if I should fall in love in the process of getting a degree and find a life partner, please be happy for me. Please. I will behave with propriety for I have seen the consequences first hand when one does not.

Your devoted, adoring sister,

Mariah

Now it was my turn to cry. Rhi had humbled me in a way that no one except a best friend can. She had spoken the painful truth lovingly. I wrote her back the next day saying, something to the effect that she had always been such a "perfect child," helpful, kind, generous. I told her that I never really thought she would behave in any way that was improper, but that emotions can distract even the most conscientious of us from our goals. I also said that I should have remembered that she was one of the most practical persons I ever knew. She would graduate, and if a worthy young man came along in the meantime, she would find a way a way to include him in her future beyond graduation. I also assured her that I knew she would never look twice at someone who was not worthy of her.

CHAPTER 11: REPERCUSSIONS
OF CORRESPONDENCE

On Helen's cheek all art of beauty set,
And you in Grecian tires are painted new:
Speak of the spring, and foison of the year,
The one doth shadow of your beauty show,
The other as your bounty doth appear;
And you in every blessed shape we know.
In all external grace you have some part,
But you like none, none you, for constant heart.

from Sonnet 58,
William Shakespeare

The next day I received a very strange letter from a stranger source addressed again only to me.

October 10, 1893

Messrs. Marc Fortier, Marc Fortier, Jr., Roger Fortier, et Eugene Travers

67 David Street

New Orleans, Louisiana

  Miss Sara Gilley

  Raven Lea, Virginia

  My dear Miss Gilley:

  Please be advised that you have placed yourself in jeopardy of being named as a defendant in an alienation of affections lawsuit considered by Mme. Joseph Thierry of New Orleans Parish, Louisiana. You are advised to cease corresponding with her husband, M. Joseph Thierry, who currently resides in Washington D.C. Mme. Thierry is reluctant to bring this action given, from what we can gather, your general inexperience.

It is Mme. Thierry's wish that she and her husband be reconciled and reunited. Mme. Thierry believes that due to a fanciful notion M. Thierry has that he is your personal savior, M. Thierry will not consider reconciliation with her so long as you are receptive to his attentions. Please understand that an alliance with you is harmful to his ambition for a U.S. congressional seat in the December election. As you are no doubt aware, the fact that you are negro eliminates the possibility of a more permanent connection between you and M. Thierry in either Louisiana or Virginia.

If you break all connections, either by correspondence or in person, with M. Joseph Thierry, Mme. Thierry will abandon the idea of an alienation of affections lawsuit against you.

Very truly yours,

Marc Fortier, Jr., écuyer

If this was meant to intimidate me, it succeeded. When I wasn't shaking because of this threat, I was moping with my guilty conscience gnawing away at my self-respect. How *dare* I give my sister advice? Here I was, never having been more than 30 miles from where I was born, cooking for a family who liked my cooking fine, but for the most part didn't give two figs about me as a person - well, Maybe Mr. Robert and Miss Ivy did, but the rest? Well, maybe Lucy, Minnie and Andy also.

I was engaged in a morally questionable and evidently *legally* questionable relationship with *a married man* who seemed to have neither ambition to divorce a woman he and Clay both described as evil, nor to marry me as he continually hinted. Rhi had moved on and up in just a month of leaving us. Already she had experienced more than I might in my entire life. I had no experience to support any advice I might give her, and certainly no ethical high ground from which to preach. I saw myself shamefully as a hypocrite.

But I had found in my short life that some action is better than wallowing in fear and self-loathing. So either out of jealousy, loneliness, frustration, fear, *or all four*, I wrote Joseph a bitter letter, telling a lie for what I thought was *a good reason*. I do not have to rely on memory for what I wrote as I got the letter back quickly enough.

October 20, 1893

Raven Lea, Virginia

Dear Mr. Thierry,

I want to thank you for your friendship and counsel the last few years - your letters have meant a great deal to a lonely girl. I have learned much about the inner workings of Washington D.C. politics from them. I have also learned much about prevarication, obfuscation, and smooth-talkers who would amuse themselves with poor, ignorant girls. You alone are not to blame. I accept and deeply regret my own sinful, vain behavior in allowing myself to be so gulled and, especially, for coveting another's husband.

I will no longer write to you as, against all hope, I have met a nice young man who is not comfortable with our corresponding, even though I have assured him there is no reason for him to concern himself about it. He has asked me to marry him, and although I have not yet given him my answer, I am inclined to accept. I beg you, for my sake, do not write to me again as it would only cause complications. I am so very sorry if any of my actions have prevented you from developing a more felicitous relationship with your wife. It is towards her that you should be addressing flowery sentiments.

Thank you for years of friendship, and, with all sincerity, I wish you success in your run for congressional office.

Regards,

Sara Gilley

I knew as soon as I left the letter at the post office that I had made a *terrible* mistake. I never imagined though what wrath would fall on my head because of that letter.

The first hint I had of repercussions came in a scathing letter from Clay.

October 31, 1893

Corsicana, Texas

Dear Daughter Sara,

I can only assume that missing your sister and too much hard work have caused you to develop a blister on the brain! By Jehosphet! Why have you written to Joseph Thierry telling him you are going to marry someone else? If I am wrong in thinking that there is no one else, please forgive me, but I have never known you to so much as look at another man.

I must blame Joseph himself partially for this. He should have told you months ago that he has filed for a bill of divorcement and a request with the Catholic Church for an annulment from Olivia Marie. He has tried diligently to keep this information from the newspapers, but it was not wise to keep it from you. A divorce can take a long time if it is uncontested, but Olivia Marie will see him bankrupted before she will agree. You know, of course, that everyone who still has any money, is keeping an eye on their bankbook these days. I presume that the Thierry Lines have suffered with this panic, too.

Joseph has a deposition in hand attesting that Olivia Marie had at least two abortions. This same maid also has given a deposition that she knows of at least one man who was present in Olivia-Maria's bed when she took chocolate in at 10:00 AM. 'Course the maid's word is questionable because Olivia Marie fired her, supposedly over a theft. Olivia Marie's own personal physician knows as well that she has had several abortions. He won't implicate himself in a crime by acknowledging that he knew it, and, of course, the old Voodoo witch won't put herself in jail to help Joseph. Still, I believe enough people dislike Olivia Marie and they will come forward with sufficient evidence. It may, however, take a while.

Olivia Marie might have been a very wealthy woman. More money came to her than Joseph had when they first married, but the Napoleonic Code in Louisiana gives him almost total control over what she has. Joseph was initially very lenient with her concerning money, then he became tight-fisted when he learned she was gaming for large stakes, and losing more often than not. She may well try to take more than half of his estate as she likely needs it. For the first years of their marriage Joseph hoped that she would relent and have a family, but, if anything, she became more hardened against the idea, fretting over her freedom, her figure, her health! Had he made her completely dependent on his generosity, she might have acceded to a divorce readily. The shame is that he wanted a family badly, but he was content to let her go her own way, creating no further scandal by asking for a divorce - until he met you. Olivia Marie is alluring to a certain kind of wealthy roué who will help her as long as she rewards him with her charms. This includes at least one of the judges who might hear the divorce proceedings if they come to trial.

Joseph is angrier than I have ever known him to be, and he has this election coming up very soon in addition to the fact that he has been working night and day on the Plessy case. The outcome of the case could decide the fates of colored folks for decades. He needs to be able to work without distraction. Go to town and send me a telegraph telling me that you are straightening this mess out!

I await your telegram, or failing that, your letter.

Disappointed, but affectionately, your step-father,

Clay

I had barely put Clay's letter away in my apron pocket when Vaz burst into the kitchen, dropping a bucket of shelled black walnuts on the big table and kicking at imaginary objects. He was flailing his arms around as he began pacing, "Sara, you are a *complete ass*!" he declared angrily.

I stepped farther back away from him, fearing he might strike me! He was behaving like a lunatic. I was just about to protest his name calling when he interrupted me and went on.

"What in God's name is *wrong* with you?" He blasphemed unapologetically as he poked his finger at me emphatically. "One of the *smartest men in the country* holds *you* in high esteem - a man who will soon likely be a U.S. Congressman - and you dismiss him as if he were an unsatisfactory servant! *Where in the world* did you ever learn such high-handed behavior? You're a *cook*, for God's sake!"

I didn't even try to act as if I didn't understand what he was talking about. "How did you learn this?" I demanded loudly, my own arms up in the air out of frustration. Nothing here was ever private!

"How do you think? Daddy wrote me. It seems Joseph sent him a telegram to ask him if there is another man in your life." Of course, Clay told his son, the spit of himself. Two of a kind they were!

"Damn it all, Sara, " I wondered where he had learned all this profanity as I stood there stunned, "You and I and *the whole damned world* know you don't ever meet a man you might remotely be interested in! You have no chance of doing so!" He was now circling me. I was penned in. I couldn't escape without an undignified struggle with my little brother who stood nearly a foot taller at 14, without his full growth, than I did at 20.

"Vaz, you calm down now!" I ordered, "*Who* do you think you are to use such language around me? Are you a *field hand or po' white trash*? Surely I deserve *some* respect from you!" I was beginning to cry and because I didn't want him to see me swamped in emotions, I pushed him gently, hoping he would let me go past him. He resisted.

All of a sudden it seemed his anger melted and he wrapped me in his long arms that were fast becoming muscular like a man's. "Oh, Sara, *I love you, you goose*! And most of the time I *respect* you! I'm sorry about the language." He didn't sound sorry, but at least the words came out of his proud mouth.

"This letter you wrote to Joseph has more to do with what other people might think about *you* than it has to do with any change in your feelings for him! I understand you might *rightly* be angry with him for not divorcing his harlot of a wife!"

"Who told you she's a 'harlot'?" I questioned, trying to clear my head.

He shook his head impatiently, releasing me from his embrace, "I can't remember *who*, for God's sake!" I looked sternly at him for cursing again. He grinned.

I told him between gulps of air, trying to stem the tears that my eyes could barely contain, "There's more that you don't know. Clay doesn't know, and Joseph certainly never heard of it from me!"

I walked to my bedroom door and motioned for Vaz to follow. In my battered small chest of drawers, I kept a few personal items under my under things, including Joseph's letters. I reached into the drawer and extracted the letter from Olivia Marie Thierry's attorney. I thrust it at him wordlessly. He took it and we both sat on the edge of my little sagging, virginal bed while he took the letter from the envelope and read. He re-read it, folded it, put it back in the envelope and then threw it across the room in utter disgust as he let loose a stream of blasphemy that I won't repeat. Finally he hushed. Then he did something I had not seen him do since he was a little boy and stepped on a yellow jacket nest. He cried.

My maternal instincts swelled up. "Oh, Vaz. Please don't cry, honey. Please don't cry." The tears were freely flowing down my face now as I pulled this big boy over onto my shoulder. "This will be alright. I promise you. Somehow, I'll work this out. I'm not afraid of that witch!" I bluffed.

"Ole Mammie taught me some things, to protect myself and to thwart others. God help me, I may try them!" My fingers were crossed and I looked upward to let Ole Mammie know I was sorry for the lie. Old Mammie was the last person who would *ever* perform black magic. It was a sin she said and quoted the Bible about not allowing a witch to live.

Vaz pulled himself up stiffly and promised me, "So help me, God, if anyone *hurts* you they'll have more than Grandma Callie's old magic tricks to fear!"

Now he scared me because he was far more capable of carrying out such a threat than the boy who helped rid us of Miz 'Becca.

"Vaz," I grabbed his arm, "Please don't do anything! You'll only make things worse! If Joseph will just be done with me, she will have what she wants. She won't hurt me or mine." I spoke sadly, my heart aching as it had ever since I mailed my last letter to Joseph.

"He's a good man, Sara, and you have sacrificed *everything* to raise us. *Everything!* You deserve to be happy. *Joseph* deserves to be happy! No one so wicked should be *allowed* to destroy your future and his!"

184

I shook his arm. "Stop talking like this. You scare me. I can't bear any more worry and misery right now. Please!"

He sat silently brooding for a minute then his countenance eased as if he'd decided something and his internal conflict was over.

"You and Joseph have deep affections for each other. Haven't you learned by now that life is too short? *'Gather ye rosebuds while you may. Old time is still a-flying, and this same rose that blooms today'...*" He didn't need to finish Herrick's poem. Vaz, Rhi and I often quoted poetry to one another.

"Are you saying that at 20 *my* rose is dying?" I demanded, puzzled at his mercurial change in demeanor.

"Not at 20, sweet Sister, but if you wait until both Nora and I are out of the house, I think Joseph may give up on you! There must be some lovely, cultured women in Washington D.C. who could give him a *fine* passel of brats." He laughed, knowing I was subject to jealousy where Joseph was concerned.

"Don't wait!" Vaz ordered. "He may get the idea that your love for us is greater than your feelings for him. Affection is too fragile." He stood and walked back into the kitchen. I followed.

"How is that you know so much at 14 about affection..." I started to kid him, but a horrible thought popped into my head.

"I hope you have NOT been dilly-dallying with that strumpet Maggie Pennington - because if you have I shall tell Ole Missus. Maggie and her daddy will be *gone* from this farm by tomorrow sunset!" I threatened.

"*Dilly-dallying.* Is that what you call it, my sweet high-minded Sara?" he goaded me. "My Lord, you have become quite a *termagant* of late, haven't you?" I looked puzzled. He poked me in the arm, "Look it up! Ah, ha! Got you with that one, didn't I?"

I gave him a good shove and started to leave the kitchen in annoyance. I no longer cared about my dignity.

He caught up with me, passed, opened the door to the hallway, holding it open for me, making a sweeping theatrical bow. With an impish grin on his handsome face, he taunted, "Maggie Pennington and I have been *dilly-dallying* for about six months. She *likes it*, and *I like it* even better! Tell Grandmother if you want. 'Young men will sow their wild oats,' was all she said to me about it!"

I huffed out of the kitchen, but I was trying hard not to laugh until I got out of his earshot. That was just like Ole Missus! If I'd been "*dilly-dallying*" with someone, she'd have me whipped at the cart's tail for fornicating even if it had not gone that far. It was the first time I'd laughed in two weeks.

A maelstrom of my own making was about to submerge me completely, but first little Nora had to have her say.

Sunday after church, Nora sweetly put her arms around my neck while I was sitting in Ole Mammie's rocker on the back porch mending clothes, sewing buttons back on, re-stitching loose hems. It was a beautiful Indian summer afternoon. Soon it would be cold and, if it was a normal winter, mostly gray, but right then the leaves were at their most vibrant with the sunshine on them.

"Sara, write Joseph back and tell him you told a fib. Tell him why you told it. He will forgive you. The two of you have been close for too long to give up now." She kissed my brow and smoothed a few stray strands of hair off my face.

"Nora, what I've been doing has been sinful. I must stop before it goes further. You are old enough to understand the commandments about covetousness and adultery."

She shook her head, saying, "As Andy might say, *hogwash*! Go to Washington now! Leave! Buy your restaurant! Don't wait another four years before you go! Grandmother and Uncle Robert will see that Vaz and I are okay. Miss Ivy is here. She keeps us out of trouble almost as well as you."

I shook my head sadly, "No, honey. It's too late. I think I destroyed everything between us. But what a sweet girl you are to tell me this. I love you *very much*!"

She kissed me again and said, "We love you very much, Sara. It's not that we *want* you to leave us. We just want to see you *happy*!" With that she turned and walked toward the front of the house where the family had gathered on the porch and lawn to enjoy the lovely afternoon.

About an hour later, Nora, Andy and his oldest sister, Minnie, came around to the back porch. The family would like a pot of tea and some cookies. They offered to help carry the necessary china, sugar, milk and cookies out front for me if I'd prepare the tea and bring it around when it was ready.

As I was carrying a heavy tray with the teapot, as well as the napkins the youngsters forgot, I was thinking what a nice idea it was to have tea outside on what was likely to be one of the last days we could do so. I had just rounded the corner from the back to the front when I heard a horse whinny just beyond the front gate. For a second I wondered who had come to visit this late in the afternoon. Then the gate burst open and in rushed Joseph Thierry looking as stormy as the devil himself might. I stood frozen for a second before I dropped the tray and started running for the steps toward anyone who would keep Joseph from killing me!

He caught me before my foot hit the first step, grabbed me by my shoulders and shook me violently. I thought my neck might snap. I think I moaned in pain or fear, and he put his arms around me, growling something in Cajun French, and kissed me so hard I thought I might die from the force of it.

"If you ever make me so much the misère again, I'll…" Joseph began

187

Mr. Robert stood up as quickly as his condition would allow and barked at Joseph. "*What the blazes* do you think you're doing to that girl? Let her go NOW!" He was trying to get to the steps, having to step over and around Mr. 'Zander and Miz Anne who seemed frozen.

Joseph never let me go, but he did take his mouth off mine, exhaling loudly. Then he burst into joyous laughter. "I don't intend to *ever* let her go, Sir! She's mine if I have to *kill* half the county to keep her!"

Ole Missus spoke up in her gruff voice, "Robbie. Sit down before you fall down - and please don't bark like an angry father! Have you gotten so *old* you don't recognize a couple of love birds?"

Mr. Robert had been the only one who even tried to defend me when he thought I was being killed. I wasn't going to let him be ridiculed for it. I spoke up with a smile so big I thought my face might crack.

"Oh, Mas… Mr. Robert. I thank you for coming to my defense, but I'm in *no danger* from Joseph." I wiggled an arm free from his arms which had mine pinioned, and I stroked his face - his bronzed face with fine lines around his eyes and new ones forming on his forehead. His face that I thought I would never see again. The ardent look he gave me caused me to drop my own gaze in embarrassment.

"Well, Mr. Thierry, what makes you storm in here acting like a *wild* man when you have been treated as a respected guest in my home before?" Mr. Robert demanded.

Joseph laughed again, but it was his old familiar self-deprecating laughter this time. "My sincerest apologies, Sir, to all of you, but *I think I have been a wild man* for the last week or so! This little dove has led me to believe since last I was here that she and I will marry. Last week…"

I put my fingers on his mouth gently to stop him from telling what I had done. My eyes begged him not to humiliate me by letting them know the lie I had told. He carefully removed my fingers from his mouth and put his mouth tenderly on mine. The next thing I knew, I was lying on a blanket under the lightening-damaged oak with Joseph waving a fan in front of my face and Miss Ivy handing him a decanter of brandy and a glass. She stooped down and picked up the book of poetry she and her beau-of-the-week had been reading as they sat on the blanket before I fainted. My brother and sister were standing over me with Nora looking white as a ghost.

"Nora, don't fret." Vaz told his sister. "She'll be alright. She's not been breathing or eating right for the last two weeks. She's got the best medicine for her right here in front of her."

Joseph glanced up at Vaz in appreciation for his support. "So she's suffered too?" He asked. Vaz nodded. "Good!" Joseph said gleefully, "I hope she suffered as much as I did, the little devil!" He began to pour a little brandy in my mouth. I drank it, but I made what was most likely a horrid face.

"No, Joseph," Vaz responded defending me. "*It's not good that she suffered as she has*! She wasn't trying to get your attention or get you down here from Washington."

"I know that much about her character, you young jackanapes!" Joseph protested. "But why *did* she do it?" he demanded.

"Not here. Not now." Vaz said lowly, "But she had good reason."

"I'm right here!" I said petulantly. "Ask me!"

"Then, why?" He started to pour more brandy and I shook my head violently.

"Now, dag nab it, girl! This one's for me! I've been travelling non-stop since yesterday! I may faint from hunger, weariness…"

I managed a giggle and said weakly, struggling to sit up, "Let's go to the dining room and I'll put out supper for all of us."

It seems Miz Anne was within earshot. "You'll do no such thing, Sara! Your sister and my girls can bring food to the dining room. Mr. Thierry is *always* welcome at our table, of course, but I expect he would much prefer to eat with you in the kitchen where you may speak privately."

Joseph laughed. "You are very gracious, Mrs. Powell, and, as always, perceptive. "He lifted me off the blanket over my objections, carrying me over one shoulder like a sack of potatoes. Everyone seemed to find this amusing as they headed indoors with the sun beginning to drop behind the western mountains.

"Joseph, you are hungry and weak! I can walk. Please put me down." I protested, wriggling.

Quietly, just for my ears, "I'm hungry alright, my sweet!" He smacked me gently on my backside, but he continued walking up to the kitchen porch and into the kitchen where he deposited me in a chair at the big table.

"Understand, Sir, that I will not be manhandled and physically abused!" I protested halfheartedly.

"Nor shall you be, mon amour. Did you really mind?" He leaned down and kissed my cheeks - both of them.

"I'm not sure you should be touching my backside, Sir. Nor kissing me in front of God and creation, but if your smack was intended in jest..."

He gave me an odd look, "Good God, girl, do you think I would ever strike you in anger?" He turned completely around, then put his hands on my shoulders, leaning down, his face near my own, "No one, and *I mean no one*, had better ever put an unkind hand on you. I would never hurt you."

I reached up and caressed his face, smiling at him, "I think I know that, Joseph.

We said a great many nonsensical, loving things to one another until Miz Anne, her daughters, and Nora came into the kitchen and assembled three platters to take into the dining room. They even prepared a separate one for Joseph and me. Nora quickly set the table for us and poured buttermilk into glasses at which Joseph laughed, telling her she needed to find a decent bottle of wine. Nora looked confused and I waved her toward the dining room.

"It's good, angel. Thank you. We have all we need." I said to her.

"Yes, mon ange, we certainly have all that we need!" I never knew whom Joseph was addressing, but his eyes never left my face.

We ate silently until we were full, only looking at each other and grinning foolishly like children on receiving a first puppy.

Finally Joseph pushed back from the table, patted his stomach, staring at me intently the whole time, "You are more beautiful than you were three years ago!"

I blushed and stammered some kind of a response, reaching out and touching his face softly. He took my hand in his and demanded, "Now what was all the *nonsense* you wrote me about? What happened to change you so suddenly from my sweet, uncomplicated girl to a little hornet with a vicious sting?"

I shook my head, resisting telling him about the letter, but Vaz made a timely entrance, although at the time I certainly did not think it so timely. Vaz looked steadily at me, "Sara, if you don't go get the letter, I will. He *must* see it."

I probably uttered an ugly word under my breath. I had learned a few of late from the blaspheming men in my life. But I walked directly toward my room with Joseph and Vaz following. I stopped them at the door, all of a sudden ashamed to let Joseph see my humble room. I could see the astonishment - and anger - on his face at what he had glimpsed from the doorway: my little bed that had once slept three and four of us at a time; the faded, but infinitely precious quilt that Ole Mammie and Momma put together one winter; my plain, scarred, straight-back wooden chair; my small bureau with a kerosene lamp; a basin and pitcher on it next to my hand mirror and comb; a few jars of cream and one of hair ointment all concocted by me took up the rest of the space; the portrait of Rhi, Vaz, Nora and me that hung over the bureau; my stack of personal books, always topped with a dictionary were beside the bed; my dresses, three for every day and one for special occasions hung from an improvised clothes line in one corner of the room; my two bonnets, one for every day, the other for church, were suspended by their ribbons from pegs on the wall. The room was clean and well-aired. It even contained a small vase of asters and mums on the rickety table by the bed, but...

"By the Almighty!" Joseph gasped. "You are not a slave, Sara!" he cursed.

Vaz had probably never looked at the room in the same way. He lived in it with me until he was almost twelve. He and Nora had charming rooms, small, but well-furnished with handsome spreads, curtains, wallpaper, rugs, bed, bureau, table, and easy chair.

Vaz was embarrassed, "You are right, Mr. Thierry. This old stuff should be replaced. I think it belonged to my Grandmother Callie and came down from her cabin when she and my mother did." He spoke quietly, but I knew it was not idly.

I turned quickly, angry because I was humiliated, speaking harshly, "These things, pitiful as they are, Vastine, are *my* property! They are my inheritance - all I have in the way of material goods from *my* family!" I only called him "Vastine" when I was completely irritated with him.

"Sara," Joseph spoke softly, "no one will ever dispose of your things if you want to keep them. And of course you want something to remember your mother and maw-maw with. But no one will ever allow you to live like a slave again either. That *I promise you this day*!"

I looked at him, my eyes full of tears. All I could do was nod. I went into the bureau drawer and took out the letter from Olivia Marie's attorney. We walked back into the kitchen. Once he sat down I handed Joseph the letter and Vaz came over and gave me a hug.

"Sara, I'm sorry. I just never saw the difference in how we are treated until now. This will be changed - and soon." Vaz promised.

"Vaz, I *am paid*. I could *buy*..." I began.

"Yes, I know, but you are saving money for a business. Anyway, this still isn't right." Vaz interrupted.

"I am not Clay's child." I stated simply. "I am the child of two former slaves."

"Daddy calls you his step-daughter. He needs to do more for you!"Vaz declared.

Joseph held up a hand, "Very soon now, no one will need to do anything for her. I intend to take care of her and very well at that. *Very well indeed*. But let me read this without distraction, please."

"No one needs to *take care of me*!" I blurted out. "I have so little in there because I have been saving my earnings to open a restaurant. I can provide for myself!"

Joseph took my hands in one of his, "Ma belle, you have told me this in your letters. We have discussed it to death! There is no more to say. Certainly you will open your restaurant and you can stand independently and freely on those little feet of yours, but that will be because you *want to. Not because you have to*." He kissed my hands then took the letter from the envelope.

Vaz left the room and Joseph read, then reread the letter. Finally he put the letter back into the envelope, walked over to the kitchen stove, lifted a cover on the cook surface and threw it into the dying fire. I gasped out loud.

"Why did you do that?" I demanded, hastily trying to retrieve the letter before it became ashes. He grabbed my hand just as I was about to stick it into the fire box.

"I did that, my sweet, because you need have no fear of a lawsuit. Olivia Marie is desperate because I have filed for both a divorce and an annulment. And…" He seemed to hesitate, "Marc Fortier the younger, is dead. An angry husband called him out a week ago. The cocksure fool actually accepted a duel - illegal as it is - with one of the finest marksmen I ever met. Frank DeLonghi shot him straight through the heart, I'm told. The only reason DeLonghi is not in jail is that he fled the country on one of our ships bound for Ocho Rios, Jamaica."

"Fortier's father and other law partners know that I am fully willing to make it known that Junior also dallied with my wife for some time. It was long after I didn't give a da… I no longer cared who she populated her boudoir with, but I've kept evidence and have a witness. They want no more scandals if they are to keep any kind of reputation among decent folk in New Orleans." Joseph picked me up and walked back to the big table. He sat down with me on his lap.

I tried to stand up and he gently pulled me back. "Joseph, I don't think this is proper…"

"Are you unhappy being close to me?" He queried.

"Oh, no! But I don't think Ole Missus would like it. It is *her* house!""

"She didn't make a fuss about our kissing outside." Joseph's remark was true! When I thought of it I was shocked that she hadn't.

"I wonder why…" I started to question her acceptance of the open show of affection.

"Now enough arguing! Are you going to be the kind of wife who questions everything her husband says?" He laughed, kissing the back of my neck.

He explained that he had to leave the next afternoon for New Orleans, then Baton Rouge. Judge Ferguson's ruling in the Plessy case had been upheld by the Louisiana Supreme Court in January. Judge Albion Turgee and Samuel Phillips were planning to ask the U.S. Supreme Court to hear the case. They wanted two things from Joseph: that he help draft their arguments before the high court and that he run for office as a representative from Louisiana in an attempt to moderate the racial climate there. Just that year there had been more than 100 lynching's of black folk in the U.S., and one-third of those had been in Louisiana!

"I promise you, mon cœur, this case is the only thing that would cause me to leave you so soon. I want you to move to Washington after the first of the year."

"I won't commit adultery, Joseph, not even with you." I answered resolutely, shaking my head side to side. "And if you win this election, the whole world will soon know about me if I'm in Washington!"

"Little rabbit! So skittish! I just want you nearer where I can see you often. Rob can help you find a suitable location for your restaurant and you can live with him and his wife until we marry."

"Rob is getting married on the 1st of January. I certainly *will not* move in with him while he's still a newlywed!"

"So delicate in your niceties, my sweet!" He laughed.

"Don't make fun of me, please." I begged softly, knowing that as poor as I was, living as I did, most people expected no niceties of any kind from me. Subservience, yes, but not society manners.

He looked stunned. "Sara, I didn't mean to offend you. Sometimes I forget that you don't see yourself as my social equal and that you are so thorny and insecure about your own grace." He kissed my hands separately. "You are a *far* better person than I am, my dear. I would live with you married or unmarried. I would take you away with me today. I

195

would even lose this December election to keep you by my side! So you see, you observe the social proprieties for us both in this matter!"

I laid my head against his chest and listened to his heart for a minute before speaking again. "What *about your campaign for congress*? A divorce is enough of a handicap. Marrying a colored woman will finish any chance you might have in using your position!"

"Let me teach you how to make proper coffee," he said lifting me off his lap. "I need to think with a cooler head. I can't think of much with you quite so near!"

And so he left the next afternoon. We were unsure when we would see each other again.

CHAPTER 12: CHRISTMAS AT RAVEN LEA

I looked and saw your heart
In the shadow of your eyes,
As a seeker sees the gold
In the shadow of the stream;
And I said, "Ah me! what art
Should win the immortal prize,
Whose want must make life cold
And heaven a hollow dream?

I looked and saw your love
In the shadow of your heart,
As a diver sees the pearl
In the shadow of the sea;
And I murmured, not above
My breath, but all apart, -
"Ah! you can love, true girl,
And is your love for me?

Dante Gabriel Rosetti

Rhi arrived home late the afternoon of the 23rd of December 1893. Gone was my sweet, shy younger sister. How had she disappeared so quickly? Her attitude towards me seemed aloof, even superior. Even Ivy noticed and winked at me once as if to say, "Don't mind it."

Later as Violet and I were behind the summer kitchen dressing the eight rabbits we were having for dinner, Ivy stood with us. Ivy said, "Don't fret, Sara. She may act like this *for another six months*, then she'll be our sweet unassuming Mariah again. Wait and see. By the time she's 25, she'll be more like you *than you are*! Sometimes I think I must be standing in Mother's shadow I'm so like her!"

We had barely gotten the kitchen cleaned up after dinner, and were already working on the rabbits. Ivy asked how we could stand to work in such cold. I gave her a look that clearly must have said, "Because we have to." She laughed at herself for asking. Even dressed out, the rabbits were heavy this year. Ivy carried half and I carried the other four as Violet took the waste to the compost pile near the refuse dump.

Two big geese were hanging by their feet from the eaves of the summer kitchen next to the haunch of venison. We had cleaned the geese after breakfast, and Violet's brother, Carl Thomas, had delivered the venison, dressed out. He had shot the deer the day before. Generously, he had divided the deer five ways among the folks on the hill and the Big House. That was his gift to each of us. The geese were for Christmas dinner on Monday, and the deer was for Christmas Eve. Rob was bringing a bushel of oysters to roast on Christmas Eve. He, his fiancé, her mother and brother were arriving later in the afternoon, which was why we needed so many rabbits.

Rhi and Nora were in the house unpacking Rhi's things and making up beds for the coming company. Ivy and I walked into the kitchen and washed our hands. Ivy began to make mulled cider, using some of the oranges Mr. Robert had shipped up from Florida every Christmas. Every year at Christmas, Mr. Robert gave each of the families, or parts of families, still living on the farm a turkey, a cured ham, a large bag of oranges, a large bag of hard candies, a fruitcake that I had made in September, a gallon jug of apple cider, and $25. At one time that must have been an expensive undertaking for him, but now there were only four families living on the hill and two tenants.

The two tenant farmers lived in small houses on the farm and one of those farmers was George Avery, a black man with a large hard-working family. They lived on the other side of the hill from where the slave cabins stood. Mr. Avery and his family took care of the livestock, except for the hogs, milked the dairy cows, saw to the sheep, the goats, the chickens, and the dairy barn. The farm produced enough milk and butter to sell most of it. The Avery's were good at what they did.

The other family was white and included the infamous Maggie Pennington. They lived across the road and east of the Big House. The Pennington family tended the vegetable gardens and the orchards in the summer, slaughtered, smoked and cured the hogs in late fall and early winter and mostly sat on their backsides, the best I could tell, from mid-December until late March or early April. Mr. Robert was satisfied with their work, so maybe he thought they earned a few months of rest. I always thought they were shiftless and could have been earning a few extra dollars doing something in those months had they tried. Slopping hogs was not a great deal of work!

After bringing the rabbits in, I kneaded the dough that had been rising since dawn, adding fruit and nuts. Joseph had asked one of his numerous sisters to send me a recipe for Three King's Cake. It was different than what we usually had for the Holidays and it sounded delicious. His sister, Genivee, told me in her letter that she made a colorful variation of the cake for Mardi Gras as well. Sounded to me as if Cajuns liked any excuse to celebrate and eat! I didn't think I had any recipes for food that could equal hers since she was a grandmother of six already, but I did send her a couple of my balm and restorative recipes.

Vaz and Andy stomped the mud off their feet on one of the back steps before dragging a load of pine limbs onto the porch. Miz Anne had them gathering greens for garlands to go around the doorways and the front stairs. They took off their wet, muddy boots on the porch and came into the kitchen. Their hats, mittens and coats landed on Ole Mammie's rocker as they hurried to the big kitchen range to warm up cold fingers and toes.

"Oh, Ivy," Vaz said enthusiastically, putting his cold hands on her shoulders as she continued working on the cider, "how did you *know* I was *craving cider?*"

She pushed his cold hands away, "Vastine, you are perfectly horrid! Now *I'm frozen too!*" she protested laughing.

I looked at the boys. Both had red, chapped cheeks from the cold and wind. I wiped my hands and went into the pantry to get some balm for their cheeks. When I returned Rhi, Nora, Laurie and Minnie were in the kitchen too. Nora, seeing a job that needed doing, picked up the boys' wet things and hung them to dry behind the stove on a line we put up for just such things.

"Oh, boys," Mariah said in such ladylike fashion, "you smell wonderfully of evergreens!'" She peeked out the window at the branches. "It appears that you brought a forest home."

"Ah, Rhi, cut it out!" Vaz said, impatient with her posturing.

"If you would put this on your faces *before you go out*, you wouldn't end up in such sad shape." I waved for Andy to come to me so I could put some of my honey/honey locust blossom/aloe balm on his cheeks. I knew better than to ask Vaz first as he would likely be so uncooperative as to dissuade Andy from accepting any. I dipped my fingers into the salve and gently dabbed it onto Andy's red cheeks.

"Ooh!" he responded in relief. "That feels so much better." He gently touched his cheeks, "But it's sticky, Sara."

I had always asked the children to tell me what they thought of my potions so I could improve them, if possible. They were very free with their comments, most of them criticisms!

"In another fifteen minutes you won't notice the sticky, and your cheeks will be healed by tomorrow morning if you'll let me put a tiny bit more on later."

I waved to Vaz as Ole Missus came through the door, tapping her cane. "Your turn, young Lochinvar!"

"*O young Lochinvar is come out of the west, Through all the wide Border his steed was the best…*" He would have theatrically recited the entire Scott poem if I hadn't shushed him by dabbing salve on his chapped lips.

"Good Go... Goodness sakes!" He changed his statement seeing his grandmother in the hall doorway. "Sara, can't you make this stuff a little less *sissy smelling*?" He complained ducking in an effort to escape the last dab that I smeared playfully on his nose.

"A thank you would suffice." Mariah instructed her brother haughtily.

Vaz gave her a scathing look. "Well, *I do thank her*, but it stinks like a whor... It stinks!"

"What, my dear brother," whose language had become *far too salty for my taste* of late, "would you like it to smell of?" I was poking him gently on the arm. "Horse lather? Cigar smoke? Ambeer?"

Miz Anne and Mr. Robert came into the kitchen about the same time that Vaz lifted one arm and sniffed pointedly at his armpit, "No. Sweet Sister, *sweat*!"

We were all laughing, even Rhi despite her new found dignity, when Mr. 'Zander came in from the dining room carrying two chairs, one under each arm.

"Oh, Alexander," Miz Anne said, "you're joining the party! Good. These two jokesters," she pointed to Vaz and me, "are entertaining the lot of us!"

"Let's adjourn to the dining room where there is more space." Miz Anne said.

"Ah, Mama! I'm frozen! It will take that room an hour to warm up enough for me." Andy complained, turning his face to the kitchen stove now that his backside was warm.

"Alright son," Mr. Robert answered for his daughter-in-law, "You and Vaz help your daddy bring in a few more chairs and we'll all crowd in down at this end of the table so Sara still has some work room. She wants to hear her sister's adventures and I can tell by the harried look on her face that she has a great deal of work still to do."

201

"Laurie, Minnie, get some plates and napkins and bring them in here." Ole Missus smelled the cider now, "And you'd better get some cups as well." She turned and looked at Violet, one of the few times I ever saw her do so, "Girl, do you know where the fruitcake is kept?"

Violet had been turning her head first to this one, then to that one, trying to keep up with the conversation. She had a ludicrous grin on her face. She was so happy to be in the middle of it all!

Violet nodded an affirmative to Ole Missus. "Then bring it out here on a platter with a good sharp knife. My son never seems to have enough fruitcake. Just like his father." I nodded my chin and looked at Ole Missus pointedly.

"Please, dear." Ole Missus added more gently. It hadn't been long since I had a conversation with Ole Missus about being gentler with Violet instead of alarming her.

"You've told me a *hundred times*, Miz Powell," I had said to her, "that you can catch more flies with honey than with vinegar." My voice was sweeter than I wanted it to be, but the same adage worked with Ole Missus, too. "That's especially true of Violet. If she thinks you like her, if you're kind to her, *she will work like a beaver*. Otherwise she is almost too frightened to move."

That was the beginning of the best Christmas I ever had at Raven Lea, although I have rarely worked as hard before or since.

Before supper the crowd that now included Rob and his company took two wagons out across the fields. Mr. Robert had chosen a full red cedar that he thought was perfect for this year's Christmas tree and they were all headed to cut it and bring it home. Even Rob's future mama-in-law bundled up and went with them. Only Ole Missus, Rhi, Violet and I remained at home, and Ole Missus was napping in the rear parlor. She looked so frail now, sitting in her easy chair with a wool blanket across her lap. She napped mid-morning and mid-afternoon these days. Her heart was wearing out. I crossed the room, stoked the fire as quietly as I could, and adjusted the blanket around her legs more firmly.

"You are a good girl, Sara. Thank you. I need to talk to you soon." She whispered, never opening her eyes, as I left the parlor. She was 89 years old. It was the last Christmas that she participated in the festivities downstairs. Until her death four years later, she was in her room either on her sofa or in her bed, or, on a really warm day, sitting in the wicker chair on the upstairs porch. She was unable to navigate the stairs and unwilling to be carried up and down like a heap of dirty laundry, she said. She almost always complained of being cold.

When I returned to the kitchen I found Rhi there alone opening oysters. She looked over at me with tears in her pretty, dark-fringed eyes.

"What's wrong, sweet girl?" I asked, truly concerned. I had not known Rhi to cry since Miz 'Becca hit her, not even when she left for school.

"I wrote you that I would tell you about Thanksgiving when I arrived for Christmas. I wanted so badly to be home, but it wasn't long before Christmas vacation and my friend Rohan Clarke's family was coming from New York City to Oberlin for the Holiday. He asked me to meet his mother, father, and sister. I was to have dinner with them the evening before the Holiday and again the next day. I was so excited because it meant Rohan thought me special enough to introduce me to his family." She sighed heavily, looking down at the hand she had gouged hard with the oyster knife. It was bleeding. I took her hand, washed it and tied a clean dish rag around it as I led her over to Ole Mammie's rocker.

"Did you enjoy your dinners?" I asked, trying to smile. Something had gone badly for her.

"Oh, the food was probably excellent and Rohan's family was civil, but completely cold in their demeanor toward me. I don't think they knew I was so light-skinned! I never expected to be disliked because I am *too white*, Sara!" She whispered.

"On the walk home from the hotel back to my room, I asked Rohan if he had told his parents that I was a light-skinned girl. He said he had, but he probably had not prepared them well for how light I am. Oh, Sara," she broke into sobs, "I am the same person regardless of the shade of my skin! Why must people be so... so..."

"Bigoted." I supplied the word harshly. "What has Rohan said after this?"

"Well, I sent a note Thanksgiving morning claiming illness - which was actually true because I had not slept at all the night before and I cried most of the evening, so I did not meet them again. She looked down at her drenched, twisted handkerchief.

"Later the next week Rohan and I talked. He said that his parents have done so much for him that he cannot go against their wishes in the matter. They think a relationship between us would create many problems. People see me as white while he is a handsome dark color. They said they have no idea what children of such a union would look like or how they would be treated." She continued to twist her handkerchief. "His parents immigrated from Jamaica and began a laundry business in New York when Rohan was four. They live above their shop and work over 12 hours a day, six days a week so he and his sister can go to college and have decent lives."

"All that may be true, but if you care enough about one another..." I began.

"Evidently he doesn't care that much about *me*!" She exclaimed. "I said we would be better off not to see each other again except in passing, that seeing each other could just cause us pain. To my great dismay, he agreed *readily* and has been seeing my darker roommate, Cassander Hall. They seem to do very well together, but Cassander is so haughty about her relationship with the *handsome Rohan*!"

"Forget about him, Rhi. He doesn't have enough courage to deserve you! You are the most loyal person I know. Rohan is not! You'll meet five or six nice men before you decide on the right one." I counseled.

"Oh, Sara, I hope you are right, but I really, really liked him. He is *handsome*. He's intelligent. He's funny, and, oddly enough, in some way, I hold him in high esteem for the respect he gives his parents.

I threw a clean dish rag to her. "Oh, hush up, Rhi, and let's get back to work!" I was annoyed with her sentimentality over the unworthy Rohan.

Rhi, Nora, Laurie and Minnie kept the house clean and tidy over the next several days and helped get food to the dining room. Ivy helped me in the kitchen, though she was really no hand at cooking. She could ladle food onto platters and into bowls. She could put pots into water to soak. I had insisted that Violet take her usual Sunday off and, of course, Christmas Day. I am sure that she would much rather have been with us at the Big House, but I insisted that she be treated with respect. If I was going to leave them next year, they needed to begin to treat Violet the way I believed she should be treated.

After breakfast was cleared and the dishes washed on Christmas morning, I wrapped up warmly and took my gifts up to the families on the hill. I gave each of the men and boys two pairs of socks that I had knitted and a muffler that Nora had knitted. I gave the girls and women each a sweater. Rhi had liked hers so well that I decided these women would enjoy being in the forefront of a new fashion as well. Nora knitted mittens for each of them. I gave Violet a sweater, too, but she was special to me, so I also gave her a pair of small gold earrings. She could have used new shoes, a new coat, all sorts of *practical things*, and the earrings really took a chunk out of my bank account, but I intended Violet to have something special for once in her life.

"Carl Thomas, I can't thank you enough for that piece of venison. That must have been a *big deer*!" I said, shaking hands with him as I went inside the cabin.

"Yes'um. It was a *nine-pointer. I never seed such a buck in my life*! I had to field dress it just to git it home!" Carl Thomas was so proud.

"Did you go back and get the antlers?" I enquired, showing enthusiasm that I didn't really have, but I knew it mattered to him.

He nodded to a place in the corner of the cabin on the plank floor he had installed last year. Over the last few years, Carl Thomas had added a loft for his own sleeping quarters, re-chinked all the logs to make the cabin warmer, put down the plank flooring and tanned several skins from slaughtered cattle to use as floor covering. He had made three wonderful chairs out of wicker and devised a better fireplace for his mother to cook in. He was a wonder. He did most of the carpentry for the Big House, but he could have made a great deal more money if he had access to a larger market for his services.

The antlers were impressive. Carl Tomas was a big man and he could've stood between the forward forks of the creature.

"Oh, my! The antlers alone must weigh… "I said with new respect

"Bout 20 pounds I reckon. On Massah's scales down at the barn, that buck weighed 160 pounds dressed out! I had to create a rough sled out in the woods and hoist him onto it. I borrowed a horse from Massah Robert and dragged him home 'cause I couldn't carry him on my shoulders and I couldn't get a wagon into that thicket neither."

"Did you get any more deer this year?" I asked.

"Yes'um, two, but they tweren't nothing compared to this one." He dropped his head, embarrassed now at his enthusiasm.

I turned to Violet, "How brave are you, Violet?" I teased gently as she opened the box with the earrings. She was grinning from ear to ear. "We'll have to put holes in your ears now, you know!"

As I left, Aunt Cornelia, Carl Thomas and Violet's mother, walked me to the door. There were tears in her eyes. "I hear you planning to marry that good-lookin' feller frum Louisiana and move to Warshington. I reckon now it mus' be so 'cause you just give my gal a gift to remember you by. Look at her face! She ain't *never* had such a fine gift. I thank you, Miss Sarie. What that family goin' do without you, I' like to know!"

I hugged her with tears in my own eyes, "Merry Christmas, Aunt Cornelia. God bless you!"

As I started down the path to the next cabin, Aunt Cornelia called out. "Sarie, I want to give you something to remember *us* by, but I hain't got much in the way of cloth right now. If you can git me some scraps o' cloth, I be right proud to make you one o' my quilts."

She was known to do beautiful work. "I'll get you a box of fabric right after the Holidays. Oh, I can't wait to see what you do!" I called back. She waved and went back inside.

I walked on, finishing my deliveries. I had never spent very much time with the folks on the hill, not because I didn't like them, but because I had so little time. It was a painfully sweet morning for me because I expected this would be my last Christmas on the farm. Those folks were simple people, *honest in their very simplicity*, loving and "*real Christians, not just ones as say so,*" as Ole Mammie would've phrased it.

Amazingly, each of the families had a gift for me, too - a beautifully detailed male cardinal carved out of cedar, stained with pokeberry juice and with two small shiny black rocks set into the wood as eyes. The Carter girls had crocheted a set of four doilies for me, and Junior Dickenson had crafted a bone handled carving knife and matching serving fork to give me. I couldn't imagine where he got the steel. I knew he was a wonderful blacksmith, could do practically anything with metal, but I didn't know he excelled at carving too. The knife handle had a stag carved into it and the fork had a swan. I don't know where or when he ever saw a swan. There were certainly none around us then.

I had taken two large Christmas puddings, the ingredients for which I had paid, to the tenant farmers before church on Christmas Eve. I thought by doing that I could get back earlier on Christmas morning, but each of the families on the hill wanted to know if it was true that I was leaving, when was I leaving, and a dozen other assorted questions. I didn't think anyone except the immediate household knew of my plans. All the children, black and white, went to school and could read, so I began to think someone had *my business printed in the local newspaper*!

Thankfully Ivy and Miz Anne had corralled all the girls to help in the kitchen. Rhi knew best what needed doing, and I think she enjoyed being in charge until I returned. I had put the geese into the oven before I set out to play Santa Claus, but the remainder of the oysters from the evening before needed to be chopped, onions and carrots needed dicing, cream needed to come from the dairy, and at least fifteen to twenty other details needed attending in order to finish dinner.

When I rushed in around noon, there the five of them, Ivy, Rhi, Nora, Minnie and Laurie, sat around the kitchen table drinking more cider, but I could smell that things were progressing well without my expertise. "Oh my heavens, ladies," I playfully bowed, "You've been busy!"

It had begun to sleet, so I was hoping Miz Anne's mother, sister, and brother-in-law would decide to stay home. Laurie giggled as she told me that her grandmother's wig went askew as she was trying to take her hat and muffler off when they arrived about an hour earlier. That meant they'd be staying overnight since the weather had turned bad. That many more for breakfast tomorrow! I was running out of steam.

"You should have seen her!" Minnie, the youngest of Miz Anne's children, giggled. "The wig slid down over one eye and she looked like Ollie Dickens when he's been drinking!"

"How, young lady, do you know what Ollie Dickens looks like when he's been drinking?" Ivy asked her niece sternly.

Minnie blanched. Her mother might take a switch to her if she knew what she'd just said, making fun of the poor old soul.

"Oh, for heaven's sake, Ivy," came Nora's gentle little voice, "*even I* know what Ollie Dickens looks like when he's drunk, and I never go anywhere! He's always drunk!"

Everyone of us, except Ivy, laughed both at Nora's comment and the images of Miz Law's red wig and poor old Ollie staggering up and down the road as he peddled his lineaments and potions.

Ivy put her hands in front of her, composing herself so as not to sound angry. "I just want to tell you girls something you most likely don't know. Ollie Dickens *was a doctor* for the CSA. He worked in the Andersonville, Georgia prison camp. He saw men die from diseases that could have been avoided by good sanitary practices and sufficient food. CSA leaders expected there would be ready food there. Well, cotton doesn't make a nutritious diet and that was mostly what they grew in large quantities that far south."

She continued, "Dr. Dickens was captured himself before the end of the War. The Union officers didn't trust him with most surgical tools and supplies, but they *trusted him well enough with a saw to remove the limbs of wounded Rebel soldiers!* Dr. Dickens came home with a broken limb himself that *never healed correctly.* That is one of the reasons he stumbles so badly. That leg and his back have pained him ever since he came home, almost 30 years ago. He refused to ever practice medicine again after what he had seen *and done* in the War." She sat quietly, morosely, totally unlike herself.

"His wife, our *cousin, by the way*, left him *during* the War, allowing his farm to fall into total ruin! If Dr. Dickens drinks too much - well, the fact is, *he does drink too much*, but I'm not the one to *judge him*, and *you* are not ones to *ridicule him*!"

She got up to leave the room, turned around and said, "Ollie Dickens has been like an uncle to me all my life. Please, be good enough to *say a prayer* for the old fellow!"

We were all shamed into silence. About this time, Vaz and his shadow Andy came into the room. "What's the matter with Ivy?" Vaz puzzled, "She just passed us as if she didn't see us *and* she was *crying*."

Rhi told them about what Ivy had said. "Oh, Lord!" Vaz said, "I'm glad I wasn't in here as she would've combed my hair with a pitchfork! I know several really funny stories about old Ollie and I'm sure I would've started telling them."

Mariah stood up quickly, "I have an *excellent idea*! Let's ask Grandmother if we may ask Mr. Dickens… Dr. Dickens, for dinner. We're not eating today until 3:00 are we, Sara?"

"Yes. Rhi, I think that is an excellent suggestion. If she allows it, Vaz and Andy, hitch a horse to a carriage and ask Ivy and Mr. 'Zander - or Ivy and someone reasonably in *charge around here*, to go invite him. Girls, I need the best linen on the dining table and several sprigs of holly up and down it. Will you set the table with a place for one more, please? I doubt Dr. Dickens is in any condition to come, but…" I went to put chestnuts and sweet potatoes in the oven and to baste the geese.

Vaz drove the carriage for Ivy and Mr. Robert to Dr. Dickens' ramshackle house. Vaz said that Ivy and Mr. Robert were inside for what seemed ages. He and Andy had to drive the horse around several times as the wind and sleet were cold. Evidently Mr. Robert had helped Dr. Dickens with shaving and grooming. He said later that the old fellow wore his Civil War uniform as it still fit him and was the one presentable suit of clothing he had. Ivy took a wet rag to his shoes to clean the dirt off, even if she couldn't shine them.

They came back to the Big House about half an hour before dinner was served. Dr. Dickens bowed courteously to all the ladies, smiled sweetly at the girls and thanked his old friend, Mr. Robert, for remembering him that day. He did hobble even seemingly sober. I was glad that the children saw him having some difficulty walking. They needed to know that maybe the old man needed help instead of ridicule.

Mr. Robert handed Andy a bottle of his best bourbon to carry for Dr. Dickens.

"Son," Mr. Robert told Andy, "see that this gets safely to Dr. Dickens' table. Don't let him carry it. He may drop it and cut himself."

Vaz and Andy drove the doctor home. Vaz said the old fellow had only one small glass of wine while he was with us, so it was his guess the doctor needed to get back to his serious drinking in private. How Vaz knew that much about the needs of topers I never learned, but I expected that was how Maggie Pennington's father spent the long, dark winter days.

Mr. Robert and Ivy both told us after Dr. Dickens was being driven home that they were *thoroughly ashamed* for not thinking of inviting him every Christmas, but Ivy allowed if a lecture from her led to such thoughtfulness on the part of the youngsters, maybe she should lecture them a little more often.

Minnie, Laurie and Nora cleaned up the dining room. I had insisted that Rhi visit in the front parlor. She had worked almost from the minute she walked into the house on Saturday.

I shooed Minnie, Laurie and Nora out of the kitchen when the last of the dirty dishes, pots and pans were scraped and stacked higher than my head by the new wet sink Mr. Robert had put in when the water closet was added. They also put the leftovers away.

"Go! It's Christmas Day. Spend time with the family. You've been my Christmas angels for the last three days! I could never have fed all of us without your help!" I exhorted waving the backs of my hands as if to shoo them out. "And, *plea-e-e-ze*. Minnie or Laurie, or *both of you*, get your grandmother Laws *off the piano*. Evidently she has lost her hearing completely in the last few years!"

They giggled. I stood staring at the mountain of dishes. The floors of the kitchen and the dining room needed mopping. The back porch was covered in muddy footprints. The girls had not taken the scraps across the road and to the hog pens. I couldn't remember when last I *sat down* to eat anything. Clay's children ate in the dining room anytime they chose by then. I never had the convenience of doing so as there was always something in the kitchen that needed tending, and I'm sure that Miz Anne's family, and, likely, Rob's fiancé and her relatives would've been ill at ease with a negro at the table.

I'd been rising at 5 AM and collapsing in my bed at 11 PM or later for the last four, possibly five days. I was completely exhausted. Initially I thought that staying busy would keep me from missing Joseph so badly, but I had missed him every waking hour, and in the few dreams I remembered.

I wanted to collapse in Ole Mammie's rocker, cover my head with my apron and bawl! *This place was not my home*. My home was wherever Joseph Thierry was. For all the affection and gift giving we had experienced this Christmas, it held very little Christmas spirit for me.

Instead of crying, however, I stood and pulled on an old cape that I kept behind the stove and a pair of mittens. I picked up the heavy bucket of scraps and headed down the yard, across the road and up to the hog pens in the darkening twilight.

"This will be one good thing about moving to Washington," I thought. "No hogs to be slopped! Or I hope we won't have hogs anyway!"

Coming back, I could just barely make out the carriage back in its shed. The boys were back safely and I needed to remember to compliment Vaz and Andy for their thoughtfulness and generosity in delivering the toys yesterday for the children on the hill. Toys they bought, evidently, with their own money. I knew nothing about it until my morning deliveries, but, on reflection, it explained how all the black folks up there knew I was moving. My brother, the Town Crier!

By the time I got back to the house I was covered head to toe in snow. I slipped and fell in the freezing mud just as I got to the porch. There was a slick mess there where the boys had stood to make garlands. I kicked my wet shoes and stockings off at the door, but the floor was cold. I decided to wash up in the hopes that it would calm me down and help ease the ache in my shoulder and hip where I'd landed when I fell. I didn't expect it to help my heart, but it might help me to sleep. I picked up a tea kettle of hot water from the stove and started for my room just as Rob, Vaz and Andy came into the kitchen.

"We're washing up out here, Sara. Rob says he knows how as he did this for you a long time ago." I looked over at Rob and smiled. How very sweet of him to offer.

"Rob, *please* go spend time with your family. You are only here for such a short while. I appreciate it. I do, but I will take care of it."

"No, Little Sara! I'm helping. That way we can finish quicker and we can *all* get back to visiting." He looked around the room as if he were looking for something or someone.

"I sent your sister and nieces to the parlor to visit along with Rhi and Nora. All five of them have worked so hard for the last few days. They're good girls!" I explained the missing persons.

"They must be in the back parlor playing one of their new games. We didn't see them in the front. It's true, they've done well, but then *you did nothing*, did you?" Vaz teased.

"I don't have the energy to argue, Vaz, and I've changed my mind about you helping. I thank you sincerely if you will at least wash and dry the glasses and dishes and put the pots in to soak. I'm going to wash up a little and put some dry stockings on."

213

"Why are yours wet?" Andy asked.

"Hogs," was all I needed to say.

"Oh, Lord, Sara. I'm sorry." Vaz and Andy said almost in unison. "We told the girls we would take the scraps away!"

Vaz went to the back of the pantry where we kept the old tin tub my "children" and I had always used before the new bath was put in. It was still what I used. He dragged it to the stove, poured it about a third full of hot water and dragged it in to my bedroom. He lit a lamp for me and got a couple of gallons of cold water to add to the tub.

"Do you have everything you need in there, Sara? A towel, soap?" Vaz asked so considerately I wanted to pick him up and hold him on my lap as I did all too seldom when he was little. It was a time gone far too soon.

I was going to break out in sobs any second so I nodded and closed my bedroom door as I searched, blinded by tears, for clean under things, stockings and another dress. I happened to put my hand up to my now throbbing head and felt mud in my hair. Oh goodness. I'd have to sit in front of the fire half the night to dry my hair after I washed it!

I called out to the kitchen help, "Please stoke the kitchen fire for me, and if you would pull Ole Mammie's rocker over by the stove, I would be grateful." I could ordinarily pull that rickety rocker by myself, but tonight I was so tired.

"It's done right now!" Andy called back as I heard him sliding the chair across the floor and throwing wood in the stove.

I never knew anyone could have such a good time washing dishes! There were cries of "Oops!" "Oh, no you don't!" "Get away from me with that sopping wet rag!" and other general hilarity and scuffling. I never heard the crash of china or glass, but more than one pot clanged to the floor. I figured the floor would be wet from all the playfulness that was going on and I hoped one of them would mop it. That would at least partially clean it, although it needed a good scrubbing.

I must have fallen asleep in the tub because I awoke in cold water. The kitchen no longer emitted sounds of splashing, banging, dropping, and laughing. I got up stiffly, rubbing my hair gently with the towel I had wrapped around it after rinsing it the last time. I pulled another towel tightly around me, trying to wake up enough to find my under garments. I decided I was too tired to join the family in the parlor tonight, so I tossed the under clothing back on the chair and took out one of the pretty nightgowns Ivy had given me for Christmas. Miss Anne had given me a nice soft rose-colored wool robe this year and Teensy had knitted me house slippers in a color to match the robe. I used some of the violet-scented talcum powder that Vaz had gifted me with. It was a soothing scent, I thought as I pulled the gown over my head. I was afraid the slippers might be slippery on the wood floors as stockings can be, but Nora had sewn leather soles on them. How innovative! Mariah had given me hair ribbons and I found a white one, deciding not to try to braid my hair while it was still wet. I brushed my teeth, grabbed a quilt off my bed and went out to sit by the fire until my hair was almost, if not completely dry. The grandfather clock in the front hall chimed eight times. It seemed as if it should be midnight!

The dishes and glasses were no longer in the kitchen, so I opened the dining room door slightly to see if they were on the table. They were, meaning someone would need to sort them and put many of them away before breakfast.

"Oh, well," I sighed, "they did wash them and get them out of my way so I can start breakfast first. Violet will be down in the morning." I walked back to the kitchen and noticed that the pots had all been washed and put away where they belonged.

It was beginning to look as if I'd have to make hoecakes for breakfast to reward such great helpers. What nice young men! Their help was a Christmas gift indeed.

I sat down by the stove, with my head between my knees, running my fingers through my hair, separating it to help it dry quicker and with fewer tangles. I don't know when I leaned back in the rocker and drifted off again, but the next time I awoke it was due to a cold blast of air on my back. My first thought was who left the kitchen door ajar so it could blow open? I got up stiffly and turned to close the door. I thought I must still be asleep. I saw Joseph, stripping off his coat, hat and gloves and throwing them down on the end of the table. He was bent over, busy removing his wet boots when I cried out at the sight of him.

His head came up immediately and he kicked off the last boot. I ran straight to him, throwing my body against him, almost knocking him over. He picked me up, whirled me around and we kissed several times before we stopped for breath.

"Mon cœur! Ma vie! Mon amour!" He kissed me again, this time tenderly. "I have been trying to get here since last night! I was afraid I wouldn't make it before Christmas was over."

I stroked his face, as I loved to do. I whispered, "It's Christmas *for me now*! You are really here, aren't you?" I tugged lightly on his moustache.

"Ouch! Is that any way to treat a member of congress, cherie?" He pretended offense.

"No. It certainly is not! I do not want you to become another William Henry Harrison, dying days after you're sworn in!" I removed myself from his arms.

"I won't be sworn in until March, mon amour." He murmured trying to pull me back to him.

"This is not a matter to haggle over! Your stockings are wet, Joseph. You will catch your death! How long have you been so wet?" I began to put his wet things behind the range where they could dry. Then I led him to Ole Mammie's rocker, hoping it wouldn't break under any weight greater than mine. I gently pushed him down into the rocker, tugged off his socks, hung them on the arm of the oven door where they would dry quickly - if I didn't let them burn, and I wrapped his feet and legs in the quilt I had taken from my bed. I sat at his knees and laid my head on them, hugging his legs. He stroked my hair, lifting, letting it fall a few strands at a time.

"Do you know, this is the first time I've seen your hair loose!" He seemed in a dream state. "It's much too wonderful to keep in braids." He put a handful of my hair next to his nose and inhaled. "Oh, girl, I think you have put a *very big cunja* on me now!"

I lifted my face to kiss him when I heard his stomach growl, "Is that part of a cunja?" I asked, laughing.

"Of course," he answered at once, "When you've had a big cunja put on you, you waste away to nothing. *To nothing*!"

"What is a cunja?" I asked curiously.

"Don't tell me you don't know because you are an enchantress if there ever was one!" He laughed chucking me under my chin with one finger. "A cunja, my sweet, is a hex. A spell."

"Well I don't want you to stop telling me lovely things, but I do want you to eat." I stood up, but he grabbed my hand. I pulled slightly and he let go, laughing.

"I have no idea what was left after dinner. I had very good helpers this afternoon. They cleaned up everything!"

"Just as they should have done!" He stood, pushing the rocker back away from the stove, as we looked into the warming bin. "Aha! That was the wonderful fragrance I smelled on you. Goose and chestnut stuffing!"

I smacked at his hand as he was attempting to filch a slice of goose from the pan in the bin. "I do not smell of goose, Sir. I've just had a nice soak in a tub!"

I started to move around him to get a plate and silverware for him.

His arms were around me and he was nuzzling my neck, "Don't I know it? You smell so sweet I could eat *you* for dessert! Yum! Yum!"

I turned in his arms, "*You are the one who's put a cunja on someone!*" I declared as I tiptoed to kiss him, then snuggled against his chest. I could hear his heart *pounding* as he hugged me tightly to him. "Oh, Joseph, *one day* is too long without you. Six weeks was agony!"

"Then, *come back with me on Wednesday*. Olivia Marie has agreed, for considerable monetary compensation, to give me a divorce. We can be married *before next Christmas.*"

I was staring up at him thrilled at the news. I began to jump up and down as Vaz would have. "Oh, thank God! Thank God! That is *the best Christmas gift* I could receive!"

"Then you'll come back with me?" He asked hopefully. I shook my head "no" as I went to the dining room to collect a plate, silverware and a wine glass. He followed. I pointed to the decanter of my elderberry wine for him to carry back to the kitchen.

I put some of everything on his plate and poured a glass of wine for him. He sat down and ate like a starving man for the first few minutes. I took a good look at him. He had lost considerable weight in just six weeks.

"Joseph, have you been ill or just not eating right?" I was alarmed. I couldn't bear it if something happened to this man. God, please, no!

"Please, Sara, I'd love another one of those rolls. Girl, you make bread like no one else I know! Even my maw-maw never made such delicious bread!"

I gave him a roll and grabbed his socks just in time. I went back to him and began to put his warm stockings on his feet. He sighed heavily at the warmth against his cold feet, wiggling his toes in delight.

"No more digressions! Have you been sick?" My voice was harsh out of fear.

"Yes, sick for the love of you, ma belle."

"Don't 'ma' me this and 'mon' me that, Joseph! How much *weight* have you lost?"

"You are like a dog with a bone, non?" he complained.

"Non! I am not like a dog with a bone or without a bone! I'm worried!"

"Don't know," he mumbled with his mouth full of bread. He opened his vest to show me a pair of shoulder braces.

"All I know is that my pants would fall off if I hadn't resorted to these things! I haven't time to have my old pants taken in or new ones made!" He stared at me hard.

"When did *you* last eat? *Your face looks thinner.* I can't tell in that heavy dressing gown, but I'd say you haven't sat at a table to eat correctly in a week or more. I see some shadows under your oh so alluring eyes that I don't like either! Please sit down with me and *eat something.*"

"I've tasted this and tasted that for days." I was shaking my head. "I'm not hungry."

He didn't say a word. He simply pushed his own half eaten dinner away and pushed his chair back from the table. We stubbornly stared at each other for a full minute before I "humphed," giving in.

I placed a little bit of goose and a small spoon of sweet potato casserole on my plate. In the meantime, he grabbed a second wine glass from the dining room and poured it half full. He pulled a chair out for me, the first time in my life anyone had ever done so, and helped me to be seated. I felt like royalty.

We both started eating at the same time. To my surprise, I *wasn't hungry* - I *was famished!* Joseph and I both had seconds, including a small bowl of oyster stew.

"Oh, my dear," I said to Joseph laughing, "*I am sick now!* My stomach *hurts* from so much food!"

"That's too bad, ma chérie. No dessert, then?" He stood and walked to the cupboard where two covered cake plates stood. "Oh, this one is my very favorite - *pecan pie!*" He took the lid off the second, "Non, mon trésor! It can't be! *A Three King's cake!*" He looked at me with a raised eyebrow. "How do I decide? I love them both almost as much as I love you!"

I laughed, holding my aching stomach, at his antics. "Have a little of each, but I had better just have a cup of your delicious coffee if you will make some."

"Sacre cœur! I can only have a *little of each?*" He looked so downcast. I decided then and there that a really good attorney has to be as good an actor as my brother, possibly even better.

I was almost gasping for breath from laughing so hard, "Fine, if you must be a pig, have however much you can hold! If you eat like this when we are married *you'll soon become fat!*"

The look he gave me sent thrills up my spine, "No, my dove. I shall work off all excess food once you are completely mine!" He actually twirled his moustache in perfect villain's form!

We had evidently begun a tradition with my sitting on his lap while we drank our coffee. As always, it was delicious. While I was still on his lap he said, "I have a gift for you, mon ange, but I don't want a passel of Powell's traipsing through here while I am giving it to you. Are they likely to be in here soon?"

It must have been past 9 PM and the youngsters, at least, had to be hungry again by then. Just at that moment, Andy and Vaz opened the hall door. They took one look at us and started backing out.

Joseph beckoned them in. "You pair of young rapscallions, get food and take it thither. I have something I want to give to Sara in private. Where can we be private for half an hour?"

Vaz turned beet red. Andy was too innocent to think anything such as Vaz was thinking.

"No, you young scapegrace!" Joseph rebuked Vaz. "I may be dissolute, but even I am not about to have my way with your sister in *this house*! Can you keep everyone out of here for half an hour?"

"Yes, Sir, but wouldn't her bedroom be more private?" Vaz asked.

"Yes, it would, *but I am not allowed inside the temple*!"

Vaz turned red again.

"Oh, we can take the cider and the King's cake on a tray. The old folks are still too full to walk down the hall!" Andy declared.

"I have trinkets for each of you, but I want to give your sister hers first. Get your libations and be gone with you!" He was being very dramatic that night, almost as if he'd been drinking more than my elderberry wine!

"Oh," he stopped them as they were entering the dining room for a tray and cups, "be sure there's at least one more piece of that cake left. I've only had *one*!"

When the boys had finally collected enough food to feed an army, requiring two large trays, Joseph gently lifted me from his lap, rose and sat me in the chair again. He went down on one knee, took a small box from his breast pocket and handed it to me. I looked into his face questioning the significance of this new bit of theater.

"I can see that no one has properly asked you for your hand in marriage before." He smiled, opening the box for me. "I'm asking you now, my lady love. Will you be my wife as soon as may be? I realize I am asking a little prematurely as I do not have my divorce decree yet, but I expect it before the end of next year. Would you like a Christmas wedding?" He was entirely serious now as he took a ring from the box and put it on the third finger of my left hand. It was too big and he moved the ring to my middle finger. He kissed each of my hands in turn. I had been staring into his brilliant eyes, never having looked at the ring yet.

"Oh, yes! Yes! Yes! Yes!" I pulled his face to mine and kissed him.

Finally he pulled back and asked, laughing, "Well, are you *ever going to look at the thing*?"

"Of cour…" I gasped for breath. It was the most exotically beautiful ring I ever saw. The ring had a large square ruby surrounded by diamonds and mounted on what I then thought was silver. I later learned that the ruby was a rare 4-carat Burmese pigeon blood ruby surrounded by nearly flawless diamonds set in platinum. It was worth a small fortune and I could tell that even before I learned what it was!

I started to try to take it off, loudly exclaiming, "Oh my…" Then a terrible thought occurred to me. "Take it back! *Take it back*!" I was struggling with Joseph who was holding my hand, "You *can't afford…* You *didn't steal it*?" I asked in shock.

"Joseph, you didn't do something *dishonest* to earn the money? No! I won't keep it!" I was shaking my head 'No' violently. "Get your money back! You *take it back* as soon as you can and get your money back! We could buy a house - two houses - for what this ring must have cost!"

The whole time I was trying to get the ring off, Joseph was holding my hand. He finally pinned my arms to my side, lifted me up and whirled me around, laughing, "Well, I see that you don't *love me for my money*!" He exclaimed gleefully.

The hallway door banged open and in came, first Rob, followed by what seemed the whole family coming to see what the commotion was about. "What on earth's happening here, Joseph?" Rob asked. "You have managed to *wake the dead*!" He looked in back of him nodding at his father and grandmother who stood behind Mr. 'Zander, Miz Anne, ole Mrs. Laws, his own fiancé, her mother and brother, and God only knew whom! The dining room door flew open allowing the younger group in with Miss Ivy.

Still laughing, and giving me pecks on my cheeks, Joseph pulled my left arm free from his grasp and held up my hand to show them the ring.

"Oh, Lord in Heaven above!" Vaz blasphemed in front of the entire company. "Does Queen Victoria own anything as extravagant?" he demanded of Joseph.

"I don't know, son." Joseph answered him stoutly, "But your *sister does*! What do you do with a girl who asks you if you '*stole*' her engagement ring?" He whirled me around again and kissed me on the lips this time. "What a filly she is! There's not another one like her in the whole world!"

I heard Rob mutter, "And he would know!"

"Ah, he's lost his cotton-picking mind!" Andy informed the whole crowd, disappointed at Joseph's romantic behavior.

"No, son," Mr. 'Zander said giving one of his rare laughs, "he's just head over heels in love with our little Sara!"

"And he'd be *the biggest fool this side of the Rockies* if he weren't!" Mr. Robert said from the back of the crowd, "Look at that girl! She's a *beauty* - *and righteous* to boot!"

I lowered my head at that, embarrassed and ashamed by the compliment. There were certainly times when I was not righteous in my thoughts or my actions. Loving this man was most likely the biggest sin I'd ever committed, but I had hard thoughts about others *often*.

Miz Anne waded through the crowd, "Let me *see this ring* closely, Sara! I'm thinking someone needs to go shopping for my *next birthday*!" She looked teasingly at her husband.

"Can *you afford it*?" I whispered to Joseph. He kissed me long and hard in front of the entire room.

"Mon bébé. I can't afford not to! You are the *air I breathe*."

"Don't start that 'mon' stuff again! Can you *afford* it?" I was gruff, but my lips were against his throat.

"Yes, mon tresor. *Many times over*."

"Then *you lied* when you said you weren't rich." I scorned.

"Non. I was never rich in any meaningful way *until I met you*!"

After everyone had inspected the ring, Joseph insisted that we open the champagne he had brought along. He asked Miz Anne if her children could have a quarter of a glass. She relented, but it didn't matter. The children did not like the wine!

Someone remembered that Joseph was a newly elected congressman from Louisiana and the congratulations went on and on with much champagne drinking. There were a number of adults present. I believe at least six bottles of champagne were consumed in all. Even I had a quarter of a glass. I didn't care if they all became as drunk as Lords and Miz Laws had to be carried off to bed again. I was happier than I'd ever been in my life!

CHAPTER 13: MR. ROBERT TALKS TO SARA AND JOSEPH

To keep the song of the pain of parting
Alive in the memory,
Autumn in her dark skirt
Brought the red leaves.
Scattered them on the steps,
Where I said farewell,
Whence into the realm of shadows
You my consolation, fled.

from Drowsiness Returns Me,
Anna Akhmatova

After dinner on Tuesday, the day after Christmas, Mr. Robert asked Joseph and me to come to his office and let the younger folks clean up the dining room and kitchen.

"After all," he said, "it looks as if our Sara will be leaving us soon and we're not likely to find another cook who works as hard as you do, my girl."

He was smiling and I know he meant it as a compliment, but I could see the look on Joseph's face and I knew what he was thinking. From the scowl, Joseph was thinking they weren't likely to find another dogsbody to work seven days a week from before sunup until after sundown for little compensation. But Joseph didn't know that I *was* paid well, as cook's pay went in those days, and that Mr. Robert had promised me $500 when I left Raven Lea as an inheritance through him from Ole Mammie.

I put my hand on Joseph's arm and slightly shook it to keep him from saying something harsh to the rare adult member of that family who afforded me more than a small measure of respect. Joseph looked down at my face which was probably showing my concern. He patted my hand and said, "At your convenience, Sir."

"How about now? Sara, if you would just stick your head in the kitchen door and tell the young folks to clean up..."

We walked down the hall and into Mr. Robert's sanctuary. He locked the door behind us. "This is not a conversation for any other ears than yours, and if a question about the kitchen enters your brother's head, Sara, he will bounce in here with only a slight rap as he bangs open the door!"

Embarrassed by Vaz's imperious behavior, "I *have* tried to instill better manners..."

Mr. Robert waved a dismissive hand and laughed, "Generally, I enjoy the boy's open manners and lack of formality with me, but today, it wouldn't be suitable. Please sit." He waved us to the two armchairs near his big desk.

"Would you care for a cigar, Mr. Thierry?" Mr. Robert was rooting around on the cabinet behind him, moving objects until he could get to his humidor. "I have them brought up from Havana, probably on a ship of your line."

"I enjoy a good cigar, Sir, but Sara is not fond of the..."

"Please, Joseph. Have a smoke with Mr. Robert this once. Maybe if it's not too chilly, we could open a window slightly." Mr. Robert nodded and I proceeded to get up and open the window farthest away from us. There was a chill wind blowing, so I opened it only a bit. "I'll close this in a few minutes, but maybe I'd better stoke the fire now," I said throwing two logs in the grate. The crackle of the wood catching fire was almost merriment to my ears in this intimate environment. I sat down next to Joseph and he took my closest hand in his.

It took a minute for the gentlemen to get their cigars lit properly. As they took in the smoke, Mr. Robert sighed at the pleasure.

"The doctor says I should not smoke after my stroke. I think thwarting my desire to smoke is more dangerous to my health than smoking a cigar once a day. I know it's more dangerous to my disposition!" He laughed at his own reasoning. "If I have to give up all my pleasures, I might as well die!"

"Mr. Robert," I said gently, concerned, "unfortunately you might be completely disabled instead of dying right away. You would want that even less, I think." Joseph was looking at me, as if for the first time he realized I actually cared for this old man.

"You're right, Sara. As usual. Ivy tells me the same thing every time she smells smoke or whiskey on me." He shuffled in his chair, trying to find a comfortable position. "I am consuming much less of each these days. Don't worry about me, but I do thank you for caring. However, I am delaying talking about what I really should have told you long ago. Please forgive me. I had my reasons. I only hope they are sufficient for you to forgive me."

"There's still more to tell?" I asked in surprise, alarmed at his contrite tone. I had, of course, shared with Joseph what Mr. Robert told me about Ole Mammie saving Mr. Robert's life and part of the family fortune. Joseph was looking much less surprised than I expected.

"Yes, my girl. It may not be so grim as the last time we talked, but it may be even more significant to you. It was late when we stopped talking the last time and I lost my courage. Besides, the story is not really mine to tell. I was sworn to secrecy years ago, before you were born, but I think time has changed so many things…" He seemed to have moved into the past already.

And so began the story of how *I* was truly connected to this family.

Mr. Robert began, "I'm not sure where to start, but I will try to find the beginning and go forward from there. Our family was well-acquainted with the Gilley family who lived just across the mountain in the next county. We visited their farm often and they visited here. All of us children were friends. My sister Victoria still writes to her lifelong friend Lucy Gilley Bowen. You don't know them because the older folk have either moved or died. The estate was sold off in pieces over the years and not one of them lives there now. Lucy herself has lived in Bristol since she married ages ago. No, we are not so well-acquainted these days with Gilley's." His gaze wandered to the window as if he could see the past more clearly through the window.

"I don't know how it happened. How do these things happen anyway? Look at you and Joseph! Maybe it was that simple. Maybe my brother Holton was walking on the Gilley farm and saw Addie working. However it happened, Holton began to see old Miz Gilley's best housemaid, Addie, in secret. It had to be in secret as Addie was black. She was light-skinned, but not as light as your sisters." He sighed a heavy, uneasy sigh this time.

"Neither my daddy, Claiborne, nor Mother ever approved of white men behaving free and easy, if you know what I mean, with the slave girls. It sometimes *happened* - on many farms, in fact. But it didn't happen here at Raven Lea. Daddy would have beaten any of us for messing with the slave girls! And we all knew it! Holton knew better, too." He looked away from the window toward the bourbon bottle behind my back on the table.

"Sara, I need a sip or two to get through this. Will you join me, Mr. Thierry?"

"Thank you, Sir, but I am still so full from dinner that I will decline, if you permit."

"I ought to decline myself!" Mr. Robert laughed, "But, as I said…"

I poured two jiggers into a glass and started to pour water in. I looked to see if he wanted the water added.

"Go ahead, girl, fill the rest of the glass with water. Maybe that way I won't feel the need to have more." I did as he asked and handed him the glass. He drank half the glass before he resumed his story.

"It's not that they were so much against white folk and black folk liking one another. It was the fact that the black girls we came into contact with were all *slaves*. Mother said that a white man having intimate relations with a slave girl was the same as *rape*, no matter how else you might put it." He looked quickly at me when he uttered the word. "I'm sorry if my language shocks you, Sara."

I lifted my head and took a deep breath. "I don't know if it was *always* the case, but I think Ole Missus, Miz Powell that is, is more right than wrong about that. A person who's not free *can't freely consent nor freely decline* relations with their owners. Maybe some women found it a way to get favors. If they did, who could blame them? I am black, but I am in no position to know what their lives were *really like*."

Joseph said, "I think I'll accept that drink now, Sir, if you don't object."

Mr. Robert waved for Joseph to help himself. When Joseph was back in his seat, Mr. Robert began again.

"Well, you can probably guess that Addie became pregnant with my brother's baby. How Daddy and Mother could produce *two sons* who would act as they did, I have never understood. I can tell you that my daddy was a gentleman in *every sense of the word*. But then he and Mother married while he was practically a boy. I don't know that makes a difference as *I never…* and Holton was only a couple of years older than Daddy had been when he met Mother…" He seemed to have struggled with this question for years, never having found a suitable rationale.

Mr. Robert finally began again, "At any rate, Holton needed to talk to someone, so he came to me, his older brother. He pleaded with me to tell no one, but he wanted to get Addie off the Gilley farm. He cared about her that much, at least. The girl was barely 15 years old and one of the Gilley sons had been looking at her and making lascivious comments about her for a year or more. Holton knew that if it became obvious that Addie was pregnant, the boy would take her with or without her consent. He begged *me* to buy her."

"She had considerable skills. The Gilley's refused at first to sell her, but Victoria's friendship with Lucy Gilley came in useful somehow. I never knew exactly how the girls finagled to get Lucy's mother to sell Addie to Victoria, but that's how Addie came to live here at Raven Lea."

"I had enlisted Victoria's help without telling her that Holton had gotten the girl in the family way, but Holton eventually told her when it became clear that Addie was going to have a baby. He told her because Victoria *assumed* it was *mine*! Holton was Victoria's favorite brother and I don't think the truth about the baby Addie named Caesar ever passed Victoria's lips, not even to her husband the Reverend."

"I helped Holton on the condition that he would never touch the girl again. He cared enough about her to get her away from Edward Gilley, but he was scared enough that he was more than willing to comply with my demand. And he was right to be afraid of daddy's wrath! Daddy would have disowned him and left his share of the farm to Addie's baby! Had Daddy Claiborne known all of this before both Addie *and* Holton were dead, things would've been very different."

I stood up and paced as much as I could in the small room. I was seething with anger. "Your brother Holton was my papa's father? My grandmother was only a little older than Nora when she conceived his child! How could he treat her so shamefully?"

Mr. Robert - *Uncle Robert* - looked me squarely in the face. "You're saying pretty much what I said to him, only I said it *after I broke his nose*."

I raved, "They *could not have married* even if your brother had *wanted* to marry her!"

"My father would almost certainly have given the girl and her baby, your father, their freedom. That might not have made a huge difference in how they lived, but it would have given them both the dignity of their freedom."

"The dignity of their freedom!" I scoffed. "Look at my dignity!" My arms were practically flailing with every word I uttered. "Look at how I live and how I work!"

I pointed at Joseph, "Here sits a wonderful man who wants me to leave with him *tomorrow* and I'm as tied to this place as if I were *a slave*! I feel obligated to see that my sisters and brother are old enough to manage without me - to see that you're *all* taken care of before I leave! Clay loves them, but not enough to move them to Corsicana immediately so I can leave knowing they're taken care of by someone who loves them *almost* as much as I do!" I was so loud that I doubt closed doors kept anyone from hearing the volume if not the words I spoke.

Mr. - Uncle Robert - seemed taken aback at my words as if he'd never considered how humbly I lived.

Joseph reached out and put a restraining hand on one of my arms. He pulled me back toward the chair. I yanked myself away from him, angry at the world at that moment, unwilling to be mollified.

Joseph spoke calmly, "Mon amour, you have the dignity of being able to *show your anger*, to *vent your rage*. Without freedom, you would have to bear it silently or suffer grave consequences! There is *some dignity* in freedom. And you have enjoyed it your whole life, unlike your mother and father."

I began to cry, at first angry, hot tears, then tears of sadness for my poor papa and his little mother. Joseph stood and embraced me. I cried on his chest for several minutes before he complained mockingly, "Ma belle, you have wet me through and through, *répète,* and wrinkled my freshly laundered and nicely pressed shirt. People will look at me and *laugh* at my négligé - at my slovenliness!"

I gave him a little shove and said, "Oh, hush up, you big dandy!" At which both Mr. Robert - Uncle Robert - and Joseph laughed.

Joseph dried my cheeks and kissed me on the nose. "Be still, my little dove…"

I interrupted, attempting halfheartedly to lighten the mood myself, "This must be *really important* as you are now speaking the English, *non?*" I said with what I thought was a French accent.

The men found that funny and Joseph led me back to the chair. He sat also. "Mr. Powell, who else in the family knows that Sara is really your great-niece?" Joseph asked quietly.

"No one except my sister Victoria. I promised not to tell and Victoria must have promised as well. She and I have never discussed it after…" he mused as if this had never occurred to him before.

"Mother would have disowned Holton had *she* known. As hard-rock as she is today, she was *much sterner* about propriety and piety then! Baptists have nothing over Quakers when it comes to strict observance of the Commandments!" He took a slow puff on the cigar before continuing.

"She nearly beat the living daylights out of me with a razor strop when I was about eight for what she called *sassing* my Daddy! I had to write 100 times *'Honour thy father and thy mother, as the LORD thy God hath commanded thee, that thy days may be prolonged, and that it may go well with thee, in the land which the LORD thy God giveth thee.'- And,* it had to be written with good *penmanship*! - Try writing all those *hath's, thy's* and *thee's* 100 times! Daddy thought my sassiness showed spunk. Mother *did not share that sentiment.* Let me just say that I learned then and there to give my daddy his due respect."

He found this mildly amusing evidently as he smiled, took another sip of whiskey and another long draw on his cigar before continuing. "But I digress. Oh, I think Daddy *guessed* Caesar was Holton's as the boy grew up. Caesar looked like a darker version of Holton - and only slightly darker, at that. Your father, Sara, could have passed for white, I think, in a big city. Holton took more after Mother than Daddy physically. As a grown man Holton was shorter than Clay and I and he was wiry where we are solidly built. His appearance was deceiving though, as was Caesar's. They were both very strong men. And Caesar had a natural gift with horses, just as Holton did. Your papa, Sara, could ride any horse anywhere, anytime - *bareback*! He was almost Indian-like in that ability. And he never was harsh with a horse when he was working it. He was firm and the horse knew that Caesar was in charge, but he said the phrase 'breaking a horse' should be removed from the English language! He preferred 'training a horse'."

"Holton left Raven Lea when little Caesar was about two years of age. Holton asked Daddy for his inheritance early and bought prime bottom land in the northern Shenandoah Valley. He moved up there, and met his wife, Dorothea. Her family lived on the property that adjoined his. They married. My sister-in-law had three sons by him. Holton died before the youngest was two." Mr. Robert -Uncle Robert - sighed almost painfully.

"Addie died when Caesar was maybe seven or eight. I honestly believe the girl died of a broken heart. But we had another good black woman grieving over the loss of her husband and sons," he looked straight into my eyes.

"Your Grandmother Callie was never again my Mother's happy, humorous personal maid after Daddy sold your Granddad and uncles. Miz Callie did her job well, but *never joyfully* again. Mother had been very fond of her up until then, but something changed in Miz Callie. She was not rude. She did what she was told, but she ceased confiding in Mother and sympathizing with all Mother's little idiosyncrasies. Miz Callie was not Mother's friend after that. Their circumstances were too different."

"Mother felt hard toward Daddy over that sale. She never liked it when the negroes were sold off the farm, but this time, she was irate! She tried to stop the sale, but it was one of the rare instances where Daddy *did not bend to her will*. When Addie died, Mother *told* Daddy to move Caesar in with Miz Callie and little Nisa. She said that Caesar could never take the place of Miz Callie's own children, but he might lift some of the sadness from her heart."

"I don't think Daddy had yet come to accept the idea that Caesar was Holton's son when Caesar moved in with your grandmother, Sara, but he may have suspected even then. He really wanted the boy raised here in the house to do odd jobs for the family, like shoe blacking, wick trimming, silver polishing, escorting company in. I think Daddy wanted to groom Caesar as a gentleman's butler, but Caesar had such a gift with horses that Abraham took him under his wing during work hours. Daddy always liked the boy almost as unreasonably as Mother dotes on Clay's children by your mother."

"But no one resists Mother for very long, and Daddy was never good at holding out on whatever she wanted, except for that one time when he sold your grandfather and uncles. They were not openly affectionate with one another, but he worshiped the woman almost as much as I worshiped Loudena! And, as Mother *enjoys being worshiped*, she loved him in return."

"At any rate, Miz Callie was happy to be raising a boy again. When Caesar and Nisa married, Miz Callie was thrilled as I never remembered her being. She loved her son-in-law very much. Your papa, Sara, was a decent, hard-working, respectful man - respectful to my daddy and mother, *of course*, but also to your Grandmother Callie and your momma."

We sat quietly for some minutes, then Joseph broke the silence, "Your mother never knew? Clay? Your wife?"

Uncle Robert shook his head, "No. I always felt guilty for not telling Loudena, but I had promised Holton."

Joseph stood up, drank the last of his bourbon and forcefully threw the remainder of his cigar into the fireplace. From the look on his face, I was surprised he didn't throw the glass into the grate as well! He was very stiff in his movements. I knew he was very angry about something, and I was afraid he would say something harsh to Uncle Robert. Instead, he turned to the door muttering in Cajun French what were probably very ugly words. He turned to me and said, "I am going for a long walk to cool my blood. I will be back when I am calm again." He bowed slightly, stiffly to Uncle Robert and left.

I stood as well, my voice shaking as I spoke, "I can't say thank you for telling me these things, but it is better I know than not know, Mr. Robert."

"Please forgive me for not rising, Sara. I am, all of a sudden, worn out." Mr. Robert said.

"I understand, and I'm sorry Joseph is in such a snit. I don't know why - I think I'll go find him." I said as I closed the window.

He only nodded as I left.

I grabbed my heaviest cape and one that Violet kept in the kitchen in case she forgot to bring her good one when she needed it. I figured Joseph didn't stop for a coat. I saw him walking fast across the frozen corn field. I ran toward him and stumbled half a dozen times jabbing my shins through skirt and petticoat on the hard corn stalk stubbles. I finally caught up with him. The look on his face was so dark that I thought at first he was going to send me back to the house immediately, but instead he caught me up in his arms after a minute's hesitation. He hugged me to him so tightly I couldn't catch my breath.

"Oh, Mon Dieu, Sara! My heart hurts for all of them! Your papa, your grandmothers, your grandfathers - all of them! But I hurt *most* for you! That cursed family owes you so much! You were denied your birthright! Look at how Ivy and Rob have been raised. God in heaven," he cursed, "look at how much better your brother and sisters are treated!" His grip on me lessened enough so I could catch my breath and I lifted my lips to his, silencing the curses, the anger, the heartache he was expressing. It was almost as if he felt it more strongly than I at that moment.

I took my lips away and whispered, "We can't change an iota of any of it, Joseph! I shall always remember that you love me enough to be revolted by this, but I don't want to ruin one more second of the time we have before you leave tomorrow in regretting what was done and can't be undone. Please!"

He stood me on the frozen ground and looked steadfastly into my eyes. "I don't know that I can ever forgive Mr. Powell for what he left untold for so many years."

I put my gloved fingers on his lips. "I think perhaps he did the best he knew how at the time and under the circumstances. My grandfather, Holton Powell, was the villain in this piece - if there was a villain." I added sorrowfully.

I continued, "And the War ended any chance of him *ever* making amends. Times were different. My mother and Clay married. It's true it was not a marriage the state of Virginia would recognize, but he married her and he acknowledged their children."

"Sara, leave this place with me tomorrow!" Joseph demanded gruffly.

"I can't leave just like that. I have responsibilities - the children. Another cook…"

"Then I will be back as soon as maybe…"

"I promise that I will be in Washington before Christmas next year, Joseph, but there are things I must see to here first..." I was pleading with him.

He started walking away from me with such disappointment on his face. I began to cry as I ran back to the house still carrying Violet's cape that I meant to put around him.

It was years before it occurred to me that the timing of the sale of my grandpap and uncles probably provided Holton with a substantial part of his inheritance. Those good people were valuable property and no doubt brought a price large enough to buy a deal of land even on rich Shenandoah soil. Joseph had come to the same conclusion that December day sitting in my uncle's office. That was the final insult that made him so very angry. The transgressor was rewarded but at the price of the *additional misery* of others. Where was the justice?

Joseph and I made up over coffee after supper that evening. He told me that the revelations of the afternoon had more firmly convinced him that the Louisiana law being contested by Mr. Plessy *must be overturned* if black people were *ever* going to be treated fairly. He would need to work so many hours and to travel back and forth to Louisiana so often that it would be unfair to ask me to move up to Washington immediately. I would be alone so much of the time. He would see me at Raven Lea as often as possible. Of course I cried.

Joseph had to return to Washington on Wednesday. He, Rob and his company all left together. Rhi went back to school the following Tuesday, and the house fell into a deep winter's quiet.

Ole Missus cornered me alone in the kitchen shortly after all the company had gone. She asked Violet to go help Nora get the house returned to its usual state.

"Sara, you will not like what I have to say, but I feel it is my Christian duty to say it. I am the closest thing you have to a mother or a grandmother." In my head I was thinking "You *are* my great-grandmother."

"Even if Joseph Thierry gets a divorce from his wife - what is her name?" she asked testily.

"Olivia Marie." I answered.

"What kind of name is that?" she sniffed. "French? Catholic?"

"Both, I think, Ma'am."

"Well, this is the United States of America for Heaven's sake!" She was shaking her head back and forth, tut-tutting. "Didn't we just have an awful war to determine that?" That day was not one of her better days. She was cranky and fault-finding. Her arthritis must have been acting up.

"Let me think. What was I going to say?" She was silent only a few seconds. "Ah, yes. Even after he gets a divorce, it may be a sin for him to remarry. He is clearly entitled to divorce this creature who calls herself a wife, but whether the two of you can then marry… ? Well, you can't, according to the way I interpret the Bible, although there are Biblical scholars who think Mr. Thierry might remarry without sinning ." She was not being unkind. Indeed her voice was sincere and had softened considerably in the last minutes.

"Ma'am, I am certainly no Biblical scholar. You know far more about these things than I do, but Joseph tells me the reason he is seeking both a divorce *and an annulment* is so that there can be no questions about our marriage being legitimate in the eyes of the Church and about our children's legitimacy when they come." I looked straight into her face as difficult as that was in talking of such matters.

I pulled my neck up as high as it would go and straightened my shoulders, "The divorce is necessary to satisfy legal authorities and to divide their property between them. Joseph says an annulment will mean that the Catholic Church has concluded that Olivia Marie acted in such a way that no true marriage ever existed in the sight of God since she lied to the priest and to Joseph before they were married. She *never intended* to have children. An annulment is actually more difficult to get than a divorce. The Church wants to be sure they are not nullifying a marriage sanctioned by God."

I added for good measure, "I am no authority on this either, but it seems as if Joseph has a dozen relatives who are priests, nuns, something or other in the Catholic Church, so I expect *he does know*."

"Sara, I like this man very much even though he is a Papist. I believe he will take care of you and protect you from a bigger world than you have known - a world that troubles me for you, your sisters, and brother. And I believe you and Mr. Thierry know one another very well through your long correspondence. In fact, you probably know each other better than most couples who have lived near one another for years! I don't believe it is simply a case of a man seeing a pretty girl and deciding to have her. You have always been such a good girl and I don't want you to jeopardize your immortal soul. Be sure of what you are about to do." She patted my hand with her pale, vein-laced hand, stood and said one last thing before she left, "I will pray for you, girl." That bit of tenderness from her made me want to cry.

I sat there thinking for a long time. I intended to marry Joseph even if the Church should refuse an annulment. I couldn't imagine that a God worth caring about would condemn Joseph to either a life of living with Olivia Marie or living celibate. In either case, he would never have the children he so badly wanted. Frankly, although I would never have voiced this to Ole Missus, I loved him so much *I would imperil my immortal soul to be with him*. What I *wouldn't do*, however, was risk our children's reputations and futures. He had to have a divorce and marry me before I would live with him. Then I'd fight against my own weak faith and pray that a just God would "look not on our sins" but on our love for each other and forgive us - even if the Church wouldn't.

January seemed six months long that year, but Vaz, Ivy and I traveled to Washington D.C., staying with Rob and his bride Lizzie from the 10th of March until the 18th. We were able to see Joseph sworn into office and tour the town. Lizzie was very proud to show us the sights. She had grown up not far from Washington and knew the city well. It was wonderful to spend a week's worth of evenings with Joseph, but he was torn between spending time with me and working. He didn't want me to leave, but he *needed* me to go back to Raven Lea for a time.

CHAPTER 14: PREPARATIONS

… Icicles filled the long window
With barbaric glass,
The shadow of the blackbird
Crossed it, to and fro.
The mood
Traced in the shadow
An indecipherable cause…

… When the blackbird flew out of sight,
It marked the edge
Of one of many circles….

from Thirteen Ways of Looking at a Blackbird,
Wallace Stevens

We only saw Rhi again in 1894 at the end of her summer tour and her summer service work. What a changed girl! Actually she was more like a young woman then, although she was just 17 years old. The immigrant children she had seen that summer living in inner city poverty struck her heart deeply. She told us that however modestly she had been raised at Raven Lea, she was *always* warm, clean and well-nourished. *None of that was true* of the children she saw, especially in Boston, New York and Philadelphia.

She said they were making great strides in Chicago to educate the children and to improve the conditions of poor women and children. Although there were attempts to develop similar kinds of neighborhood guilds and settlement houses in Boston, New York and Philadelphia, the number of people needing services far outstripped what was available. The cities had waited too long to begin to get a handle on the problems and the immigrant populations had burgeoned.

Joblessness was still high in many European countries and their own populations were growing rapidly. Many people poured into the U.S. Those who could afford a ticket, boarded a ship and came to America. "The Land of Opportunity," "The Golden Door." Some would find work and send for family members. Some would even do well. But most would never again see the families they left behind.

The two weeks that Rhi was home at the end of the summer before the beginning of the fall term, the dressmaker made her a few new gowns. Thankfully, she had not grown more and she had worn her clothes "gently" the past year. It seemed that she had reached her adult height of five feet ten inches. She said she felt like someone who belonged in a freak show, but I thought her stately and quite pretty, especially her glorious hair and straight, white teeth that made her smile lovely. Her clear gray eyes were fascinating to me, as they were surrounded by such thick dark eyelashes, unusual for such light eyes. It was too bad that she had to wear spectacles most of the time. Rhi never stooped, despite complaining of her height. Ivy, almost as tall as Rhi, had been a good influence on her posture.

Nora and I had knitted stockings and sewed new under garments all summer for Rhi. Rhi needed new boots as there was so much walking from class to class and practically anywhere else she went. But *Rhi's biggest concern* that late summer was to get our local churches to support the efforts to help the inner city residents of Philadelphia. Each of the students who had travelled that summer with Dean Moore had chosen a city to support. Rhi chose Philadelphia for what reason I never knew, but it may have been due to her hero-worship of Benjamin Franklin. The old womanizer was an odd hero for such a Christian girl as Rhi, but a great deal of what we do and think does not fit into tidy categories.

"If our churches can support missionaries in China and Africa, why can't they *do more right here in the United States*?" she railed. She made passionate, effective speeches in the four nearby churches where she asked for help. None of these churches had a wealthy congregation, but they each pledged help. One church pledged five chalkboards and a gross of chalk to be sent before Christmas. Another pledged thirty wool afghans and thirty pairs of socks. The Powell's church promised to ship 25 bushels of potatoes and another 25 bushels of apples to Philadelphia. The poorest church, our own black church, collected $20 to put toward whatever the service organization most needed. I found Rhi crying on the back porch after she received the pledges.

"What's wrong, Honey?" I asked putting my arms around her.

"Oh, Sara, they've been *so charitable*. So kind! I know that almost every congregant will make *a real sacrifice* to meet these pledges." She waved the four letters in her hands. "I am so humbled and grateful, but… "

"But, what, Rhi?"

"What they're sending is *a mere drop in the bucket* compared to what is needed! The potatoes and apples won't feed the needy for a week even. The chalkboards will help, but we could have used another 20. As for the afghans and socks - well that's enough for 30 people. There are *hundreds* in need. I don't know what they'll do with the cash, but it will be used up immediately as well, probably in postage for letters asking for support."

"Hush! Hush right now, Rhi! Those who do receive these things will be *better off*! It sounds to me as if we need to send *knitting supplies* to every family and get some local land near the tenants so they can grow their own food!" I tried to buck her up.

"You have been a wonderful help for these people." I went on, "If the other students do as well as you have, you will have made a *real impact*. Next year, this project can grow - and the year after that. You will get better at fund-raising, but it sounds to me as if these folks need some equipment, some tools to help themselves. I'm sure that they want to do for themselves. A skill is much more reliable than charity!"

"Sara, many of these women actually *know how* to knit. They unravel old tattered garments *and reuse the wool.* Maybe slaves once did that here. I don't know, but in my lifetime I've never seen it done before. But then we have sheep and wool right here on the farm."

"Well, *I have done it myself,* Rhi. Before Momma passed." I laughed. "We must have been as poor as I thought we were! Ole Mammie had me unravel garments and she would knit something out of the salvaged wool. It's really a smart use of what little you have when you're poor. Maybe we could send some castoffs to these folks so they can unravel old wool garments and send cotton things for quilts. You can even make rugs out of sturdy rags! Look at that big old rug in my room. It's a braided rug made from rags and it's warm to my feet in the winter and *attractive!* Ole Mammie and I made it one winter. Old clothing that is no longer fit to be worn won't cost the church members anything. Nora, Vaz, and I can pay to ship what we collect wherever you want us to ship it. I'll see that the things arrive clean, if washing doesn't *totally destroy them.*"

I pulled the ring out from inside my bodice. I wore it on a ribbon because I didn't want to put my hand inside a chicken or shape sausage, or knead dough with such a ring on my hand. I looked at it. "This would probably feed 500 people for six months, maybe longer."

"Don't even think about that, Sara! Joseph gave you that ring as a sign to the world of his love for you, and, who knows? Bad things happen. Your papa died. Momma died. There may come a time when you need the money you can get for it." Ever practical, my Rhi was back.

"Well, I don't even think I could *ask* Joseph to help because he has taken this Plessy thing pro bono. You know the exact Latin meaning, of course, but for an attorney it also means *free of charge.* He oversees his family's legal affairs and is well paid for that, but right now he pays Rob and another attorney to do most of that work. Joseph brought Rob into the firm as he can no longer manage by himself with this case coming up. He just has so little time right now. The Thierry family also supports an orphanage in New Orleans. As a matter of fact I think they fund it *entirely*."

"Joseph doesn't have the kind of money it takes to handle the Plessy case this long without compensation does he? What is the family business that he is paid so well that he can do all this work for free?" Rhi asked.

"Shipping. They have warehouses in New Orleans, Galveston, Tampa, Miami, Charleston, Baltimore, Philadelphia, Boston, and Portland, Maine. Oh, and Halifax, Nova Scotia. They are building new facilities in Long Beach, California, Seattle, Washington and Vancouver, Canada. Their ships travel to and from about 20 different countries! He has told me how many tons of freight they transport per year, but I can't remember all of that!"

"My heavens! I had no idea they had such an enterprise! No wonder Joseph could give you a ring worth a king's ransom! How do they keep it all functioning?" Rhi was finally impressed.

"There are nine *children still alive* in Joseph's family! Between the brothers, the brothers-in-law, the nephews, and nephews-in-law and even *one niece*, at least one family member lives near each port and manages the overall business for that facility. Joseph is chief counsel and chief executive officer. He is paid a salary rather than relying on a percent of the profit as do the rest, which is most of them in one way or another. He is the oldest brother, but I think his sister Rosemarie's husband, Jacques, is the general manager for the East Coast facilities. They live in Boston with their *12 children*." I laughed. "They are *the most prolific bunch* I've ever heard of! Joseph is the only one with no children, and the smallest family is his *youngest brother* Louis.' Louis is only 28 and he and his wife *already have three children*. Henri, the brother closest to Joseph in age, will oversee the West Coast facilities from Seattle once they're operational. I'm so overwhelmed with all of it." I shook my head.

"I'm just *a cook*." I concluded.

"Listen, Sara, you've raised us *since you were ten* and *managed to keep us together* and reasonably *sane* living in *this mad house*! I think that qualifies you as considerably more than *just a cook*!"

We laughed at that and began to recall some of the funnier experiences we'd had over the years in the "mad house." Some of the stories we had told Vaz and Nora because they had not been old enough to remember themselves. Others they had shared as well.

"Do you remember, " Rhi began, "when Ole Missus ran Reverend Pickle off because he insulted *her oh-so-innocent Vastine* by calling him 'insolent'? Reverend Pickle was livid with anger and slammed the front door so hard on his way out that it cracked the leaded glass in the door. Ole Missus deducted the replacement window from his last pay, which made him almost angry enough to slam the door again! Vaz gave a slight bow as the Reverend was leaving just to torment the man."

I jabbed her gently in the ribs, "Do you remember when Ole Massah was first becoming senile and losing his eyesight, but still took a couple of jiggers of bourbon before supper every evening? The old man thought he saw a deer inside the stock pen near the stables, took out *his father's old musket loader* and killed the expensive jersey bull calf Mr. Robert had just bought that day! Shot it from the front porch! Mr. Robert took the gun away from him, threw it so far it practically landed in the road, breaking the stock of that Revolutionary War musket!"

"Yes," Rhi completed the story laughing so hard tears were in her eyes, "and Grandmother railed at him for disrespecting his aged father! Uncle Robert retorted that if Granddaddy Claiborne shot one of us thinking we were a bear or something, would he then have her permission to throw the gun out? You, Vaz, and I hid in the dining room and laughed and laughed, covering our mouths, hoping they wouldn't hear us. Grandmother and Uncle Robert were arguing so loudly they couldn't have heard Gabriel blow his horn!"

I gasped for breath, "The funniest thing about it to me was that after about 20 minutes of wrangling between Mr. Robert and Ole Missus, Ole Massah asked them quite calmly when supper would be ready!" We whooped for a couple of minutes.

"I remember a real doozie!" Rhi exclaimed. "The day S'rena waxed and buffed the front stairs because Grandmother wanted them shinier. Did you see Mr. 'Zander slide from the top step to the landing on his backside?" I shook my head no. "Well, I did!" Rhi said.

"I saw him cursing and chasing Silly S'rena with her own broom." I started to laugh, remembering the sight of her running, scared for her life. I added to the story, "She hid on the roof of the back porch! I'm not sure how she got up there quick enough to keep Mr. 'Zander from seeing and catching her, but she didn't come off that roof until after dark and she was nearly frozen stiff!"

I went on, "Andy and Vaz played some mean tricks on Miz 'Becca to get rid of her. I don't know which was worse. A dead, half-eaten rat during her morning Bible studies or a locked privy?" I giggled, in my mind seeing Miz 'Becca hurrying to find Violet and asking her to retrieve the chamber pot for her room.

Rhi started laughing and began, "Do you remember how Ole Miz Laws got so drunk on fruit cake three Christmases back…"

I picked up the story as Rhi was laughing too hard to finish, "Yes, she bit Miz Anne on the arm when Miz Anne suggested she not have more cake. Miz Laws' dentures fell out and chipped the top front teeth. Mr. 'Zander and Andy carried her upstairs. Andy had her feet and Mr. 'Zander had her arms. Her wig slid off on the stairs and one of them stepped on it, slipping and nearly dropping the poor old thing! They put her to bed with every stitch of her clothing on!"

"Yes," Rhi finished the tale, holding her stomach she ached so from laughing, "Miz Anne finally felt sorry enough for her mother to go up and partially undress her before covering her with a quilt. But Miz Anne didn't get to her mother's wig before Vaz snatched it up and hid it under a chair cushion in the front parlor. It took an hour the next morning to find it before we could get Miz Laws on her way home! Miz Laws has accused us all, including her daughter, of lying about the events of that evening. All I can say, Sara, is you make a pretty powerful fruit cake!"

"Let's not forget Joseph showing up in a rage threatening to kill half the county, nearly shaking me to death!"

We laughed until we hurt, so we stopped short even though we could have told at least a dozen other similarly crazy things we'd experienced at Raven Lea. Over the years when one of us remembered something we had not mentioned before, we'd write and say, "Remember when…"

Rhi went back to school and I began having my trousseau made. Mr. Robert insisted that he would pay for it. I think Vaz must have spoken to his uncle and to Ole Missus because in addition to the trousseau, I received a large cedar chest, a large leather trunk, and Miz Anne was put in charge of seeing that I was properly outfitted. Ivy was teaching new subjects that fall with heavy preparations to make both evenings and weekends - in addition to getting Vastine ready to go to college the next fall.

"No penny-pinching, Miss." Miz Anne said to me the first time we traveled to the nearest large city to shop. "You are going to be the wife of a highly distinguished, well-known man. We can't have you looking like a farmer's wife. At some point we will need to go to Philadelphia, I expect, as I doubt we can get all we need here."

"I may not be a farmer's wife, Miz Anne, but I *will be* a cook. I need suitable clothing for work."

"Is it suitable for a man in Joseph's position to have a wife who is a cook?" Anne asked aghast.

"I don't know if it is suitable or not, but I intend to do this! My father and mother died, leaving me with *nothing. Things change.* Joseph's business could flounder for some reason. He could *die*, God forbid. As long as I am physically able, I won't ever allow myself to be in a position again where I must rely on the generosity of others, however kind and open-handed they may be."

She looked at me as if I had slapped her. For a moment I was sorry for having spoken so bluntly. Then I decided it might be time for these privileged, albeit well-meaning, white people to see things from a different perspective.

I did try to smooth things over a little since she was putting herself out to help me. "Anne, Joseph and I have talked about my owning a restaurant for several years now. He understands and he *still* wants to marry me." I decided then and there that I would call her Anne just as she called me Sara! Her nose went up in the air at my familiarity and I laughed a little. She gave me a long cool blue stare down her straight patrician nose, then her face softened and she laughed too.

"I hope to Heaven that he knows what he's getting with *you*, Little Sara! I think you are more than a match for him!" Anne said firmly.

Since I intended to operate a restaurant and would be working, I needed several practical, plain dresses, no leg-o-mutton sleeves, but close fitting, three-quarter length sleeves. A hot stove and pots and pans full of hot grease and hot liquids are dangerous if you wear too much clothing. I wanted two dozen new aprons in white, of course. I couldn't stand to wear an apron after it was soiled.

Anne decided that black was the most professional color for a work dress, but that I *must* have white collars on the dresses to frame my face. I refused to wear "widow's weeds," so we compromised on dove grey gowns with white collars, piped in charcoal grey. My patrons would be professional people and clerks working around the capital. I intended to serve breakfast and luncheon Mondays through Saturdays, so I insisted on having *six dresses* for work. I would have no time for laundry during the week We chose cotton as it was easiest to wash, but Anne insisted I needed heavier petticoats to wear under cotton dresses in the winter.

"You don't have to have work-a-day underwear too, do you? You can be a bit more extravagant with what no one but you and Joseph will see." At this I blushed and she laughed.

I wanted a cloak and bonnet that could be worn over the grey dresses so I could go straight to the market and order supplies right after luncheon. Anne said I should have two cloaks, one lightweight and one heavier. We ordered both in charcoal grey with dove grey satin piping. She also encouraged me to buy a charcoal grey bonnet with the dove grey ribbons, lined in white satin that framed my face. It was ornamented with one white satin cabbage rose. The fashion of the day was for hats to "perch" on the head and be covered with feathers and flowers that reached almost a foot above the wearer's head. The ornamentation on those hats made women appear a foot taller than they were. I was too small for all that folderol and I didn't think it would make me look older or more professional, both of which were important to me. A bonnet was just passé enough to do that, but I did give in and buy a straw "boater" with no ornamentation except a white ribbon around the crown that hung down the back. I bought white cotton gloves, black kid gloves, and long white evening gloves by the half dozen. I also purchased walking boots and evening shoes. I decided I needed an additional trunk.

The gowns to wear away from work were exciting. I bought goods to make two walking suits, one in linen for the summer and one in wool for cooler weather. The shirtwaists we chose were white linen lavished with insets of white lace. I hated the current style of large shoulders. I refused to have them on my clothes. Anne just sighed. By then she had grown used to my definite opinions.

After about two shopping trips with me, Anne seemed to be tired and lose enthusiasm. The morning she had Vaz stop the carriage to let her get out to throw up, I began to worry about her. She looked very pale and was not eating well. At first I thought it might be some illness one of the children had contracted and transmitted to their mother, but she never ran a fever and the malaise seemed to linger. Miz 'Dena's illness had started the same way, and I grew really fearful. I told a lie the next time we were scheduled to shop. I told her that *I* was feeling unwell. She looked so ashen and thin. She simply smiled at me wanly, almost certainly because she knew what I was doing.

To my great surprise, Eliza and Clay arrived the following week. Eliza and Clay felt they could safely leave Lou Issa at home with Lupe and Jorge now that she was a little older and less susceptible to childhood illnesses. They had a telephone in the house and the servants knew how to use it to telephone a doctor. Lupe and Jorge were under strict orders to telegraph them at one of several locations if Lou Issa should become ill while they were away. I never knew, but I think Ole Missus wrote her son that I needed Eliza's help because Anne couldn't help right now.

Eliza, Clay, Nora, Vaz and I took a train to New York to shop. Nora and Vaz were thrilled to be going and, of course, so was I. If it hadn't looked undignified, I would have been up peering out windows, getting out at every stop to look around, and in general behaving the way Vaz and Nora did on the trip.

Eliza *insisted* we go to New York. "I need to see for myself what people are wearing to the opera in New York. Clay has some business to conduct there as well." I never learned what business Clay had, but, by then, he had his hand into all sorts of enterprises. Joseph's sister Claudia invited us stay with her. Claudia was a widow, living alone in an apartment across from the new large, urban green space in the city, Central Park. I never realized an "apartment" could be so large and I voiced this to her.

"Bébé, I have *twenty grandchildren!* I need the space when they visit, and *I enjoy their visits so much!* In fact, I crave company. My son, Gervais, and his wife dine with me on Wednesdays when Gervais is in town, but that is not much company. It's unfortunate that the one child of mine who lives nearby has *no children*, but I am well blessed by the other five!"

Claudia was warm, chatty and helpful. She gave us cards of introduction to her favorite dressmaker and other merchants. "I am *much too lazy*, ma chère, to go with you, but I would enjoy seeing the things you buy, if you don't mind."

Her dressmaker couldn't do enough for us. Eliza had three gowns made for herself and picked up fabric for Rhi to have a special dress made over Christmas. She insisted that Nora have a new warm coat as well and several new dresses. While I was being fitted and pinned one afternoon, Eliza went to F.A.O. Schwarz's Toy Bazaar to pick up things for Lou Isa. I had no idea that stores existed specifically to merchandise toys! I never saw the toys as she had them shipped directly back, but I assumed they could not be purchased in Corsicana. That same afternoon Clay took Vaz and Nora to ride in Central Park on horses belonging to Claudia's son, Gervais Mayeux.

I had an evening cloak made of black velvet, lined in white satin with jet beading on the collar and down the front. I liked a satin rose-pink gown with a large ecru lace collar, a black cabbage rose corsage on the side of the collar and a black band around the waist so well that I wanted a second one made in velvet. Eliza put her foot down. I was marrying a man who could afford to clothe me in a different gown for every day of the year. There were too many beautiful fabrics and designs to bother replicating any.

I thought some of the gowns indecent, as there was so much bare neck and shoulders. Eliza laughed. "Just you wait, Sara. I give you a year of living in a city before you'll wonder why you had necks put on *any of your gowns!*"

We ordered day dresses for summer, day dresses for winter, a magnificent ball gown in gold-colored silk with three different kinds of lace, silk shawls, wool shawls, day hats, evening hats, three skirts, half a dozen additional shirtwaists, and a full length blue fox coat! I was starting to feel like an organ grinder's monkey - with too much finery for such a simple creature!

"It *doesn't get cold enough in Washington* to wear this coat!" I protested to Eliza as I turned to look at my back as I wore the coat.

"Law, child! *it doesn't get cold enough south of the North Pole* for this coat, but what has that to do with *anything*! Take the hat too! It's stunning with your coloring." She adjusted the hat slightly to one side on my head.

"But it is so extravagant that it must be quite costly. Mr. Robert can't afford all of this…" I waved my hand around the salon.

"Of course he can't!" There was no hemming-and-hawing. Eliza was often brutally honest. "But Clay and Joseph have talked it over. Joseph says to present Robbie with half the bill and he will pay for the rest."

I began to remove the hat, shaking my head "no."

"I will go to the altar in my best petticoat if that is all Mr. Robert can afford. Joseph can spoil me rotten in years to come, but not now. It is indecent!" I protested, probably too loudly.

Eliza put her hands on her hips, pursed her lips and shook her head at me. "*Your - best - petticoat, indeed*! Hear me now and hear me clearly, *Miss Sara Gilley*! You are young and quite lovely with a perfectly proportioned figure even for such slight stature. Wear fine clothes *now* while you look best in them! Babies may add weight to your figure. They often do, you know." She turned her back to me and patted her hips as well as she could wearing a bustle. "I have *saddlebags* where I once had hips!"

She faced me again, "Your hair will turn gray at some point, like it or not, and you may, heaven forbid, even get a few wrinkles."

"I swear by Zeus, if our ship ever comes in, Clay Powell is going to buy me a coat like this!" She stroked the fur coat lovingly.

She continued, "Joseph wants to show the whole world how lovely you are. Love him enough to do what he wants."

"If he thinks he's buying a doll…" I began in a waspish tone.

Eliza sighed in exasperation. "Sara, just *hush your pretty mouth* and do as you're told. He's not buying *you* - only *some* of your clothes! And if the man doesn't know by now that this doll," she gently poked me in my midsection, "has a sharp tongue and sharper teeth, then he deserves whatever aggravation you give him!" There was no use arguing with her. She was tenacious. She began to giggle - there's no other word for it - in her mid-40's she was giggling like a girl.

"My dear Sara, I wish we lived near enough to see Mr. Joseph Thierry get his come-uppance from you *on a regular basis*! He's been overdue for a lesson in humility for a long time!"

I was defensive for my sweet Joseph, "I have no intention of trying to humble him! He's a wonderful man just as he is!"

She patted my arm, still laughing a little, "You won't be able to help yourself! It's the way you are made, Sara. No one rides rough-shod over you, do they?"

"Well…" I didn't know what to say. Finally, "I have no intention of mistreating…"

She laughed again slightly, "You won't be mistreating him, my dear. He needs to be brought down a peg or two *for his own welfare*!" She walked me over to another area of fabrics, "But please don't mind me. *I actually like the scoundrel* and he's been a good friend to Clay! Anyone Clay likes is fine by me!"

I needed underclothing, Eliza said, and the kind of underclothing that *ladies wear*. She insisted I buy two corsets that I *swore I would not wear*, warm stockings, lighter stockings, slippers, boots, frilly nightgowns, and *indecently sheer* robes.

Then there was the matter of a wedding gown. Presumably the wedding would be around Christmas, but in the event that it was delayed until spring, she had a plan. The wedding gown was not really a dress, but a skirt with two bodices, one bodice suitable for winter, the other suitable for warmer weather. There was a long sleeved, high necked bodice for cool weather. The skirt was simple in front, but fuller in the back with a short train. It was cut in simple lines that did not swamp my figure in swathes of fabric. The second more summery bodice was made similar to the first but it had small cap sleeves. I thought it was the most elegant gown I 'd ever seen.

I had addressed my insecurity with our hostess at breakfast the morning after we arrived. "Mrs. Mayeux, does it…"

"Stop. I am Claudia to ya'll. These are my *favorite brother's* dear friends and you are his fiancée. I believe I can call you that even though he is still married to that *creature*!" I began to wonder why he had ever married Olivia Marie as I had yet to meet anyone who knew and liked her.

"What were you about to say, ma chère?"

"Marrying me won't help Joseph's political career." I stated outright.

"Oh, Sara, don't let that…" Clay started to say something when Claudia put up a hand and pointed to a photo I hadn't noticed before.

"Clay, would you please bring me the photo that's setting on the table over there? Isn't he handsome?" I was wondering if she was getting a little senile because I didn't see how this fit in with what I was trying to say. When she handed me the photo that Clay retrieved, I was still somewhat confused. It was a picture of a black man, light-skinned and distinguished looking, but clearly with African features. I looked at her, puzzled.

"He was *the love of my life* and my husband for 35 years. Gervais Mayeux, Sr. He was born into slavery and ignored and scorned, in turns, by his white father, but something about him caught his white grandmother's eye. She taught him to read, write and count when he was still young. *Illegally taught him*, I might add. When he was 10, she *bought* his freedom from *her own son,* gave him an introduction to my father and recommended him as an employee."

"Our family never owned slaves." Claudia continued. "We had plenty of black help, but they were free and they were paid. Not everyone in Louisiana believed in slavery and my father was one of those who didn't. It was known by those closest to the family that our help was not indentured. They were free to leave whenever they chose, and a few left hoping to find conditions more favorable somewhere else. Gervais' grandmother knew that *my grandmother* was a mulatto, the same as Gervais. My father, who was one-fourth black himself apprenticed Gervais at that tender age to a sea captain to learn sailing and ports of call."

She wiped her spectacles to better see the photograph. "By the time he was 18 Geri, as I called him, could sail *anything that wouldn't leak* and he had been to forty or fifty ports of call south from New Orleans: Kingston to Cartagena, Caracas, Recife, Maracaibo, Rio de Janeiro, Buenos Aires, Port-au-Prince, Havana, San Juan, Nassau, and everything in between. He had also gone as far north as Halifax, Nova Scotia. What *he had not done* was to sail east to Africa or Europe, not because the company didn't trade there at the time, but because my father feared, probably irrationally, that Geri might be captured and re-enslaved. My father found him to be hard-working, intelligent and loyal, and since he had no sons at that time, Père loved him like a son. About 1850, my father built warehouses in Baltimore placing Geri *there* as head of the Baltimore operations. I still had never met him. "

"At that point, Père had a house *full of daughters* and it did not look promising that he and my mother would ever have sons. My father took my next younger sisters and me with him on a trip up the east coast to visit our warehouses in about 1852."

"Something alarmed Father, *even that early,* so he *slowly,* so as to alert no one in the South, began moving most of his operations to Baltimore and points north, namely Philadelphia, New York, and Boston. He still owned warehouses in New Orleans, Tampa and Charleston, but by the time the war started there was very little in the nearly empty warehouses. That was good because the warehouses *were burned* during the War. He had moved all the ships to northern ports and Havana. When the War broke out, he moved those of us still living in Louisiana to Philadelphia."

"But I am ahead of myself. I met Geri when I was 18, Vivienne was 16 and Rosemarie, who was with us on that trip, was 14. I loved him *the moment Vivienne declared herself smitten* with him!" She had us all chuckling.

"Unfortunately for me, Geri preferred Vivienne at first, but at 16 a girl is apt to be fickle, fond of this beau today and another tomorrow. I must say he didn't pine over her very long either. Father sent Geri to Boston to get that office into proper shape, and we actually married there where race was less of an impediment to matrimony."

"The year my first child was born, Mere gave birth to our first brother, Etienne. Etienne died in infancy, but after five girls in 12 years, my mother birthed six sons in a row! Of course I've got grandchildren nigh as old as my youngest brother. My mother was a work of nature! Men can procreate forever, I reckon, but mother was almost 50 when Louis was born. She passed almost 15 years ago at the age of 62, having birthed 11 children and reared 10. She was sharp as a pin until the day she passed. And our old Maw-Maw Bethel, who helped raise us - she was the mulatto - was 97 when she passed! Maw-Maw lived with Vivienne and my two youngest brothers in Baton Rouge after Père died. I had moved to Philadelphia by that time and the two youngest brothers, Michel and Louis wanted to attend school in Baton Rouge. Vivienne had a full house for years. We can never give Vivienne nor Maw-Maw enough credit for what they did for the family! I can't recall how many children Maw-Maw had because by the time I was born several of them had passed, but I believe Maw-Maw had 18 or 19 children of her own. Then she helped raise us. She lavished attention on us all, but she had *one favorite* and that was Joseph - there was no one like *her boy*!"

Vaz was enjoying this family history immensely. Eliza and Clay were both enjoying it as well.

Clay interjected, "When I found out Louis was so young, Joseph and I started sharing family stories. I must say we have a great deal in common. My mother is still alive and will likely live *forever*. She's too ornery to give up or give in!"

"Ah, Daddy, *don't say mean things about Grandmother*," Nora said sweetly. "She is becoming very slow."

"Yes," I added to this conversation, "physically her body is wearing out, but don't ever try to get the better of her. You *will* lose. *Every time*!"

"So, young lady," Claudia looked pointedly at me, "Do you want to know if I think your being part black, or part white, or *whatever it is you are*, will hurt my brother's political career?"

I lowered my head at first because I didn't want her to see the fear in my eyes of her answer. Then I lifted my head and looked her squarely in the eyes.

"The undeniable answer *you already know*."

Clay gasped, surprised at the bluntness of her answer. She laughed and held a frail hand up toward him, "But Joseph Thierry *doesn't give a hoot and a holler about a political career!* I doubt he will *ever* run again as soon as this Plessy case is decided. When it becomes known that he has helped the New Orleans Comite des Citoyens - The Citizens' Committee - he couldn't even be elected dog catcher again in Louisiana. Of course," she laughed, "I'm not sure that dog catchers are *ever* elected and I'm fairly sure they don't have any in Louisiana as I saw so many mangy dogs everywhere the last time I was there!"

"But I keep digressing," Claudia laughed at herself, "Joseph will be as good a representative as possible, given his convictions, so long as he holds office. He is also reasonably sure that the Supreme Court won't hear this Plessy case before the 1896 session. That leaves, at most, a year for you to *be discrete*. I will say this, he *refuses adamantly* to delay your marriage another year. Six months maximum, he said. 'Come hell or high water' he told me, 'I'm marrying that girl in the next six months.' And, from the last time I saw him, I hope you marry him as soon as possible. He's on the verge of being ill. He needs you to see that he *eats and sleeps* right. He's certainly not doing it for himself!" She was passionate.

Eliza was quick, "What did he mean by *six months*? We were fairly sure the divorce would be completed by early December?"

"I can't answer that, Eliza. I only know what he told me last month." Claudia said so matter-of-factly there was no more discussion about it.

I was more tired at the end of the third day than any day I could remember since last Christmas' activities. I just wanted a bath and a bed, but Claudia Mayeux enjoyed talking about our adventures, so I could not disappoint her. After I had spent several hours in her company, I came to realize she had a difficult time walking very far. I didn't want to ask why she became so winded and tired, but she finally confided to Eliza and me.

"I don't go out with you, mes amis, not because I am *lazy*." She had the same kind of self-deprecation that I loved in Joseph. "By now you probably have seen how little effort is required to tire me out." She tapped her chest lightly. "My heart is not strong. The doctors can only give me this nitroglycerin for my pain, but they can't stop the pain from happening and they can't fix my heart. So, here I stay, waiting to die, it seems." Again she laughed, "Rusting out instead of wearing out! You can't know how much I enjoy your visit as I seldom go anywhere!"

I took a hot bath after our third day of shopping. I was so tired I fell asleep in the tub. A maid came in around seven to turn my bed down and see if I needed help dressing. She found me still in my dressing gown trying to dry my hair before I went to the parlor for a glass of sherry before dinner. New York City was *a sooty place* and my hair that I had washed on Saturday before we left on Sunday had needed shampooing again today. That much shampooing isn't good for curly, dry hair such as mine, so I was also rubbing a tiny amount of glycerin into the ends.

"I see you bought a few gowns off the rack. Would you like to be awearin' one tonight?" The maid asked in what I was told was a thick Irish brogue.

I smiled at her warmly. She almost sounded like country folk from back home.

"You choose one, Maeve. I'm so tired I couldn't tell a morning dress from an evening gown right now!"

"Ah, miss. It wudna matter if *you* wore a grain sack. Yure so beautiful."

"That coming from you! Take a look in the mirror, Maeve!" She was a scarlet haired angel with huge round blue eyes and just the right amount of rose in her cheeks. She was fashionably plump for the times whereas I needed both height and weight. I guessed her age to be about 18, but as I learned, she was only 15 years old.

She dropped her head and curtsied, "Ah, miss, if ya were anyone else I'd accuse ya of akissin' the Blarney stone!" She went to the wardrobe and chose a plain wool high neck gown in lavender with black cording and a pleated bodice and lace across the shoulders and at the sleeves. She pulled out underclothes and a pair of black silk slippers.

"Ah, yur har is too wet to be aputtin' up. Leave it down. Have ya a broad black ribbon?" I nodded toward the dressing table drawer. She wove the ribbon in and out of my hair, pulling it back slightly off my face, but allowing the curls to fall freely down my back to my waist.

When she finished she said, "Thar!" and turned the dressing stool to the mirror.

I couldn't stop smiling at the beauty who sat there in front of the mirror. I'd never thought of myself as anything other than moderately attractive, and most of the time, I didn't give it a thought one way or the other.

"Oh, Maeve! What a gift you have with hair!" I reached out impulsively and hugged her. She pulled away a bit. I never knew whether it was because of *my color or her station in life*. I liked the girl and her reserve hurt me.

"Ya'd better hurry up, Miss. I think they're about to go to dinner."

I grabbed my new paisley grey and silver shawl and removed the ring from the gold chain Eliza insisted I swap for the ribbon. I held my hand out to view the full effect, *dress, hair, ring and all* in the mirror and I had to say, "Not too shabby for a poor ignorant Black cook!"

I hurried down one hall, down another hall and down a small flight of stairs to the drawing room.

"Finally!" Joseph proclaimed as he walked quickly to me, picked me up, whirled me around and kissed me thoroughly in front of God and company.

"Ma belle!" He exclaimed standing back from me a moment. "Mon Dieu! Where is my little country girl?" He demanded.

"Do you want her back?" I asked timidly, thinking he didn't like my new found fine feathers.

He was laughing and twirling me around again, "No, on second thought. I think she's still here, just dressed up in city mouse clothing!"

"Oh, Joseph," his sister chided, "just stop your nonsense and tell the girl how beautiful she looks!"

He pulled me tight against him, "Ma soeur, she *doesn't just look beautiful.* This girl is the real thing. *She is beautiful!*" He pulled me up for a sweet, gentle kiss this time.

"I didn't know you were coming…" I said softly.

"No, Sara, and neither did we." Claudia said. "The last thing I knew he was in Louisiana."

Clay walked over to his friend and clapped him on the shoulder. "If this isn't love, I don't know what it is other than insanity. You have my consent to wed my step-daughter, although you *never asked for it*, you dog!"

Eliza came over to us. "She really was just a little thing last time I saw her. My goodness, she looks like an Egyptian or Persian goddess! No wonder you've been raving about her since you first saw her!"

Joseph never released me, but he leaned toward Eliza and kissed her on the cheek. "Well, you are not exactly a hag yourself, 'Liza! You are looking more beautiful than ever! And that blue gown becomes you very well!"

"Oh, hush up, you sweet-talking rogue!" She scolded, smacking him playfully with her fan.

Clay put an arm around his wife's waist, "Eliza is one of those fortunate women who becomes better looking with time and she started out well enough!"

He and Joseph were laughing, "You're right about that, Clay!" He looked around, "Speaking of pretty girls, where's my little soon-to-be sister?" He enquired. "I just now noticed she's absent."

"She ate earlier and went to bed." Claudia informed him. "She's not used to the hours we keep and her father rode her and Vastine around Central Park all afternoon. I take it she hasn't been riding much lately?" She asked Clay.

"Evidently not. I'm going to speak to my son about that!" He nodded directly at Vastine who was looking everywhere but at his father.

Joseph spoke up, "You young rascal, you need to spend more time with Nora. She's going to lose her sister's society as soon as we marry unless she agrees to live with us, *which I've suggested*."

Eliza spoke up, "Now, you listen here, you high-handed scoundrel! If that child leaves Raven Lea and her old granny, she's coming to *us*!" She was joking, but not completely.

"Do you mean that, Eliza?" Clay asked.

"You ought to know by now, Clay Powell, that *I don't talk nonsense*! If I say a thing, I mean it! I'd take that girl home with us *in a heartbeat*." She hit his arm lightly with her fan. "That son of yours," she glanced at Vastine meaningfully, "is another thing altogether. I don't think I could keep the girls away from him with a *bullwhip*!"

And, I knew for a fact, we couldn't keep Vaz away from the girls. Vastine did have the decency to blush, knowing that *I knew* where he was spending his extra time. He looked at me as if to beg me to keep my mouth closed about Maggie Pennington and his new amorata, Florence Bishop.

We were all laughing as we went in to the wonderful Louisiana-style dinner Claudia had the chef prepare for us. I learned some new culinary tips that evening.

After dinner Claudia excused herself for bed, "I am so sorry not to take better advantage of this lovely companionship, but the doctor says I must pace myself. Clay, Eliza, Sara, Vastine, you are all staying the rest of the week. Right? My brother says he must be off tomorrow!"

"Unless you chase us off!" Eliza answered. "It might help them realize down at the farm that they need to start looking for a new cook a little faster than they have been!"

"Who *is* cooking?" Joseph asked. "I hadn't even thought about that. I was just so happy to see mon bébé."

"Her name is Hermione Parkinson. She's contrary and hard headed, but she's *not* a bad cook." I told him. "She doesn't like taking instructions from me, a 'nigger,' and she has taken a great disliking to poor Violet. She says Violet is *too slow* to be of any use. She calls Violet a '*slow* nigger.' I came within an inch of hitting her with a frying pan when I heard her!" I told them vehemently.

"Violet was standing right in front of her. I think Hermione - I refuse to call her *Miz Parkinson* since she won't address me as *Miss Gilley* - believes Violet is so slow she doesn't understand the mean things said *about* her!" It made me angry even to tell what happened.

"Sara, what did you do?" Claudia asked.

"I told her *in front of Violet* that if she ever called Violet 'slow' or a 'nigger' again, I'd see her big back side going out the back gate *for the last time*. She said I didn't hire her and I couldn't fire her. To my own amazement that made me laugh! I think my laughing brought the whole thing home to her more than anger might have. *Finally!* I told her to just repeat that name-calling once again and *she'd see* whether I could fire her or not!"

"That's my feisty girl!" Joseph declared.

Clay looked at me straightly, "But *would they let you fire her*? I know her family. They're bigots like most every other white person in the county, but they're *hard-working, honest folks*. Good people in every other way, and, truth to tell, they wouldn't lay a mean hand on a colored person unless that person threatened them first." It was a statement of fact about race relations, in general, in the county at the time.

"Your brother and mother would back me and they still own the place! Anne is too sick right now to go to the trouble of finding another cook. I'm worried about her!"

Clay started laughing. "What's so funny about Anne being ill?" Eliza demanded, staring at him as if he'd lost his mind.

"She'll be well enough in another month or so. When I spoke to 'Zander on the telephone this morning - he called to see how we were doing and when we'd bring Sara home." Clay winked at me, "They want you back as soon as may be!" he digressed, giving me a gentle pat on my shoulder.

"What did Alexander say on the telephone?" Joseph asked impatiently. "I like Miz Powell. She's fair and honest. I hate to think she might be very ill."

Clay was still chuckling as his wife gouged him with her fan. "'Zander is over the moon about it! You'd think he was the only rooster ever in a hen house! Anne is in the family way!"

Those of us who knew her couldn't believe it. "Their youngest girl is twelve now, isn't she?" Eliza asked me.

"Yes, on her last birthday. Oh, I am so happy for them! That house needs more children! I'm so happy she's not ill like Miz 'Dena!" I was relieved.

Claudia left for bed soon after that and Joseph took my hand, excusing us from Clay, Eliza, and Vastine for the private talk he said we needed to have. He led me across the hall from the front parlor into what was probably Claudia's private parlor.

We sat side by side on the sofa, cooing and kissing for a few minutes. Joseph had some new affectionate French names for me and I so loved hearing them. But he became serious fairly soon.

"This time, I have a letter to show *you*. Don't react too soon until I have talked with you about it." He handed me a delicate envelope that smelled of flowers. When I sniffed it, he said "Jasmine."

September 21, 1894

Camilla House

New Orleans, Louisiana

Dear Husband,

I took the caution of having this privately delivered to you as I feared you would not open it if it arrived by mail without an envoy to plead that you read it. I will not waste time with pleasantries and trivial details of life here in New Orleans. You are here often enough to know what's happening even though I never see you. I would ask that you forgive my abruptness, but I know you prefer directness.

I am ill. Very ill, in fact. Three different physicians have concluded that I have cancerous tumors throughout much of my body that began in my lower abdomen. The cancer has spread so much that it is inoperable. I have no doubt that either the number of pregnancies I ended or the kinds of intimate behaviors I have engaged in have resulted in this. I take full responsibility for my condition.

Ironical, isn't it, that I feared I would die as my mother had if I delivered a baby? Well, if there is any humor to be found, the joke is on me.

I have made my peace with the Church and with God. I would like to make my peace vis-à-vis with you. I have done you grievous wrongs. I admit it freely, humbly and without reservations. You deserved better. You deserved far better. I beg you not to take any more of my pride away than I have already abandoned with these confessions. I know that I have no right to ask, but please do not finalize the divorce or the annulment. My death will finalize these things for you. If I can die married

266

and forgiven by you, maybe God will be merciful, too. You have only to wait a few more months and you will have a freedom that no one can challenge.

I ask that you donate the funds I was to receive when the divorce was finalized. I prefer the funds go to an organization that is singularly dedicated to the welfare of children. My priest has suggested that would be a fitting penance, although how it is to be a penance for me when I am dead, I cannot comprehend. I ask that you also make arrangements for perpetual prayers for my salvation.

My physicians are listed below. I met with Dr. Kirchstein in late May. He referred me to Dr. Faber whom I saw in New York in June. I saw Dr. LaFargue in early July and the later part of the same month. I am under his continuing care now. If you wish to consult these doctors to verify what I have said, they are:

Josephine Faber, M.D., Colorectal Specialist, The Mt. Sinai Hospital, Lexington Ave. East, Manhattan, New York

M. Alfred Kirchstein, Docteur de Gynecology, Professeur of Medicine, Medical College of Louisiana, Tulane University, St. Charles Ave., New Orleans Parish, Louisiana

M. Antoine LaFargue, Docteur de Gastroenterology et Hepatology, Medical College of Louisiana, Tulane University, St. Charles Ave., New Orleans Parish, Louisiana

I await your reply.

Humbly,

Olivia Marie

I handed the letter back to him. "Have you seen her?" I asked in a flat voice, afraid of the answer I would hear and even more afraid of not knowing what my future held.

"Yes, I came here last month to see the doctor at Mt. Sinai. She has had correspondence from the two physicians in New Orleans confirming her diagnosis of a large mass in Olivia Marie's abdomen. Without going into details, Doctor Faber believes the mass began in the lower part of the bowel and spread beyond it. The mass was interfering with elimination and that was what sent Olivia Marie to Doctor Faber."

267

"Then, as I needed to go to Louisiana to shake hands and kiss babies in my district, I saw the two physicians at the Medical College of Tulane. I had not yet contacted Olivia Marie. Doctor LaFargue told me that the mass has enlarged significantly since he saw her first in July."

"Have you seen your wife?" I repeated stiffly.

He didn't tease me about my persistence this time. "Yes."

"Do you believe she has repented and whatever other bill of goods she's trying to sell you?" I was angry and disgusted if he were gulled by her after all she had done to him in the past.

"Mon ange! She really is quite ill. She's dying and dying fast. She looks like a skeleton and is whiter than the paper that letter is written on!" He nodded at the letter, pleading with me to accept the fact.

"I asked her if she would submit to an examination by a physician of my choosing. I wanted her examined to be sure this is not some elaborate plot and to see if anything could be done to *save her life*. A surgeon who has removed numerous cancerous tumors in his career came over from Dallas at my request. He agrees with everything she's been told. He says there are too many small tumors that have developed in her breasts, under her arms, on her neck. His advice was to give her morphine and let her pass peacefully."

I felt mortified. I despised the woman for what she had done to Joseph, but she was a human being suffering hell on earth. "I'm truly sorry, Joseph, that she is so ill. Truly." I said quietly. "How long does she have to live?" I asked looking at my hands in my lap.

"I asked Doctor Freiburgh, the physician from Dallas, that question. He answered that he is not God. He can't predict with accuracy how long she will live, but he says she can't last more than a month at most with the huge mass blocking excretion, and she could die in as little as two to three weeks if her kidneys shut down, which is likely."

He dropped his head and lifted his hands to cover his face. "God forgive me, I don't think I ever loved her. Certainly not as I love you, anyway, but when we were first married I was so proud of her beauty and grace. I was so lustful for that beauty! I wanted to build a great dynasty with her and our children. I would have given her the moon if she had loved me as I thought I loved her. How could all that *evaporate*?" he mumbled through his hands.

For a moment I just sat with him, my hand on his knee. "Love has to be fed, I think, like a fire. She let that fire die in you. No, that's badly put. She killed that passion in you!"

He took his face out of his hands and pulled me to him hard, "Promise me! Promise me! We'll love each other 'til we die!" He didn't wait for an answer, but began kissing me with a passion that was frightening. I was lost in it. Abruptly he pushed me away from him.

"Will you allow me," his voice was strangled almost, "to wait until she dies, rather than signing the final divorce papers now? I have them in my valise." He grabbed me again, mumbling, "Tarnation! *She doesn't deserve for us to wait even one more day* for our happiness. I'm signing the papers now and having them recorded tomorrow. We can be married as soon as you say."

I could only whisper mournfully, "Joseph, if we don't wait for her to die, we will always be *ashamed* that we couldn't give her that little bit of grace. My sweet love, none of us *deserves grace;* we are simply very fortunate if we receive it."

Joseph left for Washington the next morning. Eliza and I finished shopping and returned with Clay, Vaz and Nora to the Raven Lea at the end of the week.

Joseph was in Louisiana on business the week of Olivia Marie's death. He had written her that he wanted to be fair, but he was not willing to be further abused out of pity, or guilt, or some other nameless emotion into relinquishing half his own hard-earned fortune for the expiation of

269

her sins. He would abide by her wishes for the disposition of what would have been a *fair divorce settlement*, rather than the exorbitant amount she had previously demanded in anger. He thought the amount he had stowed away of her inheritance from her father plus its earnings was fair - she had never been a real wife. He wrote that he was very much in love with me and that we planned a wedding in the new year, but we would not wait a full year. He told her since he was so happy, he could freely, without reservations, forgive her. He would not, however, see her.

Joseph arranged a simple funeral Mass, took care of bequests to her servants and to the orphanage that his family supported. His sister, Reverend Mother Superior Ann Clare, had received permission from her order to attend her sister-in-law during the last week of Olivia Marie's life. Olivia Marie asked that the remainder of her fortune - and she had very little left, only a few good pieces of jewelry - go to the convent Ann Clare headed. Ann Clare conveyed a last message to Joseph from Olivia Marie - she was grateful for his kindness and wished him joy in his forthcoming nuptials. Joseph went back to Washington, D.C. by way of Raven Lea. He was a widower.

I left with my things for Washington with Joseph, staying with Rob and Lizzie until Joseph and I married almost three months later. They were busy months as Rob and Joseph helped me locate property in an area likely to attract government workers for breakfast and luncheon.

As it happened there was a building for sale in the right location. It had two floors, perfect, I thought, for a restaurant below and a small apartment and attic storage above. The seller was an elderly white man who had run an office supply business from the first floor and lived on the second. It needed a great deal of renovation for use as a restaurant and I wanted to add a water closet to the apartment and another one for the restaurant.

Rob handled the sales transaction for me, "his sister," as neither he nor Joseph thought the old man would sell to a foreigner or a negro -

one of which he probably would've labeled me. The deed was in my name and how I rejoiced in holding that piece of paper in my hand! It was a dream I'd had for many years.

I jumped up and down when Rob and Joseph presented me with the deed.

"Lizzie, get your hat and coat!" I said grabbing and hugging her as well as I could given the advanced stage of her pregnancy. "We're going out for dinner to celebrate!"

"But, mon amour," Joseph teased, "you have yet to make your first nickel and you have just spent a great deal of money! Already you want to spend more?"

I gave him a sugary smile and said silkily, "My dear fiancé, don't you *want* to take us out to celebrate the culmination of my long-held dream?"

"Don't look at me like that!" He teased with his best salacious look. "Once you have sold your *first pancake*, then you can speak of culminations! Besides," he added taking my hands and dancing me around Rob and Lizzie's small parlor, "I thought I was your long-held dream!"

I shook my head "No." My head was bent so as not to let him see my bashfulness, "I was *never* arrogant enough to dream of someone as splendid as you!" I lifted my head and spoke quietly against his neck.

He kissed my eyes and laughed, "You always say the right thing! Yes, I want the four of us to go out and celebrate tonight. I want the whole world to see these beautiful girls of ours, Rob! You and I need a break from legal matters anyway."

The buying of the building was a large matter, but it needed renovations, equipment, and furnishings. Lizzie was heavily pregnant with her first baby. Joseph was back and forth to Baton Rouge and New

York with the Plessy case. Rob held down the Washington office and managed most of the Thierry shipping affairs, staying close to home in case Lizzie went into labor. I was left largely to my own devices in locating suppliers and making deals. I signed nothing however without first having either Joseph or Rob review it.

Oddly, I could not work with contractors and laborers. Or better put, they *wouldn't* work with me. First, I was a woman. What did I know about such things? And second, I was dark? What *could* I know of such things? I became so angry and frustrated that I sent an appeal to Carl Thomas. If he would come up and do the work I needed done, I would pay for his travel up and home when the job was finished, his room, board, and his labor - at more than he was being paid in Raven Lea.

Carl Thomas could read and write fairly well. I knew he had gone to school for about six years, but I had never thought about his scholastic or intellectual abilities. All I knew was that he was a good builder and a dead shot with a rifle. He contacted me almost as soon as he received my request. If he could bring his mother and Violet with him, he would pay for their transportation. Could I rent a small house rather than a room for him? He'd pay for food. He was a good negotiator I learned right from the start. The rented house, fairly near the property I bought, cost a little more than room and board for one, but not much, and I could use Violet's help once the restaurant opened. Both Ivy and Nora had told me that Violet had been miserable after I left Raven Lea.

And so it came about that Violet, her mother, and Carl Thomas relocated to Washington within two weeks of my asking Carl Thomas to work for me. They never moved back to southwest Virginia.

Carl Thomas was worth *every penny* I spent bringing him up and every nickel he made working for me. Not only could he negotiate with laborers, but he had a good head for recognizing what materials were needed when, and how to get them in a timely fashion. He bargained well for the best prices. The quality of materials I wanted cost less than I had expected. He assembled a team of skilled workers. They were not all black, but they *were* all good craftsmen, hard-working, and they were loyal to him. Most of them worked with him for the next thirty years. The ones who left were those who became too infirm or too old to work anymore. Over the years he had Joseph help him set up small pensions for each of them so that they had something for their later years and he helped them buy life insurance policies to help their families if they passed too soon.

Carl Thomas Peters went on to develop quite a career as a contractor in Washington in spite of racial hatred and Jim Crow laws. He and his family lived in comfort in an area among black teachers, black doctors, black attorneys and other black business owners. Over the years he became a deacon in his African Methodist Episcopal church, a Deputy Imperial Potentate (or something like that!) of the Ancient Egyptian Arabic Order Nobles of the Mystic Shrine, belonged to a black Masonic order, and was a member of the Improved Benevolent Protective Order of the Elks. He was highly regarded in the business community and in his social life - that same modest, *generous* young man who gave venison as Christmas gifts and floored his mother's slave cabin.

Seven of his eight children did very well. Four of the eight went to college. One daughter attended Bethune-Cookman and a son went to Hampton Institute. They both became teachers. Another daughter graduated from Howard University and later worked as a journalist for the Afro-American Ledger in Baltimore. The fourth to attend college went to Morehouse in Atlanta. That son later attended the University of Pennsylvania medical school and returned to D.C. to open what became a large, successful practice. Three of the other four did well also. Two joined their father's business and the third opened a highly successful green grocer's market that developed into a chain of markets throughout the city.

Sadly, one son died in the horrible race riot of 1919. He died the night before President Wilson ordered federal troops to stop the killings that had gone on unabated for four days. Carl Thomas' son slipped from the rooftop where he had gone with a rifle either to help defend a black neighborhood or to take revenge for the violence done to colored people. We never knew what was in his heart when he fell to his death. Being only 17 at the time, it is unlikely that the boy knew exactly himself why he went on that roof armed. To their credit, Carl Thomas' other children decided to live the best they knew how, and, in as far as I ever knew, they were complete credits to their parents and their Aunt Violet.

Carl Thomas and I travelled in different circles in Washington, but he was a friend as long as he lived. He sat in our kitchen with us almost every Sunday evening and drank Joseph's coffee after he brought Violet back from her Sunday with his family. Sometimes his wife Aleta came with him, sometimes one or two of his children. We knew his family well. Joseph invited Carl Thomas to join his Wednesday night poker group, but Carl Thomas respectfully declined. I knew it was because of his religious beliefs, but Carl Thomas never said so and never seemed to find fault with Joseph because of the penny ante gaming. He was a good husband, a good father, and a good brother besides being our loyal friend.

Lizzie had her baby girl mid-December, so Rob was able to help me in January to get supplies and furnishings for my business. I was torn between wanting to furnish the apartment and wanting to hold Rob and Lizzie's adorable bald baby, but it was Joseph's and my first home. He had lived in a rooming house the entire time he'd been in Washington. I wanted to create a refuge for him from work-a-day worries.

Claudia's daughter who lived in Baltimore helped me choose furniture, wallpaper, paint, curtains, the things that go into making a home. She pointed to an oversized brown leather club chair one day when we were in Philadelphia shopping, declaring that "Uncle Joseph" had to have that! It took up a great deal of space in our small parlor, but it was an excellent choice as it was his favorite seat in the house. Over the years it had to be reupholstered twice. I think he mentioned how much he enjoyed that chair in every Christmas card he sent to his niece Marie Rose over the years.

While Joseph and I were away in New York and Europe for the wedding and the honeymoon, Carl Thomas saw that everything went into place exactly as I had drawn on my plans. In gratitude, Joseph gave him a bonus sizeable enough for Carl Thomas to make a down payment on his own first small house five blocks from the restaurant.

The first black-owned bank in D.C., Capital Savings, lent the money to Carl Thomas for that first modest home as well as the capital he needed in the early years to help his business grow. When Capital Savings went under a number of years later, Carl Thomas transferred his business to another black-owned bank. Like many blacks in D.C. at the time, *including me*, these businessmen were helping their community grow and spending their money with people who had the interests of a black community at heart.

CHAPTER 15: THE WEDDING

I am the rose of Sharon, and the lily of the valleys.
As the lily among thorns, so is my love among the daughters.
As the apple tree among the trees of the wood,
so is my beloved among the sons.
I sat down under his shadow with great delight,
and his fruit was sweet to my taste.
He brought me to the banqueting house,
and his banner over me was love.

from The Song of Solomon 2:2-6

Joseph and I married in the church St. Ignatuis Loyola in New York City early the afternoon of March 6, 1895, the day after the 53rd Congress of the United States closed. The church was near Claudia's penthouse apartment. She was well-acquainted with the religious community in the city and it seemed half of them must have been present. The Most Reverend Michael Augustine Corrigan, Archbishop of New York was there as was Joseph's uncle, the Reverend Emile Thierry S.J., who had travelled from Mobile, Alabama to assist the church rector, the Reverend Neil McKinnon S.J., in the ceremony. Reverend Thierry was a faculty member at Spring Hill College in Mobile. It came as a surprise to me that priests could also be professors, but then it came as no surprise to me that the Reverend Thierry taught law!

  The Reverend McKinnon asked me prior to the ceremony if I agreed to bear and be responsible for the Christian rearing of children should we be so blessed. "Of course!"

He wanted my promise specifically to raise our children in the Catholic Church. "Yes."

Had I been baptized into the Christian faith to which I replied in the affirmative, thinking that my own immersion in the cold water of the river when I was 12 was vastly different than a Catholic baptism. However, as far as I was concerned it was certainly sufficient to suit Christian precepts as it was how John had baptized Jesus. The Reverend must have felt similarly as he accepted what I told him. Someone later told me that it was unlikely a Roman Catholic priest would consider *any Protestant denomination* to actually be *"Christian."* The priest asked - I answered as truthfully as I could, at the time not knowing any differently.

Was I taking instructions to become Catholic? Yes, I was, but due to the fact that I did not have access to a Catholic priest until I moved to D.C. just three short months before, I had not had time to finish the process. He married us even though I was not actually converted until late that summer. I was never sure whether our marriage would have been sanctioned by the Church if an independent-minded Jesuit had not officiated and signed the necessary papers, but our children were baptized, confirmed and married in the Catholic Church. Even *the Archbishop* blessed our marriage.

Clay and Vaz all walked me to the altar. Mr. Robert met them there in the first row. It seemed that the walk was at least a mile long. I was certain that no other woman ever had such handsome escorts to the altar, even if Clay and Vaz practically had to lift me along. Standing to one side of the altar, Rhi, Nora and Ivy were very lovely in their pale pink gowns, each one made differently. Rhi and Ivy were tall enough to wear the styles of the day. Nora, just as I, could not. Her dress was simple, ornamented with lovely lace insets instead of the large sleeves and bustles Rhi and Ivy had. Rob and two of Joseph's brothers stood with him, including the family scapegrace, Bertrand, who looked enough like Joseph to be his twin. He had travelled from Ponce, Puerto Rico to be present. The third brother, Michel, was in a tuberculosis sanitarium in Murrieta, California and could not attend, but his wife came.

Ole Missus simply could not make the trip, but she sent me a service for 16 of Rosenthal china, a beautiful lilac, pale green, white and gold porcelain service. Rosenthal was a new company not having earned a great reputation in the U.S. at the time, thus, Ole Missus said, she could afford such beautiful china. Over the years I needed additional place settings as we often had as many as 30 people to dinner. I don't think Ole Missus ever imagined what a hostess I would be, but it meant a great deal to me over the years to put that lovely china on the table, knowing that it was a gift from my great-grandmother, even if she were unaware of the relationship.

Anne, Mr. 'Zander, Andy, Laurie, Minnie, and Violet - whom I had asked to stand up with me, but she refused - were all there, leaving Ole Missus and the new baby to the care of the new nanny and a nurse at Raven Lea. All of Joseph's sisters, except for Mother Superior Ann Clare were there with two brothers-in-law, numerous nieces, nephews, and assorted other relatives. One brother-in-law could not get away because of business and, of course, Claudia was widowed. Claudia, however, found congenial company with Mr. Robert, allowing her daughters to mingle and dance. Rob's wife Lizzie, Eliza, Joseph's personal secretary, and half his staff were present. I had invited my staff, but they each declined, except for Violet. Carl Thomas had declined as well. Supreme Court Justice Harlan Sanders was present as well as half of Louisiana - or so it seemed! What a mixture of people of many shades. Whimsically, I thought of a field full of wild flowers - different shapes, different heights, and different colors, all blending beautifully.

As large as the church was, it was probably two-thirds full. Back at Claudia's, I stopped counting Joseph's family members at 20, but her ball room overflowed into the large dining room where a mid-afternoon buffet had been arranged with roast beef, several whole fishes, a whole Serrano ham, fresh fruits, caviar, oysters, pheasants, shrimp, crawfish, and at least 30 other delicious things, *none of which I remember eating.* A small orchestra set up in the parlor as the company ate. Someone wheeled out a five-tier wedding cake and enough champagne to float one of the Thierry ships.

Joseph sweetly fed me cake and lightly licked the icing from my lips in front of his relatives, mine and the Reverends. Only I seemed to find this in any way inappropriate, so, thinking I was simply a country rube, I responded in kind when he ate his cake. He laughed at me and pulled me so tightly to him I couldn't breathe.

"I'm sure about half this crowd thinks that was too saucy, ma petite, *but I like it.*" He whispered in my ear. "Don't let the world tell you what is or is not appropriate. Follow your heart."

He took my arm and guided me in to what was now the ball room. He made a motion for the orchestra leader to begin playing and we danced until the soles of my shoes had holes in them. I was so glad that Claudia had insisted I receive some dance lessons before the wedding.

I danced with Clay, Rob, Vaz, Joseph's brother, Louis, several of his nephews, Andy - and even Ivy and my sisters for a few minutes. Joseph's reprobate, but *very wealthy* brother, Bertrand made indecent suggestions to me while we danced - in jest, I think - I hoped!

I answered quite innocent-seeming, "Oh, Sir, I'm sorry I didn't meet you before I met Joseph." I was not sophisticated, but I could manage the likes of Bertrand, nevertheless. I smiled sweetly, directly into his eyes, "Then I could *really have appreciated* him when we did meet!"

He threw his head back and laughed loudly enough for everyone to turn and stare at us. Joseph danced his partner, Anne at the time, over to us and gave his brother a hard slap on the back.

"*She is a goddess*, Bertie, but I fell in love with her because she is so unassuming, so independent, and so *refreshingly* witty! Evidently you have discovered this for yourself! But I found her first and you're a married man with - what… eight children now - and at least one lady who plays the piano, violin… What is it she does do for you, Bertie? The new one, I mean. I can't keep up, there's a new one every time I see you." He sounded sincerely confused. He started to exchange partners. I resisted slightly. Joseph had a nerve to paint his brother with the same brush that once colored him!

"Joseph, don't leave Anne here with this… with Bertrand. I know Anne well enough to know she might walk off the floor and *create a splendid scene*! Give me another turn around the floor, Bertrand. Maybe I can persuade *you* to leave the battlefield and *create the scene*." I smiled genuinely and the four of us laughed wholeheartedly.

Bertrand relinquished my hand, bowed slightly to me, smiling at his brother sardonically, "*I know when I'm bested*, little fair one. Does Joseph really have any idea of the ride he's in for?" He laughed, meeting his brother's angry glare. "I hope to see more of you *both* in the near future." He kissed me on both cheeks and took Anne away, waltzing toward the dining room.

"He is a *complete rogue*, Sara! My apologies. He simply can't keep his hands off a pretty woman, especially if she's…" Joseph was truly annoyed with his brother. I wondered how long they had rivaled one another, but I didn't want to hear about it that day.

"Don't fret, sweetheart. I'm unharmed, unfazed, and *less* than dazzled!" At which Joseph dipped me dramatically and laughed.

We said our adieus at about 6 PM and left for the Windsor Hotel, not far from Claudia's apartment.

Several hours later I realized I was famished. "Joseph," I said, trying to pull the sheets up around my shoulders while he stood, in the buff in front of the fire smoking one of those hideous cigars he brought up from Cuba, "I'm so hungry! I was too nervous to eat at the wedding."

He looked at me, "Stop it!" He growled. I must have looked askance because he laughed, "Stop pulling the sheets up! You look like a princess out of *A Thousand and One Nights* with your hair mussed and down and your breasts bare! Don't ever cover up for me." He ordered.

"Well, Sir, may I cover up if *I'm cold*?" I asked tartly at which he laughed. He threw his cigar in the fire and came back to bed, hugging me closely and rubbing my bare cold arms briskly.

"I didn't eat much myself." He said, "What would you like, mon cœur?" He kissed the top of my head and pulled the sheets and blanket up over both of us.

"I'd *like half a cow*, but I'll settle for an orange and a banana from the fruit bowl in the sitting room until breakfast is served."

"I'm fairly sure we can get a little more than that from the hotel kitchen. It's only about 11 o'clock. If they don't have a chef this late, *I'll go make us something*!" He said emphatically.

"You are the most high-handed man I ever knew! You are *not going to tell me that you own this hotel too*?" I scoffed.

"No. I don't own a single brick of this place, but I know the owners well!" He stood up and pulled on his robe, walked to the sitting room to place a telephone call. I couldn't hear what he said, but he came back into the bedroom shortly.

"Put on your nightgown and robe. They'll bring us a small feast in about twenty minutes. The food will be cold, but I can assure you it will be delicious!" He stoked the fire and sat in a chair by the fire watching me dress. "I could look at you *until I go blind from the sight of you*." If most men tried to utter such words it would sound completely unnatural and probably laughable. Somehow Joseph could say such things and make them sound thrilling! I believe I blushed all our life together any time he said intimate things to me. I never tired of hearing him unless he was trying to *avoid* telling me something.

I sat in his lap, stroking the face I loved so much and giving him small kisses on his eyes, his brow, his cheeks until he took my hands and held them, "The man will be here with our food any minute. We'll eat first, then you may *kiss me to your heart's content*, mon amour!"

I laughed just as there was a knock on the sitting room door. Joseph answered the door and had the man wheel the cart into the bedroom in front of the fire. The waiter was black and seemed surprised on seeing me. It was not the first time someone had stared at me when I was with white people, but it made me very uncomfortable in the bedroom. He looked as if I were doing something shameful.

Joseph handed the man a gratuity and said, "I see you're admiring my beautiful wife!"

"My 'pologies, Sir! I meant no offense." the waiter started to retreat.

Joseph laughed a little, "None taken. She can't help attracting the eye. I need to have her portrait painted. Thank you for your service this late in the evening."

The man evidently had looked at the bill Joseph gave him because he looked significantly at it and said, "*No, Sir! Thank you!*" and hurriedly left.

When he left I asked Joseph what an appropriate gratuity was for such service. He said twenty-five cents or so usually, but he gave the man a "bit more" since it was late.

Later I learned that the extraordinarily large gratuity was Joseph's way of seeing that at least the black staff treated me very well. Even in New York City in 1895 not many black people stayed in such a fine hotel, and certainly not as the bride of what appeared to be a white man - not because there weren't black folks who could afford it, but because of the extreme prejudice that existed at the time *even there*. Joseph could ornament me in fancy clothes and house me in luxury, but most people saw me as "black."

The next afternoon we went down to the docks to the newest ship in the Thierry line, The Gilley Flower, named for *me*. A priest was there to say a blessing and sprinkle holy water on the ship. I was handed a bottle of champagne to break against the bow. There were a few stares as we boarded, but the general attitude was convivial. Most of the crew were old hands with the Thierry's and they knew Joseph. He introduced me to the crew, captain and co-pilot who were standing in a row, waiting when we arrived.

"This is your new commander when she's on board. This ship is named for her. You can see that she is an extraordinary flower and the queen of my heart." He laughed at himself and the crew smiled at us both. We were led to a lovely stateroom, a suite actually. Each ship had a couple of state rooms even though the primary function of their ships was to move goods from port to port.

We sailed across the Atlantic to London. The crossing took 11 days - 11 days when I mostly had Joseph to myself. We did go on deck several times each day to get some fresh air and sunshine, but we had most of our meals alone, inviting the captain to dine with us twice each week we were at sea.

Captain Jamison was a red-haired man about Joseph's age whose wife lived near London. When I first saw the captain I could barely drag my gaze from his red beard which was down to his chest, parted in the middle and curled up on either side. He must have spent at least half an hour styling that beard every morning. Joseph told me privately that the captain probably slept with hair pins in his beard and possibly a snood around it. I laughed until my side hurt at such an image, but I did regret laughing as he was really a nice man and a worthy captain.

The captain's wife came aboard when we left London at the end of our two days there. She was making the next roundtrip passage with her husband. Their three boys were all at school. The ship travelled to Barcelona where it stayed two nights and on to Marseilles for an overnight stay before turning toward New York. We stopped in Rabat,

Morocco for one night on the way home. The return to New York took 12 days because we sailed against the Gulf Stream. It was a great distance we travelled on our four-week honeymoon, and I *gawked at everything* I saw when we docked and toured the cities.

I even tried my hand at fishing when we were in port, finally learning what the attraction was for Vaz and Clay. It was cold on deck at that time of year, but I loved the fresh air and the wonderful peacefulness of the ocean. Joseph swore he never enjoyed any of the sights so much before.

"Looking at things through your eyes makes me feel like a little boy again! It's wonderfully exciting to see these things from your perspective."

As we were packing our things in preparation for our arrival in New York, Joseph called to my attention the fact that he had abandoned the shoulder braces.

"I have eaten so much that I may need to have the pants *let out* even though I have had so much exercise." The lurid smile came into play. "And I believe I see a little more bosom on you than you had at the beginning of this trip!" At which I threw a soft slipper at him. He caught it before it struck him.

"Aha, ma belle, two can play at that!" He picked up a soft pillow and struck my backside with it. I looked shocked, but I picked up a pillow and hit him in the stomach. After a few more strikes with pillows we fell onto the bed laughing and forgot about packing altogether.

Later he said, "I am the happiest creature on this Earth, mon cœur! Never! Never, did I expect to be this happy! It scares me." He pulled me closer to him. "Is God raising me up for an awful fall?" He sounded frightened, unlike his super confident self. "I have not led an unblemished life. I don't deserve someone as good as you!"

"Hush that *superstitious nonsense* and be thankful that we finally *have each other*!" I chastised him. "I'm as healthy as a horse and so are you!" I reached out and patted his chest. "And I intend to be around for a long time so you can call me sweet names and spoil me to your heart's content!" He laughed at that and we napped, lying in each other's arms, until the steward knocked on the door to ask us when we wanted our dinner served.

I never let Joseph know that I was *always* afraid of *losing him* to some calamity such as befell my father or losing him to another better-educated, more sophisticated, *white* woman.

I lay on the bed a few minutes after the steward knocked, looking at the ceiling of the room while Joseph began to dress. "When did you first know that you loved me?" I asked quietly.

"When did I first know *what*?" He turned to look at me incredulously. "That I *loved* you?"

I nodded bashfully.

"Oh, mon cœur, it came to me *quite slowly*," he answered, trying to close his shirt. "Blast these things! Sara, can you help me?" I rose from the bed and began to put the silver studs in place.

He put his hands on my shoulders, "I didn't know when I first laid eyes on you, although I began to suspect I could quickly come to love you. You were crying and I have always been susceptible to feminine tears. I was so slow that I still didn't know when you asked if my *cattle* needed attention, but that definitely caused me to think! Here was a girl with tenderness for *beasts*. I've always appreciated a female with a tender heart, but I was still skeptical. Maybe it was simply admiration. But, l'amour de ma vie, when you offered me *buttermilk* and *threw your apron at me*, I knew I would love you for the rest of my life!"

"When did you first know?" He asked as I put the last stud in place.

"Oh, Joseph! I was much slower to recognize love. I didn't know until you kissed my hand the night before you left after your first visit to Raven Lea." I tiptoed and gave him a swift kiss. "Thank you." I whispered.

"Thank me for what, mon trésor?"

"For finding me." I replied softly. "I don't think I ever would have found you."

"No, you weren't even allowing yourself *to look,* but oh, Sara, I *had* to find you sooner or later. It was *inevitable.* I was *always* looking for you!"

EPILOGUE

Sara's story evolved because of a recurring dream, some genealogical data, and family information my father passed on. The dream came first and it began well into my adulthood. I believe someone similar to the fictitious Sara was trying to get my attention.

In the dream I walked down an unpaved country road to a bend. The road and the bend exist. I walked there many times as a girl. In the dream I was alone, unafraid, emotionless, simply walking. The dream always ended when I came to where the road curved. If you round the curve, and walk another mile or so you come to the house where I grew up. In addition to the repetitiveness of the dream, the other puzzle for me was why the dream ended before I turned he curve. It always ended there as suddenly as it had begun about 20 paces back.

A few years after the dream began, my father told me that he needed to show me where the family slave cemetery was. I was ill at the idea that my ancestors owned slaves, but over the course of five years or so, I decided someone should know where those bodies lay. No one still alive would know the names or the stories of those souls buried there.

The next summer when I visited my family, I asked my father to take me to the cemetery, having no idea where it was. We trudged roughly 150 yards into the woods from an angle about 22 degrees south by southwest from where the road straightened to the east. We left the roadway at the spot where my dreams always ended. We dodged and moved briers, bent bushes out of the way, and watched for timber rattlesnakes and copperheads. My father had not seen the cemetery since he was a boy hoeing corn for an uncle who then owned the surrounding land.

More than 60 years of neglect changed the scenery considerably for my father. The large old white house that stood at the bottom of what was once a cornfield had collapsed in upon itself and had become food for termites. Beef cattle grazed in pasture surrounding the house. The corn field was long overgrown with a variety of vegetation, including large trees. The property no longer belonged to any family member.

Dad remembered a few landmarks: a jumble of rocks, many too large for a single man to move, and a large chestnut stump, five feet or more in diameter. These were near the cemetery. Since the wood of chestnuts resists the ravages of nature for years, he counted on the stump still being there.

Dad looked around for several minutes, moving first in one direction, then another. He was not young, but he was still agile, with memory intact. He located the stump, the rocks, and the cemetery which had been disturbed. I later learned that a neighbor boy had dug there in the 1960's thinking it was an Indian burial mound. That neighbor is dead now and I doubt anyone alive knows what, if anything, he found and removed.

A tremendous sense of loneliness fell on me standing there in those deep woods with an undergrowth as thick as the tall trees would allow, but I never again had the dream. I was called to that lonely place; of that I have no doubt. I have been back several times since with a few people, including a brother-in-law who is a safe guide in woods. The place has a stillness as if the dead are at peace, undisturbed by animals and birds. Someone knows where the bones lie. The dead are satisfied, I think.

- Mimi Mitchell

ABOUT THE AUTHOR

Mimi Mitchell was born in the Appalachian Mountains of western Virginia. Jim Crow laws lingered in the South long after the Plessy v. Ferguson decision was overturned by the Supreme Court in 1954, so Mimi saw great changes during her youth.

"I simply never saw the racial separation until I went to the movies in my late teen years, and recognized, for the first time, the separate drinking fountains and seating areas for 'negroes' and whites! I was confounded both by the segregation and by the fact that I had never been aware of it! I was possessed by a severe mental scotoma regarding race relations. All my life, I have feared that I may possess other psychological blind spots.

Mimi and her husband live in rural Virginia after residing for years in large metropolitan areas. They have travelled the U.S. from Maine to Alaska and Hawaii, from Minnesota to Texas. They have travelled widely in Canada, Mexico, Europe, parts of South America and Australia. Mimi says, "It's a big world! I hope our money and health hold out. We want to see it all. My husband wishes he were young enough to volunteer for the first trip to Mars. I like planet Earth. I will enjoy other people's videos!"

Mimi Mitchell's second book of Sara's story will be out mid-2015. She is currently writing and expecting to publish the third and final volume of Sara's story in late 2015.

Should you believe that you have dead relatives in the cemetery mentioned in Shades and Shadows, you may contact the author: mimi-mitchell-author.blogspot.com.

Scarce information is available on persons buried there largely due not to one fire, but to two. Official local records prior to 1933 went up in flames. There was a fire, devastating to genealogists, that destroyed most of the 1890 U.S. Census data. Although a small amount of 1890 U.S. Census data remains, none is applicable to this location. The 1860 U.S. Slave Census for the area is missing persons known to have held slaves or to have been slaves in the District at the time. The 1850 U.S. Slave Census data is intact, but slaves' names are not given. Nevertheless, the author will attempt to assist persons who are likely to be relatives of those once-loved dead.

www.ingramcontent.com/pod-product-compliance
Lightning Source LLC
Chambersburg PA
CBHW020239180626
46810CB00006B/2269